The
Wedding Menu

The Wedding Menu

LETIZIA LORINI

G

GALLERY BOOKS

New York Amsterdam/Antwerp London Toronto Sydney New Delhi

G

Gallery Books
An Imprint of Simon & Schuster, LLC
1230 Avenue of the Americas
New York, NY 10020

Previously published in 2023 by Letizia Lorini AB

First Gallery Books trade paperback edition January 2025

GALLERY BOOKS and colophon are registered trademarks of Simon & Schuster, LLC

For information about special discounts for bulk purchases, please contact Simon & Schuster Special Sales at 1-866-506-1949 or business@simonandschuster.com.

The Simon & Schuster Speakers Bureau can bring authors to your live event. For more information or to book an event, contact the Simon & Schuster Speakers Bureau at 1-866-248-3049 or visit our website at www.simonspeakers.com.

Interior design by Erika R. Genova

Manufactured in the United States of America

1 3 5 7 9 10 8 6 4 2

Library of Congress Cataloging-in-Publication Data is available.

ISBN 978-1-6680-8233-1
ISBN 978-1-6680-8234-8 (ebook)

To my readers, old and new,
who made all of this possible.
I can't ever repay you,
but I'll try by giving you Ian.

Author's Note

Thank you so much for picking up *The Wedding Menu*, and an even louder, higher pitched thank-you if you've read it in its first, self-published form. This updated edition wouldn't exist without you, dear reader.

The Wedding Menu is what I affectionately refer to as "The Little Book That Could," and I'm honored you chose to be entertained by my buttery shenanigans. Yes, she's a thick one. But I promise you two storylines filled with love, laughter, and spice—both the kitchen kind *and* the bedroom one.

Although this story is mostly lighthearted and filled with comical situations (*see: hilariously cringe*), I would like to acknowledge that it also delves into some heavier topics and has on-the-page intimate scenes and mature content, and therefore, this book is intended for mature audiences only. Please note the following content warnings: open-door romance, death of a parent (off-screen), and absent parent.

Okay, ready to dive in? Great.

You *butter* prepare for Ian and Amelie . . .

The Whine List

This book includes three chapters with explicit content. Here are some (sort of) explicit wines to go with them. Consult this list if you wish to skip any of these chapters, or if you would like to read them again.

Chapter 30
Domaine Saint Andéol Séduction Cairanne 2007
Deliciously rich and full-bodied, with a smoky-cedar finish

Chapter 32
Folie à Deux Zinfandel 2008
Savory and dark raspberry, with hints of cherry and black currants

Chapter 34
Chateau Ste. Michelle Eroica Riesling 2013
Sweet lime, tangerine aromas, and subtle mineral notes

The
Wedding Menu

Welcome & Bienvenue

Welcome to our gourmet restaurant! Here is our menu, designed to awaken your taste buds and dazzle your senses with refined flavors and bold combinations. Get ready for an unforgettable culinary experience.

We recommend enjoying this menu with a selection of fine wines, specially chosen to complement each dish. Bon appétit!

Bienvenue à notre restaurant gastronomique! Voici notre menu, conçu pour éveiller vos papilles et éblouir vos sens avec des saveurs raffinées et des combinaisons audacieuses. Préparez-vous à une expérience culinaire inoubliable.

Nous vous recommandons de savourer ce menu avec une sélection de vins de grand cru, spécialement choisis pour compléter chaque plat. Bon appétit!

LES HORS D'OEUVRE

It Starts with a Wedding

– ONE YEAR AGO –

A petal falls off the daisy at the center of the table, bright and yellow as the sun even among the many colorful flowers in the bouquet. Leaning forward, I grab it and rub my finger on the velvety surface. With the loud bass beats pulsing through my body, my bones rattle, my heart matching the daunting pace—though that could be the work of one too many margaritas.

Setting my drink down, I take in the crowd of people in cocktail dresses and tuxedos chatting around me. We've danced since dinner, and my social battery is drained. I'm done for the day, and grateful that my table is empty.

Martha hasn't been around for hours, so she must be somewhere with her fiancé, Trevor. And because I refuse to be the target of the unaccompanied gentlemen at this wedding, I've kept my awkward moves to a minimum and my drinking to a maximum.

Someone sits beside me, and I expect it to be Trevor or Martha. As the closest friends of the bride and groom, we share the table next to the one reserved for parents and siblings of the newly-weds. Instead, it's one of *them*. The single guys. The ones who scout the room with ever so much interest. Most people stick to their dates or their friends, but not them.

Sleek, smooth jaguars, prowling and stalking their prey.

He looks innocuous enough, but I'm not interested in testing my theory, so I offer him an apologetic smile. "Engaged."

As he tilts his head, his deep steel-blue eyes lighten up with amusement. "Congratulations, but I'm just looking for a seat. A woman stole mine, and she looks like she might need it more than me."

He points to the right, to Barbara's grandma. I see what he means, since Mrs. Wilkow uses a wheeled walker and offers everyone butterscotch candy.

"Oh, sorry," I say to the stranger, a hot prickle of embarrassment spreading across my cheeks. "Didn't mean to be presumptuous. Just a long day."

"We'll sit in silence, then." He leans back and smiles down at his drink, barely masking the width of his grin. He looks like a high schooler who's been sent to detention and can't take it seriously.

"Friend of the groom?" I ask.

His eyes meet mine, long lashes framing his ocean-blue irises. "I thought you didn't want to talk."

I didn't, but it'd be awkward to sit here in silence. We might as well entertain each other. "I'm Amelie," I say as I give him a tiny wave.

"Ian."

"The bride and I work together."

Lowering his gaze, he unbuttons the sleeves of his white shirt and rolls them over his forearms like he *knows* what he's doing. "Isn't it weird?" he asks as he uncovers thick wrists covered in black tattoos. My eyes follow the hypnotic movement, every other noise fading away for a moment as I force my gaze back to his face. "How, when you meet people at weddings, the icebreaker is: what the hell you're doing there. Does it establish a certain hierarchy? Like, if you're a friend and I'm their contractor, does it mean you're better than me?"

A light chuckle bubbles out of me, and with a shrug I say, "It's what me, you, and every other person in this room have in common. We know either the bride or the groom, and we're here to celebrate them."

The ice cubes in the honey-brown liquid in his glass click as he brings it to his lips. "I've never met the newlyweds. I'm sure they deserve to be celebrated, but"—he looks around—"I don't even know what Bianca looks like."

"Barbara."

With a snap of his fingers, he nods. "Right. Barbara."

My eyebrows shoot up. He doesn't even know the *name* of the bride? "Why *are* you here?"

"Our dads are friends." He points at an older man chatting with Barbara's dad and wearing yet another dark tuxedo. He stands with his back to us, only his salt-and-pepper hair visible above shoulders as wide as his son's. "He dragged me along."

I nod, noticing the annoyed undertone in his voice. He's definitely not happy to be here, and I'm reminded of Barbara's freak-out a few months back when she found out her dad had invited a lot of his acquaintances, turning her wedding into a "networking event." "Well, at least the food was great," I offer.

"Oh, yes. Worth the long-ass ceremony."

Chuckling, I hold my glass up. "The margaritas too. Life-changing."

"Yeah, looks like you loved those." He gestures to the several empty long-stemmed glasses surrounding my plate, then asks,

"What has you in such a foul mood? You're not up for socializing; you're drinking your sorrows away . . ."

My gaze lingers on his high cheekbones for a while before I avert my eyes, my fingers grazing along the white linen covering the table. He'll regret this question if I answer it. He's at a wedding seemingly against his will, and he's sitting here because someone else took his spot. "Trust me, you don't want to know."

"Actually, you'd be doing me a favor. It's either this," he says, pointing his long finger between us, "or give into the not-so-subtle interest of the only single bridesmaid, and I'm pretty sure she's a minor."

I glance at Barbara's cousin Alyssa, squeezed into a tiny purple dress barely covering her ass, who turns to Ian every couple of seconds with a coy smile. "She's twenty-one. You're fine."

"Oh." He snaps his fingers. "Too bad. I have a rule against sleeping with people a decade younger than me."

"Unreasonable."

"I know. I'm impossible to please." He leans forward, the lemony scent of his cologne overpowering my senses for a second. "Come on, entertain me. What's wrong with your life?"

I let out an unsteady sigh and feel the backs of my knees start to sweat. Truth be told, it'd be easier to discuss nuclear physics than the tangled-up mess my life is. But if he'd like a dose of my problems instead of a young, gorgeous woman wrapped around him, who am I to disappoint?

Leaning against the back of my chair, I resign myself to the truth. "My best friend is the worst."

"Wonderful." With a pleased nod, he takes a sip. "Hit me."

"Martha. She's here somewhere."

"I hate her already. What's wrong with Martha?"

His expression is one of total focus, as if his ultimate goal in life is to hear about my drama. But I want to offer him an out, so I ask, "Are you sure you want me to tell you?"

His head slowly bobs up and down. "I'm deeply invested."

"All right: your loss." Straightening, I clear my throat, as if I am about to deliver a lecture on the meaning of life. "Martha and I were born one week apart in the same hospital. Our families were neighbors. We went to the same schools, and—"

"Dated the same guys and practiced the same sports and— wait. Are you engaged to the same man?"

The pulsing lights paint his face pink, and, with a cocked brow, I ask, "Do you want me to dump my problems on you or not? Because I can call Alyssa over."

"You wouldn't dare. Proceed."

"We're very different, but we also went through many of the same things at the same time. Graduations, birthdays, first boyfriends, first time. Don't," I say when the left corner of his mouth quirks up. "Same things, same time, *not* together."

Stifling a chuckle, he says, "It's bound to get competitive."

"It never was. She always won, but I didn't mind." I drain my margarita and set the glass down. "She had the best grades, chose a higher-paying career. She got all the guys, the bigger apartment, and I never resented her for it. I always celebrated her success as my own."

"Did you say she got *all* the guys?" he asks, tipping his head to the side.

"Yeah, she's gorgeous." I straighten my dress. "Men always go for her."

"Where is she?" His head turns left and right. "If she's prettier than you, I definitely want to meet her."

Fighting a smile, I click my tongue. Though he's obviously messing with me, that's been my whole life. I've always been the friend who men approach to find out if Martha is seeing anybody. "She's engaged too."

His eyes fill with understanding, a low hum vibrating out of his throat. "Oh, I know where this is going. You're getting married on the same day, aren't you?"

With a half-hearted chuckle, I shake my head. I wish that were the problem. "I'm crazy about weddings." Fidgeting with the stem of my glass, I continue, "Martha? Not so much. She always said she was going to have an extravagant ceremony. In a casino or an amusement park. She'd arrive on a horse and wear a short red dress—not white, because white's associated with virgins, and . . ." I chuckle, waving the thought off. "She has a lot to say about that. No veil, lots of drinking games and dancing. The party of the century, you know?"

He gives me an appreciative nod, and I know Martha already won him over. "And you? What do you picture?"

"Simple. On a beautiful farm, with white flowers and fairy lights and floating candle centerpieces. Hydrangea and ranunculus, a white dress and a beaded veil."

"No idea what most of that means, but it sounds nice. What's the problem, then?"

"I'm getting there." He motions at me to proceed, so I cross my legs and look around. "Things changed when she got engaged. All of a sudden, Martha no longer wanted her crazy Vegas wedding. No, sir. She wanted the complete opposite."

"Oh." His expression shifts to one of concern. "She's stealing your wedding."

"All of it. The flowers, the photographer, the band. Every. Single. Detail."

He huffs his disapproval. "Jesus, Amelie. You can't let her."

I wish it were that easy. Resting my chin on the palm of my

hand, I look down at my empty plate while yet another lock escapes my hairdo. "Well, I can't really say anything because I'm not . . ." I venture a look at him, and he's watching me so intently, it makes me wonder if he gives his undivided attention to everyone, or if there's a deeper reason for his interest. "I'm not *engaged* engaged."

His eyes narrow. "Excuse me?"

"I'm technically . . . Hmm, I guess you could call it 'pre-engaged.'"

His gaze moves to my hand, probably to confirm there's no ring on it. "So you have a boyfriend."

I press my lips together. "*No.* I've *had* a boyfriend for fifteen years, and he's going to propose soon, so I'm pre-engaged."

"Yeah, that's not a thing."

"It's a thing," I snap, catching his smile widening.

"All right. It's a thing. So why aren't you engaged yet after fifteen years?"

Looking around the table, I search for my most recent margarita and take a sip, then I set it down and gesture broadly at the empty glasses. "Funny you should ask, because I've been playing a really fun game tonight where I take a drink every time someone asks me why Frank and I aren't married yet."

His lips open in a tight O before he manages a soft "I see."

"Mm-hmm."

"So you can't say anything to Martha, because *technically* you're not getting married yet."

"Technically," I admit, and when his eyes light up with a twinkle of amusement, I point my finger at him. "No, no. I'm still right. You see, my boyfriend doesn't get it, either, but there's an unspoken agreement. I chose a bouquet of red roses when I was ten and a dark green off-shoulder dress for my bridesmaids when I was fifteen. They're as good as booked, Ian."

"Of course. I get it." He nods as he rubs his chin, his gaze intently set on mine. "It's important to you, and your friend is being careless of your feelings. That's not cool."

"Thank you," I say in agreement. It's liberating to have someone take my side for once.

He shifts in his chair and turns my way, bringing his hand to the side of his neck as his blue eyes fill with a kindness I've never experienced before. Right then I realize I like Ian. He's definitely one of the good guys. "You said your 'preancé' doesn't agree?"

"Oh, we've had an entire season of fights lately. The latest episode aired today, in fact."

"A whole season, huh?" He leans forward, his interest piqued again. "Well, if I'm binge-watching, we're going to need more drinks."

He stands with a smile, then walks to the bar. His back is wide and inviting, and with each stride the muscles of his thighs flex under his suit pants. His broad chest stretches his white shirt to its limits, and his thick hair falls in a thoughtless manner over the sides of his face.

A few eyes follow him as he sets his elbow on the counter and talks to the bartender. Ian is the type of man who would attract the attention of the gentler sex, for sure. Plus, he's got the attitude thing figured out. There's a cocky but casual quality to his movements, his expressions—loads of self-confidence, humor, and wit. He might be one of the good guys, but if he's single, it must be because he *wants* to be.

He drops himself into the chair next to mine a few minutes later, a margarita and a glass of something that looks like whiskey in his hands. "So, is that why he's not here? Your boyfriend?"

Lips pinching, I nod. I've had to justify his absence with a sudden fever to a billion people already, bride and groom included.

"His company asked him to move to manage one of their offices, and he wants to go. It's only temporary, six months. But my job is here, so . . ."

"Long-distance?"

That's Frank's plan. Which is not ideal, but I'm willing to do it for a while. The fight was actually about him accepting the job without even talking to me about it first. To be honest, it felt like he couldn't wait to get away.

Barbara walks toward us in a fluffy white princess dress, holding her new husband's hand and waving my way as they leave the dance floor. Soon, that's going to be me, I hope, and I wish I were more excited, but the upcoming separation from Frank and the drama with Martha have sucked out all the joy.

With a long sigh, I take another sip.

"Okay, I have the solution to your wedding problem," Ian says, standing and buttoning his gray suit jacket over his crispy white shirt. Only then, his arm reaches out, his hand open and waiting for mine. "And it starts with a dance."

Unpopular Opinions

Ian's hand against the small of my back is innocent enough to keep me relaxed as we swing lightly on the spot. Though there's nothing wrong with dancing with a stranger at a wedding, the moment his hand slides an inch south or there's less than an appropriate space between us, I'm out of here.

To Ian's credit, he's kept it respectful.

"So did you like the ring?"

I tilt my head and grip his shoulder, enjoying the feel of the tequila swishing in my stomach and loosening my muscles. His hand gently holds mine as he leads us in a few basic steps. "The ring?"

"You said you know your preancé is about to propose." He twirls us around. "I'm assuming you found a ring in his sock drawer?"

"Oh." I smile, excitement pooling in my stomach. "I didn't, but he left his computer open the other day, and I saw an email from a jewelry store."

He rubs his lips in thought. "Hmm."

"He's not a jewelry guy, so it's definitely about a ring."

"Well, Amelie, not to rain on your 'pre-parade,' but it sounds like you don't even know if he *bought* a ring." He bites his lower lip. "It could have been a watch. A gift for his mom. An unwanted newsletter."

My posture stiffens. "The subject was 'The pleasure of rings,' and the first line said 'Thank you for your purchase.'"

His smile falls and his steps freeze. With a shocked expression, he studies me, his blue eyes wide and his forehead creasing. "'The pleasure of rings'?" he repeats.

"Yeah."

He opens his mouth, then closes it. Gripping my hand, he continues swinging on the spot. "And what was the name of the jewelry store?"

"Le Love Bijoux."

With a nod, he lets go of my back and grabs his phone from his pocket. He opens a new window and types away while I wait, my foot nervously tapping on the floor. When he's done, he hisses through his teeth as he sets his phone back. "Ugh. God, I hate it when I'm right."

"Right?" My heart quickens. "Right about what?"

Pinching the bridge of his nose, he mumbles, "I don't think I have the heart to tell you."

"Well, come on, now," I insist. Whatever he saw obviously wasn't good. What the hell could it be? "You know I can just check it myself."

"Nope." He avoids looking at me, his lips pressed tightly, as if he's trying to stop himself from laughing. "I don't want you to cry at your friend's wedding."

"I won't cry, Ian."

At my annoyed tone, he looks down at me. He hesitates for a few seconds, and when I prompt him to speak, he says, "'*The pleasure of rings*,' Amelie?"

"What about it!"

He leans closer as if we're about to share a secret. "Well, I'm going to assume you know what a cock ring is?"

Oh, Lord. Did he say *cock ring*? I open my mouth, and without making a sound, I shake my head.

"No?" He hums. "Solo use, then, huh? Frank sounds like a fun guy."

"What the hell are you talking about?" I whisper.

His eyes soften, every trace of amusement gone from his face. He cups my shoulder, the grip of his fingers delicate and comforting as he says, "Le Love Bijoux is a sex shop, Amelie. And a cock ring is a vibrating silicone ring you put around your—"

"Got it," I say, raising my hand to stop him.

A sex shop. A cock ring. He was never going to propose to me. Fifteen years—*fifteen*—and he's still not proposing. We'll never get married, will we? I might as well let Martha steal my wedding, because I won't ever have one.

I frown down at his suit, my eyes on the undulating pattern of his blue tie, and when his hand rubs between my shoulder blades, I force myself to smile. "Well, I guess you *did* fix my wedding problem."

"Your wedding problem is hardly fixed. If anything," he says with a dismissive gesture, "Martha will be all the more selfish now." He looks deeply into my eyes as we resume gently swinging on the spot. "Which brings me to your solution." There's a beat of silence. "Fuck Martha's wedding. When Frank proposes, you book the venue, buy the dress, the—whatever it is you said before. If it's important to you, have the wedding you want."

I look away with a sneer. If the solution were that simple, I would have thought about it all by myself. "I can't do that."

"Why not?"

"She'd hate me. I'd hate it too. We can't have the same wedding."

He sighs, lost in thought for a few seconds, then his eyes widen as he spins us around. "Even better: elope. Just get it done and over with. No more headache."

Once he registers my eyes bulging in terror, he whistles. "Got it. Not an option."

"*Definitely* not an option."

His shoulder slumps beneath my fingers. "I think there's only one thing you can do."

"What's that?"

"Don't partake in an archaic ritual that has, at this point in time, lost all meaning." When my eyebrows knit, he throws his palm up. "Marriage made sense when women were a burden for their fathers and an instrument for men who wanted to continue their bloodlines." He clicks his tongue. "The fathers would get three cows, a goat or two, and off the women went."

"Jesus," I breathe out, horrified. "*That's* your view on marriage?"

"It is. And that's just marriage. Don't even get me started on weddings."

I study his light blue eyes, which I now notice are speckled with darker spots, and wait for him to say his piece. I don't *know* Ian, but I know his piece is coming.

When his warm gaze meets mine, there's a devilish quality to his smile that's both concerning and inexplicably attractive. "A multibillion-dollar industry that has lots to do with status and power and little to do with marriage. Fireworks, carriage rides, doves. Impossibly pretentious food, increasingly ridiculous themes, hundreds of guests you've hardly even spoken to in years," he scoffs. "Weddings are for politics, not love."

Noticing that my face has gone slack with shock, Ian shrugs. "Am I wrong?"

"I don't know if you're wrong, but I'm ready to bet you're divorced."

Shaking his head, he laughs. "Sorry, never been married. I'm just opinionated."

"About weddings," I insist. Nobody hates marriage that much without a very personal story. "Why's that?"

"No reason." He spins me around, his breath fanning over my face as I land back in front of him. Whiskey mixed with something fresh. "I'm full of great opinions about anything."

"Of course you are."

"I mean it. Ask me the first thing that comes to your mind."

"All right." The song changes to a slower ballad. "Ariana Grande?"

He slowly shakes his head. "Shamefully underrated."

"The color orange."

"Not nearly as good as green."

"Really?"

"Really. Rainy days are better than sunny days, making your bed in the morning is a waste of time, pumpkin lattes taste nothing like pumpkin, and Christmas isn't the best holiday."

I take in a lungful of air as I stand motionless, watching him for a long while. He must be used to it, even take some pleasure out of the shock on my face, because his smirk deepens. "Christmas?" I whisper eventually. "You've got a better holiday than Christmas?"

"St. Patrick's Day. Green beer, cheerful leprechauns, unbearable bagpipe music that only sounds good when you're drunk." He makes a humming sound that rumbles in his chest. "Hard to beat."

I think of arguing back with eggnog, snow, and gift exchanges, but something tells me he'd have a strong and unrelatable opinion about those too.

There's a charming smile on his face as we silently dance to the rest of the song, and once the music stops and Barb's mom begins her speech, he lets me go. We've swung to the other side of the dance floor, away from most guests, and it looks as if the realization hits him not long after it has hit me.

For a moment we both stand there looking at each other out of the corners of our eyes. Should we go back to my table? Should we keep dancing? Should we just part ways?

"You want to hear another one of my indisputable opinions?"

I nod, relieved he took matters into his own hands.

"Cake's overrated. It's too sweet, too bland, too dry." He doesn't wait for an answer and instead rises on the tips of his toes to look over the crowd of people. "But tonight's cake was the only good one in history. We should find it and eat some more."

I scoff, a laugh spilling out. I'm afraid to ask whether he means we should sneak into the kitchen and *steal* some cake, but before I can, Martha's voice erupts from the crowd. "Amelie! Pictures!"

Even as frazzled as she is after sweating on the dance floor for hours, she's breathtaking. Golden-brown locks frame her round face, her catlike eyes greener than usual, and her smile filled with exhilaration. The strobe lights illuminate her dress, making the millions of golden sequins shine like she's some sort of mystical mermaid. When she shimmies—she must have also enjoyed the open bar—the fabric flows along her movements, her curves looking as splendid as ever.

"Speak of the devil," I say out of the side of my mouth with a friendly wave.

As she retreats into the crowd, Ian laughs. "*That* was Martha?"

"Yeah."

"She's not the pretty one. She's—" He narrows his eyes. "Yes, she's beautiful, but . . . come on."

When he points at me, waving his hand up and down, I stifle a chuckle. Being told you're pretty is a wonderful ego boost. Even more so when it comes from a handsome and quick-witted guy like Ian, and when your own preancé doesn't say it as often anymore. It's one of those things that happen with time, I guess. The small, everyday gestures fade as your comfort grows.

"Thank you." I straighten my dress, then throw a look behind me. "I'm afraid I have to . . ."

He waves in dismissal. "Of course. Go ahead."

"Sorry about the cake."

With a playful wink, he drops his hands into his pockets. "We'll get cake at the next wedding."

"Right." My fingers awkwardly play with the flaps cinching my dress, and with a quick smile I offer, "It was great meeting you."

His pearly-white teeth peek through his lips. "Likewise."

With a little hesitation, I turn around, then back to him again. There's an expectant look in his eyes as we peer at each other for a few seconds, and I soak in the fact that we won't be sharing cake at the next wedding because there likely won't be another wedding we'll both happen to be at. And though I've just met Ian, the thought saddens me.

Living in a small town like Creswell, most of the people I engage with I've known since I was in kindergarten, and it's refreshing to meet someone new. Meeting someone new and getting along this well is basically divine intervention. God, I can think of at least three girlfriends I could set him up with. But he's probably not interested, right? People at our age aren't looking for new friends, and all I am is his entertainment for tonight.

"Just do it," he says, his smile so bright and joyful, it's contagious.

"Do what?"

"Whatever you're considering. Don't think about it."

We share another silent yet word-filled look. I *am* considering something. He's right. The fact that he knows only makes my decision easier.

Fishing into my bag, I take out my phone. "Give me your number. You've been nice enough to listen to my problems, and if it weren't for you, I'd still think I'm almost engaged instead of knowing my boyfriend's creative when it comes to fiddling with himself."

He smothers a smile.

"The least I can do is get you the only cake you ever liked."

His brows rise for a second, and—considering it doesn't look like he knows I'm a chef—I expect him to ask follow-up questions, but he doesn't. Instead, he grabs the phone, taps on the screen, and gives it back with a winning grin. "There. Oh, wait."

He walks to the closest table and stretches toward the center, causing the guests sitting at it to give him the side-eye suspiciously. Even more so when he grabs one of the flowers belonging to the centerpiece.

He walks back to me, then holds out a yellow daisy. "For turning my night around."

I chuckle, awkwardly accepting the flower and rolling the stem between my thumb and index finger. "Thank you."

With a dazzling smile, he waves and walks away. "Don't keep me waiting too long, Amelie."

———

Three hundred pictures later, I fetch my jacket, congratulate the newlyweds, and leave the venue, my yellow daisy in hand. The party isn't over yet, and people are still dancing to the music of the DJ, but I've been here much longer than they have, and I'm so exhausted, I'm seeing double.

Stepping into the brisk night air, I find Barbara's grandma looking down at the white steps of the venue, and with a smile I approach her. "Mrs. Wilkow?"

She turns to me, her eyes glossy and tired. When she says nothing, I say more loudly, "Do you need help to get down the stairs?"

"Oh. Yes, yes." She holds on to my arm and, step by step, we walk. "It was a beautiful wedding, wasn't it?"

"Gorgeous!" I shout. Damn right it was a beautiful wedding. Martha and I helped Barbara plan it right down to the tiniest detail. Although the photographer was late and half the flowers were a little on the sick side, Barbara looked happy, and that's the way you know a wedding has been successful.

"Did you have fun? Did that man behave like a gentleman?" she croaks.

I squint as I try to figure out what she's talking about, when it hits me. Ian gave up his chair for her; she must have seen he came to sit next to me. "Very," I reassure her with a soft pat on her hand. "Don't worry about it."

"You'll make a great couple." With another unsure step, she squeezes my hand hard enough that it might just need to be amputated. "My husband and I were one too. Everyone would turn around when we entered a room."

I can't help but frown. I've known this lady for as long as I've known Barb, and she's always been sharp. Unfortunately, things have changed in the past year. "I have a boyfriend, Mrs. Wilkow. Remember? Frank. Dark hair, glasses?"

Her mouth widens, her lost eyes focusing after a few seconds. "Oh." She brings both hands to her cheeks. "Did you reject that handsome man? Oh, it's all my fault: I forgot."

I place a hand on her shoulder, trying to ease her concern. I won't stand by as this woman has a heart attack at her granddaughter's wedding. "No, no. It wasn't like that, Mrs. Wilkow. You have nothing to worry about."

"Wasn't it?" she asks, her eyes wandering to the people walking beside us. "He asked me to sit in his chair so he'd have an excuse to talk to you. He said you were the most beautiful woman he'd ever seen."

Who's in Your Corner?

– TODAY –

With a sharp intake of air, I emerge from the water. I wasn't under for that long, but the cold has me breathless, shivering as the strong waves push me closer to the rocks on the shore. My hand clutches around my necklace and, relieved it's still there, I fight the tide. The jump seemed like a cathartic little gesture from the top, but, once below, I swam for a while to reach the surface. "What a *sh-sh-shit* idea," I murmur as my teeth clatter.

Throwing myself off the edge of a cliff and plummeting into the void for about fifty feet, not knowing what's under?

That's not cathartic; it's potentially fatal. And no matter how hard life has been in the past year, I'm far from done.

My arms move frantically to keep me floating, my clothes weighing me down, and with the stupidly tall cape blocking out the sun, the water is almost pitch-black. Note to self: pitch-black waters are terrifying. Especially because my feet can't reach the bottom by a lot. There really could be anything down here, couldn't there? A shark. A whale. A kraken.

Shaking my head as if to propel myself from such thoughts, I slowly make my way toward the shore, which happens to *also* be farther than it looked like it was from the top of the cape. Of course, I was dry, warm, and not about to be eaten by a kraken back then.

Other note to self: the possibility of being eaten by a sea creature makes one severely reconsider distances.

It takes me many more minutes than it would if I wasn't awkwardly flapping my arms and feet around and actually swimming, but I eventually escape the shadow cast by the cape. I'm quickly and brutally aware it doesn't change much in terms of temperature or visibility through the water, but it's something. My need to be surrounded by fellow humans has never been stronger, and at least now I can see the shore, where people are sunbathing or swimming. With more confident strides and warmer muscles, I reach shallow waters, where finally my feet touch the sand and I stand upright.

"Holy fuck," I whisper in relief. I'm not sure if I'm technically out of kraken territory, but it definitely feels like it now that I know where the ground is.

I drag my feet forward, curious eyes meeting my gaze as I emerge fully clothed and wobble out of the water like someone from *The Walking Dead*'s cast.

I'm not sure the jump was worth it. I figured it'd be liberating. That I'd let myself go and leave all my problems behind. Maybe that my sorrows would drown and I'd come out a new person with a thicker, tougher skin.

But I feel exactly the same empty shell of myself.

"Darling, are you okay?"

I turn to the left, where an older woman is staring at me in my jeans and shoes. She's holding a child's hand, keeping him slightly behind her as her expression becomes one of concern. It's imperative I go back for my bag and get home; I'm starting to scare the civilians. "I'm fine, thanks. Just took a swim."

"You might want to take off your clothes first next time."

Nodding, I squeeze my T-shirt, water rippling down on the sand. "Yup, you make a fair point."

She smiles, her eyes still suspiciously scanning me as she walks away. With a resigned sigh, I walk until the beach is behind me, then begin the long trek back up the hill. At least the sun is unseasonably warm, so my drenched clothes aren't even that bad, even with the weight of them.

Look at me: finding positivity in the little things.

I just hope I'll also find my bag and keys where I left them.

———————

My shoes make an annoying slapping noise as I enter my building post–ocean dip and leave a wet trail behind me. A neighbor on his way out throws me a disgruntled look, similar to the ones I received walking past the city center. No amount of positive thinking can make up for crossing most of my town looking like a drowned cat.

As I jog up the stairs, the damp shirt glues itself to my body uncomfortably. My hair smells like salt as it moves in wet chunks over my face, and even with the warm summer day I'm so cold that I'm fighting goose bumps and shivers with every step.

Once on the second floor, I grab the keys out of my bag and walk toward my apartment, but I stop in my tracks when I see Barb's red curls jostling from side to side as she knocks at my door. "Barb?"

"Oh, Ames." She turns around and stalks toward me, holding a hand to her baby bump. Her arms lock around my neck and squeeze; then, as quickly as she crowded me, she pulls away. "Are your clothes . . . wet?"

With a sigh, I look down at my jeans and T-shirt, a tone darker than they're supposed to be, then shrug. "I took a dip off the pier. I've always wanted to."

"The pier?" she asks worriedly. I unlock the door and enter, leaving it open for her to follow. As she joins me inside the apartment, her eyes scout the dusty, crowded space, then dart to me. "How are you feeling?"

"I'm . . ." The last few hours flash in my mind. You'd think I'd be crying my eyes out or cursing the journalist who wrote the most degrading words that have ever been said about me, but I haven't spilled a single tear since the magazine was delivered to me two hours ago.

When I sit on the couch and bring one of the cushions to my chest, Barb yanks it away. She might be five inches shorter than me, with sweet, big brown doe eyes, but neither matches her superhuman strength. "Are we really not going to talk about it?"

I flinch when I realize she's read it. I wonder how many people have so far—how many will in the next hours and days. "I don't think there's anything left to say."

"*Ames* . . ."

"You've seen it, Barb." I press a finger over my temple. "By tomorrow, everyone else will have seen it too. My career, my life— I *failed*. My worst mistakes, the most painful humiliations of my life, have been made public. And now . . ."

She swallows, her wide eyes filling with the same sadness enveloping my bones.

". . . now . . . it's over."

"Ames, it's not that bad. Yes, the article was . . . harsh," she whispers while trying to mask her disgruntled look, "but it's not too late for you to bounce back. You can't give up."

I chuckle. I understand Barb's just trying to help, but it's pretty safe to say my career is over. No one will ever hire me again, not with what *Yum* magazine said about me. My only shot at getting back into the kitchen would be working at my dad's restaurant, and I wouldn't go back for anything in the world.

It's fine. I will retire from my career as a chef and explore something else. And I'll do that while retaining as much dignity as I can.

"So . . . that's it?" she asks, awkwardly shifting positions as she holds a hand to her bump. "You're one of the most talented and promising chefs in this part of the country, and you're giving up?"

When I give her a distracted nod, she carefully lowers herself onto the couch, leaning back with a tired exhale. "What about the ICCE?"

My eyes widen as my arms fall limply down my sides, droplets of water still dripping from my short, dark brown locks onto my shirt. The International Cooking and Culture Expo, a global cooking conference for newbies and professionals alike, as well as a great networking event. With my life tumbling down a hillside for the past few months, I completely forgot about it. "When is it again?"

"September seventh," Barb says. When she notices my expression, she adds, "Right before Martha's wedding, remember?"

Oh my God. I barely know what month we're in.

"Ames? It's in a week." She studies my face. "Have you been sleeping?" Her eyes barrel down my body. "Or eating?"

Avoiding both questions, I study the mess of my sad studio apartment, the dust and plates and clothes accumulated everywhere. I've been to the ICCE twice before, and when I was invited as a speaker for this year's edition, I was more than thrilled. So much has changed since. "We should definitely withdraw. I'm sure they'll be relieved. With that article, the drama would follow me to the convention."

"Are you sure?" she ventures. "It might be good for you. Give you something to distract yourself with. Maybe motivate you."

Or, more likely, someone will bring up the last six months of my life and ask what gives me the right to teach anyone anything at all. "I'm sure."

"Okay. I'll order dinner." Her finger swipes over the coffee table, and as she shows me the dust on her fingertip, she adds, "We can clean up a little while we wait, then binge something." Patting my knee, she gives me a smile that reaches up to her warm eyes. "How does that sound?"

Like I should have called her sooner. I've been avoiding her and everyone else for months, and now that she's here, I forget why. "Yes, please," I tell her as I squeeze her hand.

"Great. Let me just call Ryan."

"Why? Did you guys have plans?"

Her dismissive gesture is as convincing as my recent smiles, and as her eyes drift to her wedding band, I suck in a surprised breath. Martha's getting married on September fifteenth, a day after the weeklong conference will be over, so today must be September first. "Barb?"

"Hmm?" she asks as she taps on her phone.

"Is today your anniversary?"

She waves me off again as she makes a *pfft* sound. "It's fine, Ames. I'm stuck with Ryan for the rest of my life. We'll have many more anniversaries."

It feels like my brain is shutting down, my fingers and toes tingling until they feel entirely numb. Just when I'd started to think the sorrow in my soul was at maximum capacity, a new wave hits me and leaves me breathless.

It's been a year since her wedding. A whole year since . . . *him*.

"Ames?"

Swallowing the lump in my throat, I hold a hand over Barb's phone. "Don't be ridiculous. It's your first wedding anniversary, and you'll spend it with your husband."

"But—"

"No buts." I squeeze her into a side hug, wetting her T-shirt with my damp hair. "Congratulations, Barb."

Her shoulders slump, and she gives me a half-hearted nod. "Thank you. We won't do anything special anyway. The baby only allows for a few nausea-free hours at a time."

"Did you have another ultrasound?"

"Last week. You wouldn't believe how much he's grown already. We saw his little fist this time." She takes out her phone, then shows me a picture. Then a video, then another picture. I grin at the happiness pouring out of her and can't help thinking that their baby boy might be the only good news to come out of the past year.

"Go on, get out of here," I tell her. Knowing she feels like she's abandoning me when I most need her, I put on a mask of cheerfulness and stand. I walk her to the door, then squeeze her into a hug, her belly pushing into mine as I hold her close.

"Ames," she says as I let her go. Twisting a sticky lock of my hair away from my face, she gives me a strained smile. "I haven't seen you happy in so long."

My lips purse as I study the billion freckles on her face, praying whatever she has to say won't take long.

"You know I'm not wrong. Is there someone in your life you like? Someone you're close to? A person you trust?"

When I wink at her, she chuckles, squeezing my hand. "Same, and although I wish I could be there for you more often, when the baby comes, I'll be barely holding up myself."

"I'm doing just fine, Barb."

"*Really*?" She rolls her eyes and raises a small hand, thumb extended. "You and Martha aren't on speaking terms. Your dad can't think of anything but his career, your mom is on the other side of the world"—she shakes her head as she continues listing off each item with her fingers—"and after Frank . . ."

"I don't want to talk about him."

She lets loose a sigh. "I know. All I am saying is . . ." She looks around, as if trying to find the right words. "Who's in your corner, Ames? You need someone you trust. Someone you love, someone who gets you smiling and is there for you. You *need* someone in your corner."

When I say nothing, she kisses my cheek and squeezes my arm, then walks away.

Closing the door of the apartment, I let the question poison my mind.

Who's in my corner?

I thought Frank was, but things went the way they did. Martha was, but I can think of so many instances during the past year when she wasn't. Then I think of *him*.

He was in my corner.

He stayed in my corner, protecting it with everything he had, until I forced him away.

Ian.

4

Mayfield, Here I Come

– TODAY –

I get off my bike and park behind La Brasserie, the scent of garlic and onions telling me dinner service has begun. Unclipping my helmet, I follow the voices I can hear around the corner and find Jeremy, Thomas, and David smoking at the back entrance, their black chef coats on.

"Gentlemen," I say as I approach my former colleagues. "How are we doing?"

"Good, uh . . . we're just—we're . . ." David trails off as they all glance in different directions.

So they've read the article.

I'm not surprised. It's been almost a week, and pretty much anyone in the business has read it. It's everywhere.

After standing awkwardly for a few seconds, David throws his cigarette away and enters La Brasserie. Thomas and Jeremy follow, and with a deep breath I enter the kitchen too.

Immediately, I'm welcomed by the familiar clinking noise of pots and pans, by the butter sizzling on the stoves and the kitchen staff moving around like soldiers. My father's restaurant has had the same menu for as long as I've worked here, and the stainless steel kitchen has never changed. It feels more homey to me than most places I've actually lived in.

"Ames!" Barb calls out from the other end of the long kitchen. Everybody's eyes meet mine before they look away and whisper words into each other's ears.

My body temperature rises so quickly, it feels like my skin is steaming.

They've all read it. They all know.

Barbara steps closer and plops her oven mitts on the counter by my side, a wary expression taking over her face. "What are you doing here? I thought we were meeting at five."

"My dad wants to talk." Unfortunately, this is only one of two very unpleasant tasks today, because Martha also texted on the group chat and asked to meet us for a coffee at Beans, our usual café. "We can leave together."

Sasha, one of the latest waitresses to join the staff, walks beside me with an entrecôte and a bowl of onion soup. My gaze follows the tray until she disappears around the corner, my hands itching to stop her, because the meat looked a little overdone.

"Would you like to cook something?" Barb asks with a soft voice. "For old times' sake?"

With a glance at the black chef's coats hanging on the entrance wall, I wave her off. "I'll just go see what the man of the hour wants. Where is he?"

"Dining room," she says, patting my hand twice before stalking toward the fryer, then turning back and pointing a finger at me. "Don't spoil the customers' dinner with murder."

"I'll make sure the only red stains are left by the sauvignon," I call before entering the dining room.

Though the sun is beaming outside, the tinted windows absorb most of the natural light. A dim yellow glow comes from the chandelier and provides a soft ambience for the small groups sitting at beige linen–covered tables across the room.

My father, in his chef's coat and hat, is talking to the people sitting by the front window. There's an affable smile on his face as the soft strains of "Non, je ne regrette rien" by Édith Piaf accompany us.

I wish I could say I'm surprised to find him at the front of the house, but these days, he spends more time talking to customers in the dining room than cooking. The rest of the time, he travels from one location to another for an interview, a cooking show, a competition he'll judge—whatever it may be. Three seasons on *The Silver Spoon*, and everybody has come to know his less-than-amicable working attitude, earning him the nickname of "Le Dictateur." He loves the name so much, some days I think he might have a golden plaque engraved with it hung at the entrance.

As soon as he sees me across the room, his expression falls, and he excuses himself and walks closer. Taking off his black chef's hat, he passes a hand over his balding head. Once he reaches me, his dark brown sunken eyes—the same color as mine—scan me with a disappointed look. "*Ma fille.*"

"You wanted to see me?"

"You're working the dinner service tomorrow," he says in his usual cold voice. He gestures at me to follow him, then struts into the kitchen, all eyes on us as he approaches the serving counter.

"I don't work here, Dad."

"You don't work anywhere." He pierces me with a cold gaze. "After that article, you'll never work again."

Surprise, surprise. Father dearest has read the article, too, and he isn't pleased.

"We've already had this conversation. I don't work at La Brasserie, and at the moment, I'm not looking for a job in any kitchen."

I glare at one of the waiters, fidgeting with a bottle of champagne while he eavesdrops. "Yesterday's article changes nothing."

"Are you aware of what it means for me? What they wrote?" he says, seething, lowering his voice as he looks left and right.

"Yes. Everyone in the world of fine dining knows your daughter is a failure. They know I didn't take after the great Hammond Preston. I don't have your talent, your experience. I'm just a nobody who's used her dad's connections."

My tone is flat, and, surprisingly, saying those words out loud didn't hurt half as much as it should. It's almost liberating.

If I had known giving up would feel so good, I would have done it much sooner.

When his chin tilts toward his chest, I wonder if he'll contradict me. If, for once, he'll say I'm a fighter and he regrets being the parent he's always been to me.

But I don't wonder for too long.

"Your best chance at a future as a chef is to come back to work for me. With time, people will forget. Hopefully." His jaw tenses and his words slur, as if pronouncing them is hard, the LED lighting accentuating the sweat on his broad forehead. "I still need a head chef to take my place."

I lean against the counter and look deeply into his tired eyes, my fingers mindlessly fidgeting with the chain of my necklace. "Dad, I'm done with cooking," I say with a firm voice. This must be the fiftieth time we've talked about this, so I should have imagined this is why he called me in. "I won't be your head chef. Hire externally if there's nobody in this kitchen who can meet your expectations."

He grunts and, without another word, walks straight to Trent, one of the line cooks, then barks something about his knife technique.

For a few seconds I'm glad this isn't my life anymore. Then I squeeze the strap of my bag and walk toward Barb, who's bent over the stove and working on a pot of lobster bisque. Wiping her hands on her apron, she straightens and throws me a worried look, her red curls trapped under a black hairnet. "All good?"

"Yeah. He just wanted me to come in for the dinner service tomorrow." With an eye roll, I point at the door. "I'll see you outside."

Skillfully avoiding the cooks and busboys who shift from one side of the kitchen to the other, I get to the back door, only to stop when I notice the article from *Yum* magazine taped to it. There's boisterous laughter coming from behind me, but I don't bother turning around, my gaze laser focused on the worst parts.

My eyes fill with words like *embarrassment* and *shame*. I close them, but I can still see more of them. *Nepotism*. *Incompetence*. And, of course, *failure*.

"Seriously? You people have nothing in your brain, do you?" Barb shouts.

She comes closer, her fingers pulling on one corner of the page to strip it off the door, but I'm quick to wrap my hand around her wrist. "Wait."

"What is it?"

My eyes scroll through the lines of text. I've been staring at this article for the past week, but I was so stuck on the reputation smackdown, I didn't notice the red bubble at the bottom, prompting the reader to reveal the piece about the International Cooking and Culture Expo. "The ICCE," I huff out as my heartbeat quickens. "Did you withdraw us already?"

"I called, but they said they need me to send an email. Don't worry, I'll do it tonight."

"No you won't," I tell her. "We *have* to go."

"Do we?"

Yes, we do. I meant what I said: I'm done with cooking. I'm done with restaurants and with my dad and with everything

French. But the red bubble caught my attention for a reason. I missed some things, including the email where they announced the conference's location.

But location is key, and this year the ICCE happens to be a mere two hours away—and, coincidentally, where *I* want to be.

In Mayfield.

———————

Barbara and I sit at the first available table at Beans, our local café. We've been coming here for so long, we've seen three different owners come and go.

The waitress takes our order, and instead of the usual macchiato, Barb gets some type of herbal infusion. Our lives have changed from the days when we'd sit here and chat about boys over our frappuccinos and mochas.

"Do you miss coffee?" I ask, crossing my legs under the iron table. "I don't know if I'd be able to give up sushi and—" I stop speaking. "What?"

She shakes her head dramatically, her bright copper hair bouncing. "*What?* What do you mean, *what*?"

"I mean—"

"Martha is five minutes away, so cut the crap, Ames. How did you pass from 'not interested' to 'I'm in' in half a second?"

The ICCE. Wiping away a few crumbs from the table, I try to feign indifference. She's known me for ten years, so I'm not sure she buys it. Plus, she's sensitive. She always knows when there's more than meets the eye.

"Oh my God. It's that guy, isn't it?"

I mentally curse myself. Martha and Barbara know little about Ian, but I've shared a few bits of information here and there. Mostly under coercion.

"What guy?" I ask placidly, avoiding her gaze as I dig around in my purse.

"*What guy?*" she mocks. "*That* guy. The 'mystery texts' guy? The guy you crushed hard over?"

Okay. No point in feigning ignorance. "Ian?" When she wiggles her eyebrows, I ask, "What about him?"

"He totally lives in Mayfield, doesn't he?"

When I shrug, she laughs loudly, letting me off the hook only because the waitress is approaching with our order. But once she walks away, Barb's pointed look forces me to answer. "I don't know if he still does. We haven't talked in forever."

"But that's the reason you said yes, right?" She gasps. "That's why you don't want me to fix you up with anyone. You still like him."

I sigh. "Like him" seems a bit of an understatement, but that's not the only reason I don't want to be set up with anyone. Frank's equally responsible for that.

"Do you know what this is about?" I ask as I point at the table. Though I'm eager to change the topic, I'm genuinely concerned about seeing Martha.

"She hasn't said a word to me." Barb shrugs. "I know that she's been having issues with the wedding, though."

The wave of nausea that hits me as I remember when she planned her wedding the first time, alongside me, is swept away as her voice reaches us. "*Heeeeeeey!*"

We both turn and spot Martha's bright smile as she approaches in a flurry, presses loud kisses to our cheeks, then sits down. The collection of paper bags in her hands crinkles before she drops them on the floor, and there's an awkward exchange of looks as we all fall silent.

"My God, I'm exhausted," Martha eventually says, trying to break the tension with a forced smile as she pushes her long, dark blond hair over her shoulders.

Eyeing the name of her favorite boutiques on the sides of the colorful bags, I ask, "Shopping?"

"Yes. Just needed to forget about the wedding for a minute."

"Is everything all right?" Barb asks.

With a groan, Martha gestures at the waitress. "Honestly, I'm so over it. A wedding isn't meant to be planned twice." She puckers her lips, her green eyes lacking the usual gleam. "This second time around, it's been even more of a nightmare."

Barbara gives me a look that I translate to *Martha should stop complaining about having to cancel her wedding the first time around, since the reason for it was that Trevor's mom passed away a few days before the ceremony*, and, discreetly widening my eyes, I pat Martha's arm. "Well, let me know if you need anything. Barb is a little occupied at the moment," I say, directing a grin at her bump, "but I'm happy to help."

My stomach boils with sludge as Martha responds with her pity smile. I've seen it plenty during the years—most recently, when things with Frank went south. I can guess what this one is about. "I figured, with what happened, you'd want to stay away from anything love, wedding, and couple related," she says, tilting her head, her wavy hair gently swooshing over her white T-shirt.

Maybe it's not pity but compassion.

"I can be miserable about the train wreck that is my life and still be happy for you," I say.

"No, Ames, I know—"

"Let me know if I can do anything," I insist, this time with a full smile.

Barb tactically uses the moment of silence to change the topic back to shopping, then work, and then the baby, but something's noticeably stiff. Within one hour our cups are empty and silence is once again acting like a brick wall between us.

"So, the reason I asked you to meet . . ." Martha starts, her bottom lip disappearing under the upper one as her nose wrinkles. She wants something. "Ames, I know we've been having our problems, but . . ." She rolls a lock of her hair around her finger, as she does every time she's nervous, the light streaming in through the window and casting it a golden color. ". . . I just . . . I really miss you. Thirty years of friendship, and now we haven't hung out in months. Are you even coming to my wedding?"

I can't deny that my life without her has been easier. Lighter, even. After all the drama, there are cracks in our friendship that may heal only with time. But it doesn't mean I don't miss what we were before, and besides, she's right. We've been friends for our whole lives, and that counts for something.

"Of course," I reassure her. "I wouldn't miss it."

"Then . . . if you really mean it, there is something you could do for the wedding."

My shoulders dip. "Of course I mean it."

With an excited clap, she smiles. "You could . . . cook."

The blood in my veins freezes as her fingers wrap around my forearm. She can't be serious, can she? I haven't truly opened up to her in months, but she knows everything that's happened in my life. She must know, once again, she's asking too much of me.

"The caterer blew me off, Ames. The wedding is in ten days, and I've got no food." Her grip tightens. "I don't know what else to do."

"I'm sorry, Martha." I pull my arm back, freeing it from her hold. "I won't cook, but I'm happy to suggest plenty of chefs who could—"

"But I don't want other chefs. I don't know if I'll like their food!" she complains.

"Well . . ." My shoulders rise in a shrug as if to say, *That's* your *problem.*

"Seriously, Ames? You're my best friend," she insists. "Make me happy on my special day, *pleeeeease*."

"I can't. Anything else."

"But—"

"No," I say firmly. "I'm sorry."

She crosses her arms and tilts her chin up in a pout. "God, you're so selfish."

Oh, I am. I'm selfish, confrontational, stubborn. And I fucking love it. After spending my life failing to meet my father's expectations, adjusting to suit Frank's needs, and worrying about Martha's whims, I now put myself first and won't apologize for it.

The best part? Ian is the reason for it. Though he's technically also the reason I have no job, boyfriend, best friend, money, or plans for the near future.

Her frown becomes a bitter smile, and I realize she's not done pestering; she's simply done for today. Before she can add anything else, I stand. "But call if you need anything else."

Barb and Martha follow, collecting their belongings in a hurry, until, with a sour expression, Martha waves. "Yeah, okay. See ya."

We walk, Martha going one direction, while Barb and I walk the opposite way. A perfect metaphor for what happened to our friendship over the past year. But it's a drama I'm not eager to face, so I keep trudging without turning back.

I walk away from someone who's been my best friend for most of my life and is now nothing more than an acquaintance. Away from the person *I* was until my life got upended, my certainties shattered, my principles challenged.

I have only one goal for the immediate future. One idea in my mind.

Tomorrow I'm going to Mayfield.

And I'm going to find Ian.

5

The Wrong Type of Ring

> **Amelie:**
> You tricked me. You TRICKED me, you deceitful man.

I gawk at the screen of my phone. I can't believe Ian lied and I asked him for his number. His number! I asked a handsome man I met at a wedding for his number after he tried to hit on me.

Setting the daisy on the entryway table, I climb down from my heels and unzip my dress. "Frank?" I call. No answer. I haven't seen him since this morning, but it's late, so he must be sleeping.

When my phone buzzes, I glance at the screen.

> **Ian:**
> One hour and fifteen minutes.

> I was thinking about you, too, through most of it.

> **Amelie:**
> Mrs. Wilkow sold you out, you doofus.

> I KNOW you asked her to sit in your spot.

Ian:
Yes, I helped a fragile old lady who was a step away from crumpling to the floor.

I'm selfless like that.

He's *manipulative* like that, he means. I can't believe he made me think I was flattering myself when I told him I was engaged.

Amelie:
How about telling her I'm the most beautiful woman you've ever seen?

Ian:
I technically said that before seeing Martha, but I stand by my initial impression. No comparison.

"Jerk," I say as I rock back on the heels of my feet, then walk to the bedroom. Frank's dark hair peeks out from the duvet, and, leaning closer, I tuck the blanket under his chin and kiss the side of his head. I'm still angry at him, but I hate it when we fight. Just as I leave the bedroom, my phone vibrates again.

Ian:
Fine. I admit I wasn't transparent about my intentions, but you asked for my number.

Amelie:
Because of the cake.

Ian:
Cake as in . . . you'll give me a piece of that cake?

Amelie:
Cake as in cake.

> I was ONLY going to send you the name of the bakery.

> Of course, at the time, I wasn't aware you were a deceitful liar.

Ian:
Oh, yeah, of course. Makes sense. Totally.

Except . . .

I wait for another text, but it doesn't come. No matter, because whatever he's about to suggest is way off. Sure, we got along, and you'd have to be blind not to notice how handsome he is. But I'm basically engaged, aren't I? I'm not about to throw the last fifteen years of my life out the window for a twenty-minute conversation with a stranger.

I was *just* trying to be nice.

Amelie:
Except what?

When no answer comes, I set my phone on the coffee table and slip into my pajamas, then enter the bathroom and brush my teeth.

I'm pretty sure he'll answer at some point. Maybe he's trying to make me beg for it. He wants me to send him a hundred messages asking him to explain what the hell "*Except . . .*" means. He must be laughing at his screen right now, taking his sweet time answering.

I glance at the dark living room, my teeth sinking into my bottom lip. The temptation to check my phone is strong, but I won't play his games. I don't need to. My boyfriend is in bed, and all I truly desire after such a long day in heels is to curl up beside him and fall asleep to the rising and falling of his chest.

Once I turn the corridor light off and walk to the bedroom, Frank's heavy breathing is the only noise in the apartment. Fitting under the blanket next to him, I inhale his comforting smell of pine and sandalwood, the aftershave I got him on his last birthday. He doesn't wake up when I kiss the tip of his nose, only moves a little.

With a satisfied exhale, I rest my head on the fluffy pillow and close my eyes.

Except . . . that's not why you asked for my number.

Maybe that's what Ian will say. Well, to that I'll say he's a cocky idiot. Or I'll block him. Problem solved.

Except I know you work as a chef and that's why I brought the cake up? Except I could see how much fun you had with me? Except I could tell my weird-ass opinions made me irresistible in your eyes?

What the hell is he going to say?

With a grunt, I push the blanket away and head to the living room.

He texted.

I sit down on the couch and rub a hand over my face. I shouldn't look. If I read it six minutes after he sent it, I'll make him think I'm interested. And I'm not.

"Fuck me," I say, unlocking the phone. I need to know. My heart's beating out of my chest in anticipation.

There's a screenshot. It's my contact. *Beautiful*, with a red heart. He saved my number.

Amelie:
So? You can save my number as "wife number three" for all I care. It doesn't change the fact that I'm not interested.

Ian:
You're missing the point.

When you asked for my number, you didn't know I lied. But when you texted me, you knew. Yet you texted anyway.

And now I have your number.

Ian:
Good morning, Amelie.

I think I was promised the name of a bakery?

I drop my phone on the counter and continue whisking the eggs. It's Sunday, the sun is shining bright, and I found an excellent '90s playlist I'm currently dancing to. Though I have to work later today, I'm looking forward to spending some time with Frank before that. It'll be a great day.

"Good morning," Frank says, entering the kitchen.

I turn to him with a full smile, showing off my wifely apron. "Good morning, love."

When my lips softly graze his, he steps back, his chestnut-brown eyes softening from behind his thick glasses. "Looks like you're in a good mood."

I am, though I understand his surprise. The last words we said to each other before I left for Barb's wedding weren't kind, and I don't usually get over our fights without some sort of reconciliation.

Of course, all that went out the window when I found out I *accidentally* gave my number to a guy who turned out to be hitting on me. The bastard made me an involuntary part of a sketchy situation.

"How was the wedding?"

"Great," I say in a forcefully chirpy voice as I shake the thought off. "Barbara and Ryan were the portrait of happiness, and everyone missed you. Especially me." As I walk back to the frying eggs, my phone dings again, and I pick it up with a tsk.

> **Ian:**
> You're really not going to tell me the name?

> But the raspberry jam. And the lemon ganache.
> And the macadamia nuts!

What is he talking about? Raspberry jam and lemon ganache? *Nuts*? Oh my God, this guy didn't even eat the damn cake. The *idiot* totally played me.

Once I set the phone down, Frank says, "I'm sorry I didn't come. And I'm sorry about the fight we had. I should have told you about the move before accepting the position."

Or maybe asked?

I turn the stove off and walk over to where he's sitting. I bend forward so I can wrap my arms around his neck and stare into his eyes behind the black-framed glasses he started wearing a few years back. "Thank you," I whisper on his lips, and, pressing a kiss on his cheek, I continue, "You know I'll always support you. I just want to be part of the decision."

Our mouths meet for a moment, and after quickly brushing my tongue with his, he leans back so his face is out of reach. "So you're okay with it? With me going?"

I walk to the counter, then set bacon and eggs on two different plates and bring them to the table. I can't say I'm thrilled about it, but I understand better than anyone that ambition comes with its healthy dose of sacrifice. "I am, yes. Just six months, right?" When he nods, I smile. "I'll miss you, though."

"I'll miss you too."

I sit down and watch him dig his fork into the scrambled eggs. I guess it's time to bring up my own uncomfortable topic. "So, I met this guy at the wedding yesterday."

"A guy?"

"Ian. I think his dad is friends with Barbara's."

"And?"

"And we talked for a while. He was really nice. We were supposed to get cake, but I got called for pictures." I wave the thought off. "So I asked him for his number. I figured I could find out the name of the bakery and send it to him."

He nods like he's waiting for me to get to the point.

"Well, turns out he was—" I break off, fidgeting with the fork in my hand. "I don't know. Interested."

"Interested in *you*?"

I take a sip of coffee, avoiding his gaze. "Yeah."

"Oh my God, Ames." His shoulders drop. "I'm so relieved to hear you say that."

Relieved?

Before I can ask, he keeps going. "I went out with the guys from work last night, and this woman gave me her number." He sputters out a chuckle. "I was feeling so guilty."

My teeth grind as I force out a smile. I don't care about a woman giving him her number: he's a handsome guy, it's bound to happen. But why was he feeling guilty? "Well, if you did nothing wrong, you shouldn't feel guilty."

He hesitates, and under the weight of my stare, his teeth pinch his bottom lip. "Well, you asked some guy for his number. Is that not wrong?"

"What did you do, Frank?"

Avoiding my gaze, he digs into his eggs again. "Nothing, Ames. I just . . . I thought it was kind of . . . nice."

"Nice how?" I ask as my chest tightens. I guess there's nothing wrong with enjoying being desired. It's human, even. And he knows I'm not typically a jealous person. So there's definitely more to this story.

"Just . . . I liked the chase, I guess? The thrill?" He licks his lips, throwing me sheepish glances that do nothing to hide his discomfort. "I enjoyed flirting a little with someone new. I had a crush on you by the time I was ten; you know you're the only woman I've ever dated, kissed. Anything."

Setting my fork down, I inhale and exhale much quicker than necessary until I'm lightheaded. I think of my conversation with Ian at the wedding, of how I spent most of it discussing Frank and our pre-engagement. All the while, he was playing single dude at a party.

It's hardly the same thing.

"You know why I asked Ian for his number?" I ask, pressing my lips together tightly.

He shakes his head. "You said something about cake?"

"The cake was a thank-you for listening to me whine about Martha and being kind about it." I raise my index finger. "Oh, and for informing me of the fact that Le Love Bijoux is not a jewelry store but the place where you buy your cock rings."

His jaw snaps open, but he says nothing for a moment as his eyes bulge out. "A—a jewelry store?"

"Yeah," I confirm. "Instead of shopping for inventive masturbation techniques, I figured you might be thinking of proposing." I bite the inside of my cheek. "Turns out, you were too busy enjoying being single."

"Ames," he groans. His hand finds mine on the table, and when I pull it back, he follows, not releasing his grip. "Come on, stop it. This is exactly what I'm talking about!"

"I have no idea what you're talking about." I stand, grab my plate, and shove it in the sink. "I was asked twenty-seven times why I wasn't engaged last night." With a squeak, I turn to Frank. "Twenty-eight, actually, because Ian asked too. Did you tell your lady friend that I exist? Because you're the first thing I told Ian about. Even before my name."

"Ames, you want me to propose, but we've never experienced anything else." He comes to stand in front of me. "I know I want to end up with you. Fuck, I love you. But I also want to know what else is out there, or I'll wonder my whole life." His lips purse into a straight line. "Now that I'll need to relocate to Mayfield for a while, maybe you'd be willing to let me . . . experience something else?"

My fingers press against my forehead, now slick with sweat. This isn't happening, is it? He can't be serious. It's all just a nightmare I'm about to wake up from.

"Ames?" His hand is warm on my shoulder. "Look, I know that I'm asking for a lot here, okay? I understand that. But it'd be good for you too. This guy, Ian, did you like him?"

"I—no!"

"Would you have slept with him if I wasn't in the picture?"

I scoff, panic swirling in my chest. My first instinct is to answer *no*. That I wouldn't have. But the truth is, I didn't even consider it, because I can't imagine a life without Frank. It's not something I want. What I want is to be engaged, to marry my boyfriend. "This is a stupid conversation," I blurt out. "If you want to break up, then just do it already."

"Of course not!" He cradles both sides of my face. "Of course I don't want to break up with you," he insists. "I'm just saying, since I'm meant to spend six months away . . ."

"No." I push his arms away and leave the kitchen, tears pooling in my eyes as I smother a sob against the meaty part of my hand.

"Ames, please. Don't walk away." Frank follows me into the bedroom, and once I realize I have no reason to be there, I sprint around the bed and head back out to the living room. "Okay, listen. Listen to me."

I halt when he steps in front of me and holds both hands up. He inhales deeply, then throws me a cautious look. "If we *do* get engaged . . . can you plan the wedding in six months?"

I sniffle, rubbing the back of my hand under my nose. I never thought it'd get to this point, but I really don't want to talk about our hypothetical wedding right now. When he keeps staring at me, I shrug. "I don't know. Maybe."

He attempts a light smile. "So, until the wedding, we could do our own thing. I'll have to move out anyway, right? We could use this time apart to . . . experience a little of the single life we've missed out on when we were younger. Then we get married."

My stomach drops, the same free-falling sensation as a roller-coaster ride.

"Plan the wedding of your dreams, and in six months I'll be there, in a tux, waiting for you at the altar. I'll be yours forever and you'll be mine. No looking back. No regrets."

Squirming away from his hold, I ask, "And what happens in the meantime?"

"We're still together. But I'll be in Mayfield. New colleagues, big city. If I go out, and a woman flirts with me—"

"You'll sleep with her," I say, gingerly cutting him off.

"No, it's not about that." He runs his fingers through his hair. "It's about knowing that if I want to, I can. About experiencing being single. But I won't start sleeping with a new girl every day, Ames."

"But it might happen," I insist.

With a sigh, he nods. "But we'll both know that no matter what goes on in the next six months, we'll be back here." He pushes his glasses up, his eyes softening in that way they always do when there's something he wants. "It'll make us even stronger, because we'll still choose each other over everyone and everything else."

I study the white-and-black pattern of the rug. Never in a thousand lifetimes would I have imagined that I, Amelie Preston, the woman who's been obsessed with weddings since she attended her first at age nine, would be proposed to in the way it just happened. Even less would I have expected she'd consider it. In fact, I'm not even sure Frank realized he's done just that: proposed.

"No, Frank. I—this is crazy." My fingers are in my hair, grasping it at the root. This *has* to be a shitty nightmare. There's no way my boyfriend turned my dream into a weapon used to placate me so he can get his way. "What if I say no, huh? What happens then?"

He brings his arms out wide, a pinched expression on his face. "I don't know, Ames. Then I'll need to think about whether I really do want to commit to a marriage when I've never known anything else. We've been together for half our lives, and I want to spend the rest of it with you, but not if I know I'll never stop wondering. It'll ruin our marriage, too, eventually." He joins his hands as if he's praying. "Do you really want me to marry you when I'll be doubting and pondering forever? Knowing that I could resent you for it?"

I let my hair go when my phone vibrates against the kitchen counter, loud in the otherwise silent apartment. I can't be sure, but I *know* it's Ian. Throwing a look at Frank, I strut toward the kitchen with a rolling heat in my stomach.

"Ames?"

I pick up my phone and hastily skim Ian's texts.

Ian:
Fine. If you just ignore my messages, this friendship is never going to work.

> I hope you can live with the awareness that a bakery somewhere is losing an order of a delicious raspberry-lemon-macadamia cake I intended to eat with a spoon.

Showing the screen to Frank, I warn, "You understand that if you can flirt and text and sleep with other women, I can do the same with other men?"

"Yes, I do," he says, his eyes focusing on the screen for a few seconds before he looks back at me. "Text him back if you want to."

"Oh, so it doesn't bother you at all." I shove the phone closer to his face. "Ian is a big guy. Tattooed arms. Handsome, fun. You don't mind him wrapped around me and rocking my world?"

Shoulders sagging, he purses his lips. "I mean, I don't exactly want to hear the details, but . . . I'm okay with it. I don't just love you because I'm the only man you've ever slept with, Ames. That's never been important to me, and it's not now, as long as in six months you're walking down the aisle, toward me, in your wedding dress."

My heart aches at the awareness that it feels easier to accept this idiotic agreement than to let go of the man I've spent half my life with. I can't lose Frank. I don't know who or what I am without him at this point. Which, I guess, to some extent, is what he means. "I'll think about it."

His lips part, a small smile tugging at his lips. "Really?"

"Yeah," I mumble. I don't even feel in control of my mouth, my face numb as I speak. I figured today I'd spend the day with my preancé. That maybe we'd go out for dinner or watch the game on the couch. What I didn't expect is his confessing to flirting with a stranger, then agreeing to marry me after an open relationship. How long has he been thinking about it? Are there other girls he flirted with before? And if I'd never met Ian, never asked for his number, would Frank have confessed to what he did and how much he liked it?

"Ames, thank you so much." His arms envelop me, but they feel like a straitjacket instead of the usual comforting hold. "I swear it won't be so bad. In six months we'll be promising each other for-ever, and we'll mean it even more than now."

Slipping away from his warm body, I smile stiffly. "Sure. Unless you fall in love with someone else. Or I do. But hey, should that happen, we can totally invite them into our marriage, huh?"

"Jesus, Ames . . ."

"Nah, sorry," I say, holding up my phone with a fake smile. "I'm busy. Getting ready for my precious six months of freedom so I can find out what a cock ring feels like with Ian."

He rolls his eyes. "Seriously, if you're going to be this way—"

"Can't hear you. Too busy texting."

He stares at me with his arms folded across his chest and a look in his eyes that implies I'm being ridiculous. Petty. Childish. I know I'm being all of it and more, but the awareness does nothing to stop me from theatrically unlocking my phone and tapping on Ian's contact. "I'm texting him."

He sweeps his hand through the air. "Go ahead."

"Great." I look at the screen, then think for about two seconds. Then two more. Until eventually I've got nothing to say and I'm look-ing like a fool, so I type the first thing in my mind and send. "Done."

"Okay." We stare at each other in total silence for a while. Then my phone pings and I'm done with this game.

"I'm going out."

"Ames—"

"Bye." As I walk to the door, I look at my text conversation with Ian.

Amelie:
Unpopular opinion: the worst thing at weddings is the groom.

Ian:
Especially if he brings the wrong type of ring.

6

Not Exactly Mayfield

"Wait . . . what?" Barb's mouth hangs open for a while as the train moves along the rails. We're halfway to our destination, and, after talking about her pregnancy, the conference, and the TV shows we've binged recently, she inevitably asked for the thousandth time what happened with Frank. And though I'd kept it a secret till that point, I finally came clean. *"He asked you for an open relationship? Is that—"* She shakes her head, shock widening her eyes as she leans forward. "Ames, why didn't you say anything? Why did you accept?"

My lips twist with a sad smile as I shift in the faux-leather seat, the back of my thighs sticking to it uncomfortably. Barb is the second person to know about this besides Frank and me, and I'm quickly reminded of the reason why I've kept it a secret until now.

Because it's fucking humiliating.

My mind sinks back to the darkness it was soaked in at the time, my conscious brain trying to put into words the way I felt. Every time I think about it, it's like being back there, crushed by that same sense of hopelessness and inevitability. "I know it sounds crazy, but—"

"I'm not judging you," she rushes to say, and with a bitter chuckle I look out the window.

"Trust me, Barb. I judge myself harshly enough for the both of us."

"You shouldn't. I mean—"

"I let that man walk all over me," I say in a firm voice. "I let him dump his emotional garbage on me, use it to manipulate me into doing what he wanted until I was in such a fucked-up, exhausting situation, I couldn't find a way out." Swallowing, I focus back on her. "Trust me, I deserve to be judged, but I won't make the same mistake ever again."

Her hand rubs over her bump. "I *have* noticed a change in you lately. You've been a little . . ."

"Bitchy?" I offer.

"No, not bitchy. Just . . . you won't take any shit. I like it."

She's right. I won't. I think I took all the shit one can take, and I'm overloaded. "I'm done living my life to please others is all. Because do you know what I was left with at the end?" I shake my head. "Nothing. I spent years running after my dad's approval and never got it. I withstood months of Frank's bullshit, and we broke up anyway. And though I let Martha have basically everything she wanted, we're hardly friends anymore."

Barb nods solemnly.

"I can't live my life for anyone else, because in the end I am all I have."

Her hand squeezes mine in a silent *You have me too*. And I know I do, just as she knows that's not what I'm talking about.

Turning to the blurred scenery outside, I inhale. "I said yes because I was afraid. I didn't know how to let Frank go. And with everything else that happened . . . The prospect of losing my best friend, my fiancé, and my dad all at once was the most terrifying thing I'd ever been through, so I just . . ."

"Chose them over yourself," Barb whispers.

I nod, hugging my arms around myself. Unfortunately, they don't feel like the shield I need right now. "At some point I realized it was all too far gone—that while I was desperately trying to keep one part together, the other one was crumbling. I pretended not to see it. I tried to make it work, to make myself smaller and smaller so that everything else could fit."

Barb sighs loudly, something close to anger in her expression.

"But someone wouldn't let me."

She tilts her head up, an eager smile ghosting her lips. "Ian?"

Watching her wishful eyes, I nod and look away, and she must know the conversation is over, because she settles against the headrest and turns to the window.

Ian.

Every time I tried to ignore my instincts, he shoved the truth down my throat. Every time I tried to pretend nothing was going on, he forced me to face the music. And somehow he did all of this while making me laugh and smile and feel not completely alone in the world. In some magical, inexplicable way he made the darkest time in my life the one I can't regret.

My friendship with Martha, my job, my relationship—he demolished and dismantled it all.

He destroyed my life. And by doing that, he saved *me*.

"Oh my God, I'm too pregnant for this."

I turn to Barb, scattering the contents of her handbag across one of the beds, after heaving our two enormous suitcases through the hotel room's door. The trip from Creswell to Mayfield is only two hours long, but in this heat it felt like much more. "I'm convinced we were on that train for days."

With a nod, she awkwardly lowers herself onto the bed, lying on top of makeup and tissues, as I throw a look at the window. Turns out, I really should have read the email they sent us about the location, because we're *hardly* in Mayfield. We're deep in the countryside, with fields of wildflowers on every side of the property. There's a pool I'm definitely planning to enjoy, and, based on what I've seen, the Whispering Willow hotel is just as beautiful as promised, with high ceilings and a French grandeur that reminds me of La Brasserie.

Not bad at all, but there's not a hint of gray, concrete buildings and busy crowds walking in every direction, so it's not Mayfield.

I sit on the other bed, my shoes sinking into the thick dark red carpet as I face a flat-screen TV that I wish I had in my own apartment. The double beds that take up most of the space are covered in fluffy pillows and what looks like a warm duvet, and the wall opposite the room's entrance has two large windows that look onto acres of white daisies. It's breathtaking.

I remove my sneakers, sit cross-legged on my bed, and power up my laptop. The air here is so humid, you can almost chew it; desperately fanning myself with my hand, I click on the browser. As I stare at the white page, all the conviction that brought me on this trip goes out of me.

Sure, I want to see Ian. But will he want to see me? After what happened, I'm not so sure. And how will I explain everything? Plus, I don't know what he does or where he lives. I know plenty about him, but not anything that can help me find him.

After typing "handsome Ian in Mayfield," I shut the laptop. Mayfield is a big city, and I'm sure he's not the only Ian around here.

"Ames?" Barb says softly from her bed. She tucks her hand under her cheek, her frizzy curls flattening against the pillow. "You know the results only come up if you press 'enter,' right?"

I give her a half smile.

"What's the plan?"

Scooting down, I rest my head on my pillow and face her. "I don't know what he does for work, I don't have his address, and he's not a hobby guy."

"Not a hobby guy?"

"No. He's an opinion guy."

She gives me a slow, uncertain nod.

"No sports that I know of, no favorite spots around town he ever mentioned. I've been racking my brain, trying to think of anything useful he might have told me, but there's just nothing. I have no idea how to find him."

"No surname, either, huh?" Her lips twist to one side. "Are you sure he's not, you know, hiding something?"

"Uh, well . . ." I give her a small shrug, my shoulders drooping. "Actually . . . I was hiding something." Her eyes bug out, so I quickly hold a hand up. "Not— Back then, my dad was quite popular on social media. Remember? The fourth season of *The Silver Spoon*?"

She sucks in a sharp breath. "Oh, right."

"If I told him, I figured he could connect the dots and . . . well . . ."

"Nobody wants to be known as the 'Dictator's' daughter?"

"Pretty much."

She hoists her head up, holding her weight on her elbow as her hair cascades down one side of her body. "I might be missing something, but . . . why don't you just call him?"

"He blocked my number. Plus, if we're face-to-face, he'll have to listen. He won't be able to tell me to get lost." So much about my rashly thought-out plan relies on the assumption that he doesn't completely hate me. Even more, that he feels about me the same way I feel about him.

It's a huge, *huge* assumption, considering he made it impossible for me to reach out.

"So," she says, sitting up. "The plan is . . . no plan."

Throwing a glance her way, I bite my bottom lip. "Is it crazy to hope that fate will bring us together?" I let out a single chuckle. "I've already given it a huge boost by coming all the way to Mayfield."

"Fate?" She smiles wide, then gets up, walks over, and gestures at me to make space. "Like destiny?"

"Like . . . like I'll walk down the street and he'll be there. Or tomorrow I'll need an antihistamine and he'll be the pharmacist. Or his dog will run off his leash and leap into my arms."

"Oooh." She lies down next to me, then pokes my side. "A meet-cute."

Yeah, sure. Or a meet-ugly. Any type of meet would work, really.

"You could pick up his coffee by mistake."

"He could be driving by when my car stops."

"You don't have a car."

When I shrug, Barb chuckles. We both stare at the ceiling for a while in companionable silence, and the endless possible scenarios swirl in my mind, each one more glorious than the last. I'd even be happy to crash my nonexistent car into his.

"I can't believe you talked to this guy for so long and you don't know what he does."

I open my mouth to explain, then think better of it. "I'm crazy, huh?"

Her head rests against my shoulder. "Well, the odds are against you. It's, what, a million inhabitants to one very handsome guy?"

Yeah, it is.

"But what were the chances of my grandma taking his spot at the wedding? Of him sitting down next to you? What were the chances he'd love my cake and he'd bring it up with you, a chef?"

Turning to her, I let out a small, thoughtful sigh. "He asked your grandma to sit in his spot so he could talk to me, and he didn't even eat the cake."

"It's *really* difficult to comfort you." She taps her fingers over the back of her hand. "Can I at least know if you two . . ." Her coffee-brown eyes widen suggestively.

When I look away, she gasps. "Oh my God, I knew it! Did Frank find you together? Is that what—"

"We didn't even kiss, Barb," I grumble. I've done so many things in the past year that I've come to regret, but cheating isn't one of them. Though I guess it wouldn't have been cheating anyway. "Look, all there is to say is that the instant Ian sat down at my table, I knew he wasn't just a random person who'd leave a shallow imprint on my life. I knew he was different—that he wouldn't be a stranger for much longer. That he was going to stay." I pause, struggling to explain it with words. "It was the way he looked at me. I didn't recognize it right there and then—it took me a while, actually—but it was like he'd been searching for me his whole life."

"Ames . . ." Barb says with a shaky voice.

I smile, though my first instinct would be to do the exact opposite. Maybe the day will come when we'll be together, and letting him go the first time won't hurt as much as it does now. But regret is a merciless feeling.

"I know it's crazy. Coming out here knowing there's a ninety-nine-percent chance I won't find him. But it's easier to run after that one percent than to let him go."

I notice tears running copiously down Barb's cheeks, snot smearing her upper lip as she tries to sob on the inside.

"Wha—oh. Oh, I'm sorry. Hormones, huh?"

"*That one percent*," she whimpers, exploding into more sobs. Unable to help a snort, I stand and walk to the bathroom.

I'm fetching toilet paper when I hear a gasp bounce off the ugly wallpaper in the room. "Ames!"

"What?"

"Ames! Ames!" she shouts. I dart out of the bathroom, expecting to find her on the floor or in a puddle of her own water, but she half runs toward me, a hand on her bump. "I know how to find him! I know how to find Ian!"

"What?" My heartbeat spikes, fear and adrenaline mixing dangerously in my mind. "How?"

She swats my arm over and over again. "We asked the guests at my wedding the names of their plus-ones for the placeholders! Ian was his dad's plus-one, right? His surname will be there!"

The toilet paper roll falls from my hands to the carpeted floor as my brain registers her words.

The guest list.

That's how we can find him!

7

A French Feud

When my phone beeps, I finish buttoning my chef's coat and fish it out. Maybe a tad too excitedly.

> **Ian:**
> This one you can't possibly disagree with, so here it goes. The whole thing about sleeping apart the night before the wedding is ridiculous. Hello?! Most people move in together before they get married these days.

I loosen a jagged breath at the relief washing over me. Like a light wind on a warm day, it soothes me from the inside out, and like every day since Barbara's wedding it quickly fades away when I realize just how happy I am that Ian hasn't stopped texting. It's been a week, and he's sent me his unpopular opinions about weddings every day. "Why is it called a honeymoon if neither honey nor the moon are involved?" and "Never mind. It comes from the Scandinavian practice of drinking fermented honey during the first moon cycle of the marriage to help with conception." And, of course, "I'm happy to ask the bakery if they have some fermented honey for you as soon as you tell me what it's called."

I haven't answered since the day of my fight with Frank, but he keeps going with a new message every day, and despite myself I'm getting used to the steady stream of witty one-liners about weddings. I suspect he'll stop soon: he must be getting discouraged by my lack of response by now.

The phone beeps again and I wrinkle my nose, surprised he's texting twice in one day. But it's not him. It's Frank.

> **Frank:**
> Just got into the new apartment. Love you.

There's a new notification in the Find My Phone app, so I tap on it, and Frank's picture is somewhere in the center of Mayfield, but it's gray instead of the usual green.

"Last seen two hours ago."

I guess he stopped sharing his location with me.

I shove my phone back into my pocket as my heartbeat quickens, and Tanya, one of the line cooks, enters the kitchen. "Chef Preston wants to see you in his office," she says as she passes by me.

Great. That's just what I need this afternoon, after I haven't talked to Frank on the phone for a week and then he stopped sharing his location: texts from a stranger that shouldn't feel as pleasant as they do, and a conversation with my father.

I turn to Barb, who's putting on her jacket. She winks, pressing her lips tight to contain a smile, and with my heart beating fast, I turn around and walk to my father's office.

I guess it's time.

He's been hinting at wanting to retire from the kitchen for a while, and we've all been waiting for him to name his worthy successor. He's also made it perfectly clear that he won't hand me the head chef position and that I am on an equal footing with every other chef in his kitchen.

But we also know I'm the best chef in his kitchen.

When I knock on the door, my dad, in a muffled voice, tells me to come in. The large space feels crowded on account of the busy shelves and stacks of paper cluttering his dark wooden desk, and though he's squinting all the time, he insists on keeping a soft yellow light in here. "You wanted to see me?"

He motions at me to enter the office, and as I sit, my phone beeps. Once again, it's not Ian; it's just a notification. He's kept it to one daily message, riding the dangerous line between endearing and creepy, and so far coming out a winner.

Glancing at my dad, who's bent over his desk and studying a thick folder, I swallow. This is definitely it. He's going to give me the position.

I love La Brasserie. I basically grew up in this kitchen and have worked with my father for fifteen years. But I'm also not as thrilled as I should be at the prospect of becoming the head chef.

It's not that I don't want the position, because I do. The thought of being the captain of my kitchen is thrilling. It's what I've worked so hard for. But I have this horrible feeling that if I do become the head chef of La Brasserie, I'll be stuck here for the rest of my life. I'll never work anywhere else. Never try anything different. I'll always be living under my father's shadow.

When a whole minute passes and my dad still hasn't looked up at me, I scroll through seven days of Ian's texts.

Ian:
Wedding without kids? Totally fine.

Tossing the bouquet is horribly passive-aggressive. Not all of us are dying to get married, and it's like throwing garbage at your single friends.

Destination weddings are the last frontier of selfishness, aren't they?

"Am I interrupting all your posting?"

I look up at my dad, his eyes narrowed and his thick gray brows taut, then put my phone away. I guess another reason for not exactly dying to work here forever is that, though he's undoubtedly talented, my dad's a bit of an ass. "What's up?"

"Did you see the Marguerite's latest campaign?"

"Hmm?"

"The Marguerite." He drums his fingers on the desk. "It's William Roberts's restaurant."

I nod, perfectly aware that he's talking about some restaurant in Mayfield, over a hundred miles away from here. "I know. William Roberts is the Lex Luthor to your Superman." His eyes narrow. "Your archnemesis. I remember. What about his campaign?"

He huffs out a breath, the light disdain now turning into a teeth-baring sneer. I know I shouldn't enjoy it as much as I do, but my blatant indifference to this stupid little feud with some irrelevant chef—and my equal indifference toward all his public endeavors—frustrates him. And frustrating him is my petty way of getting back at him for being the absent, cold father he is.

"Look." He takes out his phone, then proceeds to aggressively tap on it. On the screen, there's the Marguerite's Twitter profile and their latest tweet.

The Marguerite ✔
@Themarguerite

@LaBrasserie: open since 1967 and still stuck there.

10:00 AM · Sep 08 · Twitter for iPhone

💬 220   🔁 590   ♡ 3K   ılı 5K   ⬆

Biting my lower lip, I fight as hard as I can to hold back a chuckle. "Hmm." I give him back the phone, and the muscles in his jaw flex when he notices my enjoyment. "So what, Dad?"

"*So what?*" His neck stiffens. "It's distasteful, Amelie. How dare William Roberts and his vulgar little enterprise come at me and La Brasserie? We're a staple of French cuisine—a staple! *Fils de pute!*"

Crossing my arms, I ignore his cussing and wait for his skin to tone down a few shades of red. Pointing out that he's making a big deal out of nothing won't help: I've tried before. Saying that this competition to see who has the biggest dick is ridiculous because Roberts's restaurant is in Mayfield, a whole other city? Also pointless. But it's always been more about the two of them butting heads than the restaurants, and who am I to stop two grown men from wasting their time? No one, that's who.

Once the muttering of French swear words subsides, I sigh. "Dad, it's just a marketing campaign. It's called competitive advertising, and if our manager weren't six hundred years old, maybe he'd be able to do it too."

Leaning forward as if he's about to deliver instructions on how to detonate a bomb, he joins his hands. "I'll do it: I have the perfect comeback." He snickers, then proudly announces, "'At least we know how to cook.'"

"That's terrible," I say in a bored voice. "Hire a social media guy."

"How about, 'Learn French, jackass!'"

"Hire a social media guy."

"Amelie, we have to respond. The post already has hundreds of comments and likes and . . ." He frantically points at the phone. "And the other buttons."

Taking the phone from his hand, I fight a groan. "First, this is a tweet, not a post. And you mean retweets." He rolls his eyes, the usual frown just a few inches deeper. "Are you sure you want to start a social media war with William Roberts? With the Marguerite?"

He mutters something that sounds like "We're already at war," and with a resigned shrug I tap on the "new tweet" button.

My dad's right: they've been at war for years. But it was a passive war, started on a cooking show when William Roberts had the audacity to comment on the thickness of the crust on my dad's crème brûlée. A war fought with snarky comments thrown at journalists during interviews, with heated discussions at various culinary shows, and with gossip passed along by other cooks and mutual acquaintances. This would turn it into a full-on active war fought in the most public arena of all: social media.

Boy, I hope we don't go viral.

Pleased, Dad walks away, his cheeks still red and puffy, but that's his usual state when William Roberts is involved. I've never met the man—never eaten at his restaurant, either—yet I've heard his name about twenty billion times since they opened their restaurant a decade ago. I'd be happy to never hear the name Roberts again.

I think of the latest critic's review of the Marguerite I read and chuckle to myself. I think I've got it.

La Brasserie ✔
@Labrasserie

@Themarguerite Fun fact: Marguerite is actually French for "too much onion."

06:22 PM · Sep 08 · Twitter for iPhone

💬 0   🔁 0   ♡ 5   ılıl 10

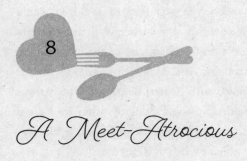

A Meet-Atrocious

We walk down the stairs toward the clinking of glasses, plates, and forks. Barb texted Ryan and asked to be sent a picture of their wedding's guest list, then we left our room for an early dinner. After the train journey, all I'm craving is a bite to eat and a good night's sleep.

We approach the dining room, which follows the same French splendor theme of heavy beige curtains pulled back to reveal double glass doors overlooking the pool. The sun setting outside paints the dark wooden ceiling and floor tiles with an orange light, and tables covered in white linen are peppered across the room and filled with formally dressed guests.

"We might have underestimated the dress code," Barb says once we halt at the bottom of the stairs. She must feel as self-conscious as I do, because she stares down at her worn-out sweatshirt. With my gray oversize *I'm not as think as you drunk I am* T-shirt and the pair of faded jean shorts that come mid-thigh, I can sympathize.

Noticing the familiar faces of the chefs at the first table to my right, I'm reminded of Pamela's email about having an introductory dinner tonight.

"We have to run back and change," I say, trying to magically stretch the fabric around my legs. I hold on to Barb and back up toward the stairs, but before we can turn around, a crashing noise comes from behind us, jolting the room into silence.

"Amelie?"

My muscles, sore from the long day of carrying luggage and traveling, tense and turn into rock. My mind explodes like a dying star, the fragments of it flying around my head as every sound disappears in the background.

That voice.

It can't be.

I turn, the movement resulting in a stab of pain, with my neck as stiff as it is, and when my eyes meet his blue-speckled ones, it starts all over again. Like a fireworks factory just exploded in my brain. "I-Ian?"

He's motionless, gaping as he stands in front of the hotel's revolving doors, a bottle of champagne that must have slipped through his fingers in broken pieces on the floor around him. He's wearing a light blue sweater, and he's so handsome—even more than I remembered. His ash-brown hair sweeps the top of his left eyebrow, and the stubble he had on his cheeks the last time I saw him is gone. The same speckled-blue lakes that represented a source of safety radiate, too, though at this very moment they're bugging out, wildly terrified.

He walks around the glass shards, staring at me as if I'm a ghost from his previous life. And maybe I am. Once he's standing a couple of steps from me, he stops. I'm almost certainly imagining it, but the citrusy, clean smell that's integral to my memory of Ian envelops me. His warmth, his comfort.

Am I dreaming? This can't be real, right? It's almost too good to be true. Too fortuitous to be casual. Too fateful even for fate. "You—" My hand clasps Barb's arm. "You—"

"Yes, I see him too," she breathes. "It's a meet-cute."

Ian's eyes haven't moved from me at all. He obviously didn't expect to see me, either, but what is he doing here at all? Why is he in this hotel, so far outside Mayfield? How is he in front of me?

"What—what are you doing here?" he asks in a warm, velvety voice.

Words. I need to say words. My brain has forgotten how to form them, or maybe the cable connecting it to my mouth has been severed and now information can't get through. Though the whole sentence in my mind goes, *We're here for an international conference about fine dining, and I'm one of the speakers*, the only strangled noise that comes out sounds like "Work."

He nods, silence stretching again for more seconds than necessary, until Barb clears her voice. "Hmm. I'll . . . I'll be in the dining room." She brushes past me, her back to Ian, and frantically mouths, "Get it together," before waddling away.

But how can I get it together? I'm alone with Ian. Well, the hall is filled with people who froze in their position at the commotion and now resume walking from one side of the room to the other, but we might as well be alone. Just as a hotel worker approaches the mess of glass and champagne with a broom, Ian takes a step closer. "You look good."

"You do too," I offer, and he really does look good. Elegant, excruciatingly gorgeous, and he's certainly maintaining his composure better than I am. All of a sudden, I'm aware of the weight I lost since he last saw me. Of my hair, which could use a nice trim, and the fact that I haven't smiled in a really long time; I wonder if he can see that just by glancing at me.

"I'm sorry, I just . . ." His hand moves to the back of his head, stretching his lovely sweater over the waistband of his jeans. "I guess I never expected I'd see you again." My expression must be conveying my feelings about that, because he quickly corrects himself: "I just mean . . . I'm a little . . . *a lot* surprised."

Likewise. I mean, I was obviously hoping this would be the outcome, but I didn't expect it to happen like this. On my first night here. With no effort on my part. Now it dawns on me: I should have probably prepared a speech of some sort, because he definitely deserves one. A carefully crafted explanation, a declaration of feelings, and an admission of mistakes. After the way I treated him, I'd beg him on my knees if he asked me to.

"Well, how's . . . how's everything?"

There you go. The most innocuous yet unwanted question he could possibly ask. How's everything? Shit, pretty much. I've got no job, no relationship, basically no friends. My life, compared to when he last saw me, is a whole lot better and worse at the same time.

I'm sure he'd understand if I explained it, but it's hardly a conversation to have in the middle of a hotel hall, one second after reconnecting, when I'm struggling to get two syllables together.

"It's . . . um . . . good."

He nods, his eyes darting away for a moment.

"What about you?"

"Good. Great." His jaw tenses, the lines so sharp they could cut concrete. "Everything's great."

An uncomfortable silence stretches yet again as we study each other with tentative smiles. God, there was a time when Ian was the only person I could talk to. The only one who was there, who made an effort to understand; the only one who truly cared. And now we're back to being strangers.

"It was nice seeing you," he says, awkwardly looking away. "I should probably—"

"Would you—" I blurt the words even before my brain fully

puts the thought together. I just know he's about to leave, and I'll be damned if I let him disappear from my life again. "Would you get a coffee with me? Or dinner, or . . ."

His eyebrows knit with suspicion, as if I just asked for his credit card details.

With a slight shrug, I ignore the bite of nausea in my stomach and say, "I still owe you drinks, don't I?"

"Hmm." He looks down between us, then back up at me. The tension in his shoulders tells me he's either about to say no or he'll say a very displeased yes. It's unfair of me to expect he'd be thrilled to see me—not at first—but it's a punch in the stomach anyway. "Yeah, of course. Of course I would." He smiles softly. "We should catch up."

Oh. He almost looks like he . . . like he means it. "That's—I'd love that."

"I'm staying here for a weeklong conference. When do you—"

"A conference?" My heart beats a thousand times faster. "You're attending the ICCE?"

"Yeah. Are you?" he asks with a confused smile.

"Yes." I grin widely, my posture relaxing now that he's less tense. "I'm one of the speakers."

"You are?" His expression brightens with surprise, and when I nod, he replies, "Me too."

My smile dies as my throat turns dry. "You're a chef?" Everything I know about him points to *Fuck no*. Hell, the man has the weirdest eating habits I've ever heard of. But the possibility terrifies me anyway. If he *is* a chef, then he either knows who I am or he's about to find out. He'll know what the past six months of my life have been like, and not from me. He'll hear about the article, about my father, about Frank and—holy fuck, I'm going to be sick.

"Actually, I manage and co-own a restaurant here in Mayfield. Wait—you're a chef." He chuckles to himself. "Right. You're a chef. It makes sense."

And it makes sense he's a restaurant manager. Much more than his being a chef, anyway. He said his dad is friends with Barb's father, and Mr. Wilkow is a chef. My money is on Ian's dad being a chef too. "So, hmm, what restaurant—"

"Amelie! Ian!"

A woman approaches us with a tentative grin, and when we smile back, she offers us her hand to shake. "Hi! Oh, it's so nice to meet you both. Pamela Gilbert—I work for the ICCE. Was the trip all right?"

When I nod, Ian affably says, "My trip was short, actually. Are we late for dinner?"

"No, you're not." Pamela gives his shoulder a squeeze, then prompts us to follow her. "We're still waiting on some members of the team." We walk through the busy dining room as Ian and I throw curious looks at each other.

Even though I wish I could have told him about everything that happened myself, I don't mind so much that he'll hear all the gossip about me. Ian's never judged me once, and I'm far too happy he's next to me again to care about anything else. "Come. I'll introduce you to everyone."

We walk to one of the last tables, where I see a few familiar faces beside Barb. Phil and Gianni, two chefs of That's Amore, a nationally famous Italian restaurant, as well as Rosalia, a Mexican chef I've met only once before at a similar event. Pamela mentions the names of two more chefs, and after they all wave, the group continues chatting and eating.

Barb has saved us two spots, but once I sit down, I notice Ian took the chair on the opposite side of the table, the one that's farthest from me. My shoulders slump as my eyes meet his, and with a light smile he looks away.

I guess not all walls have turned to dust.

Pushing the sadness down, I exchange polite glances with the seven other people at the table, but the vibe is definitely weird. I'm certain they've read the article. They all know: they're judging me, and on top of that, they're all wearing dresses and blazers and pants. Not a single inappropriate T-shirt in sight.

I shrink into my chair, but when I glance back at Ian, I notice he's also worriedly looking around. Because the people at the table are staring not only at me but at him too.

There's no way they know, right? They can't have any idea that Ian and I have met before—that we're much closer than any other person at this table is to the next one. But then, what's going on?

Pamela clears her voice, her head bobbing from him to me a couple of times. "Obviously, you know each other already. I'm aware your fathers don't always get along, but . . ."

I tune the rest of it out. Our fathers? Who's *his* father?

He must be asking himself the very same question about me, because his eyes narrow, and just as I put the pieces together, he opens his mouth too. "Ian *Roberts*?" I ask at the same moment as he exclaims, "Amelie *Preston*?"

Oh, this is definitely a meet-atrocious.

9

My Wedding Dress

– Two Weeks After Barbara's Wedding –

The door of the apartment closes behind me, and with a sigh I drop the keys on the entryway table, then slip out of my rain boots. Since Frank moved out, we haven't had a single conversation. I've been telling myself it's because of the move, but maybe he's already started his . . . break from me, even though I haven't agreed to it yet. I've done no wedding planning, either, while Martha continues to pick at the carcass of my dream, stealing all my favorite details. This week she took rice paper save-the-date cards and monogrammed cookies.

I take out my phone to send him a text as I collapse on the couch, but I find one from Martha, the bubble taking up most of my screen. I haven't told her or Barb about my potential engagement, and if he wants to stay alive, Frank didn't either. Cringing with fear anyway, my eyes scroll through the lines as I prop myself up.

Martha:
Hey, babe. Please don't kill me, but I went to the bridal shop with Trev's mom today and saw this dress that the designer was working on. We completely fell in love, but it turns out it's the one she's working on for you! Do you think since Frank hasn't even proposed yet, I could buy it from you? Pleeeeeease? Love you love you love you.

I scoff, the text filling me with such anger, I don't even know where to start. Tossing the phone on the couch, I get up and pace on the rug, my stomach twisting again and again at every step.

No. There's no way in hell I'll give her my dress. It's the one thing I started planning even before Frank's "proposal," and it's mine. I don't care how many fits she throws, how upset everyone gets. My dress is mine—end of story.

God, I can't *believe* she'd do this.

Why! Why in the world would she want my wedding dress? My ankle-length, classic, *white* wedding dress? What about the short, crazy, red wedding dress she once loved? For Christ's sake, she lectured me for two whole hours about veils once.

And she's my best friend! My sister, basically. I've known her my whole life—have been there for her through thick and thin.

With quick movements, I grab the phone and tap on the most recent contact, my heart thrumming so hard and fast, I might just have a heart attack. I hear the ringing, my fingers squeezing tighter and tighter around my phone, increasingly convinced she won't answer, until eventually I hear a male voice say, "Hello?"

Unbelievable. She's making Trevor pick up the phone for her? And he's playing along? "Are you fucking kidding me?"

"Whoa."

I try not to let my voice reach a fever pitch. "Whoa? *That's* what you have to say?"

"Okay, look," the voice says, unusually deep for Trev. "You kept reading my texts, so I figured you might be having a laugh. I shouldn't have persisted. You didn't answer, and I didn't mean to force your hand. I'm sorry."

Eyes wide, I stare at the phone, the name "Ian" on a black background. "Shit," I mouth as I grit my teeth. I bring a hand to my lips, mentally cursing myself for just blindly tapping on the last contact. Ian must have sent me his daily text during my freak-out, and now it's one a.m. on a Sunday and I'm screaming at a stranger.

My finger hovers over the red button, then I stop. It'd be mighty shitty to ignore him for two weeks, then call him in the middle of the night to scream at him and hang up in his face.

Preparing for an awkward conversation, I bring the phone back to my ear.

"Amelie? Are you there? I'm truly sorry."

"Yeah—hey. Hmm . . . no, *I'm* sorry. I didn't mean to call you."

"Oh. So you weren't—oh. Who's 'fucking kidding' you, then?"

With my eyes darting left and right, I hesitate, then say, "Sorry again to bother you this late. I'll—um, bye."

"Is it Martha?"

I press my lips tightly.

"Frank?" he offers. "Come on. It's either this or a documentary about penguins. Entertain me. What's wrong with your life?"

This time I chuckle. "That was lame the first time you said it."

"My lines, just like wine, get better with time."

"I guess they need more time, then."

His laughter makes me smile wide, and my shoulders begin to relax after the burst of tension from a few minutes ago. "So . . . Frank? Martha?"

"God. You're relentless, you know that?"

"I do know," he says proudly. "Out with it. Come on. Who were you planning to scream at at one in the morning?"

"I'd gladly scream at the two of them, actually," I say, frowning. It's crappy to be mad at both your best friend and your fiancé. I'd normally go to one to bitch about the other. And with Barb busy with the last arrangements before her honeymoon, the possibility of talking to someone who's already proved to be a good listener doesn't sound too bad. "Martha has another unreasonable claim, and Frank, he . . . well, he proposed, actually."

"He did?" he asks, his voice laced with surprise. "Congratulations, then. Or not, since you're angry at him."

Angry at him. I could almost laugh. Anger is what I felt before, but now? Now it's mostly resignation, disappointment, loneliness, doubt. I question myself, him, our relationship. And then try to push it all down until it turns into a stomachache. "Yeah, no. It's great."

"Sounds like it."

I brush my fingers over the frame of a picture of Frank and me at our high school graduation. "He just . . . he suggested that we change a few things before the wedding."

There's a sigh, then he observes, "What a vague, nondescript dilemma you got there, Amelie."

"He . . . he shifted the paradigm of our relationship."

Annoyingly amused, his warm voice whispers, "Vague and nondescript."

"Well, anyway," I say, more than ready to change the topic. "I was planning to scream at Martha right now."

"Right. What else does *she* want?"

With a long exhale, I sit back down on the couch, dragging a blanket over my lap. "My custom-made dress."

"You don't mean your . . . *wedding* dress, do you?" Ian is silent for a moment, then he clears his throat and asks, "Doesn't 'custom-made' literally mean it's made for you?"

"We wear similar sizes. She could get it altered." I lean back against the cushion. "But I love this dress. It's a mix of all my favorite details from my favorite dresses of all time. Intricate floral lace appliqués, four thousand beads and sequins, illusion plunge corset, and a soft skirt with a double slit."

"Wow."

"I commissioned it months ago, long before the engagement, when I walked by the shop and saw that they'd hired a designer and were taking custom orders. I've dreamed of it since then, and I'm not giving it up. I don't care how many fights it causes."

"Good for you."

I bite the inside of my cheek, knowing full well that I say this now, but Martha won't make it easy not to crush under her pressure.

"Amelie, it's your dress. Four thousand . . . threads, was it? Anyway, it's yours. No matter how much of a bully this Martha is."

I take my head in my hand and close my eyes. God, what a positive impression my little group and I must be leaving on this person. "She's not a bully," I breathe out. "She's . . . she's like a sister to me."

"Well, some families are toxic, Amelie, and your sister sounds like a bit of a bitch."

My lips pinch. Of course he'd think that: it's the only thing he's seen of her through my eyes. What saddens me is that sometimes I think that too. "There's more to her than that," I say, more to myself than to Ian.

"Really? Like what?"

"Like . . . like she's strong. And she cares about things—she's always fighting other people's battles." My mind fills with memories of the marches and protests she dragged me to when we were growing up, and a smile pulls up one corner of my mouth. "And she's affectionate. All hugs and kisses and gifts. You know the big mall in the city center in Mayfield?" When he says he does, I smile. "Every time she happens to go there, she grabs me a box of candy from this shop I really like. Just because."

"What else?"

Settling with my elbow on the armrest, I inhale deeply. "She's quick to forgive. We've never had a fight last more than a couple of hours. And she's smart, passionate, fun."

"Damn," he says. "Now I kind of wish she was single."

With a chuckle, I insist, "I just didn't expect she'd ask so much of me. But she deserves this and more. I owe Martha a lot."

"I don't know, Amelie," he says. In the background, there's the squeak of a mattress, and I picture him getting out of bed. "Unless she gave you her kidney, asking for your wedding dress is bold."

"Ian, I should let you go to sleep."

There's a click, then the sound of a door opening. "No. What you should do is tell me what exactly you owe this person that would justify not having smacked her in the face. And I'll get some chocolate milk."

Chocolate milk? I set the thought aside and insist that we hang up. "It's late. Really, I should—"

He yawns dramatically.

Rolling my eyes at the way I just catapulted into this man's night with my drama, I say, "Okay, fine." I pull my knees to my chest under the checkered blanket. "So . . . my mom lives abroad. When she left, and for a long time after, we weren't on good terms."

"I'm sorry."

"She divorced my dad when I was nine years old, and by the time I was ten, she'd left the country without any plans of coming back. My dad isn't an easy person to be around, and they brought out the worst in each other. But he also wasn't willing to let her take me away, so . . ."

"She left you behind."

"Yes," I confirm. "I grew up with my dad and talked to my mom on the phone regularly. Then for a long time I didn't talk to her at all. Now we're in a good place. A better place."

He's silent for a moment before remarking, "Damn. That's not easy to forgive."

"I didn't forgive her," I say. "We found a good balance, because after twenty years of her absence, I realized I don't need her now.

But for the longest time I did need her, and she wasn't there. You know who *was* there, though?"

He groans, and his next words make me suppress a grin. "Damn Martha."

"Mm-hmm. I was not fun to be around for a long, long time, and Martha always stuck by my side. She never let me feel bad for myself, always pushed me out of my comfort zone. Her family welcomed me into their home and . . ." I pause when I feel my emotions crawl up my throat. "Really, I have her to thank for the happiest memories of the first fifteen years of my life."

"Wow. That's *more* than a kidney."

"It is."

"It still doesn't justify her snatching your wedding dress."

"It doesn't, but—"

"If I may, Amelie," he interrupts, "I suggest you adopt the same merciless approach with Martha as you have with my texts. Set a boundary."

I fidget with the hem of my shirt and let out a strangled laugh. "Sorry I ignored you. I'm engaged: I can't exactly text single strangers who—"

"Whoa, whoa, wait a minute, Amelie. You're quick to make assumptions, aren't you?"

"Do you have a girlfriend?"

He snorts. "Hell no. But you're assuming I'm interested in you, and that's not the case."

Yeah. Except that at Barb's wedding two weeks ago, he was, and no man ever continuously texts a woman for friendship.

"I might have approached you with the intention of hooking up, but that's it. I'm not here to steal you from your fiancé and make you my wife or something." He snickers. "Some of us are actually happy in our single lives."

"All right. Then why do you keep texting me?"

"I don't know. You seem fun. And I keep coming up with reasons why weddings are the worst." He clears his voice. "But I'll stop if you want me to. I won't even get offended or anything. I get it."

Ugh. He's cute. I hate that he's cute, because despite what Frank is doing or will do, I have no intention of carrying on as if I'm single. But he seems sincere. And his texts are something I've started to look forward to. "I *am* curious to see how many of those unpopular opinions you can think of."

"Endless. What's with the rice throwing? And the public proposals—God, they're tacky. Worst one yet? Apparently, engaged women aren't allowed to make new friends. It's madness."

Fine. He's cute and charming, I guess. There's something endearing about him—something I can't really explain but speaks to me. "I guess us engaged women can make friends. As long as those friends realize that *if* they have an ulterior motive, they're wasting their time and ours."

"I'm sure those friends are happily single and well-intentioned."

Tucking some hair behind my ear, I smile. "Cool. Then . . . don't keep me waiting too long, Ian."

———

My phone is still in my hands, Ian's voice not yet out of my mind after my accidental phone call, when another text notification comes through. Thinking it could be Frank, I check the screen, and my face involuntarily splits into a wide smile.

Ian:
You know what I need?

He really didn't let me wait too long. Or at all. I burrow deeper into the cushions, my knees falling to one side, and type.

> **Amelie:**
> I'm afraid to ask.

> **Ian:**
> Photo proof.

I frown down at the phone. What does he mean?

> **Ian:**
> I need to see the dress.

There's a pinch of excitement in my stomach at the idea of showing Ian—or anyone, really—my dress. But he'll tell me it's the most beautiful dress in the world and looks made for me, because it is. I'm honestly not in the mood to hear any of it.

> **Ian:**
> You know I can be relentless, Amelie . . .

"Fine, fine." I open the cloud and tap on the wedding folder, subcategory "dress." I have measurements, pictures, price. Everything's on here. With a nostalgic smile, I open the picture and send it.

> **Amelie:**
> Here. Let your eyes feast, but don't you dare tell me it's beautiful or I'll kick you. I'm NOT in the mood.

I wait for the three dots to appear, but it takes forever, so I open the picture.

This whole thing is so stupid.

Ian's right. A wedding is just a party, a wedding dress only a pretty, expensive white thing. I don't know why I care about it so much, why I always have. It was my favorite game when we were kids. Martha and I would set all our plush toys along her parents' corridor and wear fluffy white towels, with veils made of toilet paper and bouquets of dried flowers her mom had by the entrance. We'd walk down the aisle and get married to each other. Then we'd start again.

But I'm not a kid anymore, so it shouldn't matter. I should hate the idea of all those people watching me pronounce private words to my fiancé, asking us to kiss or give speeches. Of turning such intimate moments and feelings into a spectacle for others to enjoy.

I should recognize that, though beautiful, this is nothing but a dress. A long-sleeved wedding dress with a crystal-beaded waistband and jeweled buttons down the illusion neckline. Nothing more than a gorgeous dress.

For some reason, this is so much more than a dress.

Ian:
Meh.

"*Meh*?" I straighten, a river of hot rage flowing through me. "What does he mean, *meh*?"

Amelie:
Have you no taste, sir?

Ian:
It's all right.

Amelie:
All right?! Did you see the waistband? The appliqués?

Ian:
The what?

Amelie:
The white flower- and vine-looking things on the gown.

Ian:
They're fine.

"Oh!" I swing my legs over the side of the couch and squint at the screen. It's not like I care what Ian thinks about the dress. Still, it's a matter of principle. He can't "Meh" the perfect dress.

> **Amelie:**
> You must be looking at some other unimpressive, ugly dress.

I send him a picture of me in the dress. Because, yes, I've got plenty. Of course I do. I might have shown up at the shop in my pajamas the day the dress was ready for the first fitting.

> **Amelie:**
> Look at this. I look divine. No, I look almighty. I look like that dress was draped around my body and I was coated in perfection. No, I look like an enchanting, angelic goddess.

> **Ian:**
> Gee. Low self-esteem much?

> **Amelie:**
> Am I wrong?

I stare at the phone, waiting. Sure, beauty is in the eye of the beholder, but he can't deny that the dress looks amazing on me. The designer *wept* when she saw me in it. She asked to take pictures of me to hang on the shopwindow, for crying out loud. They're *still* there.

> **Ian:**
> Do you really want my opinion?

> **Amelie:**
> Yes.

After all, I'll love it either way.

> **Ian:**
> Are you sure? Because I remember some sort of threat being thrown my way.

Oh. So maybe he *does* like it, and he's lying because I told him he couldn't say it's beautiful. Now I want to know.

Amelie:
Just tell me.

Ian:
All right. Honest opinion.

If you're not wearing that dress, you shouldn't bother getting married. Forget about how good it looks on you. How divine, enchanting, or perfect you look in it, though you do.

That smile, right there, is the reason you should wear it.

The way your eyes sparkle is the only excuse you need.

That, Amelie, is your wedding dress.

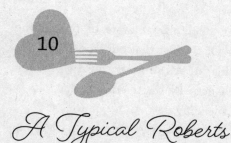

10

A Typical Roberts

Ian is . . . a Roberts? How is that even possible? How did I not know this?

The dining room, filled with patrons chatting loudly and clinking forks and knives against their plates, feels distant, especially as every person sitting at our table seems to have gone still. It feels like time has frozen.

Ian blinks once, twice, three times. He swallows, then remains completely still. Horrified. As horrified as I am. We'll spend the next week in this hotel, going to the same places, attending events together. We'll sleep under the same roof. It's much more than I could have hoped for, but that was before I knew *my* Ian is Ian Roberts.

The son of the man who ruined my life.

When Barb's elbow sinks into my hip, I notice the table has gone silent and everyone is gawking at the two of us as we gaze at each other in disbelief.

"Nice to officially meet you," he eventually says, his voice hesitant, as if he's not sure of his own words. "Ian Roberts, co-owner and manager of the Marguerite."

"Amelie Preston."

People start murmuring, hopefully unaware of the staring match going on between us. Of the fact that our whole lives just shifted. I'm the daughter of his father's sworn enemy. He's the son of my father's sworn enemy—actually, scratch that.

William Roberts is *my* archenemy.

Ian must know what happened to me. At this point, everyone in the business has read the article about the daughter of Hammond Preston falling into disgrace. Now he knows that's me. He must be putting two and two together, which means he surely knows about Frank too.

The chain around my neck and tucked under my shirt feels heavy, the air saturated and thick. Ian is here, in front of me. I've wanted to see him every day for the past six months, and now he's here.

And he's a Roberts.

Pam talks of the other speakers coming in tomorrow from all over the country, then points at two of the nearest tables and explains who's who. Her voice vibrates with an excitement I honestly can't bring myself to share. Food isn't that necessary, is it? Maybe I could just skip dinner and spend my night hyperventilating with my face hidden in a pillow.

"So, how have you structured your seminars?" Pam asks, turning to Ian. She's sitting right beside him, but he doesn't appear to hear her: his eyes are on me, a cryptic expression on his face. He's definitely not happy, though I can't tell if it's because he can't stop looking or because he doesn't like what he sees.

Discreetly widening my eyes, I look toward Pam, hoping to redirect his attention.

"Oh—sorry. What?"

"Your seminars? There are so many interesting ones this year. I forgot what you'll be delighting us with."

He nods, straightening the collar of the white shirt under his sweater. "How to cook and sell affordable French delicacies that can relate to diverse palates. The Marguerite was the first restaurant to spread low-cost French cuisine on a national level, so—"

"*Tsk.*"

Seven sets of eyes turn to me, and it's the first hint that my mocking noise *wasn't* internal. Barb's strong grasp of my thigh is another great one, but Ian's glare takes the cake. "Yes, Amelie?"

Focusing on the menu between my hands, I shake my head. "N-nothing. Sorry."

"Right. As I was saying, we've—"

"It's . . ." My eyes meet his, the murmurs at the table flattening out. "You weren't." Everyone stares at me, waiting for what will come next. "The first ones to bring French cuisine to this country."

"That's not what I said."

"It is. You said—"

"I *said* we were the first to do it at affordable prices."

The waiter pours some wine into my glass. I could—I should—let it go. Except I can't, because despite the intensity of my feelings for Ian, I am fighting with the hateful monster that takes over my brain every time William Roberts is involved. Though not long ago I didn't care about him in the slightest, the past six months have irrevocably changed my mind. Ian's father is the devil incarnate. "Same thing. And you weren't."

His lips disappear behind his teeth, as if he's trying to hide his amusement. "All right, then. Who was?"

"Jaques Moreau? Even my father started long before William Roberts decided he was done doing taxes and got into the restaurant business."

The clinking of forks and knives stops in a second as the whole table stills, Barb hiding behind her menu and mouthing, *Shut up.*

Ian, whose eyes narrow to slits, takes a long, deep breath, then rubs his hands on the napkin at the side of his plate. A line of white teeth peeks through his lips as he fights rising laughter. "Amelie, your father's restaurant is not affordable. It's pretentious, ancient, tedious." Threading his fingers through his hair, he shrugs. "But not affordable."

"I guess it depends what you mean by 'affordable.' See, La Brasserie doesn't compromise on the quality of the ingredients. It's based on the assumption that people would rather spend a few more bucks and be served high-quality food instead of overly seasoned grub—"

Barb's nails dig into my thigh. I might have taken it too far.

Everyone's head at the table ping-pongs from Ian to me, different degrees of shock etched on their faces. When I look at Ian, I expect him to be livid, but he's not. His eyes are wide, his eyebrows arched, and there's a full, jubilant smile on his face. With a loud snort, he pinches the bridge of his nose. "The Marguerite placed first in the 'Best New Restaurant' category at the Fine Eats Awards. We won prizes for our marketing, our design, our inclusiveness, and our dining experience. We're listed among the hundred best French restaurants in the country." He fidgets with the cutlery. "Your father is a successful man, a damn skilled cook, but despite what you Prestons believe, that does *not* mean he's the only one."

Why am I not surprised there's no food-related award on his long list?

"You're right," I say, taking a sip of wine. "My father isn't the only talented chef around here." Nonchalantly, I add, "In fact, you've got plenty of examples at this very table." After a quick look around, I set my gaze on him again. "But you won't find any in the Marguerite's kitchen."

It's Ian's turn to be stared at as I try to control my rising anger, and, judging by his expression, he's thoroughly enjoying pushing my buttons. It doesn't surprise me in the least, and it doesn't make what I said less true. The only reason the Marguerite is so damn successful is because of how much smoke is blown in the customers' eyes. Circus-like performers hanging from the ceilings, QR code menus, champagne fountains, and many more attempts to distract the diners from a simple truth: their food is substandard.

"By the way," Ian says, snapping his fingers. "Looks like your language skills are a little rusty." When he's met by my dubious gaze, he explains, "Marguerite isn't French for 'too much onion.' It means daisy, and it's my mother's name."

The tweet.

I avert my gaze, making myself small on the chair, as the silence between us stretches.

"Well, this is surely an explosive start to our week," Pam says in a tentative, cheerful voice after a while. Everyone half-heartedly laughs, and soon the chatter is back in full force, except for Ian and me, who continue to glare at each other until, eventually, I lower my gaze.

God, what a shit show.

"You know, I've met your dad." Ian speaks over the others' voices, and the laughter and chatter die down as people realize we're about to start round two.

Barb raises her hand, frantically looking around the dining room. "Where is the damn waiter?" she asks worriedly.

"Have you?" I ask.

He slowly nods, sucking his cheeks in. If he thinks there's anything he can say about my father that will upset me, he's way off. I'm very much aware of his flaws and limitations. So aware, in fact, that I could list them alphabetically.

"And?" I ask with a fleeting smile.

A slow chuckle bubbles out of his lips. "Let's just say . . . I get it." He gives a cold, assessing look. "Why you're like that."

———

By the time the waiter approaches the table, Ian hasn't uttered another word, and neither have I. I also haven't been able to really grasp anything written on the menu, so whatever Barb's getting, I say I want the same. Considering she's pregnant, I hope it's not too weird.

At some point, other brain functions kick in. I smile and respond when asked a question, then examine the little ceramic flowers on the rim of my glass until I'm served a chicken fried steak. After I've eaten half, I go back to staring at the flowers.

I get it. Why you're like that.

I can't believe he'd half insult me at a table full of colleagues. Actually, I can't believe he'd insult me at all. Sure, I wasn't exactly kind when I spoke of his business, but he's attacking my personality. The very fiber of who I am. *Like that.*

As soon as he's done with his soup, he stands. We throw each other a sullen look—a pissed-off, frustrated, sad look. This isn't the end of it; we'll have an entire week of these delightful exchanges, now that we're more than Ian and Amelie. Now that we're a Roberts and a Preston.

The thought of it makes my stomach churn.

Ian was a friend for a while there. The best one I've ever had, despite having only really met him a few times. And there was also something more, though we messed that up. I sure as hell won't be his enemy, and he won't be mine, so once he wishes the table a good night and walks away, I stand and follow him.

"Ian," I call.

He turns to me with a glare, then looks away.

"*Why I'm like that?*" I mock. I realize this isn't the best way to bury the hatchet, but I can't let it go.

Strutting toward the stairs with his shoulders closing in on his neck, he doesn't bother turning around as he says, "Hmm."

"How am I, Ian?"

He stops on the carpet, which covers most of the hotel's hall. After a long, deep inhale, he begins walking away again as if he's changed his mind.

"How am I?" I repeat, loud enough to cause a couple of heads to turn.

Once again he halts, but this time he grabs my arm and pulls me toward the corridor opposite the dining room.

"What are you doing?" I ask.

He opens a door, and once we're both inside, closes it behind us. Even with the low light of a lamppost filtering through the large windows, I can see the clean, polished white flooring and the beige walls. We must be in one of the conference rooms. We stick by the door, and he towers over me, his fresh and clean scent making everything else seem unimportant. Though it's the very opposite thing I'd like to do, I cross my arms over my chest and wait for his explanation. Starting with why he dragged me in here.

"*How. Am. I?*"

This time I sounded aggressive.

"You're a Preston. You think you're better than anyone else. You're pretentious, critical, and stuck-up." He leans forward as he speaks, his cold eyes piercing mine. "Just like your father."

My legs turn weak as a chill moves up my spine. "You—"

"Unlike your father," he continues in a sharp tone as my vision tunnels, "you value everyone else's wants more than yours, Amelie. You can't fight for yourself. You're a coward and—"

With my ears ringing and my muscles tensing, I beat his chest with the side of my fist, barely creasing his shirt. His lips compress as if he's trying not to laugh before he looks down at my hand. "Was that supposed to be a punch?"

Well, yes. I've never punched anyone before, and it's not like I want to physically hurt him. I don't know what I was going for *exactly*, except maybe hoping that, unlike a jukebox, the noise would stop if I hit him.

I'm unsure of where to go from here, and his derisive look embarrasses me, so I go for a second mock punch. But he grabs my wrist, his fingers delicate but firm around my skin.

"Stop it," he says as I try to free myself from his hold. The man must have sixty pounds on me, and my squirming does nothing to break his grip, now on both of my wrists. "Stop being ridiculous, Amelie."

"Is that what you think? Do you really believe I'm . . . everything you said?" When he averts his gaze, I pull myself free. "Or are you just angry because I didn't choose you when you asked me to?"

As his chin jerks down, his eyes shoot through me like a bullet. There's hurt and disappointment in them, and they're painfully familiar, because despite all my big talk, that's exactly how I feel about myself. "The problem isn't that you didn't choose *me*. The problem is that you didn't choose *yourself*."

I swallow, trying to hold back the swell of emotions twisting my stomach.

Ian is right here in front of me, he's a Roberts, and he hates me. It's all too much to process in the span of one meal. Especially because he's right. He's so right, it hurts. I've failed myself in more ways than I can count, and by doing that, I've disappointed Ian. I've hurt him too.

So, he's right. Except that he's also completely wrong.

"I told you I couldn't," I breathe, my voice so weak and shaky, it's barely audible. "I was engaged. I never led you on and—"

"Ha!" His eyebrows rise. "You never led me on?"

"No! You asked and asked. And I said no. I kept saying no! No, no, *no!*"

I stomp my feet, halting at once when bitter laughter bubbles up from his lips. "I remember you repeating 'yes, yes, yes' on occasion too."

My face grows hot and tingly, the memories clouding my mind much too painful to bear. "Fuck you," I whisper. "Fuck you for using that against me." I try to walk past him, but he blocks me, not motivated *at all* by my deadly glare to let me through. "Move!" I shout. "Let me out of here."

He doesn't at first, instead running a hand over his face, then steps to the side. Finally free, I open the door and run all the way upstairs to the safety of my room. Only then do I hide my face in the pillow and burst into a snot-filled, desperate crying jag.

I bawl for all the times I dreamed about seeing Ian again, because none of them went like this. I don't know what I expected, exactly. Maybe that, like in a movie, our eyes would meet across a busy street and we'd walk straight into each other's arms. That we'd fit into each other's lives as magically as we did before. That, like in a fairy tale, one kiss would be enough to mend us, to make up for what we damaged and lost.

But this? Insults and hurtful remarks to wound each other? It's certainly not what I envisioned.

So I weep.

For Ian, for me. For everything that has happened since Barb's wedding. For everything that happened since mine.

11

Why You're Like That

– FIFTEEN DAYS AFTER BARBARA'S WEDDING –

The Marguerite ✓
@Themarguerite

@LaBrasserie The saying goes "Everything's better with butter," not "Everything's butter with butter."

04:29 PM · Sep 16 · Twitter for iPhone

💬 890   🔁 2.2K   ♡ 5.1K   ılıl 7.4K   ⬆

I snort, studying the Marguerite's latest tweet. Whoever's writing these is good, I'm gonna give them that.

My turn now.

Just as I tap on the "retweet" button, the apartment door opens and my stomach plummets. My gaze flies to the door through which, with a cautious smile, Frank enters with his suitcase. He's been gone for two weeks, which is also when we properly talked last. But he's back for the weekend, and it's finally time to face the music.

"Hey," he says, closing the door behind him. He kicks his shoes off and drops the luggage, turning to me a couple more times. "I thought you'd be at work."

"In half an hour," I explain. "Welcome back. Was the trip okay?"

"Got stuck in traffic for a while. But it gave me a lot of time to think about, um . . . what I asked you."

So we'll get right into it, huh? Sounds good. I've been thinking, too—every day and night for two weeks. And I think—I *know*—I'm ready to have this conversation. "Yeah. If you're not too tired, maybe we should talk."

"Of course. But let's not fight, please?"

"Uh-huh." I rub my hands together, trying not to get immediately annoyed. If he doesn't want to fight, maybe he shouldn't act like an idiot.

"Look, Ames, it's not that bad. We can set our own rules and boundaries. Adjust this to our needs as a couple and—"

My eyes narrow at his words. "Did you research this?"

"Yes," he says, looking down at the floor to avoid my judgmental expression. "I just checked a couple of websites, you know? To help you—us."

"Yeah? Perv.com and How-to-ruin-my-engagement.net?"

"You said we wouldn't fight," he says. "I'm not in the mood, Ames."

"Fine." I cross my arms and click my tongue. "So enlighten me. What results did your research yield?"

He hesitates, glancing around for a rescue. "There isn't only one way to do it. It depends on what we want."

"And what *do* we want?"

"I want nothing emotional," he says with a firm shake of his head as he paces in front of the window, warm light peeking through and highlighting the beads of sweat on his neck. "I'm in love with you, and I want to marry you."

"Just sex, then," I say with a dramatic sweep of my hand as I cross my legs on the couch. "No big deal."

"*If* it should happen." He opens his mouth, then closes it. For a few seconds he says nothing, then he meets my gaze, an apologetic smile on his lips. "Ames, the sex we have is kind of . . . basic."

I swallow and look away, because he said something I can't possibly disagree with. At this point in our relationship, we just meet at night under the blanket and have missionary sex. If we're feeling wild, I might give him a blow job. That's it.

"Ames? It's not an attack on you." He sits next to me, his legs coming to rest beside mine as he holds my hands. "There are certain things that I'd like to try, but I can't do them with you."

"Why not?" I ask.

"Because you're . . . you." He shakes his head when my jaw drops. "No, not like that. It's just . . . I see you as a . . . mom, I guess?"

My head jerks back, a cloud of shame and anger taking over my mind. Sliding my hands out of his hold, I yelp, "A *mom*?"

"No, not *my* mom. Just like . . . the mother of our future children. Or . . . or my future wife." He nervously scratches the back of his neck. "I respect you is what I mean. I can't do that stuff with you."

God almighty, what in the world does he intend to do with these poor women?

He hesitates, then pushes his glasses up the bridge of his nose. "I need to do this, Ames. I feel this huge weight pressing on my chest at the thought of never being single again." As soon as I open my mouth, his voice rises. "Look at it this way: if I get it out of my system, then there won't be any of that once we get married." He pauses. "Can you think of any rules that would make you more comfortable if I . . . meet up with a woman?"

Burying the feeling deep down, I focus on his question, but it feels like discussing sci-fi. Rules. "I guess . . . don't . . . don't have sex with anyone I know," I say, since it looks like common sense has been lacking in this household recently. "Whoever you sleep with, you can't ever meet again after we're married. And use protection, because I don't need syphilis from my fiancé." I ignore his sigh. "Don't tell anyone about it."

"Okay, yes." He nods. "It's all fair. Consider it done." Leaning closer, he whispers, "And in six months we get married. Do you think you could do this? For me—for *us*?"

I nod. It feels like I don't have a choice—though, really, I guess I do.

"Can I have a kiss now?"

I press my lips against his, but I'm hardly feeling it, and when he leans closer for a second peck, I stand and walk into the corridor. "Frank?" I call. He turns to me, and with a frown I say, "One more rule."

"Anything you want."

"Please, keep it to yourself. If you do sleep with someone, I don't want to be informed."

I step into the wooden gazebo in front of me, then lean against the railings and look down at the pond where a swarm of red fish is thrashing around. Most of the spaces available at this venue are way too vast for our fifty-guest wedding, but it might also be the best location I've seen so far.

My phone vibrates, my pulse racing as I check Ian's answer to my pictures.

Ian:
Nice. Better than that shack from last weekend.

Amelie:
But that terrace . . .

Ian:
No terrace. You can't get married next to a bowling alley.

A light chuckle bursts out of my mouth. Though Ian is the anti-wedding man whose kryptonite is marriage, he's been nothing but supportive since we started texting. I'd even go so far as to call him a friend. And I'm ashamed to say I might have been taking advantage of it, texting him at odd hours with potential flower, menu, and photographer options.

> **Amelie:**
> Are you sure I'm not bothering you with this?

> **Ian:**
> Don't ditch me right before we get to the good part.

> **Amelie:**
> What's that?

> **Ian:**
> When you tell me what's wrong with this place.

> **Amelie:**
> I have no idea what you're talking about.

> **Ian:**
> Pff. Please.

Fine, he's right. Despite the cold September day, I can just imagine how perfect this garden would look like during my March wedding. The indoor spaces, though . . . they're so luxurious and stuffy—nothing like the simple ceremony I envision. Nothing like the Kent Farm, which Martha has already stolen.

> **Amelie:**
> Isn't it a little too country club–y?

> **Ian:**
> Golfers would feel right at home.

> **Amelie:**
> Right. I don't want that.

> **Ian:**
> No shit. Golf is boring.

With a groan, I walk toward the villa's entrance. I'll never find a location that isn't either impossibly big or absurdly expensive or just a total dump, will I?

Throwing a last look behind me, I text him that I'm driving and make my way home. Once the door of the apartment closes behind me, I find a missed call from Martha, and the usual weight settles in my chest. It's been two weeks since her text, and though she's been moaning through most of it, I haven't given up my dress.

I haven't seen or talked to Frank, either, since his visit, but I'm trying not to think about that too much.

Thankfully, something—or rather someone—has been keeping me distracted.

Fetching my phone, I take my usual place by the armrest of the black leather couch and notice Ian answered my last text ten minutes ago.

I know it'll say what he always says when I tell him I'm driving.

Ian:
Text when you're home safe.

Though I obviously appreciate his presence in my life, it also makes Frank's shortcomings bigger by comparison. Ian is so sweet, so thoughtful and available. But no one is so damn perfect. There's a catch, and I'm dead set on finding it right now.

Amelie:
Are you unemployed?

Ian:
No. I work for the family business. Why?

> **Amelie:**
> You always answer all my texts within minutes. Even at night. Don't you sleep?

> **Ian:**
> You always text me late at night. Don't *you* sleep?

Yes, but I'm a chef; I often fall asleep at three or four in the morning.

> **Amelie:**
> I don't always answer immediately.

> **Ian:**
> I sleep. When you text, I wake up.

"Oh, come on," I say to myself. I roll my eyes and walk into the kitchen, grabbing a bottle of white wine and filling a glass. "Just be despicable already. Show me your true colors."

> **Amelie:**
> You don't need to do that. Wake up to answer.

> **Ian:**
> I know. I enjoy doing it.

"You're just so very unhelpful," I mumble.

Enjoying the fresh taste of the chardonnay, I stare down at my phone. He definitely has commitment issues, and I know there's a story with him and relationships—no one is *that* against weddings for no reason—but there must be something more. Something terrible and disgusting about him.

I'm not giving up on this.

> **Amelie:**
> Are you a racist?

> **Ian:**
> I'm more of a love person than a hate person.

> **Amelie:**
> Aggressive tendencies?

> **Ian:**
> Are you trying to find out what's wrong with me?

> **Amelie:**
> Is it aggressive tendencies?

I already know that's not it. I bet he's never thrown a punch in his life. Maybe he's been arrested for public urination? Or his mom is a huge bitch? Because Frank's almost too proper, and I love my future mother-in-law.

> **Ian:**
> I was caught cheating on a test in college, if it helps.

> **Amelie:**
> It doesn't. I cut my own bangs in college.
> Everybody does stupid shit.

> **Ian:**
> PFP.

PFP. He's sent me about a million *PFPs* so far. I've sent a couple too. When he said he was eating at an underwater restaurant, and when he was at Mayfield's Beckett Bridge.

After a deep dive into my social media, I find a cute picture of me with bangs. It's very *Little House on the Prairie*, but the memory warms my chest.

> **Amelie:**
> There. Picture for proof.

> **Ian:**
> Still hot.

My lips pout as I think of Frank's shocked expression when I showed up at his dorm with my home-cut bangs. *I preferred you without*. We had a big fight afterward, and I hate that I'm reminded of it now, because a very immature, very petty part of me wants to send him a screenshot of this conversation. Maybe text something like "Another man thinks I'm hot" with several exclamation points.

I wish that he'd flip out or warn me against other men or even just . . . check in. Be curious and ask if I've met this guy, kissed him, slept with him. A healthy amount of jealousy shows passion, doesn't it? Why doesn't he care?

Dropping my head against the leather cushion, I groan and angrily tap on my phone.

> **Amelie:**
> PFP.

> **Ian:**
> Of what?

> **Amelie:**
> Your hairline. I want to see if it's receding.

He sends me a picture, and I tap on it. It's a ridiculous shot from the top, his blue irises looking up as he sticks his tongue out. His hair is exactly where it's supposed to be, thick and a shade darker than wheat, and he's wearing a white sweater and jeans. I'm pretty sure he's at a restaurant, maybe a bar, and he's not alone, because from the weird angle I can see the bottom half of another man's body.

Stupid Ian. He's obviously doing something, yet he always finds time to answer.

It's *really* annoying.

> **Amelie:**
> You're out with someone. You should have told me.

> **Ian:**
> Why? Did we agree on an only-at-home texting policy?

> **Amelie:**
> It's rude to spend lunch with your nose buried in your phone.

> **Ian:**
> It's just my dad, and I'm a great multitasker.

Of course he is. And he must be rich and successful, with sweat that tastes like cotton candy and farts that can cure cholera.

Wait. I think I got it.

> **Amelie:**
> The problem must be south, then.

> **Ian:**
> Are you asking if I'm well-endowed?

> **Amelie:**
> As if a man ever answered "No" to that question.

> **Ian:**
> PFP?

I burst out laughing. Maybe that's what's wrong with him. Unsolicited dick pics: I hear some guys do that.

> **Amelie:**
> Shut up.

> **Ian:**
> Just tell Frank to buy you flowers.

> **Amelie:**
> Flowers?

> **Ian:**
> Tell him to surprise you with them next time he visits.

I haven't said a word to Ian about my arrangement with Frank. We've agreed to be friends, and despite what I told my fiancé, that's all I intend for us to be. And he's a flirt, but I've got a feeling that has much more to do with his personality than with me. He knows I'm engaged, and he's not looking for a relationship anyway.

We're good.

Still, the comparisons I can't help but make worry me. No matter how well-intentioned, Ian is making Frank look worse than bad, and I don't need more doubts when my relationship has already taken such a huge hit.

No. I can't let a random guy who gives me an ounce of attention be what breaks us.

> **Amelie:**
> I think we shouldn't keep texting this much.

There's a hole in my heart the second I send him the text. I almost wish I could unsend it, but I know it's for the best. He's become the highlight of my day, and that's not healthy.

> **Ian:**
> Okay. I get it.

Not the answer I expected. Something tells me he's sad: we've been texting enough that I can almost pinpoint the messages he types with a smile and the ones he sends with a frown. This feels like one of the latter. But even now he gets it; no need to explain.

I don't want this to be the last time I talk to him.

> **Amelie:**
> We can still text sometimes,
> but not all the time.

> **Ian:**
> Sometimes.

> But remember one thing?

Amelie:
What?

Ian:
It's your rule. You can break it if you need me.

I exhale, slowly and so deeply that my whole body deflates. I need him so much all the time. He's making this whole nightmare less stressful, and God knows I could use a friend. But right now he's the *only* person in my life, which means some stuff desperately has to change.

Amelie:
I can't need you this much. It's not fair.

Ian:
It's not fair that you're so alone either.

Amelie:
Ian, you said you understood.

Ian:
I'm not saying you should text me, Amelie.

I'm saying you should talk to Frank and Martha.

Amelie:
Why are you like that?

Ian:
Like how?

Amelie:
Why do you care so much?

Ian:
Don't worry about it. I'm not that well-endowed.

12

The Door Between Us

"What the hell was all that about?" Barb asks, closing the door of our room behind her. Once she notices my crouched position and the tears on my face, she frowns. "Oh, Ames."

She sits beside me, her hand rubbing up and down my arm. "I don't understand. What happened between the two of you? I thought—"

"He hates me," I whisper as his eyes, normally warm and loving, flash before me. Today, they were filled with enough poison to kill. "No, more than hates me—despises me. Is that more than hate?"

"I'm not sure." Barb bites her lip—probably on account of the many questions she's dying to ask. Lots of questions she asked before but I never truly answered. How could I, when I couldn't even explain it myself?

"He's a Roberts," I say, facing the ceiling. At the very least, this bed is far more comfortable than my own ragged mattress. "How is he a Roberts?"

"I was going to ask you the same thing. Did you really not know?"

My temples throb with pain as I wrap my mind around the huge mess I'm in. "I knew William had a son. I never knew his name, though. I never cared about the Marguerite and Dad's stupid feud, so I didn't bother learning anything about them."

She nods, knowing all of this as well as I do. "Yeah. I knew he had a son, too, but he's not a chef, so . . ."

So we never truly gave him a second thought.

She presses a hand to her bump, and sighs. "What . . . what did he say?"

Thinking back to our conversation, I sit up, my gaze falling to the fluffy-red-carpeted floor. "That I'm arrogant. And a doormat. And unassertive, and a lot of other things. That I led him on."

"Did you?"

I cup my cheek. "Not with my words. But maybe . . . maybe I did with my actions."

"Okay, well, at least Ian's here. That's what you wanted. Maybe he isn't as thrilled as you pictured him being, but you have a whole week. You'll change his mind, right?"

But now I know he's a Roberts. William Roberts's son. And . . . well, this changes nothing about my feelings, but it complicates the situation considerably.

Barb must be clued in by my expression, because her shoulders shrink inward. "Oh, come on. I know your fathers have a whole Capulets-and-Montagues thing going on, but you always hated your dad's war against the Marguerite."

I did; she's right. But Barb has been gone for most of this year. Between the honeymoon and the pregnancy and simply being a newlywed, she's missed a lot. She doesn't know anything of the shitstorm Ian's dad threw my way.

I stand and enter the bathroom, then come out with my toothbrush in my hand. "Barb, things changed a lot in the past year. I didn't care; you're right. But I never told you that . . . well, William Roberts is responsible for a lot of what resulted in the article."

"The article?"

When I nod, there's a knock on the door. It's him. It must be Ian. Who else would show up at our room this late at night?

With my heart beating its way out of my chest, I scurry to the bathroom and shut the door behind me, then cringe. I don't want him to see me looking like this; he'll know I cried. I wait for a few seconds, then flinch at the sound of the door opening.

"Hi," Barb says.

It's him. I can tell by her greeting—the same sad, hesitant "Hi" you'd say at a funeral.

"Hi, Barbara, right? Sorry to barge in at this hour. Is Amelie . . ."

God, his voice. It breaks my heart and glues the pieces back together with every word. I've been thinking about him every single day since the last time I saw him, but I've only just fully realized how much I've missed him.

"She's—um . . ."

"Amelie? Can we talk?" I hear him call in a louder voice.

I stand by the door, silent. What can I say? Ian knows every nook and cranny of me; he *actually* knows me. If he thinks I'm all those horrible things, then how can I face him?

When there's a knock on the bathroom door, I jump back.

"Hey," he says from the other side. His tone is much gentler now, but I press my lips together and wait, as if he'll hear it if I breathe, if I move. It's not like he doesn't know I'm in here. This makes no sense. "I'm here to apologize."

The lump in my throat is as fiercely stuck as before.

"I shouldn't have said those things. You're not any of that . . . well, you're not *most* of that." His smile penetrates the door, and I can't help a small one too. "And I'm sorry about—uh, the thing I said about . . . The 'yes' thing."

Oh, thank God he's not saying anything more in front of Barbara, because I wouldn't be able to take the questions. Although it's true that, technically, we've never shared so much as a kiss, I'm not ready to talk about that specific situation.

Leaning against the sink, I stare at the door.

"I was insensitive. You—what happened was my fault."

"It wasn't your fault," I rush to say.

There're a few beats of silence, then: "You know, you always answer when I think you won't."

I smile down at my shoes. "And you never give up when I think you might."

The wood of the door creaks as he leans against it. "Well, I've been told I'm relentless."

"That you are." I approach the door, the tips of my fingers touching the glossy wood.

"How come we always end up talking without looking at each other's face."

A rush of memories surge through me, each one tugging at my heart, as I clasp my necklace. "At least it feels familiar, doesn't it?"

"Yeah. Like old times."

My smile weakens. Old times. As crazy as it sounds, I miss those times. Though my life was otherwise miserable, he was part of it. I'd kill for a version of our future in which we're part of each other's life again.

The yearning grips me so tight, it's almost smothering as I say, "A little *woebegone*."

"Woebegone, huh?" His chuckle is muffled, but sweet as honey to my ears. "I thought we'd banned that word."

We did. All W-words.

Be assertive, Amelie. Take what you want, say what you think, express what you feel. Do it now, before the closed door between you won't be as easy to open.

"Look, things are different now," he says. "We can be friends."

My stomach clenches. "Friends" is something we've always tried to be but never quite managed. "Friends?"

His voice reaches me again. "Yeah, friends. This time I'm not letting it turn into anything more."

No W-words Allowed

Eyeing my reflection in the mirror, I turn from one side to the other, then check the way the chiffon off-the-shoulder dress wraps tightly around my hips. The forest-green fabric looks even darker on my fair skin, the flowy elastic sleeves are sheer, and there's a deep slit up the side. Suspiciously similar to one I wanted Martha and Barb to wear for *my* wedding.

"What do you think, babe?" Martha asks from the couch behind me. Barb and one of Martha's colleagues, Danielle, are wearing gorgeous dresses in the same color, though one's considerably shorter, and the other has a soft tulle strap over one shoulder. Martha, in her regular clothes, is looking at us appreciatively.

"It's beautiful, M." I adjust the elastic around my waist and meet Barb's eyes. I'm sure she's noticed the similarity between the dress I wanted for my bridesmaids and the one I'm wearing today, but she says nothing, and neither do I.

"Come on, twirl! Strike a pose!" Martha squeals excitedly as the shop assistant hands her a glass of champagne. With my own glass in hand, I spin, showing off the way the dress follows my movements, the split reaching my knee as the light fabric caresses my skin.

"God, you look great," Martha says, gently squeezing my hand. "Are you happy with it?"

"So happy." Stepping off the pedestal, I stare down at the bubbles in my flute, trying to really *feel* happy, but I guess my efforts are all going toward not causing a scene today, because my chest feels utterly hollow. Martha and I haven't discussed the wedding gown yet, but, considering where we are, I know what's coming for me.

As she follows Barb and the shop assistant to the back, I sit next to Danielle on the white couch and take out my phone. No new texts. I'm not surprised, because the last time I heard from Ian was only a couple of days ago, and texting him right now would mean breaking the rule.

"Did you get it?" a voice calls from the changing rooms.

"Excuse me?" I ask Martha.

"The invitation. We sent them all out on Tuesday."

I stall with a sip of champagne, trying to get the weight in my chest to settle. My progress with wedding planning has been abysmal despite all of Ian's help, and all the joy I thought I'd feel at this point has either been smothered by Martha stealing everything or by Frank. "Didn't get it yet!"

"I can't wait. Trev and I will go talk to a caterer upstate next week, so I might not have time for a call, but text me the moment it arrives. I want to know what you think."

I roll my eyes and, immediately feeling a deep sense of guilt, take a long, calming breath.

Jealousy is such an ugly, unwanted emotion. So what if she copied my wedding and now I need to settle for plan B? So what if her fiancé is involved in the planning the way I wish Frank would be? I should be happy for her. I've always believed there's enough sun for everyone, even though lately it feels like there's a perpetual gray cloud following me everywhere. Maybe I'm just a horrible, small person.

Stomach churning with remorse, I stare down at my phone.

I'm probably smaller than a small person, because though I said I shouldn't, all I want to do is text Ian. Let him distract me.

Amelie:
Unpopular opinion: bridal shops are depressing.

Staring at the screen, I wait. He's always quick to text back, so if he doesn't, I'll take it as a sign. We shouldn't break the rule.

Ian:
A huge scam too. They talk you into spending months of income on a dress you only wear once.

Ridiculous, don't you think?

I can't help the sense of relief that overcomes me, my lungs filling with air.

He answered.

Amelie:
Totally. And no other shop encourages day drinking.

Ian:
Oh, and strawberries and champagne?

It's not a great pairing, and someone needs to come out and say it.

Amelie:
Right?! How about some cheese nachos instead?

Ian:
You're reading my mind, Amelie.

Plus, cheese powder is surely easier to get off white tulle than strawberry juice.

Fighting back a smile, I scour my thoughts to try to find other absurd reasons for bridal shops being so bad. Really, they aren't. They're fancy, with soothing music, comfortable couches, and gorgeous dresses. Plus, there's always this cheery atmosphere of new beginnings.

But I don't want to stop texting.

Just as I begin typing, he does too.

> **Ian:**
> PFP.

I'm guessing he thinks I'm here for a fitting for my own wedding, so I approach the mirror and snap a shot of my reflection.

"Oh, yeah," Martha says as she enters the room, adjusting the forest-green ankle-length dress Barb's also wearing. "Send it to me too. My future mother-in-law needs to approve."

Her lips twist, but as she quickly turns to the mirror and talks with Barb about her upcoming honeymoon, I check the picture. My smile is wide, my hip tilted, and I hope it's enough to distract Ian from the fact that I'm at a bridal shop. I can't keep talking about my nonexistent wedding planning.

> **Ian:**
> You're gorgeous enough to marry.

> If one was inclined to that sort of nonsense.

> **Amelie:**
> Still no story, huh?

> **Ian:**
> Nope. No story.

I mentally stomp my foot. There *definitely* is a story, and seeing as he's all up in my business all the time, I won't rest until I know it. But just as I prepare to type my next text, Martha squeezes my shoulder.

"Ames?" she asks in her whiny voice, and, even before meeting her begging green eyes, I know what this will be about. "Do you think, since we're here, I could try on the dress?"

"*My* dress, you mean?" I ask, turning to face her.

With her shoulders drooping, she nods. "Yes. Could I try it on? Because I can't find anything else I like, and Trev's mom keeps asking. It's just so stressful, and since you're not engaged yet—I mean, by the time Frank proposes, who knows? Maybe you'll have changed your mind. There'll be different trends and dresses and—"

"Actually, Frank proposed before leaving for Mayfield." I set the flute down, my arms bowing at my hips. "So, no. I'll need my dress, and I'll need it soon. Six months, to be exact."

Barb and Martha stare at me, open-mouthed and speechless. When Martha got engaged, she planned a whole party where she got us to dress up and announced it over a microphone. It's one of the few memories I have of that night, before the Jell-O shots started being passed around, but I'm fairly certain there were fireworks. The news of her wedding certainly wasn't sprung on people during an argument.

"You're engaged?"

"Why the hell didn't you tell us?"

"Ryan didn't say anything either!"

"Let me see the ring!"

The saliva in my mouth thickens. God, I've got no ring. I have no ring, and I didn't even think about it until this very moment. I doubt Frank even remotely planned for it, seeing as he's busy living his best life.

"It's . . . it's being resized, actually." I fidget with my dress, tugging and pushing as if it doesn't look perfect already. "And we didn't want to make a big deal."

"But it's your wedding," Barb says softly. "You love weddings, Ames. You've been dreaming about this moment for—"

"And *you* have dreamed the exact opposite for just as long," I say sharply, turning to Martha, and feeling a pang of remorse at cutting Barb off in mid-sentence. "Care to tell me why you're after my classic white dress now?"

She hesitates, shifting her weight from one foot to the other. "I just . . . I realized it's not appropriate to get married in a short red dress." With an uncomfortable giggle, she shrugs. "And you have such good taste with these things. I don't have a shred of a clue."

"Not *appropriate*?" I throw a disgruntled look at Barb, who shrugs. This is the woman who only seven months ago, at her birthday, was hanging upside down from her boyfriend's shoulder and drinking from a keg of warm beer while everyone shouted, "Drink." She complained, demanding everyone shout, "Swallow," instead.

"You're obsessed with weddings!" Martha continues. "You can find other things you'll like. Please, Ames, your dress is the first one I don't hate." As her eyes well with tears and her lips wobble, she continues, "I've tried on hundreds. Hundreds!"

"Martha, I'm sorry, but—"

"You're always saying how much you owe me, right? How much I changed your life and how without me you would have had a depressing childhood," she says with a pout. "Can't you do this *one* thing—just one—to pay me back?"

"Martha, that's not nice," Barb interjects as she stands. Considering her soft-spoken nature, so unlike mine and Martha's, this is a full-blown scene for her. "You can't manipulate her into doing what you want."

"How am I manipulating her?" Martha shrieks.

She's using my gratitude to guilt me into giving her my wedding dress, that's how. And it's bad enough when I do it to myself, but that she would? This is so unlike her. "Martha, what the hell is going on with you?"

Sitting on the couch, she begins sobbing wildly. Danielle pats her shoulder, and Barb meets my gaze with an apologetic expression, then holds out some tissues for her.

"Please, Ames, just this one last thing," she says through a wall of tears. "I promise I wouldn't be asking if I wasn't desperate."

I don't know what's going on. Frank is acting like the very opposite of the man I love, Martha is basically unrecognizable, and the *one* event I've been waiting my whole life for is turning into a nightmare. It's an avalanche, burying me alive and leaving no escape whatsoever. Wherever I turn, there's just more and more weight keeping me trapped until I can't breathe.

I speed toward the changing rooms, the need to get out of this place overpowering. I slam the door behind me after spitting out, "Just have the dress."

I navigate the aisle of the store, throwing random glances at gardening products and vases. There's a cute black ceramic one with a white rim, but never has a plant survived my care, so, with a yawn, I move forward and take my phone out. The last thing I feel like doing is choosing a bunch of crap we don't need for our registry.

On the other hand, I've been thinking about my comeback to the Marguerite's last tweet almost obsessively, but nothing has felt right so far.

I tap on Twitter, and once the app opens, their latest tweet is the first thing that shows up. It's a retweet of That's Amore's update, where the Italian restaurant wished the Marguerite a happy tenth anniversary.

Seizing the opportunity, I click on the "new tweet" button.

La Brasserie ✔
@Labrasserie

@Themarguerite Thank you for ten years of competition. Try
to make the next ten interesting.

06:47 PM · Sep 18 · Twitter for iPhone

💬 1   🔁 5   ♡ 15   ۱۱۱ 30   ⬆

I glance at the shopwindow, a pathetic little rush of excitement
making me giggle, and stare at the rain still pouring down in buckets
outside like it's been doing for the entire month of September. When
my phone vibrates, I peek at the screen, a certain disappointment settling on my chest as I notice it isn't Frank. But it lasts only a second
before my eyes widen and the humming in my veins quickens.

Ian is calling me.

His name blinks as I wonder what to do with my hands, my
heart rate spiking. He's never done this before.

My hand trembles, and after a long moment of hesitation I answer and press the phone to my ear. "Hello?"

"Hi," he says in his warm, deep voice. "Hope you don't mind me
calling. I was thinking about you."

With a newfound lightness, I walk along one of the aisles of
the shop, glancing at the items on either side of me. "No, of course
not." A couple starts making out on my right, so I turn left and
keep going. "I couldn't remember your voice, you know?"

"Couldn't you? Way to bruise my ego."

"It's a beautiful voice," I offer.

"Do you remember my face? It's my most striking feature and
biggest source of pride."

I grab what looks like a mug but on second thought could also
be a soap holder and shake my head. "Really? Not your personality? Your sense of humor?"

"Nope. With these eyes? This dashing smile? My face is the best I can offer by far." There's some noise of plastic crinkling. "Anyway, I figured I should check on the bride-to-be."

"That's nice. Thank you."

Someone next to me picks up what's either a lamp or a record player, the scan gun in their hand beeping obnoxiously.

"What was that?"

"Oh, nothing. I'm . . ." I check the price of the "could be mug, could be soap holder" and shiver. "I'm making the wedding registry."

"Fuck—sorry. I can call back," he says. It sounds like he's got his mouth full, and the awkward-sounding words make me smile.

"No, no. Actually, I could use some company. Based on the number of guests, they suggested I find about a hundred items, and even with my list I only got to fifty. I'll be spending some time here." Setting down what I'm increasingly convinced is neither a mug nor a soap holder and rather a paperweight, I walk to the cooking equipment.

"Well, send me the list. I'll call the items. You look for them."

"Seriously?"

"Yeah. And turn on the camera so I can help choose."

What sounded like a terribly boring afternoon has a whole different meaning if I'm hanging out with Ian, so I don't even think of protesting. After sending him the list, I turn on the camera and smile.

He *is* eating.

"Hello." He waves, his beautiful blue eyes framed by light wrinkles as he smiles. Setting the hot dog on the paper in front of him, he brings his thumb to his mouth and sucks off some of the condiment. It's my first time seeing him in a T-shirt, and it fits him nicely, the solid black lines of his tattoos disappearing under the gray sleeves. "Ready? We've got a lot to go through."

"Hot dogs and chocolate milk?" I ask when I notice the colorful box and straw. "Like a toddler?"

He spreads his arms, his hands opening wide as he frowns gently. "Hey, I'm here to help you. And you suggested cheese nachos and champagne."

"I was joking!"

"Well, I was not. Strawberries and champagne stink, and chocolate milk is perfect at all times. Now"—he clears his voice and grabs a tablet by his side—"we're looking for . . . throw blankets." With his nose scrunched, he focuses on me. "Really?"

"I don't know," I complain. "I found this checklist online and—"

"Sure, throw blankets." He claps, back to his infectious smile. "You can throw them on Frank."

I roll my eyes, which does nothing to stop his chuckles, but I can't say I'm truly annoyed. Not with how I feel about Frank. Though I have the decency not to say it out loud, I would like to throw something at—*on* him.

Turning around, I see pillows, and I walk in that direction, assuming I'll find blankets. "Don't you have something better to do on a Friday evening than tend to my wedding? Parties? Dates? TGIF and all, you know?"

"I keep my partying for Tuesdays and my dating for Thursdays. Boring days of the week," he says, biting into his hot dog. "Friday nights are when mundane chores become epic stories."

"Hmm. All about that single life, are you?" I ask.

"Absolutely. Being single means that I *can* help you out with your wedding planning. I choose what to do whenever I want to. And my happiness only depends on me, which isn't too bad either."

Though it's in no way unreasonable, I just have this gut feeling there's more to his complete rejection of relationships. But I've insisted plenty before to no avail, so I switch to the back camera, then point it at the throw blankets. Narrowing his eyes, Ian slurps from the straw. "The gray ones look cozy."

"Don't you think there should be some vegetables on your plate?" I ask. "Hot dogs and chocolate isn't exactly a balanced meal."

"I don't eat anything green."

"Excuse me?"

"No vegetables. And fruit . . . fruit isn't great either. But I'm a fine snack connoisseur."

"Huh," I say, surprised. "You're a junk food junkie." When he hums in agreement, I grimace. "How does someone not like fruit?"

"I don't mind the taste, but most of it has a weird texture. Apples are fine, but bananas? Persimmons? *Mango*?"

I can't help laughing. He sounds personally offended by mangos' texture. "Tell me more."

"More about my eating habits?" He looks away, then clicks his fingers. "Water. It's a very disappointing fluid."

"Is it?"

"I don't understand why someone would choose, among all the fun drinks out there, to drink water. Soda is better than water. Juice. Beer. Coffee. And of course—"

"Chocolate milk, sure." I think of saying something about his health but don't. "What else?"

Letting out a long "Hmmm," he stretches back. "Unpopular opinion? The best foods are the ones you can eat with your hands."

"All right," I say, though it comes out sounding like a question.

"And cheap food. Cheap food is *the* best food. And, mind you, it's not about money. It's just . . . processed, cheap, boxed food tastes much better than anything fresh. Always."

I scoff loudly. He's insane. No one—and I mean no one—in this world would agree with him. "You're out of your mind."

"And you're out of . . ." He stares down at the list. "Patio furniture? I thought you lived in a condo."

"I do."

He leans forward, dramatically hitting his forehead against the table, then sets the list down. "How about luggage? It's useful, expensive, and you can use it with Frank. To hide chunks of him."

I switch to the front-facing camera and give him a pleading look, nonverbally begging him to drop the topic. It's sinking my already horrible mood.

"All right, all right." He bites into his hot dog. "Any progress on the wedding, then?" he asks. "Besides this?"

"Don't want to talk about it."

"Why?" He dramatically brings a hand to his chest. "Is your long-distance engagement not as peachy as it sounds?"

I shrug and look around the store. Where the hell *is* the luggage?

"Fine. What about the dress? Are you still holding on to it?" When I say nothing, he groans. "Oh, come on. Seriously, Amelie? What the hell happened?"

"That's not a good topic, either, Ian. Drop it."

He laughs, the sound oddly familiar and heartwarming, as if he's someone whom I've known for a lifetime, who's happy. It certainly feels as if I know Ian better than most people in my life. "See, Amelie, that's not going to work for me. I allow my friends one taboo topic. And you only get one, so choose carefully."

I see suitcases, and like a mirage in the desert I sprint toward them. "Is that so?"

"Yes. Take Andres, my high school buddy. He demanded we not talk about his hot younger sister. Since that day, he's had to answer whatever question I come up with about his bowel movements. It isn't funny for either of us."

Stifling a laugh, I switch to the back camera. "I might have to go with bowel movements, then. Save us both some discomfort."

"Is that your final answer?" he asks, deadpanned.

I tilt my head to the right. Bowel movements sounds like an undeniably good taboo topic to settle on, but talking about the wedding is becoming dreadful. As for Frank . . . every time Ian asks about us, I can't answer.

A notification on the top of my screen distracts me, informing me that yet another one of my dad's moments on the last season of *The Silver Spoon* went viral. That's all it takes to sway me into a certain answer. "Work," I say, walking in front of the rows of luggage. "I choose work."

Ian grabs his phone and brings it closer to his face, his eyes squinting. "The red set looks nice. Check if it's sturdy. Oh, and a lock. See if it has a lock."

This close, he's excruciatingly gorgeous—though, to be fair, he's handsome from every angle. His light brown hair looks scruffy and soft, and the stubble on his cheeks makes him look a little older. I almost get a whiff of his scent—*that*, I remember clearly. Like fresh, clean clothes.

Looking away, I tap on the luggage, not sure how to verify its sturdiness.

"So . . . work, huh?" comes from my speakerphone.

Yes, work. Work is my taboo topic. Ian lives in Mayfield, where *The Silver Spoon* is shot, and besides, chances are that he got bombed like everyone else with useless "news" about my dad's latest hot comment or unjustified lashing out. If I can choose to keep one thing secret, that's it. I want Ian's impression of me to be unencumbered by the aura of hatred my surname carries. The less he knows about my career—and my family tree—the better.

"Why?" he continues.

I tap another piece of luggage to see if I notice any difference. "Isn't the point of choosing it as a taboo topic that we won't talk about it?"

"Yeah. Just . . . you're not getting fired or anything, right?"

"I'm actually up for a big promotion, but the decision hasn't been made yet."

He sucks from the straw of his chocolate milk until it makes a slurping noise. "Well, then tell your boss to drop the dumb act and give you the job already."

With a grin, I inhale deeply. I wish it were that easy, but it never is when it's your dad. Even though I'm his best chef, he's stalling.

"I work for my father," I explain. Seeing as he also works in the family business, I'm sure I don't need to say more.

"Oh . . ."

He knows. When family is involved, it's much more complicated. Silence. Then: "Fine. Work it is," he says. "So, how's the wedding planning going?"

"What's yours?" I ask, pointing my scan gun at the red set. Frank and I will find out if it's sturdy on our first trip with a low-cost airline. "Your taboo topic?"

"Well, if you don't want to confess the dirty secrets about your job, you'll miss the awesome anecdotes about mine."

I smile. Though I had zero interest a minute ago, now I kind of want to know.

"Will you ignore my questions about the wedding again?"

Bringing a hand to my left shoulder and loosening up the muscle, I say, "Yeah. Weddings and work are some of my least favorite topics these days."

"Sounds like it's a W-problem." He snaps his fingers. "We should ban all W-words from our vocabulary."

"Right. 'Wackadoodle,' 'whippersnapper,' 'wigwam.'"

His laughter hits all the right notes in my ear. "And 'whemmel,' 'wheeple,' 'woebegone.'"

"Ha!" I snort. "'Woebegone.' Especially 'woebegone.'"

14

A French Cooperation

– TODAY –

"A taboo topic, you say?" Barb asks before fitting a large piece of cantaloupe in her mouth and chewing.

My eyes don't leave the scrambled eggs in front of me. It's my second plate, so it's fair to say I'm emotional eating. "Yeah. A topic we were allowed to avoid," I explain again. I set my fork on the small wooden table, then steal a look at the breakfast room. Ian is nowhere to be found. Maybe he slept in. "We made a deal about it."

"Well, it's still crazy that he didn't know who you were. That *we* didn't know who *he* was." With a "Humph," she shakes her head. "You know William Roberts congratulated me at the wedding? It was the first time I ever spoke to him. He said his son also wished me the best, that he was somewhere around, but I never saw Ian. Never talked to him." She smiles to herself. "Seriously, it's crazy. Especially since the—" She widens her eyes, cutting herself off with a visible shiver. "I mean . . ."

She means since the article. And, of course, she has a point. Though I managed to distance myself from my father's very public career, the few instances I spent online in the last days have been

---

excruciating. That article is everywhere. How did he miss the *huge* picture of me that comes with it?

Almost as if summoned, Ian walks into the breakfast room, and the whole atmosphere shifts. Logic tells me he's too far for it to be possible, yet I could swear I'm enveloped by his fresh, comforting scent as he walks to the buffet.

Dark shoes, blue jeans, a pressed shirt that looks like it's just waiting to be wrinkled. Ideally by me. He's heart-stopping, but what steals my breath away is the gorgeous woman at his side, whispering something in his ear.

"Is that their chef?" Barb asks. The woman looks like she should be welcoming people into paradise rather than working in a kitchen, but yes, that's her. Isabella Clarke.

She's far more gorgeous than I imagined, but to be fair, in most pictures or videos I've seen of her, she's always been in her red chef's coat, with a ridiculous red toque on and a sheen of sweat over her face. The woman in front of me right now is *wildly* different.

Barb blows a raspberry, a pretty unmistakable sign that she's noticed her too. Just as I slap her hand, prompting her to stop staring, Ian turns around, and his eyes find mine.

Oh, my heart.

He waves, and I can almost see an ethereal light around him, wind blowing through his hair despite the closed windows. Sexy music in the background, slow-motion effects. The whole thing.

I wave back. Casual, not like the psycho I am. Once he faces the woman, she glances at me, and I'm seeing her in slow motion too. High cheekbones, perfect blond beach waves, and a gorgeous resting bitch face. She looks like a *Vogue* model. She's as tall as he is, slender and tanned. And her *outfit*. She wears it with such grace, the short lilac dress should thank her.

"I think I hate her." With the way she smiles at Ian as they study the breakfast buffet, I can't help it. They're obviously close, and though I adore Jules, La Brasserie's manager, he's a sixty-year-old grandfather. It's not quite the same thing.

Barb steals a look and lets out a low whistle. "Oh, this is going to be a long week. A long, excruciating week."

Fuck. I know what this is in front of me. Karma. One would think I paid enough, but it looks like the universe disagrees. This man obsessed over me for six months, and then I vanished for half a year, so he shows up here with a hotter version of Natalie Portman.

"She's so beautiful," I whisper. It's all my mind can process. Every single one of her movements is sheer grace. How she fills her glass with apple juice, how she chuckles at something he said, how she tucks a strand of perfectly curled, bright blond hair behind her ear.

How was Ian ever attracted to me with someone like that woman beside him every day? She and I don't belong to the same world. I live in the land of fuzzy hair and a touch of makeup, in the kingdom of baggy sweaters and knee socks. She's from the realm of people who sleep in lingerie and wake up with zero need for makeup.

"You're staring," Barb says. When I force my gaze on the plate of food in front of me, she adds, "Now you're fuming."

I look up at Barb, pleading for help, and she squeezes my hand with hers.

"It's too late to cancel, Ames. Unless I fake a pregnancy-related issue and you say you're my doula."

When a chuckle bursts out of my mouth, she points at my plate, but I don't think I can eat anything. Instead, I ask her about the nursery, and though I grasp a few words about paint colors and stuffed pandas, I can't process any of it as my fingers pull at my necklace and my eyes study Ian and his gorgeous chef.

Barb groans, slapping her forehead as she grumbles a string of curse words. The introductory meeting just ended, and Ian and the blond goddess are sitting a couple of rows behind us in the conference room. Though I can't see them, I'm sure their expressions resemble mine as I stare down at my copy of the schedule we've all received.

I stand and walk to Pamela, my stomach in a knot. "Pamela? What's this?"

She stares at the paper, then smiles. "The schedule. Do you have any questions?"

Questions? Yes, I have questions. Though the schedule is fairly clear, with ten to twenty classes taking place in the conference rooms every day for the next week, there's one *teeny tiny* problem. "Why am I paired with Ian Roberts?"

Her eyes move somewhere behind me, to Ian. I don't get it. These people are aware of the hatred between our fathers. Especially after the scene we made last night at dinner.

"Since you both work with French cuisine, we figured . . ."

"But he's not a chef. And we have very different views on food, opposite work ethics. The food that comes out of the Marguerite isn't in the same universe as what I do."

"Do you want me to see if we can move you around?"

"I . . ." I think it through for a moment. Ian hasn't approached her at all, so he must be okay working together, and if I complain, it'll look bad after he said he wants us to be "friends." "No, I guess it's fine. We'll manage."

"Okay, then. Let me know if there's anything else."

With a nod, I turn my attention back to the paper. Maybe it won't be that bad. According to the schedule, we'll teach three two-hour classes every day. Six hours a day, the two of us bouncing ideas off each other, smiling, reconnecting. Maybe becoming *more* than friends.

"Amelie?"

Ian's warm, deep voice brings me back to reality. Tucking some hair behind my ear, I turn to him, my dreamy smile shifting into a polite grin when I notice Isabella is by his side. "Hi," I say, scanning both of them and hating how good they look next to each other.

"Seems like us four will stick together," he says with a formal, tight-lipped smile. It's nothing like his real one.

Barb nervously chuckles as she appears at my side. "It's going to be fun." She's met by a stony silence, yet she continues: "So fun."

Everybody looks tense and uncomfortable, stealing glances at one another without knowing what to add. Though Isabella's definitely glaring at me, I figure I should introduce myself. "Nice to meet you," I say, extending my hand toward her. "Amelie Preston."

"I know." She glances down at my hand like it's a piece of fish gone bad. "The *famous* Amelie Preston."

My eyes shoot to Ian, asking a silent question. Why did hotter Natalie wake up and choose violence today? "Not a fan of my father's?" I ask.

"Your father and his little restaurant don't bother me in the least." She tilts her head, her eyes studying me as if she's deciding I couldn't possibly have spent more than twenty dollars on my whole outfit. I probably didn't. "But I *am* a fan of your personal work. Few people can make so many mistakes in so little time."

"Quit it," Ian mutters in a tone I've never heard him use before. Aggressive, abrupt. It's probably the same one I'd use if a staff member from my father's kitchen acted in such an unprofessional way toward a colleague.

My hand is still outstretched and waiting for hers, and with a stiff smile I pull it back. I expected the article to come up—of course I did—but I didn't think it would be on my first day. During my first interaction with a stranger.

I'm pondering what to say when Isabella's arm locks with Ian's as she leans against him.

Not like a colleague.

Maybe she's not talking about the article at all, and the mistakes she's referring to have nothing to do with my career. Maybe they're about something much more personal. Someone much closer.

Maybe Isabella isn't only a colleague.

Maybe she's Ian's girlfriend, and she's telling me to back off.

As I look from one to the other, my smile withers. "Well, anyway, I—" My chest tightens as the realization fully hits me. "We'll only work together for the next seven days. For only six hours a day, so . . . forty-two hours." Everything around me begins to blur, my panic at this point probably obvious in my expression. "And you and Barb will be there too. And the audience. We'll all be there together. The four of us and . . ."

Barb gawks at me in a desperate attempt to shut me up.

". . . and them," I choke out.

Nobody utters a word, awkwardness hovering between us like an uninvited guest. This empress of beauty is Ian's girlfriend, and oh my, I look like a rat next to her.

"We should use today to go over our notes, make sure we can come up with cohesive lectures before we start," Ian offers, placing a hand into the front pocket of his jeans.

I nod, staring at the deep-blue flecks in his irises. It makes even more sense now that he only wants to be friends; after all, his new girlfriend looks Louis Vuitton, and I'm Forever 21. "Yeah, okay," I say, in a tone of abject defeat. "Sounds good."

"Great. We can meet this afternoon." Ian turns to Isabella, but her mocking, ice-blue glare is still on me.

"Fine." She holds her hand out, and almost automatically I grab it and shake. This time, though, I don't smile. I couldn't even if I wanted to. "I look forward to seeing what you'll *delight* us with." She looks down at me from her impossibly high heels and grins, though there's hardly any honesty in her expression. Instead, her smile is malignant, arrogant. In a sickeningly mellifluous voice, she adds, "Ella Clarke."

My jaw snaps open, my eyes darting to Ian as every single thought disappears from my mind.

Isabella Clarke . . . is *Ella*?

Ella . . . *Clarke*?

15

Family History

Another tweet has come.

It's stupid, really, but I've been craving one since their anniversary, and I'm shaken by a jolt of adrenaline when I grab my phone and find it waiting for me.

I wonder who's behind it. William Roberts himself, or, much more likely, whoever his social media guy is. Making a mental note to check the restaurant's website, I open the app and read.

The Marguerite ✓
@Themarguerite

You want to eat at The Marguerite and your boyfriend suggests @LaBrasserie? Don't despair! There are plenty of fish in the sea.
12:29 PM · Oct 02 · Twitter for iPhone

💬 2   ↻ 8   ♡ 26   ᴵᴵᴵ 61   ⬆

Pulling the apartment door open, I snicker and set my gloves down. There's a box by the door, so I pick it up and see it's for Frank. "Here's hoping it's not a new cock ring. Lord knows, he'll need one in Mayfield," I mumble as I close the door behind me and set the box down. Though we've hardly talked at all in two weeks, I can't say I'm looking forward to his coming to visit. Until the wedding,

I'm happy to use an "out of sight, out of mind" kind of approach.

I know it's insane. Rationally, I can totally draw that conclusion. I'm stuck, and the more I plan for this wedding, the more I can feel the pressure of expectations weighing on my shoulders. The more I hope to rekindle my relationship with Frank, the further I feel it slip away. It's like a sinking ship, relentlessly taking on water, and whatever cracks I manage to patch up are replaced by new, deeper ones.

But the alternative is worse. Throwing myself off my familiar yet sinking ship in favor of a frozen ocean of unknowns. Alone to face all difficulties. My fiancé is my one certainty, and I won't stop trying to fix our relationship until there's nothing but water in my lungs.

I enter the kitchen, placing the food I brought from the restaurant in the fridge, and my phone notifies me of an incoming text. I expect it to be Ian and nearly topple over when I see it's Frank.

Heart tumbling, I tap on the notification as one more message comes through.

Frank:
Something got delivered for me today. Open it, please?

Sorry this engagement isn't exactly what you wanted.

I walk back to where I placed the box and open it, finding a black ring box inside. My bottom lip stings, and I realize I've been nibbling it; the metallic taste of blood floods my mouth. Without hesitating, I pull out the box, lift up the top, and find an engagement ring perched on black velvet.

It's beautiful. Classy, simple. A small oval white diamond and a thin white gold band. Exactly like I've always wanted.

Settling on the closest chair, I slide it on my finger. It feels foreign, though I guess that's somewhat normal at first. I think of sending Frank a picture, then sending one to Barb and Martha, but for a while I do nothing except stare at my hand, at the ring.

It's good. Great, even, that he remembered the type of ring I wanted. Maybe it's a sign of what he promised, that although I might not get the engagement I've always dreamed of, or the wedding I've always wanted, I'll get the marriage I deserve. And that's what counts the most.

My phone vibrates on the wood coffee table, and I throw a quick look at it.

Ian:
Send help right fucking now. There's a spider on my desk.

I huff out a laugh, then open the message just as I receive a picture of the tiniest brown spider next to his computer.

Amelie:
It's so small. Don't kill it.

Ian:
I won't, but I'll need to move in with you.

Amelie:
Too late for that. I'm officially engaged.

Ian:
Officially? Did you submit papers?

I send a picture of the ring, and though he sees it immediately, no answer comes for a while. Then he types and stops. Then he types again, and for the second time the three dots vanish.

Until eventually:

Ian:
Congratulations, beautiful.

Are you happy?

Yeah, I guess. No, I'm definitely happy about the ring. It's gorgeous, and Frank clearly put thought into it. I guess I didn't imagine my engagement ring would come in a box. Or with a text.

> **Amelie:**
> Yes, very happy.

> **Ian:**
> Good.

> Did he do the champagne thing?

> **Amelie:**
> What champagne thing?

> **Ian:**
> The cringe proposal thing where he plops the ring in the champagne glass?

> **Amelie:**
> Yes, but he used a Bloody Mary.

> **Ian:**
> Much better. You can use the celery stick to fish it out.

Snorting out another laugh, I switch to my chat with Frank, then stare at the keys on my phone, not sure which one to tap first. I should say thank you, that the ring is beautiful and I love him, but every word I think of sounds wrong. Not enough, or just too much.

I get a voice message from Ian and, curious to hear what else he has to say about proposals and celery, I tap on it.

"Not that you don't sound absolutely over the moon," he says, his voice dripping with sarcasm and filling the silence of my apartment, "but I figured I'd cheer you up anyway in case the engagement was cringier than I'm picturing. Because, dear Amelie, I have *the* cringiest engagement story for you. I hope you're ready."

"All right," I say as the recording goes on.

"More specifically, this is the story of my parents' engagement. They married later in life, so I was an unfortunate witness to all of it."

I'm already smiling as I settle back against the chair.

"Well, I'm ten. My dad drags my mom and me to this fancy hotel for the weekend. Rain, fireplace, chocolates. The whole thing. The fucker makes me light up about fifty tea candles and spread them all around the room while my mom is at the spa."

I bite the inside of my cheek. "See, *that's* a proposal."

"He sends me away, but I steal my dad's camera and hide somewhere in the room, because I figure my parents will love the video of their proposal, right? So he comes in wearing the hotel's white fluffy robe, and when my mom enters the room, he's there, holding the ring." He snickers. "But because he's always pranking her, she thinks it's bullshit. She grabs the ring from the box and throws it across the room. And the ring, defying all laws of physics, hits one of the fifty tea candles a ten-year-old me *might* have placed just a little too close to the edge of the table."

My eyes are wide as I listen, anticipating what happens next.

"And I'm still making a video of my mom crying, my dad screaming." He sighs. "Eventually, he gets on one knee, begins his speech. But the robe is a hotel robe—one size fits all. Well, turns out it does *not* fit all. So now my dad's kneeling in front of my mom, giving her this very emotional speech, and his dick and balls are hanging out for us to enjoy."

My shoulders shake from so much laughter, it's hard to breathe.

"And that's when the whole room turns into a fiery inferno. The carpeted floors catch on fire, the flames spread to the curtains, the hotel's alarm starts blasting." He groans. "Oh, Amelie. You have no idea."

God, the way he says my name, though.

"And any type of self-awareness has gone out the window, my dad's dick is still swinging left and right like he's trying to hypnotize us with it." He laughs so hard and for so long, he struggles to speak, until eventually: "Oh, and . . . funny thing? My mom hated the ring. *Hated* it. My dad has no fucking taste: it's this thick golden band with yellow topaz stones around a white central diamond, like her favorite flower. *Gah.* Of course, after we all risked our lives for it, she couldn't exactly exchange it." There's a little pause. "So there you have it. Whatever Frank did, I'm sure he didn't flash you and a ten-year-old, nor did he set a hotel on fire, causing hundreds of people to evacuate their romantic holiday."

The message ends, and, still chuckling, I press on the microphone icon. "Oh my God, Ian. Please tell me you made it all up."

As soon as I get his answer back, I press "play." "Hell no. I almost died, Amelie. In fact, I remind my dad every time we go out for lunch. We're close, which I guess is bound to happen when you know how to recognize your father's ball sack out of a lineup. So close that if *you* were to propose to *me*, you'd have to ask him for my hand in marriage."

I smile down at the phone. Though I didn't need cheering up, I feel better. And I'm happy to know Ian has someone in his life who has his back. Pressing on the microphone icon again, I twist a lock of hair with my fingers. "You'll have to send me a picture of that ring. You know, to verify the truthfulness of your story."

Immediately, I receive an image. I open it, and the démodé ring isn't even the first thing I notice. I think it's his hand, which the ring is resting on. His tattoos wrapping around his wrist. Or his disgusted expression as he looks at it, his chin pushed down. He's purposefully being ridiculous, and yet he's painfully handsome, with his soft brown hair falling down his forehead and eyes so blue, it's like being underwater.

Eventually, though, I look at the ring. The tear-shaped topaz stones surround a small circular white diamond, just like a yellow daisy.

The fact that Ian has it, though, *could* mean that his mom doesn't want that ring anymore.

Amelie:
Still no story with you and marriage?

Ian:
Just opinionated.

No story.

"How was your week?" Ian asks as he lets out a long sigh. He said he got home five minutes ago, which means he must have had a long day, because it's eight.

I hold my phone against my ear and chew my lip. "My week was . . . exhausting."

"Did you get that promotion?"

"Not yet."

"Why not?"

I let myself fall back against the chair, then glance at the poster-sized paper on the table, peppered with black and red pins. My guests and Frank's guests. I have to say that out of all the things I've planned for my wedding so far, figuring out how to place his homophobic uncle as far as possible from my lesbian cousin—and everyone else, really—is the most challenging by far.

"Dad making you jump through hoops, Amelie?"

I drag my cousin's pin all the way to the right, then rethink it, because she's known to become a little too flirty when she's had a few drinks, and Frank's sister is having a bi-curious moment. His uncle would not like *that*. "I have a vague memory of us discussing taboo topics."

"Fine, fine. But it has been two weeks already, hasn't it?"

Since I told him, yes. Since my dad announced he was retiring and would be choosing the next head chef? Embarrassingly longer than that. Though I'm still not dying to get the job, it's all types of insulting and infuriating. As such, it's a thought I'd rather avoid. "Taboo topic."

"Come on," he says with a loud groan. "I'll trade you. Just this once."

I stab the bridal table with my pin and throw my head back. "Fine. But I don't want to know about your job."

"No? Are you sure? It's really fun. Plus, I'm blanking and I could use a good comeback—"

"*No*," I say pointedly, refusing to let him distract me. "You know what I want. The true reason behind your hatred for marriage."

"Fine." He clears his throat. "It all started a long time ago, in a faraway land."

"Ian . . ." I scold.

"There once was a kingdom—"

"Come on! Be serious."

"—whose queen and king—"

"Oh my—goodbye." I hang up, my lips twisting with a smile I can't undo when I receive his text.

Ian:
Well, that was rude.

Now you'll never know my story.

I see the messages, then tap my fingers on the table as I wait.

Fine. The queen and king had a handsome, gorgeous, hilarious, good-spirited, merciful, impossibly smart prince.

With an eye roll, I press on the call button.

"And one day, the prince met a princess. She was . . . all right, I guess. Blond or something."

"Oh, for the love of—"

"Yes, love! They were in love. Or so the handsome prince thought."

"How old were you?" I ask, settling my feet on the chair and hugging my knees. Something tells this will be a *long* story.

"Me? I'm telling you a story about a handsome prince."

"Fine. How old was the dorky prince?"

"He was in high school." He waits for a hum of confirmation, then continues. "The prince and the princess dated for years, throughout their royal studies and until graduation, when the prince decided to do something really, *really* stupid."

"Let me guess: he proposed."

"Hey. This is *my* story." He clears his throat again. "The prince proposed."

"My, oh, my, I'm shocked!"

"And the princess wasn't as condescending as you, so she said yes. Blissfully in love, the two of them planned their wedding. The whole court was invited, and the king and queen were thrilled. Flowers in the kingdom sprouted higher, their colors were fuller, honey was sweeter, and—"

My shoulders slump as he rambles on. "I'm hanging up."

"—until one day," he says, his voice turning grave, "the princess was kidnapped and taken to a tall, dark tower from which she could never escape."

My thoughts run wild as I try to understand exactly what he means.

"Hmm . . . Wait, that wasn't dramatic enough. The princess was taken by an ogre who brought her to his kingdom of sad sex and gray flowers, where honey tastes like gasoline."

"I'm still—not sure—"

"I caught her fucking my best friend."

I hiss through my teeth. "Shit. How long before the wedding?"

"Two months. He was going to be my best man."

My shoulders fall, the cheerful and good-spirited Ian I know now mixing with a younger, heartbroken version of him. "God, Ian . . . I'm so sorry."

"Don't be. Best wedding gift she could have given me. I saw her true colors; his too. Cut them both out of my life, and it was for the best."

Still, he was fresh out of high school. I can't imagine how hard that must have been. "And that's when the prince swore off marriage?" I ask in a tentative voice. I just assumed he was playing around as usual when he started with the whole fairy-tale thing, but maybe he wasn't. Maybe it's just hard for him to talk about these experiences as his own.

"That *is* what the prince did. He decided he would never trust another woman, or have another relationship, and, most of all, he would never *ever* get married."

My eyes widen. "Well, that's hardly fair to women. Or to the prince. He could be missing out on a lot by swearing off the gentler sex."

"Oh, trust me, the prince did not swear off any type of sex."

"Funny," I say flatly.

After a pleased chuckle, he inhales deeply. "You're right. It was quite drastic. A little overdramatic, maybe. The prince was young."

"But the prince hasn't changed his mind. Has he?"

"He has not. But the story isn't over yet."

"Aw, that's nice." I stand and clean up the table. Frank will figure out where to seat Uncle Tony. "You're right. The story isn't over. You've got many more chapters to write, and I'm sure you'll find your princess."

"What?" He laughs. "No, that's not what I meant. The story isn't over because I'm not done speaking."

"Oh? There's more?"

"There's more. But I'll tell you after the commercials. It's your turn."

Abandoning my position at the coffee table, I enter the kitchen and take out the lasagna from the fridge. "Fine. The promotion. I've been groomed to take over my dad's position since before I left school, and he's decided he's retiring. But despite what some of my colleagues think, he's not a nepotist."

"So you have to prove you deserve it."

My lips pinch as I set the oven timer, my mind roaming to all the extra shifts and courses and hours of practice I've put into becoming a chef my father would be proud of.

Once the oven is set, I lean against the countertop. "Basically, yes."

"You don't strike me as someone who'd want a hand-me-down."

"I'm not," I confirm, drumming my fingers on my arm. I don't know exactly how to put this into words, but here goes my best attempt. "I don't mind working hard. And though I've already proved myself plenty, I don't mind doing it again every day."

"Okay."

"It's the stupidest thing, but . . . what if I want to be *offered* the position but I don't want the position itself?"

He hums. "Didn't you say you work with your father?"

"I do."

"Yikes."

Yeah, yikes. He's right. If he did offer me the position and I refused it, it'd probably break his . . . well, it would give him an upset stomach, at least.

"Sounds like you want your dad to recognize your efforts," Ian says, while munching on something. I swear the man's always snacking. "And based on your long-ass, late-night shifts, it sounds like he should."

"Well, he hasn't yet." And he probably never will either. All he cares about is this stupid fight with William Roberts. Which reminds me, I'm still waiting for the Marguerite's tweet. "Anyway, commercial's over." Sitting down at the kitchen table, I rest my chin on my knuckles and wait.

"Fine. Where were we? Oh, right. I swore off love and marriage forever." He clears his voice. "Then my mom got sick."

My hand lets go, my arm slowly falling on the table as my brows pinch together.

"The woman was . . . a bomb. My dad says I'm just like her, but imagine this much energy and these few fucks to give as a woman. She was"—he snorts—"fucking fierce. A hurricane. A complete nutjob."

I both smile and frown, my thoughts returning to my mom, a whole world away and so terrifyingly absent throughout most of my life.

"She had absolutely no time or patience for my heartbreak. And she was not okay with my 'nonsense about marriage.' That's what she called it." He takes a deep breath, then lets it out with a sense of resignation. "Anyway, as I said, she got sick, and it was one of those diseases that's long and debilitating and known to be fatal since the beginning. In the end, she was nothing like the woman who raised me. And seeing her like that . . . I wished she would just die."

"Ian . . ." I whisper.

"I know. It sounds horrible. It took me a lot of therapy to accept the way I was feeling."

"It's not horrible," I tell him. Not for the first time in the past few months, I wish there were no phone between us. That he was here, or I was there, and right now I could hug him tight and whisper in his ear that his feelings are perfectly normal. I can't imagine what it would be like watching someone so exuberant lose all their light. It's even harder to imagine seeing someone you love go through that.

"Well, the dumbass decided if she was not going to be by my

side for the next fifty years to remind me not to give up on love, she'd motivate me enough to remind myself."

"O . . . kay?"

"So when the queen died and the whole kingdom mourned her loss, the prince found out he'd been left fifty percent of her inheritance, and he'd only receive the other half on one condition."

Bursting into a smile that takes over my whole face, I say, "He had to get married."

"Mm-hmm. Can you believe this lunatic?"

"Not only can I believe her, but I love her."

Ian mumbles, "Yeah. I love her too."

As I get up to set the lasagna into the oven, I ask, "What about the princess?"

"What about her?"

"Well, did she end up with the ogre? Are they still having sad sex? Or did she come back for the prince?"

"No, she never came back," he says. "And by the way, she's anything but a princess. Maybe one of those wrinkly witches with a dark hood over their almost bald heads and huge, hairy warts on their noses."

"Not a princess. Got it." I bite my lower lip. "So, then, what should I call her?"

"You could call her a bi—" When I laugh, he sputters an amused chuckle too. "Ella. Her name is Ella."

LES PLATS DE RÉSISTANCE

16

Ratatouille Equals War

"Ella isn't just the Marguerite's chef, is she?" Barb asks, following behind me as I quickly ascend the stairs. "Is that why we're running away?"

We're not running away. Ella introduced herself. I shook her hand and said I'd meet them soon enough. Then—well, then I guess we ran away.

"Ames? Pregnant women should never exercise," Barb says with a quick pant.

Halting and turning around immediately, I stare at her bump, my hands hovering over it as if it'll fall off. "Shit. Are you okay?"

"Yes," she says with an amused grin. "Don't you know anything about pregnancy? I said that so that you'd stop." When I glare, she tilts her head. "Come on. Who was that?"

"Isabella—*Ella* Clarke, of course," I grumble as I make my way up the stairs.

"But you know her."

Passing a hand over my face, I hop onto the last step and turn to Barb. "I've *heard of* her. She and Ian were . . . engaged." As her eyes widen, I clarify, "No, not when I met him. A long time ago."

"But they didn't get married?"

I shake my head.

With a long exhale, she says, "Oh, this keeps getting better."

She doesn't need to tell me. What happened to all that talk about her being a witch? He doesn't seem to be acting as if she has a wart on her nose, whether literally or figuratively.

I haul Barb along the corridor and into our hotel room, where she sets up for a nap. I'm in no mood to discuss any of this, and—if anything—I'll show Ella I'm a better cook than she is.

I try; I really do. For two hours I read my notes, go through the lectures I prepared for the week, and force myself to think about recipes and cooking techniques instead of Ian kissing Ella. Undressing Ella. Laying her down on his bed. Turning her world upside down.

God, it's like bugs are crawling all over me; I'm going to lose my mind.

By the time I meet them again, I'll be a bundle of nerves, but I'm sure of one thing: I won't let him see it.

We head down to the conference room, and as we enter, Ian leans back and rolls his chair a few inches away from Ella. He turns to me, the usual twinkle in his eyes replaced by an annoyed look.

"Hi. Come in."

I sit, keeping my eyes down on the glossy black table that occupies most of the room. After Barb and I take out our material, silence blankets us again, the chattering from outside becoming louder as people walk past our meeting room.

"Well, let's try to make this as painless as possible." Ella takes out a single sheet of paper. "These will be the topics of our lectures. Prepare your material based on our plan."

Accepting the paper she's offering, I inhale deeply. How to Run a Profitable Restaurant, class for beginners held by Ian. French Cooking for Beginners, held by Ella. Master French Sauces, Ella.

Bistro Charcuterie for Beginners, Ella. The Art of Marketing, Ian. The list goes on.

They're much better organized than I am. They have a list of the topics they'll cover, the ingredients needed for each class, and a level of difficulty set to a five-star scale. It's insane.

Barb shoots me a worried look.

I won't be rude—not when my annoyance can be mistaken for jealousy—but I also won't bend over to please Ella. This whole meeting seems to be more about us following their orders than a collaboration, and I will never follow rules set by a member of the Marguerite's kitchen.

"Interesting." I set the paper down and offer her my own. It's handwritten, not a fancy Excel sheet printed out in four exact copies. And there are no ingredients or difficulty levels, only lots of notes and ideas. Some doodles, too, because that's what I do when I'm focused. Doodle.

With a harmonious chuckle out of her perfect cherry-red lips, Ella holds her hand out. Even her fingers are enviable. Long and elegant, with a fresh coating of pink nail polish and cute golden rings. Before she can get her claws on my notes, Ian fetches them.

My eyes meet his, and he briefly smiles before focusing on the paper, his forehead creasing as he goes through the few lines of text I've put together.

I don't know what to expect. My Ian of a year ago would cheer me on over the silliest thing, though he's also always been one to dish out tough love when needed. But a Roberts? I'd expect him to spit on the paper, crumple it into a tiny ball, and throw it into the nearest bin, then sing a hymn to the devil.

When the tapping of my fingers on the table becomes the only sound in the room, I tuck my hand out of sight, trying to hide how nervous his lack of reaction is making me.

"This is good," he says, passing it to Ella. "We should incorporate—"

She sets the paper down, her nails clicking on the table's surface. "No. Our ideas are better."

"We'll incorporate our ideas," he repeats without looking at her. "Get rid of half our topics and introduce half of Amelie's."

Ella glares at him, and as he returns her hateful look, I clear my throat. Not only is this not the way I'd expect Ian to behave toward his girlfriend, but it's hardly a positive example of a healthy relationship between colleagues. "We could join our seminars on desserts and—"

"Do what you want but stay out of my way." Ella stands, her chair screeching against the wooden floor. Grabbing her bag off the table, she turns and leaves the room in a cloud of sickly-sweet perfume.

"Sorry about that." Ian holds on to the papers in front of him, an awkward smile bending his lips. "She's a little . . ."

"Temperamental?" I ask.

He rubs his chin. "Passionate."

Right. Passionate. She's rude and nasty, that's what. Nothing like him, for sure. But then again, I struggle to see his usual joie de vivre, his exuberant enjoyment of life. I'd assumed it was me, but, considering the exchange I just witnessed, maybe it isn't.

Barb desperately tries to break the tension, saying something about chefs being some of the most stubborn and overbearing people ever, but it's all background noise to me, because as I shoot Ian a questioning look, he stares back in a way that's much too familiar.

His eyes glimmer, shining like they always have. And I may be projecting, but it feels like he might have missed me. I wonder if he, too, has thought about me every single day since the last time we spoke. If he's replayed our conversations in his head a thousand times over like I have, changing the parts he regrets the most. I wonder if he has any regrets at all. I have so many.

"Ames?"

I turn to Barbara, whose gaze moves between me and Ian.

"Should we . . . ?"

"Right, yes." Ian clears his throat. "Let's . . . let's just all try to get along."

"I don't think you need to tell *me*." He throws me a dubious look, and my stiff smile falls. "Seriously? Did you miss the way she's been treating me since we met?"

"No, I didn't. But Ella, she's—"

"Passionate," I say mockingly. "I got it. But passion is for the bedroom, not seminars, and she shouldn't direct it at me."

His eyes squint, and his posture stiffens. "Jealousy, Amelie? After everything? How's Frank, by the way? I don't expect we'll see too much of him around here, huh?"

Wait—what? *Frank*? With wide eyes, I glance at Barb, the beating of my heart slowing until it's like a faint knocking in the back of my mind.

Ian doesn't know. He has no idea Frank and I aren't together. How is that possible? It was right there, in the article. With the most blatant unprofessionalism I've ever experienced, *Yum* magazine mentioned all my recent failures, my relationship included.

My eyes widen. It's obvious, yet somehow I completely missed it.

Ian hasn't read the article.

"Don't make that face," he says. "If Frank turns out to be husband of the year, by all means, apologize to him for me."

"Actually, Ian, you should know that—"

"I should know *nothing*, Amelie. Let's just focus on this." Pointing his pen at the paper, he turns to Barb. "So, where shall we begin?"

17

A British Snake

Kicking the door closed, I glance at my reflection in the entryway mirror. My hair's a tangled mess atop my head after the quick but exhausting jog I just went on, and the cold fall wind has my cheeks burning. "Can I ask you something?"

Ian's voice crackles through the phone, warm as if he's the most relaxed he's ever been. "If you don't, this'll turn out to be an incredibly dull conversation."

"You know, some people just say yes."

"Incredibly dull people," he says. "What's the question?"

With a shake of my head, I walk down the hall to the kitchen. I'm not exactly comfortable discussing this with anyone, but is it crazy that I'd go to Ian before Martha or Barb? I don't feel judged when I talk to him. Not ever. Or like I'm interrupting something more important.

"Do you ever not—hmm, if a man doesn't feel like . . ." I roll my eyes and open the fridge. "What's the best way to make him want to, *you know* . . ."

Ian clears his throat. "Some people just say 'have sex.'"

"I'm serious, Ian."

"So . . . Frank isn't putting out?"

I grab a bottle of water and head to the living room, flopping onto the couch. The black leather is cold against my sweaty thighs, and it isn't by far the most uncomfortable thing going on. Frank and I haven't seen each other in a month, but even before he moved out . . . things weren't exactly *hot*. Physical contact between us had already been at a depressing low for a while.

But I'm trying this new thing where, instead of letting the thought send me crashing into a ball on the floor, I fight for my relationship. He said sex between us was boring, so I'll just make it not boring.

It might sound horribly desperate, but it's not. It's only *moderately* desperate.

"Is that it?" he insists.

"Uh, yes. Sort of . . . yes."

He exhales deeply, then his chuckle melts my insides, warm and throaty and calmness personified as Ian always is. "That's . . . funny," he says, as if he doesn't think it's funny at all. "That is really, *really* funny."

"How so?"

"Because, Amelie, that's insane. You're hot—and that's not just my opinion. You're universally hot, objectively hot. Long legs, amazing ass, and you have the face of an angel, which most men appreciate on a primordial level."

"A *primordial* level," I echo.

"Yeah. So innocent and angelic. Our primal instincts tell us to mess you up." When I let out a laugh, he continues. "I mean it! Turn you into a sobbing, desperate, dirty mess. We want to defile you," he insists, his voice fluid and joyous, as if he's smiling.

"Thank you, *friend*," I say pointedly. He'll say stuff like that every once in a while, but always with a painfully playful tone. If

I'm so desirable, how come Frank doesn't want me? "I think the problem is how *angelic* I am." I grimace. "How *innocent*."

"Hmm. And how much is that? Paint me a word picture."

I cross my ankles over the coffee table. "Ha-ha. What should I do, Ian?"

"I'd suggest switching your current model for a more advanced one, but I'm afraid that wouldn't be well received."

"It would not."

He hums, and in the few seconds of silence that follow, I fidget with my engagement ring. "Okay. How about . . . get yourself into a tiny lingerie set and wait for him in bed." There's a clap. "Done."

"Hmm . . ." I doubt it'd be in any way more interesting than the girls he's probably sleeping with right now. He's seen my bras plenty of times.

"No? Okay . . . how about . . . role-playing? Tie your wrists to the bed and tell him you've been a naughty, *naughty* girl. No way he says no to that."

With a snicker, I say, "I don't know."

"I guarantee he's not going to be able to resist you half-naked and whispering dirty shit in his ear." When all he gets is an unconvincing "I guess," he continues. "Come on. Pretend it's him. He comes in and you say . . ."

I get up and head to the bathroom, grabbing a brush to disentangle my hair before I take a shower. "You? No, Ian, I'm not—"

"'*Hi, Amelie,*'" Ian says in a weird nasal voice. "'*Work has me really stressed-out, but blimey, doesss it help to sssee you in that ssssexy red bra, mate.*'"

Snorting in amusement, I lean against the bathroom sink. "He sounds nothing like that. And why did you morph into a British snake?"

"I don't know. Come on. What do you say?"

I let out a whiff of air, setting the brush on the marble counter. "I say . . . 'Hi, Frank. Do you . . . I want you to come to the bedroom with me.'"

"Mm-hmm. Okay."

"'And I—'" Shaking my head, I close my eyes and blurt out, "'I want to lie in bed together, get naked, kiss, then touch you and—'"

"'*Crikey, Professor, thank you for the lecture! I've always wondered where babies came from.*'"

"Your Australian accent is terrible."

"So is your dirty talk," he says flatly. "Where's your bar graph? How are you grading his paper?"

"Just leave it be." I look into the drawer under the sink for . . . nothing, really. "I told you I'm not—I don't—" I groan, snapping the drawer closed. "I told you I don't know how to do this."

"Okay, okay, calm down." He sounds far less amused now, his voice returning to the usual dark timbre, and after a couple of seconds of silence, he speaks again. "He comes in, and you say, 'I've been thinking about you all day. About how much I want you inside me.'"

In the mirror, my eyes widen, the deep brown looking even darker against my red cheeks as I press my lips together tightly so that no noise comes out.

"And then you say, 'I want you to take me against the wall and make me forget everything else but your name. And once you shove me on our bed, I want you to bend me over, push my face against the pillow, and use me like I'm your dirty little fuck toy.'"

"Ian," I scold weakly, my stomach clenching. My whole face has turned a crimson red I'm not sure I can blame on the run, and it feels like my heart is beating in places it's not supposed to.

Why is this so damn hot?

"*That sounds delicioussss, Amelie. Come here: I'll give you the besssst orgasssmsss.*"

I don't even know what accent he was going for this time, but my arousal and amusement have me sputtering out a weirdly high-pitched giggle that I promptly rein in.

"Did I leave you speechless?" he asks in his normal voice.

"A little." Swallowing away the tension, I shrug. "Did you come up with that on the spot, or . . . ?"

His sudden guffaw is raspy and *way* too sexy. "Are you asking if I fantasize about using you as my dirty little fuck toy, beautiful?"

My jaw unhinges as I grip the counter to keep me steady, the cold surface burning against the heated skin of my fingers. "No, not me. That's not what I—no, I—"

"Relax, Amelie. I'm just messing with you." He lets out something between a chuckle and a sigh. "I've been told that and much worse in the bedroom. Really, telling your fiancé you want him to fuck you hard is nothing special."

"Figures you'd say that," I say, trying to divert his attention from me. "You're a fuckboy."

"Maybe. But if you were my fiancée, you wouldn't be asking another man how to get me into bed," he says in a firm voice. "In fact, I'd keep you pinned to that mattress until it's worn out, and then we'd move to the couch. Or the floor."

Ignoring what his words do to my stomach, I trap the phone between my shoulder and my ear, then squeeze some toothpaste out of the tube.

"Plus, your mouth would probably be too busy for questions."

"Ian!"

"Just playing. You basically repulse me, and anyway, I'll never have a fiancée." He clears his voice. "Look, Amelie, my experience with these things is that the more it turns *you* on, the more it'll turn *him* on." I can almost hear the mischief in his voice. "So . . . tell me, beautiful. What turns you on?"

"Nice try."

"Come on, I mean it," he says with a chuckle. "What is it?"

"I'm not saying, Ian," I say. "It's inappropriate."

"Is it? Or maybe—hear me out—*maybe* what you like is *not* pure and angelic. Quite the opposite. *Maybe* Amelie has an angelic face and a filthy mind."

I begin brushing my teeth, switching to speaker and placing the phone down next to the faucet.

"Just all sorts of nasty kinks."

I say nothing.

"The dirtiest fantasies."

He can be *so* annoying.

"No hard limits."

"Ugh—stop it! I'm not saying!" Little drops of toothpaste pepper the mirror at my outburst.

"Come on! *Show me yours and I'll show you mine*," he singsongs.

With my stomach plummeting, I sigh. He's like a child on Adderall. "Fine. You start, then."

After a quick cheer, he clears his voice. "All right. So I'm into a *lot* of things. All that pure and angelic stuff? Not me. Oral sex— love that. Even more if my face is being ridden like a train. And you remember I'm great at multitasking, so sixty-nine is one of my many talents." He hardly takes a breath before continuing. "I'm into any type of role-playing, edging. I'm definitely a switch. Threesomes are fun. Anal—"

"Okay!" I shout, my cheeks tingling so hard I don't even dare to look at my reflection in the mirror. "Okay, I got it. You love sex."

"Don't you?" he asks, the question drenched with such shock I consider not answering.

"Just tell me one. One thing you've never done and you really want to."

There's a long exhale, which—if I know Ian as I think I do—means he's frustrated and has some opinions about my sex life. "Okay," he says. "We're out somewhere public."

"*We*?" I mock.

"Yeah, me and you. Hypothetically."

I roll my eyes and fight back a smile. I *have* to stop smiling. "Right. We're *hypothetically* out somewhere public."

"Yes. You go to the restroom, and when you come back, you put your panties in my hand. You don't say anything, only look at me and sit down. But I know you're naked under your dress. That you're wet and warm and tight, and that I can reach my hand out and touch you, but I can't because there's just too many people around." His voice darkens, his words coming out slower. "And I stare at your thighs, hoping to see underneath, terrified that someone else will. Unable to think about anything else, obsessing over how ready you are, how close, but unreachable." He inhales, then exhales slowly. "That would drive me insane. Hypothetically."

Am I breathing? I think I'm not breathing.

There's a minute of silence in which my body throbs to life. In which I feel like a woman, a desirable one too. In which my skin heats and feels raw, my throat dries up, and the saliva thickens in my mouth. It's been months, and I'm—how should I put it?—horny.

I press my thighs together, losing myself in the thought of Ian's fantasy playing out. My underwear in his pocket, his blue eyes darting to my legs, my thighs slick with—

"Amelie?"

"No. I mean, no—yes." Heat moves past my cheeks and all the way to my ears. "That sounds—that's definitely not basic."

"Nothing wrong with basic if that's what you like," he says. "Okay. Your turn."

"Hmm." I smirk at the mirror. "I'm not saying."

"Unbelievable," he says. "'Innocent and angelic' my ass. You tricked me!"

"I did," I confirm as I shove the toothbrush into the holder and pick my phone back up. "Considering you deceived me during our first interaction, it's only fair."

"That's fine," he says, followed by a low chuckle. "I think I've got a pretty good idea of what you like anyway."

"Really?" My brows arch. "And what would that be?"

"I'll tell you what it's not," he says in a cocky voice. "It's not the lights-off, under-the-blanket missionary sex you're used to having with your fiancé."

18

Out of Business

– TODAY –

I stifle the fourth yawn in a row, the sun filtering through the window of the conference room warm on my skin, then throw a look at my watch. Ten fifteen. I already heard this seminar yesterday, and though I'm not looking forward to learning about the Robertses' marketing and management techniques, Ian is pleasant to ogle as he explains to his eager audience how to run a restaurant. His dark gray sweater looks so soft, his blue jeans wrapping his ass ever so perfectly.

He gestures a little. Not too much, but enough to keep people entertained. His light brown hair mostly stays in place, but a few lovely strands fall over his eyes when he tilts his head forward, and his ocean-blue eyes squint every time he's deep in thought.

And his smile. He throws in some grins that he should keep to himself. They're distracting as hell.

When he turns to me as he walks up and down the room, I avert my gaze, focusing on him again once he looks away. We haven't spoken since yesterday, when his girlfriend nearly bit my head off.

And I'm happy for him. I'm *trying* to be happy for him. Okay, I'm not happy for him at all. There's not a single reason in the world I can think of that justifies getting back together with an ex who slept with your best friend. Not one, except the not-so-basic things she probably lets him do to her.

Ella's sitting on the other side of the room, lazily scrolling through her phone. Her blond hair is perfect—not one single strand out of place—and, God, she has impossibly long legs. No wonder he enjoys keeping them entangled with his own.

A round of applause echoes around the room. It looks like people appreciated Ian's seminar, though I suspect the most enthusiastic claps belong to women who also appreciated the speaker.

With a light smile, Ian nods in silent appreciation. "Any questions?" he asks, and boy, there are many. People would ask the dumbest things to see him move around a little more, smile a few more times, look into their eyes. Though that could just be me.

"What's the most important thing you shouldn't be cheap about when managing a restaurant?" someone asks from the back.

Biting his lower lip, Ian leans against the desk behind him. "Just one, huh?" There's a general chuckle, which elicits another one of his heartbreaking smiles, and after rubbing his chin he continues. "I'd say . . . location. Location is the single most important thing when opening a restaurant."

"Well, I disagree," I mumble, which makes Barb smile. It's a "Who would have guessed it?" smile that has me rolling my eyes. "Barb, come on. You know he's wrong."

"Care to share your opinion with the rest of us?" Ian asks in a loud voice.

I turn to him, his brows raised and one corner of his lips quirked up. "N-no, sorry."

"Come on." He motions at me to come stand with him and turns to face the audience. "This is the head chef of La Brasserie, Amelie Preston."

Now that I'm aware he hasn't read the article, even the incorrect introduction makes sense. But even so, what game is he playing? Because I'm not about to shy away from a confrontation with a Roberts, not even if it's Ian.

Tentatively, I stand and join him as a few people clap lackadaisically. Of course, there isn't nearly as much enthusiasm as when *he* showed up. Most of these people probably read the article about me.

"What's your take, Amelie?" he asks, crossing his arms with his usual playful smile. "What's the one thing you can't skimp on?"

After lingering a second longer than I should on the infinite blue of his irises, I turn to the audience and smile at the many faces staring back at me. "Well, as a chef, I can't say anything is more important than food quality."

There are several nods of agreement from the crowd, but as I turn to Ian, his mouth is twisted in a dubious grimace. "True. Food quality is a big one." He shrugs slightly. "But I still think people would rather eat a sandwich in the city center than a lobster next to a dumpster."

And what does *that* have to do with anything?

I try to keep my smile unfazed, but a flash of irritation has me raising my hands and blurting out, "Have you ever even entered a kitchen?"

When his eyebrows rise, I look down at my shoes. That was rude.

"I mean . . . food quality has nothing to do with sandwiches and lobsters. It's about choosing the best ingredients for your dishes."

"I understand that. I was exaggerating to prove a point."

"Location is very important, as is a cohesive interior design, a unique selling point, and trained staff." I clasp my hands together and keep them over my stomach. It's better than furiously waving my index finger at him as I'd like to. "But *unpopular opinion*," I say pointedly, "people go to restaurants to eat. The most important thing is the quality of the food."

A man in the back raises his hand, so I start to return to my chair. The last thing I want to do is intrude on Ian's seminar, and it looks like we're done with this topic.

"I disagree."

My head turns back to Ian so fast, he must think we're reenacting scenes from *The Exorcist*. "You disagree?" I ask.

"Customers come in for an experience, not to eat."

"They want to eat something *better* than they would at home. Hence, food quality—"

"They want to sit in a pretty room and be served by competent staff. They want to feel important. Food's the least relevant thing."

"What?" I ask, my ears ringing. "You can't be serious."

"I am." Resting his hands on the desk behind him, he smiles, as if my outrage amuses him. "Food is sustenance. People go to a restaurant to be entertained."

A low murmur spreads through the room, and to be honest, I'd be surprised if there weren't such a reaction. It's crazy that anyone in the restaurant business would say something like this, but him? How can someone believe food is just *sustenance* and work as the manager of one of the most famous French restaurants in the country?

Oh, right. They don't serve food at his restaurant. They serve overly seasoned sludge.

"No wonder *you'd* think that," I retort as I stride to my seat. If this conversation continues any longer, I won't be responsible for my words.

"You seem to forget—"

Oh, here it comes.

"That you have won a bunch of irrelevant awards?" I finish for him, with a snap, and spin like a whirling dervish to face him. "Oh, I remember. And every item on your menu tastes like the same generic thing. You serve a facsimile of French food that I wouldn't recommend to my worst enemy."

As he throws a look at the crowd, he chuckles, unbothered by my tantrum. "Amelie, have you ever even eaten at the Marguerite?"

I open my mouth, then close it. To him, it probably looks like he's won this round—and he has, but by default. I've eaten at the Marguerite before, though I can't share that with him.

When he smirks, I know I have to say something. "The Marguerite is a French fast-food joint, Ian!"

Ella gasps, quickly standing. "How dare you give your unwanted opinion on the Marguerite after you couldn't keep your own restaurant afloat for four months!"

I swallow, my mouth instantly going dry as my heartbeat thunders in my ears. It's like the whole room has gone dark, and the only light is shining down on me, exposing my rawest parts for everyone to judge. Showcasing each and every one of my failures.

"Amelie?" Ian asks in a questioning voice.

I straighten my shoulders. My restaurant may have failed at the speed of light, but it doesn't change the truth. "The only reason the Marguerite is successful is that you serve people-pleasing, simple recipes." I glance at Ella's hateful glare, then turn to Ian. "You have a standardized twenty-dollar menu. You work with frozen, low-quality ingredients. You microwave precooked food, for Chrissake."

As I catch my breath, I swallow. I'm making a scene in front of a hundred people, but I don't care. It seems all I've been doing for the past year has been humiliating myself anyway.

When I'm met with stony silence, I grab my bag. I need to get out of there. "I'm sorry, but . . . Actually, I'm not sorry. You are both living off the vulgarization of French food. Of food in general. What is art to me, you treat as mere business. I—" I take a step toward the door, then turn to the audience. Most of them are staring at me, wide-eyed and in complete silence. "Sorry. Business advice? You're in the right hands. But if you treat your food as art"—I point at Ian and Ella—"this isn't what you're looking for."

The wine is fresh on my tongue, rich and sweet and accented by fruity, ripe flavors. Cabernet, about ten years old. Setting the glass down, I turn to the counter as I pull at my necklace with my finger. The bar is open only to lecturers and other people working at the event, and even so, the dimly lit space is almost filled to the brim except for the seat in front of me.

I close my eyes and tilt my head back, exhaling deeply. But even with my eyes closed, I sense him coming to stand beside me. It must be his smell, or maybe the shadow his body casts over me. Whatever it is, I'm equally eager and terrified to open my eyes.

But I do, and Ian's looking down at me, as handsome from my upside-down perspective as he is from every other angle. His nose, straight and pointy, his shapely jaw, the lovely curve of his chin. And he's smiling. God, how I constantly miss that devilish smile. "I got you another glass."

"Oh, thanks." I pull myself up as he takes a seat in the chair next to me. Silently, he studies me, every muscle and organ and bone in me squirming under his inquisitive gaze. "I should . . . I should probably apologize for what I said."

"Don't worry about it." He waves me off.

I can feel my brows scrunch up. Is he feeling bad for me after my scene, or does he really not care?

"So you opened a restaurant."

As heat blossoms on my cheeks, I nervously fidget with the hem of my shirt. "Spoiler alert," I say in a dull voice. "It failed."

"I've gathered." Looking away, he shrugs. "Doesn't matter, though, does it? You still took the leap."

Yeah, and landed face-first on cement. I usually love Ian's contagious positivity, but it *does* matter. It's what matters the most. Certainly, my restaurant failing is what got me here, with no money, no job, and no hope of having a successful career as a chef.

"But it does make me wonder . . ." After setting his glass down, he rubs his jaw. His eyes roam from left to right, as if he's trying to solve a puzzle. "How . . . how did it happen exactly? How did Amelie Preston open a restaurant and fail?"

My throat tightens as I try to swallow.

"I mean, you've been a chef since, hell, probably since before you were a fully formed adult." He smiles lightly. "I'm sure your dad taught you all the ropes. That he has the right contacts and gave you plenty of guidance throughout the years."

Shifting uncomfortably in my chair, I turn my gaze away. I can't tell Ian what happened after the wedding. I just can't. I'd love to tell him the truth: he's the only person who can possibly make me feel better about any of this. But I remember our conversations about his father. They're not just close: with his mom being gone, William is all Ian has. And if his son knew what happened between us last year, William would lose him. And Ian would lose his father.

After stalling with a sip of wine, I ask, "How come the manager of one of the *best* French restaurants in the country doesn't care about the quality of his food?"

Leaning back against his chair, he studies me, his soft, gorgeous sweater stretching over his wide chest and revealing the white shirt underneath as he takes a deep breath. "Smooth change of topic, Amelie."

"Location?" I ask, throwing my hands up in the air. "That's what matters in a restaurant? Entertainment? How about extra-virgin olive oil and vegetables in season? How about grass-fed livestock and authentic—"

"I never said all of that wasn't important. I said—"

"You said food was the least relevant thing, Ian." I cross my arms. "How can you think that?"

"Results speak volumes," he says with a cheery smile. "One of us at this table is the owner of a successful restaurant. The other one . . ." He shrugs. "Well, I don't know the details yet, but she isn't."

Wow. I've always appreciated Ian's honesty. He says what he thinks, and no sugarcoating it. Only now I realize what a double-edged sword that can be.

I try to hide just how deeply his comment stings behind a smile. "*Well*, one of us at this table also knows how to recognize fast food." I narrow my glare on him and swallow the lump in my throat. "And the other one sells it."

After wetting his lower lip and opening his mouth, I expect him to retort, but nothing comes out, and with a quick shake of his head, he grabs his drink and downs it. "I should go find Ella." He stands, and the last words I hear are "Frank must be looking forward to blowing you off again."

19

The Cheesier the Better

– Four Months and Two Weeks to Amelie's Wedding–

"Number 86, Croque Monsieur!" Dean shouts at the pass before walking back into the dining room with a filled tray.

Drying the sweat off my forehead, I stir the pot in front of me, then glance at my phone. The Marguerite hasn't reacted yet, but I'm seriously hoping my latest move pissed some people off big-time.

With a pleased chuckle, I study the large, bubbling vats of meat, covered in a crust so dark that it's almost black. Under it, beans swim in a rich, gelatinous broth with bits of tender duck leg, cured pork belly, pork shanks, and sausages.

"Are the cassoulets ready?" the waiter asks.

I nod, gesturing at him to take them, and as he walks away, I shout that I'm taking five and step out of the kitchen. My shift is almost over, and I haven't had a chance to take a single break. It's ten; Ian must be falling asleep, but I never answered his last text.

Ian:
Did you find a band?

Amelie:
Not yet. Is yours interested in the gig?

The cool night air sends shivers down my spine. Shrinking inside my black coat, I look at the busboys taking a smoke break by the dumpsters. Is it too late to start smoking? Yes, it's a terrible habit, but people say it's relaxing. I could use some of that.

Martha paid me for the dress, which is currently with the designer, being altered, and Frank has been texting sparingly. I'm pretty sure I know what *that* means.

My phone beeps and, glad for the distraction Ian's always ready to provide, I glance down at his text.

Ian:
For sure. But we only play death metal.

Amelie:
Too bad. I only listen to Christian funk.

He sends me a link, and after opening it I scroll through the page. It's the website of a cover band, somewhat like the one I originally planned to hire for my wedding. Four members with a voice lead, a guitar, drums, and a bass. There's a video, so I press "play" and listen to them playing a cover of "Crazy in Love." I like them.

Ian:
The marriage virus is spreading and taking new victims every day.

> I heard them play at a friend's wedding last week, and they're coming to your neck of the woods for yet another wedding next Saturday.

> **Amelie:**
> Do you know where?

I get a screenshot of a text conversation between Ian and Dan, who, based on the website, is the lead singer. They're playing at a venue I've actually toured for my wedding, and Dan told him the newlyweds don't mind me and my fiancé stopping by.

> **Ian:**
> Get Frank and go check them out.

Frank? God, for a second I forgot he's coming to visit this weekend. But I swore I'd make a genuine effort, and I can't think of anything better than dressing fancy and drinking champagne while we listen to some romantic music and see love blossom before our eyes.

Maybe a date would help us rekindle our romance a little. Maybe being at the Quinns' wedding would make him see the beauty of it all, and he'd care about ours a little more.

> **Amelie:**
> Will do. Thank you, wedding planner.

> **Ian:**
> Of course, Bridezilla.

> **Amelie:**
> Two more hours before I'm off.

> **Ian:**
> Time to show your dad how it's done.

> Text me when you're home safe.

After making my way through a loud crowd that smells like perfume and champagne, I find the small table reserved for me to the left of the large outdoor space. Not what I expected for a November wedding, but the Quinns were awfully nice, saving me the table, so I'm hardly complaining.

I place my coat on the chair next to mine. Finding another one would prove impossible, because the entire venue, filled with clear plastic chairs, long wooden tables, and white lanterns, is peppered with groups of people drinking and dancing to the music of the DJ. Not that I'm expecting anyone else, seeing as Frank never made it back to Creswell for the weekend.

Must be busy doing who knows what with who knows who.

The stage in front of me is empty except for the instruments, but I can see some people with headphones messing with a soundboard, so the band must be about to start.

When the waiter approaches, I ask for a glass of white, then turn to the stage and realize someone's standing beside me. I never took the coat off the chair, but they must want to sit. "Oh, sorry, I forgot—"

Light brown hair. Blue eyes with even deeper blue flecks. A soft cream sweater with a white square pattern. Ian smiles in that dashing way I've spied countless times in photos and video calls, then looks down at the chair with a mock scowl. "Frank, I don't want to fight you for this spot, but I will if I have to."

"Ian?" I ask, my heart stuck in my throat. My skin tingles as a fluttery feeling awakens in my stomach. "How—what—"

I know it's him, of course. While I haven't seen him in the flesh since Barb's wedding, there's no mistaking that flirty grin, the perfect line of pearly-white teeth peeking through, his gorgeous hair, shorter at the sides and longer at the top of his head. But he can't be here, can he? *What is he doing here?*

"Whoa, whoa," he says, stumbling backward as he glares at the empty chair. "What did you say about my mom?"

I can't believe he's here. "What—what are you—"

"You said you'd come with Frank, Amelie. You're . . ." His posture relaxes as he snaps his fingers. "What's the word I'm looking for?" He smirks. "Is it . . . cunning? Dishonest? No, that doesn't sound right . . ."

Shock prevents me from feeling the slightest bit of shame at being caught red-handed in a lie, and a hysterical chuckle bursts free. "How are you here?"

". . . Distrustful? Mendacious? Disingenuous?"

"Why didn't you tell me you were in town?"

"Specious? Fraudulent?"

I stand, and even with the chair between us, he's as close to me as he was when we danced at Barb's wedding. "Deceitful. That's the word you're looking for. And you're deceitful all right!" I playfully swat his arm. "Why didn't you tell me you'd be here?"

The right corner of his mouth curls upward, a lovely warmth settling in his eyes and making them look a shade darker still. "Hi, beautiful Amelie."

"Hello, deceitful Ian."

"May I?" He points at the chair, and when I nod, he holds my coat as he sits. He makes a gesture at the waiter and turns to me as I take my seat next to him, his focused, unwavering gaze making me squirm.

Ian and I have been growing close over the past few weeks; it's undeniable. But only now does it hit me just *how* close we've gotten. How he's quickly become the most present person in my life. One of my favorite people in the world. But is that how he feels?

Or is there more? Why is he sitting in front of me right now, a long drive away from home?

"If you keep thinking so much, your brain will need a new hard drive," he says, crossing his fingers over the soft sweater he's wearing. God, the way it frames his shoulders, and the collar of his shirt raised around his neck. How the fabric falls over his thighs, wrapped in dark jeans. Has he always looked this good?

"Why are you here, Ian? Was all this a trap?"

"A trap?"

"Yes. You get me here, then show up." I shake my head. "If you wanted to meet, you could have asked."

The band is setting up on the stage, the harmonic strumming of the guitar mixing with the clinking of glasses and the surrounding voices. "You're forgetting I told you to come with Frank," Ian says, a hint of a smile on his face.

"He couldn't leave Mayfield this weekend. Why are *you* here?"

"Because *I* could." He smiles. "Are you happy?"

I am. So much. And I'm not just happy to be in someone's company. There's hardly anyone else I'd rather be here with than him. "Yes," I say.

We study each other for a moment before the man onstage calls the audience's attention, and we both turn to the band.

Bursting into a loud fit of laughter, I look up at the dark sky peppered with shiny stars. Ian's lucky I'm fond of him, because his latest unpopular opinion would send teeth flying if shared with the wrong people. "Being a man is just as hard as being a woman." The audacity.

"Seriously? Your best argument is that men are constantly criticized?"

"Mm-hmm. You would have never called a woman a toddler for drinking chocolate milk."

"I absolutely would have," I say as he lets some peanuts fall out of his fist and into his mouth. "You're just trying to rile me up, but I can end this discussion with one painful, bloody word."

"Always with the period," he grumbles. "Women have more antibodies, live longer, and can cry in public without being called wusses."

"You can cry if you need to," I tease. "I won't call you a wuss."

With a chortle, he pokes my side. "They're also less likely to suffer from cardiovascular diseases, antisocial behavior, alcoholism, and our suicide rates—"

"Did you prepare for this?" I ask, resting my feet on the third chair at our table, the split in my black dress baring my legs. Either that, or this topic comes up a tad too often in his life.

"I'm winning, am I not?"

I roll my eyes, and when I notice his insistent stare, I take a deep breath. "Pregnancy, labor, physical inferiority, sexual harassment. Men never get called sluts for sleeping around or frigid for not putting out. And what's with female nipples? They look just like men's do, yet they're basically forbidden. Men hardly get catcalled, aren't expected to have children, and are praised for focusing on their careers." His eyes land on mine, but I only stopped to catch my breath. "We get paid less, we get interrupted more, and men never need to fake an orgasm, do they?"

He tilts his head as though he's considering my words. "Looks like I didn't prepare enough." Then, taking a sip of his drink, he nods. "Your turn."

I brush my hands together to get rid of the salt from the peanuts Ian stole from somewhere, then hum as I think of my next unpopular opinion. After "A man's hands represent half his physical appeal" and "The fun part of watching a movie is talking through most of it," I need a good one. I settle on "Pickup lines are cute."

"Pickup lines?"

I nod. "The cheesier the better."

"Huh."

His brows bend in a silent question, and as I smile down at the table, heat creeps up my cheeks. "I don't know. They're cute. It's not like I'd bring a guy home who approached me with a line. But if Frank used one to make me smile, I think I'd like that."

"I have the perfect one for you."

My eyes dart to him. Great: now it looks like I was begging for pickup lines. "I didn't mean—"

He holds his hand out, and when I hesitate, he extends it a little more. With a sigh, I rest my hand in his, preparing for what I'm sure will be the cringiest thirty seconds of my life. But his skin is warm, softer than I pictured it being, and my breath catches in my throat in response. We haven't touched since Barb's wedding, and this somehow feels different.

Then he looks at me. His eyes are so full of depth, I could get lost in them. His smile is so genuine, so young and carefree, it radiates all the joy that's been missing from my life lately.

It's like something flips inside my mind. I almost hear it click— like a switch. And I see something more in him than I did a few seconds ago.

Maybe he feels it, too, because his eyes drop to our joined hands, and his thumb presses lightly over my knuckle. It's the softest touch, but it makes my head spin, my heartbeat slowing down as my whole body tenses and I wait for what he'll do next.

Eventually, he clears his throat, his eyes burning into mine. "I think there's something wrong with my phone," he says. "Your number's not in it."

And just like that, the tension eases off. I break out into a sharp, nervous chuckle, sliding my hand out of his and ignoring the tingle spreading through every finger. "Yep, that's cheesy."

"I'm sure I can come up with worse ones." He laces his fingers together over the table and leans forward. "My turn, Amelie."

I give him an uncertain nod, his weirdly serious tone sending chills down my spine.

"Unpopular opinion. If your fiancé can't bother to drive two hours to see you, he's probably not treating you the way he should." Met by my glare, he shrugs. "Am I wrong?"

Why is he bringing this up now? We were having such a great night, listening to the band first, then swapping unpopular opinions. Why, out of everything we could talk about, does he choose to bring up Frank?

"Is that why you're here, then?" I cross my arms over my chest, unable to help a scowl from forming on my face. "To tell me how terrible my fiancé is?"

He presses his lips tightly, trying—and failing—to suppress a sly smile. It aggravates me even more.

"Seriously, Ian?"

"Come on, Amelie," he says, his voice warm and sweet in a way that tells me he knows exactly what he's doing. "Of course not."

"Because if that's what's happening . . . If you're acting as if we're friends, but you're just waiting for the opportunity to sleep with me—"

"No," he says, cutting me off. After pressing a finger to his lips, he continues. "Look, I'm not going to say I'm not attracted to you, because I am. And I admit that when I approached you at your friend's wedding, I figured I'd shoot my shot. But I didn't plan all this. Us. Our friendship." He smiles lightly, almost melancholically. "I meant it when I said I'm not looking for a girlfriend, Amelie. But you . . ." He shrugs. "You're my favorite notification."

It feels like a live wire is stretching between us. A connection I can't explain, one unlike any other. His eyes are simultaneously hard to stare at and impossible to look away from.

With a nervous nod, I look over the dissipating crowd, then at a couple sitting at a nearby table. They're both gorgeous, and there's almost a glowing bubble around them. A circle of happiness and love that's impossible to ignore as he leans closer to her, whispers something in her ear with a cocky smile, and makes her laugh. Or the way his eyes light up when she does.

"We've . . . we've been having problems," I breathe out. Immediately feeling guilty, I add, "But it doesn't mean he doesn't love me. Or that I don't love him."

"I know," Ian says.

Reassured by the look on his face, I nod. "Since the engagement, though, some stuff has been . . . off."

"Hmm." Out of the corner of my eye, I see him shift position, but I continue staring at the couple intimately chatting as if nobody else is around. It's the first time I've said any of this out loud, and it's hard to hold back tears. "Did you talk to him about it?"

"Yeah. He says he needs this time before the wedding to himself. To have some new experiences."

"Okay," he concedes. "Everybody needs a little privacy once in a while."

Swallowing, I nod. "Right."

Except he's after anything but solitude. He's after nights out with friends, dates, sex.

"So what kind of experiences is he looking to have?"

There. That's where the problem lies, and though I started out with the intention to once again vomit all my issues at Ian, now that I glance at his gentle and curious expression, I can't bring myself to tell him the whole truth. "Just, you know . . . friends and stuff," I mumble as I carefully avoid his stare. "Anyway, we've been together for fifteen years. Wanting a few months of independence doesn't mean anything."

"But?"

My eyes meet his. "But what?"

He brings a hand to the back of his neck. "It doesn't look like you believe any of that. More like that's what he's told you over and over again. What do *you* believe?"

I study his eyes for a while, considering how deep I should go to answer his question.

"Amelie," he insists. "Just because yours is an unpopular opinion, it doesn't mean it's less valid than anyone else's." When my face relaxes, he tilts his chin up. "Let's hear it. Come on."

I sigh deeply, turn back to the couple a few tables away from us, then discreetly point at them. "You see that guy?"

"Dark hair, blue suit?"

"That's the one." The man grabs the woman's hand, kisses it as she speaks, then whispers something back, his face radiating joy. "See how he looks at that woman? As if a piece of his soul belongs to her?"

"Yeah. It's intense."

"*So* intense. And the way she looks at him too." I pause for emphasis as the brunette woman stares dreamily into the man's eyes. "It's like they're competing at who loves the other more."

"Looks like they're both winning."

"It does." There's a moment of silence, and in it the thumps of my heart overpower the music, the laughter, the clinking of glasses. It's the only noise in my brain. "My unpopular opinion is . . . Frank doesn't look at me like that. Not even . . . not even close."

Ian says nothing.

"Unpopular opinion," I continue. "He cares more about having fun than being with me. He never calls, and I'm planning this wedding by myself. He's selfish, and he's definitely not being honest about his feelings. Not with me, and maybe not with himself either." I inhale a quick breath, then power through. "Unpopular opinion. I'm scared, and I should be, because I don't know when it happened or why, but I think he's fallen out of love. I don't know if it'll last forever or if it's just a phase. If he got comfortable and now he's become complacent, or if he just doesn't want to marry me or . . . or . . ."

Ian rests his hand on my forearm, lightly squeezing as his thumb rubs a spot on my skin. "I'm sorry, beautiful."

I look into his eyes, almost hoping to catch him in a lie. To see that it doesn't bother him in the least that my relationship is dying, but instead he's quite thrilled. It's stupid, of course, because that'd mean our friendship was nothing than a ruse to get me into bed. But for a second or two I want it. I want to see *someone* love me.

"I believe you, Amelie. If you think something's wrong, then something's wrong." His voice is as soft as cashmere, as warm as the spring sun, and at the accepting expression on his face, the dam I've put up to keep my tears at bay takes a serious hit. "But look"—his eyes dart left and right as he thinks—"those two," he says, nudging his head toward the couple, "they've probably been together for a couple of weeks. I bet they won't be together in—"

The man stands as the woman brings a spoonful of cake to her lips, then approaches a stroller to the right of him, which I didn't notice until now, and takes out the most beautiful baby in a pink dress. He gently brings her to his chest, her little head resting on his shoulder as he bounces on the spot. Once again, in the woman's eyes, there's such an all-encompassing and consuming love, it's hard to witness without feeling overwhelmed.

"Okay," Ian says. "So nine months and a couple of weeks."

When I chuckle, he does, too, and my sadness dwindles enough for me to cock my brow at him. "I don't know, Ian. That girl looks older than two weeks old."

"Three weeks tops."

"I'm pretty sure she just spoke."

"Look," he says with a serious expression, "I know close to nothing about love. I told you my mom died young and my dad is my best friend, but he's not exactly been lovey-dovey since." When I nod, he keeps going. "As for women . . ." He forces a laugh. "The only one who lasted long enough was Ella, and she certainly didn't love me." With a sweeping gesture, he shakes his head. "My point is, I'm not the best person to tell you how your fiancé is supposed to look at you. What I *can* say is . . ."

He hesitates.

"What is it?"

"I don't think I . . ." He takes another look at the couple. "I don't think I'd ever stop looking at you that way. If you were mine." When I look away, he clears his voice. "'You' as in—not *you*. Just . . . the woman I love."

My eyes bug out.

"Who is not—" He blinks, his mouth moving soundlessly. "I'm just saying. Hypothetically. A woman—any woman. No woman, really, because I—"

"You don't want a girlfriend," I interrupt with a smile.

"No. I mean yes. I don't." He pinches the bridge of his nose and slowly shakes his head. "That was painful for us both. How about I get you another drink?"

Sinking into my chair, I watch Ian walk to the counter, then wait for his turn to be served. He glances over his shoulder at me and smiles, so I tilt my head in a silent hello.

That smile. There's something about it. It's caring and full of adoration, a smile that melts ice better than the sun itself. It takes over his whole face, his eyes alight and his lips stretched. He's handsome at any given moment, but when he smiles, he's bottled perfection.

Does he always smile like that, or is it only when he smiles at me? And even more importantly, how do *I* smile at *him*?

20

The Baguette Humiliation

– TODAY –

"And that's how you prepare a baguette," Ella says as the audience claps. "As you can see, it's not complicated at all."

"Humph."

"Ames," Barb scolds, but I quickly raise my hands in mock surrender. I have no intention of fighting Ella, not after what happened yesterday at Ian's seminar. Though it *is* fascinating to see how I disagree with almost anything she says. Every time she opens her mouth, it's like nails on a chalkboard.

Ian stalks closer, looking splendid in a mustard-yellow sweater. He wears it over his usual cotton shirt, the hem of it peeking out over his light jeans. I know why he's here. He's monitoring me, protecting his girlfriend and chef. As the person who was previously on the receiving end of his attentive care, I know how that feels. It doesn't make me like Ella any more.

"I've never seen a baguette prepared with warm water. What's the reasoning behind it?" someone from the audience asks.

I can't help another humph, which immediately causes Ian's eyes to flick toward me.

"That way, the dough rises faster. You should also prepare it in a warm room," Ella says in her entitled voice. "It'll quicken the fermentation process."

"And reduce the flavor," I say under my breath.

"Amelie," Ian warns. He's sitting beside me now. I turn to him, expecting to find him scowling. Giving me a look that says, *I'll physically drag you out of this room if you dare to disagree.* Instead, he's fidgeting with his phone as he patiently smiles. Almost as if he's amused. A little frustrated, too, but mostly amused.

"Slowing down the fermentation process results in a complex flavor and improved taste," I say, keeping my voice low so that Ella won't hear as she answers the next question. "She's telling them to rush it and compromise on the quality—"

"*Amelie.*"

With a sigh, I look down at my feet. Fine, I won't say anything. Even if it means teaching a hundred people an approximate, incorrect way to approach French cuisine. Even if she's the very last person who should teach this class.

Ian's leg bumps mine, his lips pouting dramatically as if he's calling me a big baby. God, he's so handsome, especially when he's dorky. With his eyes squinting, his bottom lip starts wobbling as he brings his fists to his eyes and sniffles.

"Stop it."

"*Wah-wah. French baguettes. Wah.*"

"French baguette is redundant. There's no Austrian baguette."

He shrugs. "I have a baguette that's not French."

Snorting out a laugh, I roll my eyes. "Technically, it's half-French."

"Fair." His brows bunch up. "Wait, did I tell you my mom was French? How do you know?"

Holy shit. Deep dark eyes flash before mine, but, trying to keep my nausea at bay, I shrug. Seeing as Ian knew nothing about the article, my restaurant, *or* its failure, it's fair to say that his father didn't tell him much about what went on between us in the past six months, and I won't be the person to break his heart. It's not my place, not when we're hardly even friends. "I read it online."

He pretends to gasp. "Stalker."

"You're such a child."

"Me? You're all bent out of shape over nothing. It's just bread."

With an annoyed look, I say, "Stop trying to piss me off, Ian."

His eyes widen. "Stop making it so easy, Amelie."

I focus on Ella, set to ignore him. He really is a handsome idiot. In two seconds' time his leg is pressing against mine obnoxiously. I throw him a look, and there's a teasing smirk on his face that makes him look so fucking sexy. He's nothing like most men I've dealt with in my life. He's never taken anything seriously, always smiling in spite of everything. Always happy and positive and good.

His expression softens with affection when he notices mine. Since the day I met him, Ian has had the power to turn my mood around no matter the situation. I love that it's still true today.

My leg presses back, and once again his smile changes. His eyes dart to our legs pushed together, then back to me. Now his lips are slightly open. Every version of him is better than the last, and this one doesn't disappoint. It's so good, in fact, that my hand itches to touch him, to travel up his thigh and see his breath catch. To see how that makes his face change, his eyes darken. To see how he looks when he wants me.

When his gaze dips to my mouth, my chest heaves. I have to remind myself we're in public, in front of his girlfriend, and—regardless of her being a princess or a witch—this isn't going to happen if he's with someone else.

When there are no more questions, it's time for my take on baked French products. I tackle the croissant, and, God, it takes me forever.

Granted, croissants are complicated. If you don't refrigerate the dough in between each fold, the butter melts. If you don't let it rest enough, you end up with a cookie instead of a flaky pastry. But I'm pretty sure Ian's gaze, never once moving away from me, has something to do with my discombobulated lecture. I can't focus.

He's not looking at me because he's interested in anything I have to say about croissants; he's made that plenty clear. And he's sitting with one leg thrown over my empty seat, his shoulders relaxed against the chair back, his arms crossed at his chest and his tattoos peeking from the sleeves at his wrists.

Fuuuuuuck. He has to stop looking at me like that.

It's different from what he did last year, before our fallout. He used to look at me as if I were the most precious thing that had been put in front of him. Now he's looking at me like I'm breakfast. I don't know if that's a good or bad sign, but he's currently turning my brain into mush, my body is aching so much for him.

A hundred questions later, the audience retreats, and we're left with two hours to kill before Ian's class. With a mix of dread and excitement, I grab my bag. After yesterday, I'm worried about another argument breaking out between us, but I'm also looking forward to staring at him for a while. I'm sure he was sitting there being extra sexy on purpose, so maybe I can do the same during his class. Show him a little shoulder or— Wait. No, Amelie, he has a girlfriend. Goodness gracious.

Once we're back in the conference room, waiting for the next crowd of students to arrive, Ian discreetly nods toward the door, then walks out into the corridor. Ella is writing something down, and Barb is on her phone. Quickly mentioning I'm going to the bathroom, I leave the room and join him by the window. "Hey. Everything okay?"

"Can we try to have *one* smooth seminar?" he asks, his voice velvety as he casts a skeptical eye on me.

I hesitate, turning to the window. "I don't think you should ask me, Ian. You keep provoking me, and your girlfriend hates me."

He tilts his head. "No, she's only a little—"

"If you say she's passionate again, I'll lose it," I warn.

He holds on to my elbow, his touch soft but firm. "One smooth seminar? Please?" he asks. "Pamela has been complaining."

I can't pay attention to anything he's saying, only to his grip. It's delicate, and the contact sends shivers up my arm and to the rest of my body. My eyes flick to his wrists, the black ink peeking out as a reminder of the Ian he is outside of the conference room, the Ian he is outside of Ian Roberts.

My Ian.

How many times have I wanted to talk to him in the last six months? How often have I imagined hearing his voice again? Seeing his face? Waking up to one of his texts?

Well, now he's here in front of me, and I can't let this chance go to waste, because I'm not sure I'll get another one. He needs to know how I feel. That Frank and I are over, and if I could do it all again, I'd choose him every day.

"Head tables with the bridal party are the worst," I burst out.

He gives me a blank stare, his eyebrows angled upward.

"Because the plus-ones of everyone in the bridal party end up separated from the one person they know at the wedding," I explain. "And . . ." My mind roams, the saliva in my mouth thickening. "And it's better not to have many bridesmaids, because friendships end and your wedding pictures are forever." I snap my fingers. "The first dance! It shouldn't last more than a minute. Nobody wants to watch you awkwardly dance through a whole song."

Light slowly fades from his eyes as something dark and wounded draws over them.

"The garter toss makes everyone uncomfortable, and the groom not seeing the bride before the wedding is a ridiculous superstition."

"Amelie," he whispers, his smile disappearing. "We can't."

I study the sad curve of his mouth. "I just—I wanted you to know my unpopular opinions about weddings."

"I don't *want* to know."

Tears stinging my eyes, I look away. He doesn't want to know.

People walk past us to enter the class, and he smiles at someone in the crowd before setting his harsh gaze on me. "I'm not doing it again. This thing between us—it nearly killed me the first time."

I sniffle away my sadness as he walks past me, my mouth opening in a desperate attempt to fix everything. I'm terrified it won't ever be possible. "I'm sorry, Ian. I know I fucked up, and I know you don't owe me another chance, but please, I just need to tell you—"

"I don't want to listen, Amelie."

"Ian, let me say one thing and then—"

He groans, turning to face me. "What is it, huh? You want to tell me you and Frank aren't together anymore? Is that what you want to say?" When I stare at him wide-eyed, he nods. "Yeah. I know."

But . . . how? He said he didn't read the article. He didn't know only a handful of days ago.

"You don't wear a ring." He gestures at my hand. "At first I figured it's because you're a chef. Barb wears hers around her neck, and you have a necklace too." His eyes soften, his brows lowering. "But then . . . then the other day you leaned down to point at Barb's fingers when she was showing . . . something."

"Bâtonnet?"

"Whatever. And the necklace slipped out of your shirt. You were too entranced with what you were saying to notice."

With my fist tightening around my necklace, I swallow. "You saw it."

"I did."

"Do you . . . want it back?"

"No," he says firmly, and his eyes squint as if he's absorbing an invisible hit to his stomach. "But I'm happy you held on to it."

He says nothing more, and neither do I. If he knows I'm not with Frank and hasn't said a word about it—if he's *seen* my necklace—it can mean only one thing. Ella wins.

We're not friends; not rivals either. We're definitely not lovers. We're just strangers who share a few memories.

Forcing my legs to move, I walk past him and say something about needing the toilet. Though he calls my name, I keep walking until I'm on the other side of the bathroom door. My heartbeat's erratic, embarrassment creeping up at me at the realization that I've just been rejected. Not in so many words, but that's what happened. Ian doesn't want me. He knows I'm single, he knows I want him, but he doesn't want me back.

I came to Mayfield knowing there was a big possibility this would be the outcome, and now I can't believe it. Is his part in my story really over?

It feels like I've come down with the flu. My body trembles, my throat itches, my chest tingles. It might be a panic or heart attack. I've never had either, but I've never felt this way before.

Holding myself against the cold tiles of the bathroom wall, I breathe in and out. I focus on what I can see, touch, smell, and taste, until eventually my heartbeat settles. The adrenaline wears off, leaving in its place a peaceful sort of resignation. I don't think it's anxiety or a physical condition. I think it's heartbreak.

I try to tell myself it's for the best. Surely, it is. With the huge secret I'm keeping, involving none other than his father . . . this is the simplest outcome.

None of it works to distract me from the awareness that while my restaurant failed, I lost my best friend, my wedding, my fiancé, my career, my father, and so much more, *this* is the moment when my heart finally breaks.

"Your restaurant is only as good as your best chef!" I say.

Ian chuckles and rolls his eyes, then he raises a finger. "A business model"—two fingers—"a marketing plan"—three fingers—"an operations plan"—four fingers—"a financial analysis—"

"Oh my God, give me a break," I groan, running a hand through my hair as I turn to the audience.

I'm not sure how we got here. It started when he said the worst mistake one could make is to read online reviews of their restaurant. To which I countered that this attitude is as good as asking to fail. If you don't listen to your customers' complaints, then how can you get better?

It escalated from there.

"Not looking at the business side of owning a restaurant is a mistake." He pinches the bridge of his nose. "If I'm to guess, that's the mistake you made, Amelie. The Marguerite—"

"Your fast-food joint," I interject.

This time I see rage cracking him open and taking over his brain. He might have forgiven me for saying that the first time, but twice must be his limit.

He takes a step toward me until his nose is a few inches from mine, his blue eyes now so dark that they resemble a galaxy. "*One* fucking seminar, Amelie. One," he whispers. His breath on my lips is pure oxygen, like he's infusing life into me even with how furious he is. "Why can't you stop being such a pretentious, annoying—"

With a loud clack, the lights go off—all of them—and with the blinds closed for Ian's presentation, I can't see him, even though he's closer to my face than he's been in a really long time. People begin talking and chairs loudly scrape against the floor as I hold out a hand to find the desk beside me.

"Calm down, everyone. It's a power outage. The lights will be back on in a second," Ian announces. As noise and chatter cover his voice and people begin walking out of the room, I feel his arms wind around me.

"What are you doing?" I half-heartedly protest, the anger over our argument dissipating as his chest crashes against mine. It's so broad and warm and comfortable.

"Making sure no one tramples you to the floor."

I rest my cheek against his sweater as he walks back, dragging me with him to one corner of the room as people flash their phone lights around and scramble to exit. "Ella? You good?" he asks, but I can't hear her voice over the crowd. "Ella?"

Hugging him as he calls another woman's name isn't nearly as nice as only hugging him, so I lazily push myself off his chest. "Go find your girlfriend," I mutter as I take a step back.

"You're cute when you're jealous, but I can't see you right now, so cut it out." He drapes his arm around me again. "And quit calling her that."

"Calling her what?"

"My girlfriend."

My mouth snaps open against his chest, and my eyes widen enough that, even in the dark, I can see the yellow sweater I'm pressed against. What does he mean? They aren't married, are they? "Isn't she your girlfriend?"

"No?" Laughter rumbles in his throat. "I told you, Amelie. I don't want a girlfriend, a wedding, or a wife." When I don't utter a word, his chin dips. "Did you think she was my girlfriend?"

"Yes!"

"Oh." He pulls me with him as he takes a few steps back. "Why? I never said she was."

"You—she's all over you, Ian."

He snorts. "Yeah, well. You know how I said you're cute when you're jealous? Turns out jealousy makes her really annoying."

On that we agree.

"So . . . you're single?"

"Always."

Oh my God, he's single. Ian's here, next to me—at this moment, almost on top of me—and he's single. My heart palpitates, a smile taking over my face and dying just as quickly. He's not with Ella; he's not with anyone. And he still doesn't want to be with me.

I let myself melt against his chest, wanting to drown my sudden sadness in him. My hand moves to his back, and his body relaxes with an exhale. We stand still for a few seconds, his heart beating against my ear, then quickening as his other arm wraps around me.

My hands travel up his spine, feeling the corded muscles hiding under his shirt, and soon our hug turns from friendly to not so much. My whole body presses against his, my fingers rubbing the base of his neck. He locks one arm over the other until I'm squeezed tightly, and eventually my fists bunch in his hair.

Between his arms is where I belong.

"Amelie?" he whispers. "What . . ."

Letting one arm go, I use my fingers to crawl forward until my hand rests on his cheek. I'm not exactly sure of what I'm doing, except I'm very aware we won't be this close again for the rest of this week. Hell, maybe for the rest of our lives. And I might be heartbroken, and I might be rusty when it comes to intimacy, but I'm not stupid.

I attempt a light tug, pulling him closer, and when his face follows with no resistance, I do it again and meet him halfway until our mouths tentatively meet.

With a soft sigh, he smiles against my lips.

It's like being burned and healed all at once.

The second time his mouth meets mine, he takes the lead, his hand cupping the back of my head and his tongue pushing into my mouth. There's hunger in his kiss. Lust and a rushed eagerness to discover. He holds me against him, and as my body molds itself to his flat chest, he lets out a hum of pleasure.

"Ian? *Ian?*" Ella calls out, her voice so shrill and annoying, I'm tempted to throw an egg at the spot it's coming from.

But I withdraw a little, and, squeezing me tighter, he whispers, "She's fine. One more minute."

And for one more minute we continue, though it's likely much more than that. I hardly have enough experience to be making assessments, but he's an excellent kisser. I feel our kiss in my bones, in my stomach, lighting me up like a Christmas tree until I'm so receptive to him that I'm breathing heavily in his mouth with every gentle tug and rub.

It's undoubtedly the best kiss I'll ever receive in this lifetime.

With a sudden loud clack, the lights flicker on again, and in an instant his arms, his hands, his mouth are gone . . . just a second too late. Whoever is still in the room saw the way we were together. Not like friends. Definitely not like the rivals we pretend to be.

When his eyes widen as if he's seen a ghost, I return his scared look. "What—" I begin, but he grabs my shoulders and pulls me with my back to him, his hands holding me between himself and the remaining audience.

He walks backward, squeezing my shoulder. "So sorry about that. And thank you for joining us—"

Barb's roaring laughter explodes to our right, but when I try to turn to her, Ian's hold on me tightens, and I stumble back. What the hell is—oh my God, that's a boner. Yep. His cock is standing proud and pressing against my ass.

"You must be fucking kidding me," Ella says from the left side of the room. She probably has a good shot of what's poking at me, and so does Barb. My standing in front of Ian is the only reason the rest of the room doesn't.

"Th-thank you for coming," I stammer with a stiff smile as people gather their things. I can hardly focus with Ian's firm, thick erection pressed up against me. "We'll have another seminar about"—Ella flies out of the room—"about the main sauces in French cuisine. We'll do less yelling in that one. Probably."

Slowly, the crowd disperses, and when the last person leaves, Barb walks out, too, throwing a suggestive smile my way. Only when we're completely alone do I turn to Ian, who sits on the edge of the desk with his arms crossed over his chest and an annoyed expression. He glances at me, then focuses his gaze on the floor.

I get it. This must have been pretty humiliating for him and his baguette.

"Amelie, I—can't. *We* can't."

I bite my lip, uncomfortably shifting position. I didn't kiss him to change his mind, but the fact that he won't manages to break my heart all over again. Even after our kiss—our out-of-this-world, extraordinary kiss, which he *most certainly* enjoyed—he's done.

"I'm sorry. You had so much time, Amelie. I know you were engaged, that I was way over the line, but fuck, I tried so hard to show you that I was the right choice. That *we* were. I put you first, even before myself, because you kept putting yourself second. And you . . ."

"I broke your heart," I whisper.

"Yeah, you did."

I nod, still unable to look at anything but the floor. "Sorry I kissed you. I just figured it was my shot."

"You shouldn't apologize. I definitely kissed you back."

Yeah, he definitely did.

"But for our own well-being, I think it might be best if we split the seminars," he says with a stern look that reminds me of his father. "We clearly can't get along professionally, and when we do get along . . . we might do it a little too well."

God, it's like he's breaking up with me.

I nod, but the sadness that's overwhelmed me hunches my shoulders, the force of gravity pulling me farther down as if the floor is calling my name. When silence settles, I still don't have it in me to look at him, so I grab my bag and leave the room.

Leaving Ian behind again.

21

Rip Out the Weeds

– Four Months to Amelie's Wedding –

The Marguerite
@Themarguerite

Apparently, @LaBrasserie wants single people to feel less special on Valentine's Day. We invite everyone in Creswell to come visit us in Mayfield at The Marguerite. On February 14th, you'll all get a glass of champagne on the house. Couples AND solos. #Liberté #Égalité #Fraternité

06:45 PM · Nov 13 · Twitter for iPhone

7.8K 15K 25K 33K

"Amelie, did you see all the reposts?"

"Re*tweets*."

"They accused us of discrimination. Look! Look!" My dad holds his phone out. "*Quel bordel.*"

With a sigh, I grab it and scroll through the answers.

Monica said, "What about throuples? @LaBrasserie should consider there isn't just one type of family," while someone whose nickname is Lucasiisthebest wrote, "@LaBrasserie Can I come with my boyfriend? How do I prove he's not just a friend? #LGBT #QueerRights." My eyes skim over the third tweet that shows up, from Penny, that reads, "My husband is sober. Are we still welcome in your establishment, @LaBrasserie?"

Jesus Christ. How did this become about LGBT rights and alcoholism? Offering a free glass of champagne to couples was just a cute idea to celebrate the holiday, and it seemed like a good idea last February, when I came up with it. How did they even find it? I swear, whoever is behind these tweets at the Marguerite is the devil.

"We're going to have to delete the tweet and apologize," my dad says, his voice coming out more breathy than normal as he shoves his glasses somewhere on his crowded desk. "We can say we'll offer a glass of champagne to all guests next February fourteenth and hopefully everyone will forget about this."

"Absolutely not." Shaking my head firmly, I cross my arms over my T-shirt. "We've done nothing wrong, and saying that would be like admitting Roberts and the *damn* Marguerite are right."

His mouth, initially open, closes. Nothing changes his mind like mentioning William Roberts getting the upper hand.

"Fine. What do you suggest we do?" he asks, the harsh lines on his face deepening.

I'd like to find whoever's behind the Marguerite's Twitter profile and set their car on fire. But if I'm to abide by the law, I'll have to limit myself to humiliating the crap out of that disgraced restaurant. "I'll answer, don't worry."

"Amelie, I let you handle this because I thought you knew what you were doing." With a deep sigh, he rubs a hand over his forehead, the noise of his nails scraping his scalp, making me shiver. "But I might have overestimated you."

"Ha!" comes out of my lips before I have any way to stop it, and his frowning round face turns a shade redder. "That would be the first time ever."

Motionless, he stares at me. He always does this, and it has the power to frustrate me to madness. He watches me intently without saying a word, as if he's dealing with an unreasonable child who isn't worth explaining the rules to.

I endure a minute—maybe a little less—of intense eye contact before I break. "I'm not even supposed to be dealing with Twitter, you know? If I recall correctly, my very first words about this were 'Hire a social media manager.'" Rushing to stand, I grumble, "I'm a chef. That's what I do: I cook."

"That's what you do right now." He hunches over a thick pile of papers. "When you inherit La Brasserie, that's not the only thing you'll be doing."

"Will I inherit the restaurant?" I ask, my voice pregnant with sarcasm. "I assumed one day you'd announce your imminent death and explain that every chef in here has the same chance to inherit the business."

As I stalk toward the door, his stern words hit me in the back like an axe. "Throwing a fit because I didn't give you the position yet? You know how old I was before I was made head chef, Amelie?"

"Thirty-eight," I say without missing a beat. I know that and every other detail pertaining to his career. His recipes have been my bible since I was able to read, his work what I aspired to, knowing I'd never achieve the same greatness. Of course I know.

"Right. Because my father never handed anything to me." He swings lightly on his dark red upholstered chair. "He always said that La Brasserie would take priority over anything else, and I'd get the job when I excelled at it."

"Okay. You win," I say with a dull voice. Why am I even fighting for a job I'm not sure I want? Why do I always give him the satisfaction?

He chuckles as if this is all a joke. It probably is to him, but it's also my life, and it's starting to feel like he just wants me here, waiting. Stuck, not going forward or backward. I'm a grown woman, a competent chef, yet he still treats me like I'm an emotional child.

"You know, other restaurants would be happy to hire me as their head chef."

"Would they, now?" He stands, walks to his liquor cabinet, and fills a glass with his most expensive rum. "Did you inquire?"

I drag a hand across my face. I'd be flattered by his obvious displeasure, but I know it has nearly nothing to do with me. How very humiliating would it be for Hammond Preston if his daughter were to work for some other restaurant?

"Moretti has been after me for years, Dad," I point out. And his restaurant, La Fattoria, is much more in line with what I like to cook.

"Yes." He smiles, bringing the glass to his lips. "And I know you'd sooner cut your hands off than work for that *blaireau*."

My eyes narrow. "I'm competent enough to be a head chef, and Moretti might be a . . . *blaireau*, but he knows that. You don't."

"Hmm," he says distractedly. "Maybe you're right. Or maybe I'm not sure being my head chef is the right step for you."

To him, I'll never be ready. I'll never be enough. And, God, I'm done trying to please him. "Well, thanks for the chat, Dad."

"Fix the Twitter thing as soon as possible. I don't have time to worry about your messes."

My shoulders tense, my teeth grinding so hard that they might just turn into dust. "Maybe I will take that job for Moretti, then. So you won't have to worry about me at all."

"Really?" He laughs, the sound more evil than joyous. "That's what you'll leave La Brasserie for? A mediocre restaurant?"

"It wouldn't be mediocre if I was the head chef."

With his smile gone, he stands and walks to the window. "I didn't raise you as a fool, Amelie."

"No," I agree. "You raised me as a chef." Yanking the door open, I throw him one last hateful look. "Everything else I am, I did by myself."

I walk out, not even bothering to close the door, and head into the parking lot just as my phone pings.

Ian:
Dan texted me to say thanks. Apparently, you booked the band. It was a knife to my heart. What about the Almighty Lumberjacks of Death?

Amelie:
Is that the name of your band?

Ian:
Does it turn you on?

I snort my laughter, then rest my chin in my hand. Ten seconds. That's how long it took him to make me smile.

Amelie:
Uh-oh. Is it getting warmer in here?

Ian:
PFP.

Pointing the front camera at my face, I groan. My skin is ghostly, as if I spent the last few months living in a cave, and the top of my hair is pinned back; I always wear it like this at work, but it makes my forehead look huge.

I unpin my hair, then pinch my cheeks to give them some color. With a smile, I take the picture and send it.

I wait for a response, and when it doesn't come, I turn to the busboy who's smoking by the trash can. "George?"

His tired brown eyes meet mine. "Yes, Chef?"

"We're not in the kitchen. 'Amelie' is fine." I stand with a smile and walk over to him. "Could I have one?"

His hand rises, his forehead furrowed with confusion. "A smoke?"

"Yes."

He hesitates, then quickly nods and takes out his packet. He offers it to me, and I clumsily slide a cigarette out, then accept his lighter. Just as I light the cigarette up and explode into a coughing fit, my ringtone blasts from my pocket.

"Thanks," I manage to say before walking away. I take my phone out, and my camera is on. Ian's video-calling me. Why today of all days?

With a sad look at my Iron Maiden sweatshirt and ripped jeans, I answer and force a smile on my face. "Hey, stranger," I say as the call starts and his face fills my screen.

He's as gorgeous as ever. His hair has grown, falling over his face with the wind, which is making his microphone rattle. And in contrast to me, he's tan. The picture of happiness and relaxation. I often wonder what he does for a living; whatever it is, our lives must be pretty different. "Look where I am."

The camera turns, and Mayfield's Beckett Bridge stands tall against a bright blue sky. "Oh, wow, it's beautiful," I say, my voice soaked with admiration.

The camera switches back to his smiling, gorgeous face. "Frank, Martha, or work?"

"What?"

"What's upsetting you?"

I hesitate, my eyes roaming left and right. How did he figure it out? I smiled—I really tried to look cheerful. How does he always get it?

"Are you—Amelie, are you on fire?"

Glancing at the screen, I notice the smoke from the cigarette still in my hand is moving in front of the camera. "Oh, no. I'm just—" I show him the cigarette, and his brows arch. "No, I don't smoke. I've done it twice in my life and hated it both times."

"Don't tell me you're holding it for a friend," he says, cocking his head dramatically. "I'm pretty sure I came up with that one."

"I just figured . . ." With a deep sigh, I shrug. "I don't know. Stress. Smoke."

"I see. Well, what's new?"

What's new? he asks. Besides the latest battle with my dad, and Martha sending her engagement photos on the group chat, Frank continues to live his best single life and hasn't asked a single question about Ian.

"Are you on your way to work?" I ask. He's walking along the street, people rushing around him, and it looks like he's wearing one of his soft-looking sweaters. This one's red.

"Lunch break."

"Oh, Ian, I don't want to bother you during—"

"Amelie, come on." His eyes squint, the different shades of blue in his irises bright with the sunlight hitting his face directly. "If by the end of this call you're not smiling, I won't be able to focus on work. And then I'll get fired. And I'll lose my apartment and starve. No pressure."

When I chuckle, he points at the screen, joining in. "That's what I'm looking for. Come on, spit it out."

"But, Ian—"

"*Amelie*," he insists. "Don't make me beg."

"No, don't beg." It's bad enough that this man is at my beck and call for whatever emotional crisis I'm going through. I don't need him to beg for me to vomit my issues on him. "My father is playing me."

He nods. "Mm-hmm."

"He refuses to give me the promotion, although he knows I'm much more qualified for it than any of his other employees. I've worked for it much harder than they ever could."

His jaw squares as he angrily stares away. "You've been waiting for months, Amelie. You're right to demand recognition for all the work you've done."

"That's what I'm saying," I whine, dropping the cigarette onto the ground and putting it out with the ball of my foot. I can't help my relief. He sees it as well. I'm not crazy. "And I've been offered the same position elsewhere, better money too."

"But? Why do you want to stick with your dad?"

"I don't know." Lies. I *do* know. Looking in the distance, at the rows of cars in the parking lot, I twist a lock of hair with my fingers. "To prove to myself I can? To prove him wrong?"

There's the ringing of a bell, and he enters what looks like a deli. After he tells me to wait, he orders a sandwich. From where his phone is, I can see his Adam's apple, his chin, the curve of his smile. He winks down at the phone, his unbuttoned collar letting me see just a hint of the golden skin of his chest. I wonder if he has tattoos there like he has on his arms.

They're so hot. *He's* so hot.

"Okay," he says, leaving with his order a few minutes later. "Amelie, what's the end goal?"

"The end goal?"

"Yeah. Your dream."

I shrug, unsure of what he wants me to say. "To get the promotion, I guess? To take my father's place in his business?"

"You *guess*?" He sits down on a park bench, shrubs taking up most of the background as the sun highlights his ash-brown hair. Unwrapping his food with one hand, he looks at the screen. "Why is that your dream? What's the appeal?"

"Well, it's—" I open my mouth, but nothing comes out.

"Hmm. One would think that's a question you'd know how to answer."

Clicking my tongue, I pick at my nails. "I know how to answer. I want to be successful. My dad is the best at . . ." With a smile, I bite my bottom lip. "At what he does."

"So, if you were a contractor, you'd want to be the best contractor."

I study his relaxed blue eyes. "Yeah, sure, but what does—"

"That's not a dream. That's ambition." His jaw works for a while as he observes me. "Why is your dream to work for your dad and not as a contractor?"

"I can't use a hammer, for one."

"I'll teach you." Bringing the phone closer, he narrows his eyes. "Amelie, where do you see yourself in ten years? What's the passion that gets you out of bed in the morning? The imprint you want to leave on this world?"

I watch Ian's face fill my screen as he brings a napkin to his mouth. I guess there *is* a dream. Something that I used to fantasize about before falling asleep when I was younger. My own restaurant—nothing like my dad's. With simple food, a cozy atmosphere. The type of place where people would feel comfortable having dinner in a simple T-shirt and jeans. Back then, I dreamed of a place that specialized in Italian cuisine. Today I'd probably wish for something different. Maybe an intimate place by the beach that serves whatever the local fishermen catch daily. Maybe a rustic restaurant in the countryside where the food is farm-to-table.

"Ahh. There *is* something," Ian exults with his usual excitement. "Come on, I want to know. What is it?"

"Well . . . at some point, I wanted my own thing." I stare down at the ground, carefully choosing my words not to betray the nature of my occupation. "Open my own . . . *place*."

He tilts his head, his radiant smile looking only half as good as it does in real life but, even so, stealing my breath away. "Of course. Beautiful Amelie the entrepreneur." He takes another bite, and even the way he eats has me almost drooling at the screen. How his jaw snaps open and closed rhythmically, the way his tongue darts out of his mouth to lick his lips every once in a while. He's illegally pretty.

"I know we're in taboo territory," he says with a smirk, "but you can tell me it's a strip joint. I won't judge."

"A what?" I screech. "Is that what you think I am? A *stripper*?"

"Aren't you, with those hours you work? Night shifts?" He grins, his good mood so freaking contagious, I can't help but smile widely myself. "Okay, so . . . you want to open your own strip joint."

My cheeks flush again. "It's not a strip joint, and I didn't say I want to. I said I *wanted* to."

"And now you don't."

I shake my head, though the firm no I was planning on saying doesn't come out. The idea of opening my own restaurant sounds so obvious, I'm trying to figure out when I abandoned that dream and why. At some point, getting my dad's approval became more important than what I wanted. "Maybe I do."

He snorts. "Yeah, you definitely do. So . . . forget about your dad for a minute. How do you get there? How do you achieve your dream?"

"I mean, I could do it already. I have the experience I need," I say. It's not like I'd really do it right now, but I can savor the possibility. Imagine my father's shocked expression if I told him I was leaving to open my own restaurant, the sense of achievement I'd get from running my own kitchen, the freedom of choosing my own menu.

"Okay. Let's do that, then," Ian says.

With a chuckle, I study his expression. He's dead serious.

"I mean it."

"Right," I say with a cynical smile. "So I'll just pop in, tell my dad I quit, and go to the bank for a loan."

"Awesome." Noticing my bemused expression, he leans closer to the screen. Stoic. Unblinking. Ian's never stoic or unblinking. "Amelie, give me a good reason not to. If you can get a loan and have the experience to do it, then what's stopping you?"

My mouth opens, millions of reasons flashing through my mind. "I can't just quit."

"Why not?"

"Well, because my dad—"

"He'll be fine."

"But the wedding . . . Frank . . ."

"He doesn't need you to babysit him, Amelie."

I sigh, looking away. I can't believe I'm considering quitting and opening my own restaurant. It's a stupid idea, and not a decision you make in a minute. And with the wedding, I already have enough on my plate. No, it's definitely not doable. "Ian, be serious."

"I *am* serious," he insists. He leans back on the bench, holding his phone up high enough that I can see just a hint of his shirt, his coat sitting casually on his shoulders and wrapping his thick biceps. "Amelie, you need to rip the weeds out of your life. If there's something that doesn't make you happy and you have the power to change it, then you have to. You owe it to yourself."

God, does he make it sound simple.

He lazily chews his sandwich. "Promise me you'll think about it. For real."

"I promise," I say, and when I look at the time, I point behind me. "My shift is starting now."

"Don't you owe me something?"

Owe him something? Oh, right. I give him an exaggerated grin, and his serious expression turns into one of genuine joy.

Ian always makes me smile.

He nods as if proven right. "See? Gorgeous. Go, beautiful Amelie."

22

A Spoonful of Truth

– TODAY –

Someone enters the kitchen, and as my eyes meet Ian's, I quickly turn away. He's not wearing one of his sweaters tonight, just an old black T-shirt and gray joggers I want to quickly erase from my mind. We haven't talked in over forty-eight hours, since Baguette Day, and it's been miserable. If there's anything worse than not knowing where he is, with whom, doing what, it's knowing he's close, with Ella, just out of my reach.

"Sorry, I—" He points at the cabinet. "Ella wants tea."

"Go ahead," I say, staring at the oven.

"What are you doing?"

My brows pinch. "As the manager of a French restaurant, you should be able to recognize—"

"*Why* are you making macarons?"

"Barb had a craving."

Utensils clink as he scavenges for tea inside the cupboards. I know where it is, but I'm not too inclined to help. If Ella wants tea, how about she comes and makes it for her damn self? "What flavors are you making?"

"Strawberry white chocolate, mango buttercream, and blueberry mascarpone."

He walks to me, looking inside the oven with a thoughtful expression. "Damn. How long have you been here for?"

"A few hours. I'll need as many to finish and clean up."

Settling by my side, he fidgets with the bag of flour. "Ella's macarons are highly regarded by our customers, you know? Maybe we should make it a competition. You guys can let your egos battle and get it over with."

My eyes move to his. "I'm not sure, Ian. I wouldn't want to humiliate you."

"Wouldn't you?" he asks with a sly smile as his gaze drops down to his crotch.

"I've done nothing to humiliate you. I'm not responsible for your . . ." I point downward, then realize I *shouldn't* point downward and tuck my hand in my pocket. "Your baguette."

"It got just the right amount of crunchy, didn't it?"

"Ian," I say, a giggle making its way out despite my best attempt at holding it back.

"You're right." He waves me off. "It was as hard as stale bread."

"The point is"—again I try to stifle my laughter—"I don't think I'm to blame here."

He groans, hiding his face in his hands, and I watch him with a big smile straining the muscles of my face. I've been dragging myself around for two days, and in the span of a minute, look at the state of me!

"If you wait a minute, I'll give you some macarons to bring Ella with the tea."

He glances at them, then at me, his eyes brightening with amusement. "Are they poisoned?"

"I don't know. Why don't you take a bite?"

Tilting his head, he gives me a look. A "Quit antagonizing me" look. It would be easier if he hadn't just rejected me a couple of days back.

"No, they're not poisoned. They're delicious and made with the correct recipe, which I'm sure Ella isn't familiar with."

"Right. Fast food and all." He lazily waves his hand around and walks back to the cabinet. "Don't you tire of banging at the same door?"

No, not really. Not until he admits I'm right. The Marguerite serves mediocre food, and mediocre food makes for a mediocre business. "Why don't you try one?" I ask, grabbing the piping bag and pushing some buttercream onto the blueberry shell. "Eat a proper macaron made with fresh blueberries and real European butter. Done to perfection. Eat it in this kitchen instead of one of your premium locations by the beach and tell me cooking is about entertainment."

"No, thanks," he says while distractedly digging through cabinets.

No, thanks? "Come on, eat it."

As I hold out the macaron and walk up to him, he steps back. "No, I'm all right."

"Why not? Eat my damn macaron, Ian!"

"I don't want it."

"Why the fuck not? Don't you like blueberries? There's—"

"It's not about the blueberries."

"Take a strawberry one."

"I don't want it," he insists, his chin jerking back as he keeps his distance from the blue macaron in my hands.

"Then a mango one!"

"Amelie, I said no."

I stomp my feet. "*Why not? Why?*"

He draws a hand through his hair as if he's fighting to hold something back. His neck muscles tense, and as he turns to me, it's like the lid pops off. Releasing a breath, he barks, "Because I hate French food!"

He *what*?

He lets out an exhale, then shakes his head. "I don't like French cuisine. In fact, I hate it. It's disgusting. Everything tastes like butter or onions. And what's with French cheese? Why does it smell so fucking bad?" He widens his arms. "Huh? Tell me, what's so good about Brie? It smells like feet and tastes like nothing, Amelie. Like nothing."

He takes one of my macarons and studies it. "And you want me to eat macarons? They're terrible. A sugar crust filled with more fucking butter." He drops it onto the tray and turns to me, wiping his fingers on his T-shirt. "Plus, I . . ." He averts his eyes and shyly admits, "I'm lactose intolerant."

We stare at each other. That's why he didn't know who I was before we met here. How he never saw the article. Because he doesn't *care*.

He doesn't research French cuisine, doesn't study the competition, and has no qualms with my father either. He didn't know about my restaurant, didn't know I wasn't working at La Brasserie—didn't know anything at all. Because he doesn't like French cuisine, and therefore, he doesn't care.

"You . . ." My chest deflates with an exhale, and as he rubs his forehead, he chuckles. I do, too, my necklace clinking against the counter as I bend forward. "You *hate* French cuisine."

His hand cuts through the space between us in a decided gesture. "Hate it."

"But . . . bouillabaisse? Coq au vin ? *Confit de canard*?"

He grimaces. "Yeah, and snails, frogs' legs, pork feet. Oh, and foie gras." With a tremble, he brings a fist to his mouth. "Disgusting."

Holding on to the counter, I laugh so hard, my entire body shakes and my chest spasms. I can't even keep my eyes open, but as I peek through my lashes, Ian is smiling down at me.

"How can you not like fine dining? You work at the Marguerite, Ian. That makes no sense."

"I just don't." He gives me a casual shrug, then glares at the stick of butter on the counter. "I haven't eaten since yesterday."

"Since *yesterday*?" I shriek. "Why not?"

"Because Ella pissed me off right before lunchtime, and when we sat down for dinner, they served us steak tartare." He waves as if just speaking of it is making him nauseous. "Raw meat. Atrocious."

I can't help another burst of laughter, and the way he gently scolds me with his gaze makes my heart flutter. "If I cook something for you, will you eat?"

His shoulders tense. "Something French?"

"Nothing French," I reassure him with a gentle smile. "It'll surprise you to know that's not all I can cook."

He gets up and follows me to the fridge to scan the fresh ingredients. Even just the color and smell of fresh vegetables make me smile. "How do you feel about pasta?"

"One of the few dishes you need a fork for that's just as good as cutlery-free food."

As I grab shallots and asparagus, Ian tentatively hums. When I look up at him, he gives me an apologetic shrug. "Those are green."

Oh, right. He doesn't eat anything green.

"Don't you need to bring Ella tea?" I ask as I put both back.

He leans against the closed side of the fridge. "In a minute."

I shuffle back to the counter and set my loot on the wooden cutter. I put a large saucepan of water on to boil, then finely chop some pancetta. Once the pecorino cheese is grated, I grab some eggs.

"You remember I'm lactose intolerant, right?" Ian asks as he suspiciously glances at the pecorino. "That means that if I eat cheese, you want to be nowhere near me for a while."

"Hard cheeses, such as cheddar and Parmesan, and matured cheeses like Brie, Camembert, and feta, contain almost no lactose," I explain as I beat the eggs in a bowl and season them with a little black pepper, then add the cheese before setting the pancetta in a pan, stirring occasionally as it cooks on medium heat.

After I've taken out the last batch of macarons from the oven, he says, "I don't think I've ever seen you this happy." He's sitting on the other side of the counter, his arms on the stainless steel surface.

"Hmm?"

"Not when we video called or when you talked about Frank or . . ." He bites his bottom lip, lost in thought for a few seconds. "Or ever, really. I've never seen you as happy as you are right now, cooking."

I stir the bacon, the meat turning golden and crispy as the comforting smell fills the kitchen. "It's my safe space."

"So, then, why stop? Why haven't I seen you cooking once this week?"

I throw him a sidelong glance, then add salt to the barely boiling water. Ideally I'd wait longer, but I'll compromise a little on taste if it comes to avoiding this very uncomfortable topic.

"Having a restaurant fail could undermine one's confidence. I'd understand if you thought you weren't as good a cook as you figured." His gaze is trained on me in the brightly lit kitchen. "But that's not it. Is it?"

"I'm better than any cook you'll find in your kitchen," I tease.

He ignores my retort, his expression thoughtful. "And the trauma of having your dream turn into a nightmare didn't smother the fun of it, either, obviously."

"We've got you for that," I whisper. When he gives me a predatory look, I smirk and focus on the bacon.

"So you love cooking." He raises one finger. "And your arrogance hasn't diminished at all, unfortunately," he continues as he raises a second finger. "You love talking about food, you love learning about food, and you *love* being right."

With a sigh, I set my ladle down and stare into his eyes. For a few seconds that's all I do, all he does. We study each other in silence, save for the bacon fat sizzling and the water boiling.

"Are you really going to make me say it, Amelie?"

"Ian, just leave it alone."

"Unpopular opinion: you quit cooking because you're afraid of failing again."

I swallow, grabbing the bag of pasta and emptying half of it into the water. A cloud of vapor rises from the pot and, tucking my hair behind my ear, I stir a couple of times.

"Am I wrong?"

"You are," I say, and though he watches me attentively, waiting for me to elaborate, I don't speak. I don't say that he's been right all along about Frank and rejecting the possibility of failure led me to deny the clear signs that he didn't love me. That he didn't even *care*.

I'm not afraid to fail. I've failed spectacularly at everything already. But there comes a time when you need to give up and admit defeat. I've learned this the hard way in my personal life, and I won't make the same mistake with my dying career.

Once I drain the pasta and add it to the pan with the bacon, I throw in some of the pasta water, too, then the egg-and-cheese mix. Satisfied with the creamy result, I turn the stove off and grab a plate.

Setting the food in front of him, I watch him expectantly. What Ian thinks of my cooking is important, regardless of what's going on between us. He could reject me a thousand times and I'd still care.

He twirls some spaghetti around his fork, then studies it with a dubious look, like an animal that's been poisoned one too many times and doesn't trust the food it's given. When he finally chews, he does so slowly until he begins nodding. "This is delicious."

The soft, glorious tingle of victory moves up my spine. "It's because I used the best ingredients and—"

Throwing his head back, he snaps, "Settle down, Amelie. You're ruining dinner."

"Fine, fine."

He resumes eating. "So you won't tell me why your restaurant failed." He finishes chewing before going back for more. "And you won't admit you're terrified of failing again, and that's why I haven't seen you cook once before tonight." Bringing the fork to his lips, he smirks. "Looks like you're keeping a lot of secrets."

"Funny you should say that," I say, taking a sip of my coffee and making it a point not to look away from him. "Because I have a few questions myself."

"Like what?"

Like what? he says. Setting my cup down, I give him a pointed look. "Like why are you managing the Marguerite if you hate it? Do you know how hugely hypocritical of you that is?"

"*Hugely* hypocritical?" he asks with an amused smile.

"Hugely. You pestered me for half a year about standing up for myself—you called me a coward just a few days ago—and now it turns out you work a job you hate?"

His lips press together as he looks down at his plate. When he glances at me, he nods. "All right. Show me yours and I'll show you mine."

I don't even pretend to consider it, since I have about a billion questions to ask him. "Fine. Go on."

"Yeah, right. I fell for that once already."

With a groan, I sit on the stool on the other side of the island

and absentmindedly trace the rim of my cup. I can't tell him much about the last few months of my life, not without involving his father, but I can own up to my fears. "I'm not afraid to cook, Ian. I know I'm a great chef, and I'm not here because of my father. Sure, being Hammond Preston's daughter makes me privileged, but I'm a talented cook regardless of him."

"Is that what the article said?" he asks in a soft, worried voice. "That you're just your father's daughter?"

"Yeah. Among many other things." It's like the words have been burned into my brain. "Sometimes you just have to accept you failed and move on. Clinging to a collapsed fantasy doesn't magically fix it." When he gives me a sad smile, I straighten and square my shoulders. "I don't want to cook professionally anymore. That's it. Only for me and, well, for you."

He smiles down at his pasta and, leaning forward, takes hold of my wrist and squeezes gently. The gesture sends my heart into a frenzy. "Amelie, you're not—"

"No, no," I say, stopping him. "I showed you mine. Now you show me yours, remember?"

With a sigh, he pulls his hand back. "Right. Hmm . . ." He rubs his shoulder. "Where to start."

"Start from the beginning," I say as I gather the butter, fruit, and sugar I used to make macarons.

He inhales deeply, his jaw tense as he fidgets with the fork in his hand. "Okay. I told you about my mom and her stupid-ass plan to get me to reconsider marriage."

Sure. She left him only half of his inheritance and stipulated he'd get the rest if and when he got married. "What does that have to do with anything?"

"Well"—his eyes dart to the stick of butter—"her inheritance is the Marguerite."

My mouth hangs open as I piece it all together. Ian said his mom died about ten years ago, and the Marguerite was opened only a year before. "The Marguerite was your mom's?"

"Mm-hmm." He picks at a piece of pancetta. Then, suddenly, there's a look of disgust on his face. "Ugh—the smell." Using a napkin to wrap the butter, he looks around, places it in my bag, then pushes it toward me. "Oof. Much better." When I roll my eyes, he continues. "So you already know my dad used to work as an accountant."

Oh, I know. It's one of my go-to insults for him.

"My mom was the cook. She didn't come from a long line of geniuses like the Prestons," he says with a teasing smile, "but she was talented. Her family was well-off, so she never worked. We would often cook together for family and friends." He eats a forkful of pasta and sighs. "Eventually, she decided to open the Marguerite. My dad quit his job to help her manage it, and the dream was that one day I'd cook alongside her."

"You?" I can't help my surprise. "Cooking?"

"Well, don't sound so fucking shocked, Amelie." He balls up another napkin and throws it at me. "Damn chefs. I swear to God, only doctors are as self-important as you guys."

"Hey!" I half-heartedly pout, then add, "Yeah, you're right."

"Anyway," he says with a reprimanding glance, "I sucked. I was just . . . terrible. Anything I touched turned into inedible, carbonized shit, and my mom would tell me comforting lies. How I'd improve with time and one day I'd become the best chef in the world." Smiling regretfully, he shakes his head. "I lost interest after she died. Maybe I just grew out of it; maybe it wasn't fun once she was gone. I don't know. I was still basically a kid." He takes a sip of water, then sets the glass down. "When my mom passed, my dad took over. Hired a bunch of chefs to teach him the ropes and help us keep the business going, and it obviously worked."

I manage to hold back my snarky comment, and he must notice, because he chuckles, his tongue darting over his bottom lip. "The point is, I lost interest and turned to management. I love my job, Amelie. I wouldn't do it otherwise."

"But you hate French cuisine," I insist.

"I do, but I love the Marguerite. I love working with my dad every day, and I love seeing my mom's dream coming true." He inhales deeply. "It became our thing, you know? The Marguerite is my and my dad's dream. Every time I enter the restaurant, well . . ." He tilts his head. "I gag because of the smell. But then I see my mom in everything. In the floor tiles she chose, in the dent she made on the counter when she dropped a whole box of champagne bottles." He chuckles, his sad eyes glistening. "And since I won't make her *other* dream come true, I'm happy I found a way to work at the Marguerite."

Her other dream. Him getting married.

How awkward.

He must feel a similar way, because he looks down at his plate and cheerfully adds, "But I have to say, Amelie, I'd be happier to get to work every day and smell this. It's so delicious, I'm regretting the 'Everything's butter with butter' tweet."

I stand so abruptly my stool nearly tips back. "*You?*" I gasp. "You were behind the tweets!"

"I—" He glances away as he sets his fork down. "Y-yes. I assumed you figured it out."

"Stop assuming I know things, Ian!"

"Sorry, sorry!" He chuckles, raising both hands in defeat. "I *immediately* knew it was you. As soon as I found out who you were."

My shoulders rise and drop, my heart beating fast in my chest as I think of all the times I wished my secret Twitter enemy would get instant diarrhea. "Oh my God," I shout as I stomp around the island. "Valentine's Day! We got hate messages for a month, you horrible—"

He stands, too, taking a few steps back as he cackles. "Well, shit, sorry. I didn't know it was you at the time. You have to admit, it was pretty fucking funny, though."

My nostrils flare.

With his smile deepening, he bites his lower lip. "If you're going to punch me again, that's how you hold your fist, beautiful," he says, showing me the front of his clenched hand. My eyes meet his, my anger evaporating in a second, and maybe that's when the realization hits him, too, because he lowers his hand as his smile dies. "Oh, I . . . *Amelie*. I meant . . . Amelie."

I tentatively walk closer, his chin tilting down as he keeps his eyes on mine. I'm pretty sure everything in me is screaming at him to kiss me, but his pain peeks through so clearly I can feel it reflected inside me.

He's never going to move past how much I hurt him, is he? What can I do to earn his forgiveness?

I gently hold his wrist, my finger tracing the shape of the daisy tattooed on his left forearm. *Marguerite*. First one petal, then the other, then the one after that. Goose bumps break out over his skin, and once I look up, he stares at my lips with his jaw flexed.

My fingers part from his skin, though it's the very last thing I'd like to do, but before I can fully withdraw, he rubs the palm of his hand against my knuckles and leans forward.

Everything's eerily silent, so much so that I'm afraid he might notice the way my heart is beating out of my chest, and despite the defeated look in his eyes, he's definitely in agreement. I rise on tiptoes and press a kiss to the corner of his mouth to test the waters. He exhales. I do it again, and again, and I receive no answer but a puff of hot air. When I touch his cheek, he takes a step back and holds a hand over his eyes. "Amelie . . ."

"I'm sorry . . . sorry," I rush to say. I walk to the sink, grabbing my cup on the way, and begin washing it. I'm pretty sure my skin is melting from the humiliation. It's agonizing.

"No, it's not your fault," he mumbles. "But I should probably go."

Oh, fuck this.

I slam the cup on the counter, then turn to him, tears pooling in my eyes. He keeps pushing me away, then pulling me closer. Push and pull, push and pull. "Yeah, maybe you should."

"What—*you're* angry?" he snaps.

"Yes, *I'm* angry. You keep sending me all these mixed signals, Ian. You look at me as if there's nothing to save between us, you get hard for me, you let me kiss you." Tears run down my cheeks, and I quickly brush them away.

"Oh, am I frustrating you because I can't make up my mind?"

I roll my eyes at his scornful tone. "You know it's not the same thing."

He steps closer, his shoulders squared and a cold expression on his face. "You think this shit is easy for me, Amelie? You think I'm not struggling?" he complains. "We didn't end because my feelings for you changed. I didn't stop wanting you. Do you think I don't want to kiss you?"

"Then why don't you?" I ask, hating how whiny my voice sounds.

"Because everything that happened between us just proved me right, Amelie. I don't want a girlfriend; I don't want my happiness to depend on someone else. And if we were to . . ." He swallows. "It's not just physical, and I can't be with you after everything that happened. After you didn't choose me." He rubs his forehead as he exhales deeply. "But trust me, I've wished I could drag you back to my room since I saw you across the hall of this hotel." He shakes his head, a frustrated laugh bursting out of him. "Actually,

I've wished to since I saw you at Barbara's wedding, and I've never stopped. I've wanted you for a whole year, every single day."

When I say nothing, he sighs, then looks down at the floor. "It's important to me that you know this isn't a Frank thing. It's not that I don't fucking crave you, because I don't think I'll ever stop." With trepidation, he looks up at me. "Okay?"

"Okay," I whisper. Unfortunately, it offers only minimal relief.

We stand, silently watching each other for a while, until he points at the door. "Well, I'll go."

"Okay," I whisper again.

He turns to leave, and like every time he's walked away from me, it's like a knife to my stomach. As though blood were gushing out and I slowly lose my life's essence with the awareness that the only person who can save me is abandoning me. The sense of urgency, of every second that's passing and how I'm losing him more and more every day crashes over me.

"What if it was just sex?" I blurt.

He halts and watches me carefully over his shoulder, his hand on the doorframe. "What?"

"What if we agree to *just* have sex?"

He slowly turns, lips parted, until he smiles. "I don't think we could manage that, could we?"

"Me?" I ask. That's who he's talking about. It's pretty clear. "I can."

"And it's not just a way to get me to change my mind about—"

"I'm offended you'd suggest that, honestly." Sure, I hope he'll fall in love with me all over again, but that's regardless of the sex. Do I think sex could help? Yes, but it's not why I want to have sex with him.

He's Ian. I've wanted him for a whole year, despite lying to myself for so long. "Just forget about it."

I turn to the sink and continue washing my cup, the high-pitched sound of running water the only one in the kitchen. Once I'm done, I set the cup down and turn around to find Ian still there, staring at me.

After studying my questioning expression for a while, he nods. "Okay. One night."

23

Fuck It? Not?

I take in the large, dusty room. Three out of four walls in the space are made of glass doors that lead to a balcony overlooking the sea. The dark wooden deck might be the most gorgeous part of the property. When I stepped on it earlier, I could smell the sea salt, see the waves crashing against the rocks below. I could hear the seagulls calling and almost felt like I was on one of those boats I could see in the distance.

Glancing at the walls, I picture them coated in white paint instead of their actual dirty gray. They are arched at the top, with beautiful crown moldings at every corner and around the missing overhead lighting. Debris is scattered around the room, but beneath it the beige tiles are intact. It's been established I'm no contractor, but I think once polished they'd look as good as new.

I enter the large kitchen in the back and duck to avoid a big spiderweb. All the appliances in here are prehistoric. The first thing I'd trash would be the line of fridges in the back—no, maybe the microwave. But once they're all gone, there'll be enough space to equip the workspace with all the gadgets I've ever wanted.

This place is perfect.

Once I'm back in the dining room, the real estate agent points at the phone against his ear and mouths a "Sorry" as he paces back and forth on the deck. I wave to dismiss him, then take my phone out and, after tapping on Ian's name in the contact list, send him a text.

> **Amelie:**
> Busy?

> **Ian:**
> For you? Never.

Pressing on the "call" button, I bring the phone to my ear.

"Jeez, Amelie. I was in the middle of sex with a Brazilian dancer," he says in an annoyed voice. "You call at the most inconvenient times, don't you?"

"Some people just say hello, Ian."

"Hello, Ian."

"You're twelve."

He chuckles, a car horn blasting in the background.

"Are you sure you're not busy? I can call back later—"

"Not busy, Amelie. Just having lunch with my dad."

Well, that sounds like something I shouldn't be interrupting.

"To what do I owe this pleasure? You don't usually call this early."

Letting go of the thought, I glance around me. "I thought you might like to share with me the moment that could potentially change my life forever."

"I'd like that very much," he says, his voice etched with intrigue.

Walking to the back door and peeping at the short buildings and houses surrounding the restaurant, I grin. "I'm scouting locations."

"Oh," he says. He sounds somewhat disappointed. "You found something better than the barn on the Kent Farm, then?"

"No. No better place exists," I say with a sigh. "I'm not talking about wedding locations."

After a couple of seconds, he says, "No way. You're doing it?"

"I'm thinking about it."

He hollers for a good five seconds as I chuckle. "Amelie, I'm so proud of you. This is fucking amazing. It's—" He groans. "I need to hug someone. Well, I need to hug you, but you're not here. Wait, there's a lady—excuse me? Can I hug you? My friend gave me amazing news, but she's on the phone and I can't hug her. Really? You don't mind?"

I hear what sounds like an old lady say she's always up for a hug from such a handsome young man.

"Thank you. You're the best. What's your name? I'm Ian. Okay, bye, Griselle. Lovely to meet you."

"Are you done harassing strangers?" I ask.

"Actually, no, I'm not. I need to hug someone else, but Griselle *loves* strong perfume." He groans again. "Amelie, come here perfumeless. I'll get you a train ticket."

"Be serious!" I shout, stomping my feet.

"I am! This is amazing news—an early Christmas gift!"

My grin is so wide, my cheeks hurt. Stupid Ian. Stupid, amazing, special Ian. I'm only considering it, but he's turning this into such a big deal, like it's already decided.

"This is a mistake. I know it is," I say, adrenaline coursing through my body in a wave that leaves me queasy. "Frank will lose his mind, and my dad—" My throat closes. "My dad will hate me."

"You haven't told Frank?"

"No," I admit. "I need to do it in the right way or he won't support the idea."

He mutters something that sounds like "Surprise, surprise," then clears his throat. "Well, I'm honored to share this moment with you, Amelie, but I'm sure he knows you're a kick-ass woman who will succeed. And if he doesn't . . . well, that shouldn't stop you. Support goes both ways, and you've been supporting him and his needs plenty."

The sun shines through the large glass doors, lighting the room up all the way to the tall ceilings. The more details I notice, the deeper I fall in love with this place—with what it represents, and what it could be. "You're the person who inspired this, you know."

"Well, you inspire me every day."

"Me?" I say, surprised. "What do I inspire you to do?"

"You're kidding, right?" He laughs. "You've been working for your dad since you were—what, fourteen? And even though he hardly gave you any of the well-deserved recognition you need, you've stuck by his side through it all."

"Which you said I should *stop* doing," I remind him. "Remember? That's why I'm here."

"And Frank," he continues, blatantly ignoring me. "You know how many women would have dropped his ass if they were in your place?"

"Another thing you constantly complain about."

"And let's not forget Martha," he says. "Not many friendships would survive her selfishness, and yet you—"

"*These are all things you said I should stop doing!*" I shriek.

"Yes, Amelie. You need to stop putting everyone else's needs and wants above your own," he says. "Still, there's no denying your patience, your good heart, and your strength. You, beautiful Amelie, are the most resilient person I know."

I bite my lip, my eyes filling with happy tears.

Before I can thank him, his voice comes through the phone again. "But just because you carry it all, it doesn't mean it's not heavy."

God, it feels so good. For my efforts to be validated, to have someone acknowledge that I've been strong. Even if every ounce of strength I have comes from Ian. Without his comfort, I probably would have given up or gotten here feeling a lot emptier than I do right now.

Passing my hand over the dusty counter, I try to shake my emotions off. "It's your 'Fuck it' attitude. It spreads like a virus."

"Damn right. Fuck it."

Well, I still have to discuss it with Frank. As my fiancé, he has a say in the matter of our finances. "I haven't made up my mind about this, Ian."

His boisterous laugh makes my face light up, and in the seconds of silence that follow, I fall deeper in love with every detail of this place. The white windows, the beautiful sandstone counter, the glass double doors at the entrance.

"Haven't you, Amelie?"

Turning around and taking in a 360-degree view of my new restaurant's interior, I bite my lip. I guess I have.

La Brasserie
@Labrasserie

@TheMarguerite Bold of you to assume people who order your crème brûlée would want a second one.

08:44 AM • Nov 27 • Twitter for iPhone

8K 16K 26.4K 35K

I set my phone down with a loud "Ha!" and cross my arms, pleased by the number of likes and shares of this morning's tweet.

Since the Marguerite used our Valentine's Day initiative from last year to throw us under the bus, I've been waiting for an opportunity to return the favor. Imagine my joy when I learned about their "Buy one, get one free" promotion on crème brûlée. So damn tacky.

When the door rattles, I light up the two candles on the table and stand. Frank is back for the weekend, and there's a lot we need to talk about. "Ames?" Frank calls from the entrance, and a minute after I shout back, "Kitchen!" he joins my side, his eyes roaming over the table set with plates filled with cannelloni. With an apprehensive look at the meatloaf in the oven, his forehead furrows. "Are we expecting guests?"

"No, don't worry."

He heaves a sigh of relief as he takes his cap off. "Then what's this?"

"For you." I move his chair back with a grin. "I wanted to talk about something."

With a suspicious expression, he takes off his jacket. "So you sweeten me up with my favorite meal. Solid plan. Let me just change this?" he asks as he pinches his sweatshirt.

Once he's left the kitchen, I take out the documents I've prepared and set them by the side of my plate, then release a nervous breath. Though the money I'd invest in the restaurant is technically mine, we're about to be married. I can't ignore his opinion . . . despite what Ian says.

"Okay, here I am." He appears at the kitchen door wearing an old T-shirt and a tired smile. "Ready to listen."

I point at his chair, and he takes a seat. "First, food. Or my plan isn't going to work."

"Of course." He cuts a piece of his cannelloni, then brings it to his lips and closes his eyes with an appreciative sigh, waving his fork up and down. "My God, this is delicious. I haven't eaten anything since this morning."

My heart fills as he goes for a second bite, then a third. This particular joy is something I can hardly describe with words, but it never gets old. Ever since the first crêpes I used to make with my father as a child, seeing people enjoying the food I prepare is the best feeling in the world.

Which gives me more confidence for the next step.

I set a stack of papers in front of him and say, "Considering you're such a fan of my food, I'd like to present you with a proposition."

"How formal," he jokes, grabbing the papers as he goes for another forkful. He reads the first page, eyes narrowed, his chewing becoming slower and slower, until he sets his fork down on the table. "A business plan?"

"Yes. A business plan for—" I shrug. "Well, keep reading."

"Your restaurant," he breathes out, his lips parting. His eyes move left to right as he swallows, and a few seconds later he's stroking his chin and observing me with a stern expression. "Ames . . ."

"Wait, Frank. Read it first."

"I have no doubt this is a good business plan—great even. It doesn't mean it's a good idea."

"Why not?"

He sets it on the table with a deep breath. "You know why not, Ames. We can't afford a restaurant on top of the wedding."

He's right, and if he bothered to look past the first page of my business plan, he would notice that I took that into consideration. We've already scaled down a lot of the stuff I originally planned because of our six-month deadline, and to be completely honest, if it weren't for the deposits we've already put down, I would just call it off and elope. With everything that's happened, I can't say I'm particularly excited about my wedding day, and planning it has been the equivalent of a nine-to-five job you hate and get charged for.

"I'll ask for a loan. I'm a professional with loads of experience, and I've got great credit. I'm sure if I present the bank with a good plan, they'll say yes."

"A loan?" Worriedly, Frank bites his bottom lip. I nod and open the folder on the table, then point at the page with my estimate for the loan. "Whoa, Ames. That's a lot of money."

And it's not the worst part yet.

"Yes, and at the beginning I won't be able to make much, with the loan to repay. It could be months until the restaurant takes off. Maybe even a few years before I start seeing any decent profit."

His eyes find mine, and he squints from behind his thick glasses. "Ames . . ." He shakes his head, then stands. His shoulders tense as he stares at the kitchen cabinet and rubs a hand over his face. As if I asked him to build me a castle out of paper clips. "This isn't the right moment. You know I'm up for a promotion at work. Maybe we could talk about this some other time."

Ian's words come back to me.

Support goes both ways.

"So I'm supposed to put my life on pause until you achieve your dream." Pressing a hand to my chest, I ask, "It's not like we've already put our relationship on hold for your needs, right?"

"Is that how it is?" he retorts. "You'll resent me forever?"

"I don't know about forever, but you can bet it'll take more than five fucking minutes to get over this, Frank." I slam the folder closed. "What about *my* dreams? When is it *my* turn?"

"Your dream is to be the head chef of your father's restaurant."

"No it's not!" I shout. "And you'd know that if you ever bothered listening. Or asking. If you gave a crap about anything but your six months of being single, you'd notice just how unhappy I've been and for how long."

He groans, hiding his face in both hands and staring at his uneaten dinner. It feels like a boulder is crushing me to the floor and leaving me unable to breathe.

I remember our first date. Dinner and a movie. I told him about my dreams: how one day, I would love to open a restaurant not at all like my father's. A cozy, bright place to enjoy simple food done to perfection. A place where people feel free to laugh loudly and sit back, and they leave feeling like they weren't in a restaurant, but a home.

I'm sure he was listening back then. I clearly remember his smile, his comment about imagining a place like that being by the beach. It immediately made me swoon, because that was exactly what I pictured too.

I guess at some point he forgot.

"Your dad will promote you soon, Ames. You just need to be—"

Pointing a finger at him, I feel my eyes flare. "Say that I need to be patient and your weekend visit ends now."

"What's even the point of opening a restaurant and starting from scratch when you'll be handed a restaurant anyway? You'll be the head chef, and then one day you'll be the owner. You get the wedding you want *and* a restaurant."

Or maybe I'll get a wedding I don't like and a restaurant I don't want.

I look down, not a shadow of a smile on my face.

He stands, too, then cups my face with both hands. They're cold, and besides, they feel like sandpaper right now, but when I flinch backward, he doesn't let go. "Hmm? How does that sound?"

"I can give you until the wedding," I say as I take his hands and gently pull them off my face. "But then I'm done putting your needs first."

"Okay. That's fair." He kisses my lips, but I barely respond, the bitterness of our disagreement turning everything a sad shade of gray. Eventually I leave the kitchen. I can barely stand to look at him, and it's not because I'll have to put everything on pause until after the wedding. Considering the years I've waited, three months is nothing. I can do it. It's about everything else. How selfish he is, how inconsiderate and absent. How he hasn't once thought about our deal and regretted it. How he hasn't asked a single question about Ian since we met.

Approaching the couch, I grab my phone off the cushion. Of course, the only person who can make it all better has already texted me. Something between a frown and a smile blossoms on my lips as I open his text.

Ian:
So . . . fuck it? Not?

Hugging myself, I stare at Ian's name. I wish I could follow his advice. I wish his "Fuck it" attitude were as infectious as I made it out to be. Mostly, I wish he were here, right next to me, so he could hug me instead.

Amelie:
Not.

24

The Fault in the Plan

– TODAY –

We enter Ian's room in a rush, his strong arms wrapped around me as soon as the door closes. He gives me space to take the lead, to touch him like I need to. And then he does, and every single noise that comes out of him as his lips slide along my neck and his hands travel up and down my thighs is sinful perfection.

"Are you sure about this?" His mouth is on mine as I begin pulling down his joggers. I haven't even taken his T-shirt off yet and I'm shooting directly for the stars, so I'd say I'm pretty sure. There's no stopping me tonight.

"I'm sure."

"But you understand one night is all I can—"

His joggers are down his thighs, his briefs stretching in an unmistakable way. One glance is enough to know that when he said he was "not that well-endowed," he once again lied. I reach forward, careless of his warning, but just as my hand feels his hard length under the thin layer of black cotton, his fingers tighten around my wrist. He unceremoniously pulls me closer, and as I land against his chest, he whispers in my ear, "Feeling greedy, are we, Amelie?"

I shiver, his deep, raspy voice reaching corners inside me that have been shut down for a long time. Letting out a shaky breath, I hold on to his shoulder and use my hand, trapped between our bodies, to gently brush my fingers over his shaft. "Yes."

His breath, hot and trembling, fans against my ear and, taking a step forward, he guides me to the bed. He gently sits me down, his hand leaving my wrist only to get rid of his joggers, then his T-shirt.

Fuck me, I could stare at him for days.

Every single furrow and muscle in his body has been put in front of me to lead me down a road of temptation I honestly want no GPS for. Let me get lost in there. Let me roam around for hours, not knowing exactly where I am but enjoying the view greatly. His shoulders have muscles. His hips have dimples. There are even those delicious V lines that disappear into his briefs. He's all perfection. A god among humans. So good.

Almost . . . too good.

"Amelie?"

I look up at his face, my chest heaving. "Yes?"

"I feel like I lost you." He looks down at himself with a cocked brow. "That doesn't usually happen when I take my clothes off."

"No, no." I smile, though my stomach is twisting. "I'm fine. You're fine."

But I'm not fine, and he's not either. He's so fucking gorgeous.

I've never slept with someone so good-looking. I've never slept with anyone but Frank at all. How am I supposed to compete with Ella? With the dozens of women Ian must have slept with? How can I match his experience? How can I even fathom making it enjoyable for him?

"I'm fine, huh?" He smirks. "Well, I'm flattered, but I have to warn you, Amelie, that if you run for the door, I'll chase after you naked. Nobody wants to see that." He rests his hands on his hips.

"I'd probably get arrested. You'd have to bail me out. It'd be pretty embarrassing for me."

"I'm not going to run," I whisper as I stand.

"Hey, it's okay," he says softly as he leans forward and strokes my cheek. "I understand. There's a lot of history—too much for a one-night stand." He threads his fingers through my hair, tilting my head up. He smiles, then kisses me gently. "I'm kissing you. Kissing you, Amelie. After everything that happened, I never thought I would, and now I am. Sleeping with you would be . . ." He shakes his head as he stares down at my dress. "But a kissing one-night stand with you is enough."

"It's not enough for me," I insist. "Please, just give me a minute."

He studies my face, his brows wrinkled as if he's not convinced, so I kiss his lips, bite them, and when he tightens his hold on my hair, I kiss his jaw all the way to his neck and ear. Then I whisper, "Just one minute."

"Okay."

Thank God. His hands drop to his sides. I smile, quickly squeeze his hand, and walk to the bathroom. When I walk back and grab my bag, his gaze follows my movements. "Just . . . female hygiene products."

"We're on the fourth floor. *Do not* try to escape from the window."

Ignoring him, I enter the bathroom and close the door behind me. I go to the sink, and once the tap is open, I strut to the window. Phone in hand, my fingers frantically tap. Each beep that follows makes my heart quicken, my muscles tense. Until eventually I hear "Hello?"

"Martha?"

"Ames?" she asks in a doubtful voice. "Where are you? Why are you whispering?"

I release a breath, relief washing over me. I called her not even knowing why she's the person I'd run to, seeing as we haven't talked in so long, but now that I'm hearing her voice, it's crystal clear. I love Barb, but I met her later in life, when moments like this one were mostly done with. Martha? She was there when I freaked out about a boy wanting to touch me for the first time. About my first period, my first service at the restaurant. She's always been the person I call from the bathroom.

"I'm—" I imagine what I'd look like to a casual observer. Crouched next to the window, speaking into my hand, water flowing from the tap to cover the noise. "I'm about to have sex and I'm . . . I'm freaking out."

"Oh." She clears her voice. "Not with Frank, is it?"

"There isn't enough money in the world."

"Right. Why . . . why are you freaking out?"

Because he's too beautiful. Too experienced. Too different from what I'm used to. Because he's not just a random guy. He's Ian. And if it is disappointing, I won't be able to look past it, not anymore. If it is bad, it will be the end. But if it's as good as I expect it to be—if it's the best sex I'll ever have in my life . . . well, it'll be the end too. All he's giving me is tonight.

"Is he the first person you'll have slept with since Frank?" she asks softly.

"Yes."

"I see." There's a moment of silence, then: "I know this isn't the right moment to talk about it, but I spoke to him today."

"Oh?"

"Yeah. And the reason I'm bringing it up now is . . . he actually mentioned your agreement. Your . . . engagement."

My stomach clenches. Seriously, with everything he's done, now he can't even respect my wish that our friends not know that I debased myself?

"Don't hate him for it, because I basically forced it out of him. I was . . . well, I was bitching about you. Blaming you for everything that happened." She sighs loudly. "Actually, you know what? *Do* hate him for it. What do I care?"

I bite my bottom lip, sensing there's more.

"Anyway, he explained. And I see why you'd be anxious about being intimate with someone. When the man you were the most intimate with betrays you like that . . . when he . . ." She sniffles. "I'm sorry, I'm making this about me again, aren't I?" she asks in a choked-up voice. "I just wish I'd known, Ames. I wish you'd felt free to tell me, because I would have never judged you for it. I judge *him* a lot. In fact, I told Trev that if he comes to the wedding, I won't be there, so if you know of someone who wants to be a last-minute best man . . ." she says with a chuckle.

"He's Trev's best friend," I remind her, shock ricocheting through me. "You don't need to do that."

"Oh, but I do. I'll kill him if he shows up. And I'm not just saying that, Ames. I will take my heels off and stab him in both eyes." She groans. "Trust me, Trev isn't too happy about him either. How could he ask you something like that? And how did I not see it? You were obviously unhappy, and you never said more than two words about the wedding, and—"

"Martha," I whisper, "I appreciate this, but your timing is really unfortunate."

"Yeah, of course, you're right. This isn't the moment for apologies. This is the moment to leave it all behind. All the pain and the self-doubt and the heaviness of the last year of your life. You leave it here, Ames, because now it's time to reap the fruits. And I hope with all my heart that what's waiting for you is a *huge* banana."

A chuckle bursts out of me and, holding myself against the radiator, I breathe out slowly. "I haven't had sex in so long, M."

"Oh, it's like riding a bike. Takes a lot of effort and doesn't always get you too far."

Breaking into laughter again, I shake my head. God, I've missed her.

"You'll be fine, Ames. If he's a good guy, someone who cares about you, you'll be fine." She sounds like she's smiling as she continues, "Just make sure he's as far from Frank as possible."

She's right. She's totally right. Ian and Frank might as well be from different species. I'm being utterly ridiculous. "Yeah. Okay."

"Yeah?"

"Yeah."

"Good. Are you well . . . groomed?"

"Bye, weirdo," I whisper with a smile as I stand. Once the call is disconnected, I walk to the mirror and close the tap. I finger-brush my hair to one side, move it back, then smell my armpits. My breath's fine, too, and with a groan I pull my dress up and take a look under my panties. "It's fine."

"Amelie? All good?"

"Yes!" I call back, turning to the door. I let my dress go, and just as it grazes my ankles, the breath is kicked out of my lungs.

Fuck, fuck, *fuck*! I didn't shave my legs. I wore a long dress and didn't shave my legs and I'm about to sleep with a god of sex. "Holy shit," I whimper as I hold both hands against my face. I wasn't planning to be intimate with anyone tonight, and now it's all I'll be thinking about once I get naked.

I yank open the first drawer in the bathroom vanity. I could die from relief when I see a razor, but upon further inspection, there's no soap or shaving cream. With sweat dampening the back of my neck, I spin around, panic sneaking its way around my throat until I can hardly breathe.

When I see the corner of something red poking out of my bag, I stop short.

Ian's nose, scrunching, comes back to me.

He wrapped it in a napkin and shoved it in my bag.

Butter.

I swallow, taking two seconds to consider it. When I see no faults in the plan, I take my dress off, grab the stick of butter and the razor, then enter the bathtub. I really should have worn a bra today. Using the showerhead, I wet my legs, praying that I won't activate Ian's lactose intolerance, and rub the stick of butter on both. Setting it aside, I begin shaving, and my anxiety settles a little.

This is working out. Everything's fine.

When there's a knock at the door, I flinch, immediately blowing out a breath of relief when I notice I haven't cut myself.

"Amelie? Please come out. Let's have a drink and just talk—"

"No, no. I'm just"—I squeeze my eyes shut—"refreshing my makeup."

"Is it cocaine? I've heard it's a problem in the restaurant industry."

"You're exhausting."

His chuckle is muffled by the door, and once I'm convinced he's gone back, I continue. The first leg's done and washed off. When I go for the stick of butter to rub some more on my right leg, it's not where I left it. I'm getting clumsier, limbs flailing about as I look for the damn thing, until I finally spot it by the drain. Excellent. I'm working out a plan to set my foot down without slipping when the room's pirouetting around me and my body violently hits the tub. The sudden pain in my right shoulder is so severe, the breath is forced out of my chest.

Now lying on my back, I stare at the ceiling with a whimper and blink my tears away. I try to pull myself up using my healthy arm as my heart hammers in my chest, but as soon as my fingers grip the tub, they slide off.

I guess there *is* a fault in my plan, and it might just be too relevant to ignore.

Butter is fucking *slippery*.

25

A Wicked Witch

The upbeat ringtone of my phone distracts me from my conversation with one of the busboys. As I glance down at the screen, my brows furrow. "Excuse me," I say, leaving the kitchen.

Ian is calling me. That's weird. He's never called out of nowhere; it usually starts off with us texting and one of us getting tired of typing. Most of the time, him.

"What happened?" I ask, skipping *Hello* or *How are you?* If he's calling with no notice, I know how he is, and it's *not* good.

"Hey." His voice—I've never heard it like that. Soft, almost fragile.

"What's going on?" I breathe.

"I'm—it's been a shitty day. I needed to hear your—"

"I'm here," I rush to say.

Ian's never needed me, not until today. I, on the other hand, seem to depend on him for my mental stability. At every turn, through thick and thin, he's been my shoulder to cry on for the past few months. It's my turn to shine, and I'll be damned if at the end of this conversation he isn't smiling.

"How was your day?" he asks in a dull voice.

"My day was long. Not as long as yours, though, from the sound of it."

He grunts, then there's the noise of keys and a door opening. He must have called on his way home. "Work was shit. People-screaming-in-my-ears-all-day shit."

"I've got the perfect remedy for that, and it involves a pizza, a bubble bath, and a vibrator." When he chuckles, I whisper, "At the same time."

"Damn. I think I left my good vibrator at work."

Staring out of the window of La Brasserie, I ask, "What can I do to help?"

"Tell me where you are, what you're doing, what you're wearing. Everything."

"*What I'm wearing?*" I mock. "Getting a *little* creepy."

"I thought you were supposed to cheer me up."

"I'm home, about to enter the tub, and taking off my sexy nurse uniform."

He hisses. "Damn, Amelie, that might cheer me up too much."

I laugh loudly enough to get Jeremy's attention as he enters the kitchen, then I quickly turn around and say, "I'm at work, about to start my shift. And I'm wearing what I always wear to work: leggings and a T-shirt. This one says, *I'm not as think as you drunk I am.*"

"Shoes?"

"Converse."

"Hair?"

"Pulled back with pins, actually."

He releases a deep, heavy sigh. "Beautiful Amelie."

I roll my eyes. My outfit is the most unimpressive set of clothes I could have described, but the way he says that—*beautiful Amelie*—is so honest. So heartfelt.

"I—I did something stupid."

My muscles tense up as I rest my back against the window, my mind filling with disastrous possibilities. "Okay. What's that?"

"I let my ex talk me into going on a date."

"Your ex?" I ask, my heartbeat quickening.

"Yeah," he says with a joyless chuckle. "She asked and . . . I don't know, I guess I felt lonely, and when she kissed me—"

"You *kissed*?"

"Mm-hmm."

Oh. My body is licked by heat as a roaring fire bursts in my stomach. He kissed someone. Ian kissed a woman. Of course he did: we're not together. In fact, I'm pretty sure he sleeps around plenty. But now I know for sure his lips touched someone else's lips, and my insides turn into a knot.

"Which ex? What—"

"My only ex."

My eyes widen, my back tensing as I think of his fairy tale. The princess who's actually a witch and the ogre who took her away. He can't mean he's considering a date with Ella, can he? It can't be her he kissed. Not after she cheated on him two months before their wedding—and with his best friend! "You—no. Why are you even in contact, Ian?"

"Because of work. She needed a job, and . . . well, after fighting with my dad for what felt like eleven hundred hours, we hired her. It's just temporary."

"Well, it sounds like you should have listened to your father."

There's an undertone of annoyance as he mumbles, "No, I shouldn't have. Since my mom died, he's obsessively overprotective. I'm not a fucking kid: I can work with my ex and not propose to her again."

Can he?

When he notices my silence, he clicks his tongue. "It's just a date, Amelie."

My foot taps nervously on the floor. I'll admit I'm a little jealous—*a lot* jealous—but it isn't the main issue I have with this. Ian might easily be the best person I've ever met, and he should find someone as good as he is, not a woman who shattered his heart. Not one who betrayed him. "Do you have feelings for her?"

"Yes," he says with a laugh. "A few of them are *really* nasty. Most of them are just moderately negative."

I slap my thigh. "Then why would you go on a date with her?"

"Because . . . because I feel lonely, Amelie. Because the holidays are only a few weeks away, and you're about to get married, and I will never get married, and I felt lonely for a fucking minute."

I set my hand on my hip and sigh. "Ian, if you want a girlfriend or to get married, there's a million women who'd love to say yes. Find another one."

"Marriage is a scam, Amelie. I don't want to get married and I don't want a girlfriend either," he says. "It's just a moment of loneliness. Things will be different soon, once you're married. We're not going to talk as much. You're not going to be . . ." He sighs. "I don't know. It'll just be different."

I frown, the awareness he feels this way slapping me across the face. I hadn't even considered it, but I guess he's right. Things will have to change. I've let Frank believe that there's more than friendship going on between Ian and me—much more—so, according to the rules *I* set, I won't be able to keep talking to him.

No, Amelie, focus. This isn't about me. It's about him.

Tucking the painful thought away, I clear my throat. "It's time to end your crusade against relationships, Ian. Sharing your life with someone is a beautiful thing."

"Is it? Is it a beautiful thing to share your life with Frank?"

I purse my lips. "I'm not saying relationships aren't difficult. There are periods in which—"

"Periods? This period has been going on since before we met."

"We're not discussing me and Frank right now."

"Why not? Let's," he says with a firm voice. "When we checked out that band for your wedding you said something was wrong, and boy, were you right." He exhales sharply. "Your fiancé doesn't care. You're the last of his priorities, and he's the one stopping you from making your dream come true. How is that better than what Ella did?"

"So, because you believe I'm in an unhappy relationship, you'll be single forever."

In the silence that follows, my heart aches. I hate that he thinks that. How he has such a low opinion of my relationship; how he'd condemn himself to a life of loneliness.

"Look, I want to go on a date, have a chat, do something fun. Maybe end up having sex." He snickers. "And Ella might be the worst possible person to do it with, but she's *here*. She knows nothing will come out of it. Really, there's no harm."

I blink furiously, trying to stop myself from tearing up. If he truly believed that, this conversation wouldn't have started as it did. "Ian, I'm your friend, so I'll support whatever decision you make. But I wouldn't be a good friend if I didn't tell you what a dumb idea this is."

"Duly noted." He sighs.

"She doesn't deserve you."

"Agreed."

"Any other woman in the world would be thrilled to go on a date with you."

"I don't know about every single one of them, but thanks."

"*Ian.*"

"*Amelie.*"

I press my eyes with my thumb and forefinger. I should drop this, I know. After all, if he's convinced this is what he wants, there isn't much I can do. And it's not like I'm in any way an expert on functional relationships. The most stable and satisfying relationship in my life is with Ian, a man I've met twice.

"Fine," I say with a dramatic sweep of my hand. "If there's no one in this world you'd rather spend your time with, then go on a date with Ella. Have the chat, the fun, the sex." Barb enters from the backdoor, waving at me with a grin, and I quickly wave back. "I have to go."

"Of course there is."

"Huh?"

"Of course there is someone in this world I'd rather spend my time with. The person I spend *most* of my time with."

I stand still, silent. He's talking about me, isn't he? It must be: he's the person I spend most of my time talking to.

"You might know her. She's beautiful, stupidly lonely, and relentless in her goal to keep Ella away from me."

"Because Ella's a wart-nosed witch," I spit out.

"Is that so?" He chuckles. "Are you sure there's no other reason?"

My body temperature rises until my cheeks are hot enough to fry an egg on them. "Yeah."

"Okay," he says dryly. "Then I'll go on that date and watch out for spells and magic wands."

"Great," I bark.

"Awesome."

"Well, my shift is about to start, so . . ." I look toward the kitchen. "Have fun with Ella, and don't turn your back on her at family gatherings. She might go for your dad next."

"Text me when you're home safe."

"I think I won't."

"Amelie . . ."

"Bye." I hang up and shove my phone into my pocket. After walking past the kitchen and locking myself in the bathroom, I stare at my reflection, trying to get my facial muscles to loosen up and look less devastated.

I know I'm being unreasonable. I'm doing the exact opposite of what I should do. My role as Ian's friend is to warn him and advise him, not to control his life. If he's decided a date with Ella is what he wants, I should support him.

But I can't. I can hardly think of him kissing another woman, let alone one who hurt him. One who doesn't deserve him.

After taking out my phone, I type a text. *Sorry.* Then I delete it. *I'm with you no matter what.* I delete that too. I'll just text him when I'm home to let him know everything's fine.

Once I leave the bathroom and begin my shift, I burn the first plate of scallops as Ian's words keep replaying in my head. He said he'd rather go on a date with me than with Ella, and it should worry me. It should constrict my chest with anxiety that he's picturing more than a friendship with me. As should the fact that I'm incredibly jealous of his date.

But this is the first time we've fought—the first time we've hung up on such a sour note—and when Barb stops me from almost burning the scallops a second time, I leave the food in her hands and shout, "I need five," as I exit the kitchen. Standing in the same spot by the window, I tap on his contact and start the call.

"Hey," he says, his voice even sadder than before. My one goal was to cheer him up, dammit.

"Come on a date with me."

"What?"

I clear my throat, ignoring the pounding of my heart. "There won't be any sex, of course. And it'd be a friendly date, not a romantic one. I guess we could call it hanging out."

"Let's call it a date."

"A friendly date," I insist.

With a chuckle, he asks, "Do you mean it?"

I fidget with the stone on my engagement ring. "Yeah. I mean, I can't take days off right now, but—"

"I'll come there."

My brows shoot up. "But—"

"I'll drive. It's fine."

"Ian, you *do* get it's only a friendly thing, right? There wouldn't be any . . . funny business? Just dinner or a drink?"

"Is Frank coming?"

I fight really hard not to laugh. Frank? No. Frank isn't coming. Frank will be informed of this date the moment we agree to it, and he will most definitely not be aware of the "friendly" addendum.

Of course, Ian won't get the full truth either. I don't trust what he'd do if he knew I'm technically allowed to sleep with him. If he dials up the charisma a notch, I'm afraid I just might. "No, I don't think he'd want to come." My eyes narrow. "But he *can* if he wants to."

"I get it. No funny business, just dinner. A *friendly* date."

My body tingles with adrenaline. I can't believe he's serious about this, but he seems considerably more chipper than he was before, so who am I to argue? "And you won't go on a date with Ella?"

"I'll cancel on her right now."

I can't help but smile. Though there's certainly some jealousy at play, I mean it. If he were with a good person—a woman who loves him and deserves him—I'd be the first one to cheer them on. I know I have no claim on Ian. But Ella? I'd be a bad friend if I didn't do everything in my power to stop him from getting hurt again. "Okay. We have a deal."

"Next Friday."

"*Next* Friday?" I shriek.

"Yes, next Friday. Until then, I have work."

"Ian—"

"No funny business, just a friendly date. I promise."

"Okay." I have to cover my mouth with my hand to conceal my broad smile. "Friday."

"Great. I'll see you soon, then."

"You're crazy."

It sounds as if he's smiling as broadly as I am as he says, "Text me when you're home safe."

26

Don't Slip on the Butter

"Amelie? What was that noise?" The handle of the door rattles. "Are you okay?"

I wail, the throbbing pain in my shoulder only second to the gut-wrenching awareness that I can't get up. I'm stuck in a bathtub, in only my panties, with one leg shaved, the other one hairy, and the lower half of my body buttered like French toast.

"I—"

"Amelie?"

I groan, holding a butter-slick hand over my eyes. "I'm fine! I'm—I'm not fine but I'm . . . fine."

"Can you please open the door?"

Oh, God. The door is locked. The door is locked! Ian can't help me, as humiliating as that would be. He's going to have to call someone from the hotel. Hell, they might have to call the fire department. How much more pathetic will I look when they find me and I'm bawling?

"Amelie, you're freaking me out. Can you please—"

"I forgot how to have sex!" I burst. My heart is thumping in every inch of my skin, the pain in my shoulder intensifying by the second.

"You—" There's a beat of silence. "That's, hmm, fine. Come out of the bathroom. I'll . . . show you, okay? I'll show you how to have . . . sex."

Oh, just kill me now.

"No, Ian, I forgot that to have sex you need to be naked."

"You're gorgeous, Amelie, don't—"

"So I didn't shave my legs."

"Your . . . legs?" There's a light chuckle this time. "It's fine, beautiful. I never shave my legs."

"But—but I needed to, so I took your razor." He doesn't say anything, and I can only pray he doesn't deem it the huge invasion of privacy it feels like now that I say it out loud. "The problem is, I couldn't find any soap or shaving cream."

"They're here. Open the door and I'll hand them over."

Holding back tears, I clean the butter off my hand on my hip, but when I try to pull myself up, I end up only causing a screeching pain on my shoulder as my fingers slide along the ceramic tub. Settling back down, I breathe out slowly. "I used butter."

"Butter?"

"Butter," I confirm. I'm almost numb, as if my brain has shut down from too much embarrassment.

"Is it a French cuisine chef thing? Do you guys always have butter on your person?"

"I had some from before, when—" With an eye roll, I look up at the ceiling. "Yes. Yes, it's a *French cuisine chef thing*."

"Well, what's the problem? You're just gonna have to wash off really well because, well, the smell."

"The problem is butter is slippery. I fell in the tub and I hurt my shoulder. And now the door is locked and I can't get up because, well . . . butter is *really* slippery."

"You're *hurt*?" The handle rattles again. "Why the fuck didn't you start with that?"

I don't know. Maybe I was hoping I'd find a solution in the meantime. It doesn't look like he has one. He keeps trying to open the door.

When he stops, I sigh. He's probably gone to call the front desk and ask for help. Maybe if I close my eyes and wish for it really hard, this will turn into a dream.

There's a thump that makes me flinch, which also makes me cry out in pain. Then another one. "What are you doing?" I call.

"I'm breaking the door down."

"Isn't that a little excessive?"

"Remember our friendly date?" Before another thump comes, I shout that I do. "I told you that, with hairpins and the right attitude, no door is truly locked."

"I remember," I confirm.

"Well, count that as one of my lies. I don't know how to pick a lock, so it's either this or someone's going to have to screw the lock off the door. Which one would you prefer?"

With barely any thought, I answer, "Break the door down. But then . . . close your eyes."

"You're joking, right?"

"I have no bra on, I only shaved one of my legs, and I'm covered in your worst nightmare," I say as I frown at the stick of butter, which is pressed against my ankle.

I hear him chuckle as the thumps continue. On the third thump, the door opens, and my heart rate spikes.

"Okay. I've got my eyes closed. How are you feeling, beautiful?"

"I've been better," I grumble. There's a relieved smile on his face, but as he leans forward, it turns into a disgusted sneer. "Ugh. The smell. It's like a cow's living in here."

"Yeah, thanks."

"How are we doing this?"

I sigh, looking around. "I don't . . . Can you pick me up?"

"I just broke a door down. You bet your beautiful ass I can pick you up," he says smugly, then holds out both hands. "But you're gonna have to guide me."

"Yeah. Not—just a little down. No, not that hand; the other one. No, this hand is—" His open palm presses on my face.

"Oh. Hi, Amelie."

"Can you be serious, Ian?"

A chortle escapes his lips. "Right now? Not really."

"Just help me up!"

"How's this?" He puts one arm under my legs, then the other behind my back. With little effort, he picks me up and, oh my God, he's holding me against him and I'm so fucking naked. "Okay. I'll set you down now. Do you need to go to the hospital?"

"No, it's already much better now that I'm not squished inside the tub. Just pass me my dress, please."

He smiles sweetly at the defeated tone of my voice, and I set my naked feet on the floor. "Where is it?"

"Behind you, to your—"

He turns around and takes a sure step, his face hitting the extended mirror. After letting out a groan, he sighs deeply. "Yeah, I'm opening my eyes."

"Look at my face—*only* at my face."

"Okay." He grabs my dress, and as he turns around, his eyes find mine immediately. Holding a hand to my cheek, he whispers, "Are you in a lot of pain?"

I shake my head. "No. Really, I'm okay."

"Can I kiss you, then?"

"Please."

He smiles, then leans forward and drops a couple of gentle kisses on my lips. When he pulls back, his eyes run down to my breasts. "Shit—sorry."

"Ian!"

"I'm sorry! They're calling to me!" He holds a hand over his eyes, chuckles sputtering out of his mouth. "They're evil, Amelie. They're evil and gorgeous and out to get me."

"Just help me put on the damn dress."

He presses his lips tightly together and uncovers his eyes, his face tense as he stares straight at me. Now that I'm dressed, he picks me up once again. I'd like to protest, but walking on my buttery feet and no shoes would probably land me face-first on the floor.

Silently, he carries me to the bed, where he sets me down. He hands me a towel, and I clean off as much of the butter as I can. As he leans with his back against the wall and watches me, he's not smiling anymore, but he doesn't look upset either. I wonder if what happened tonight convinced him not to *ever* have sex with me.

"What are you thinking about?" I ask as I put the towel down. Ian has never once been this silent before, and it's freaking me out.

Peals of laughter erupt from him, and he bends over for a second before straightening back up and trying to contain his amusement. "Just . . . I can't stop thinking of butter pickup lines."

"Don't you dare," I say, relief mixing with embarrassment.

"I won't." He forces a serious expression on his face, his lips tight into a straight line. I know this is killing him.

"Fine. Just one."

"We're *butter* together."

"Fun."

"You're my *butter* half?"

"Hmm."

"Amelie, you really *churn* me on."

"You know, it's not funny. I do feel *some* pain," I say as he comes to sit next to me.

Gently squeezing my leg, he smiles. "Don't worry. You'll feel *butter* soon."

———————————

"What happened then?" Barb asks, eyes bulging, her spoon frozen in midair over her cereal. "Because you definitely slept in your bed. I heard you come back early last night."

Glancing in the direction of the other tables and making sure Ian isn't anywhere around, I grit my teeth. "Then I smacked his shoulder, he tickled my side, and we had one of those moments. You know, when it's clear you're about to kiss."

"Sure."

I nod, hating my next words even before I say them out loud. "Then I said, 'Thank you for everything. We should do this again,' and basically ran away without looking at him."

She inhales through her teeth and scoops up some cereal. "'We should do this again'? What, slipping on butter and breaking down doors?" At my glare, she looks away, silence stretching for a while. "What happened to the macarons?"

I snort out a laugh, her cheeks turning a shade redder as she shrinks in her chair. "I'm afraid we left them behind. Cravings are that bad, huh?"

"I'd sell you and Ryan for one of those bad boys right now."

"Damn." I fidget with the chain of my necklace. "Before we went to his room, he said he'd come back to set them aside for you."

Her eyes sparkle, but she shakes her head slightly when she sees me massaging my shoulder. "How's the pain?"

"It's fine," I grumble. God, I feel so humiliated, I wish I could peel my skin off. "Bruised, but it's my dignity that's been battered."

"That's funny, because it actually sounds like butt—"

"Don't even," I warn with a motion of my hand. I can deal with these stupid jokes only if they're delivered by Ian's perfect lips.

"So you had a little bit of a freakout," Barb says, patting my hand reassuringly. "It happens. You haven't had sex in a while. You haven't had good sex in forever. And you've never slept with Ian."

"And she never will if she keeps running away from me," Ian says from beside us.

Fucking hell. Barb giggles nervously as she throws a look at him, gives me the side-eye, and then focuses on her cereal bowl as if she'll be quizzed about it later. And I don't exactly have it in me to look at him, so I press my eyes shut and think of all the ways I'd rather die at this very moment than face him.

"Mind if I join you?"

"N-no, of course not," I mutter, opening my eyes again, and once he sits by my side and his citrusy scent wafts around me, I give him a fleeting smile. "Good morning."

"Good morning." He throws a glance at Barb. "I just wanted to say—"

"Do you—" Barb interrupts, wrapping one of her red curls around her index finger. "I . . . if you could just tell me where the macarons are, I'll be on my way."

Ian's eyes jump from her to me, then to her again. "Right. I would have brought them over, but I didn't want to risk waking you up."

"We have an extra key if you want it."

"Barb!" I shriek.

"What?" she shrieks back. "I just want him to be able to bring food should last night's events repeat themselves."

"Jesus—Barb!"

"The macarons are in the fridge," Ian says with a charming smile. Once Barb thanks him and hops up, he turns to me. "I like her."

"She's great," I confirm as I watch her walk away. I'm still kicking her the moment she pops that baby out, though.

"So, hmm . . . I wanted to say that we can pretend last night never happened. It was a bit optimistic of us to think we could have sex without feelings getting involved anyway." He pushes his hair back. "And you're not a one-night-stand kind of person, I get it."

I cross my arms. "Says who?" When all he does is tilt his head, I continue. "Yes, last night I had a minor freakout. Is relentless Ian giving up after a small hiccup?"

His smile is wide as he looks around, then leans forward. "Is that how you feel?"

"Yes."

He hums, his hand reaching into the back pocket of his jeans. He takes out his wallet, then the key card to his room. "Fine. I'll even give you a head start." Holding the key out for me, he whispers, "Take this, go upstairs, get comfortable. And wait for me."

Wait for me.

It sounds like a dangerous promise.

I swallow, my chest cavity suddenly empty and filled with rocks at the same time. "Right . . . right now?"

"Mm-hmm." His strong hand rests on my thigh. "I don't know about you, but I've waited long enough. In fact, we've had the longest bout of foreplay known to humanity."

Bolting up, I smile nervously. "We have the seminar soon. We should—"

"Barbara and Ella have it covered," he says as he stands too.

He smiles, calm and unbothered, and, boy, I could hit him in the head with one of those big plastic hammers. He's testing me, and I'm failing big-time.

When I say nothing, he slips his key back into his wallet. "I'll see you in class." And with the usual lovely smile, he walks away.

27

A Friendly Date

A white long-sleeved top with light blue flowers and high-waisted, dark blue pants. I love the big silver buttons on the front, and—I turn around and check my reflection in the mirror—yep. They make my ass look great.

What about shoes? Ian is tall, so maybe my white heels? I try them on, but I'm probably overdoing it. I opt for sneakers and put on some red lipstick. It's one of the perks of going on a date when you know you won't be kissed: you can wear whatever lipstick you want.

My phone beeps with a text, and I fetch it off the duvet as I hold my tube of mascara aloft.

Ian:
Are you a red roses woman?

Amelie:
I'm an engaged woman.

Ian:
No flowers?

> **Amelie:**
> No flowers.

> See you soon.

He's going to show up with flowers, isn't he?

Shaking my head, I dangle two different necklaces in my hands. I haven't repeated the phrase *just a friendly date* as many times in . . . I've never said it before this week, actually. But I've been saying it a lot since then.

I wonder what kind of date Ian has planned. He's been instructed not to overdo it, to keep it casual and nonromantic, so I expect a candlelit dinner and stargazing.

With my coat on, I step out the door, and a black car pulls over. Ian gets out, shuts the door, then turns to me and jerks his head back. Holding a hand to his heart, he dramatically groans. "Oh, beautiful Amelie."

"Deceitful Ian," I say as he approaches me. He's wearing a pair of black jeans and a rusty-orange sweater that looks softer than most pillows, and a black coat. You know what magazines would call that? Effortlessly gorgeous.

"How do you feel about raisins?"

My brows furrow. "Raisins? I . . . don't love them."

"Yeah? Then how about a date?" he quips.

My shoulders shake with laughter as I point at him. "Good one, good one."

"Liked it?"

"Perfectly cheesy."

He grins as his eyes roam down my body. "Did you do all that for me?"

"Well, this is a friendly date, after all."

"Blue. My favorite color." He smiles brightly. "And those red lips . . . I was right, red suits you even better than pink."

I tuck some hair behind my ear, uncomfortable at the implication that I've done any of it for him. "I—I didn't remember."

"Didn't you?"

When I shake my head, he tilts his. "Huh." Then he gestures toward his car. "Are you ready for the most romantic night of your life?"

"Ian . . ." I warn, shoulders slumped and arms crossed over my stomach.

"I'm messing with you, Amelie."

"You said—"

"The most casual date ever, I swear," he says, raising his hands in defeat. "A burping contest and some axe throwing."

"Sounds delightful." I take the hand he offers me as he curtsies, then he theatrically walks me to the car, holding my hand up daintily, and opens the door.

"What?" I ask as he slides in and turns the engine on, a smug smile on his face. He waves me off, and I pinch his forearm. "Come on! What is it?"

"Nothing. Just—you know I don't like perfume. When we met at the Quinns' wedding and you weren't expecting me, you had some on. Today you don't."

Oh, I . . . I must have forgotten.

———

As we walk across the large square, I throw a look at Ian. "Why are we here?"

He studies the mall in front of us with a thoughtful expression as a few people walk by. "You'll see."

"What do you mean?" I ask, alarmed as I step beside him. "Malls are closed at night."

"No door is truly closed if you have hairpins and the right attitude." When I halt, he chuckles and positions himself behind me to push me forward. "Come on, just joking."

I let him drag me to the tall doors of the building, where he taps on his phone and then looks up at me with a huge smile.

"New unpopular opinion," he says, raising a finger. "Road trips are better than flying off somewhere."

He gestures to me to respond with one of my own, and after giving it a little thought, I say, "Your twenties aren't the best years of your life."

"Good one." He thinks for half a second. "Beyoncé is overrated."

I scoff. "Beyoncé? I have half a mind to leave."

"Great voice, gorgeous, but her songs . . ." He shrugs, then points at me.

"The letter Q is basically useless. It shouldn't even exist."

"It's quasi-quarrelsome that you'd quench your questionable quest. Q is a quixotic, quizzical letter. Quintessential, quirky, and quaint."

My laughter is loud, and since it's so late in the evening, a few heads turn our way. God, he's like a dorky volcano of useless opinions. "Are we spending our night here on these steps?" I ask as I point around us.

"No." He looks at his phone, smiling mischievously. "Okay. He's here."

"Who's here?"

The old lock rattles, and as the heavy wooden door opens, a short, middle-aged man with gray hair peeks at us from behind a pair of thick glasses. "Hello. Ian, I presume?"

Ian nods. "The one and only."

"Come in."

The man opens the door a little more, the beam of light broadening across the dark steps. With a smile, he motions to us to enter, and despite my surprised looks, Ian says nothing as he gently pulls my arm, prompting me to follow.

We walk through the long corridor, darkened shops all around us and only the echo of our quick steps on the checkered tiles to break the silence. Our mysterious guide turns left until suddenly we're faced with a two-story, fully lit-up . . . bridal shop.

The bridal shop where I bought my dress.

"What—" I turn to Ian, my eyes wide. "What—"

As I take a step back, he follows. "Whoa. I imagined resistance but not a runaway bride."

"What are we—" I glance at the frowning man, who is following our interaction, then back to Ian. Ian, who's brought me to a *bridal shop*. "What the hell is this?"

"You're getting married in less than three months."

"I know."

He shakes his head. "You don't have a dress."

"So, wedding stuff?" My shoulders droop. "That's what you want to do tonight?"

"Fuck no." Fitting his hands into the pockets of his jeans, he says, "What I want to do is eat a quesadilla—by the way, an amazing Q-word—and bring you to the arcade. But that'd be far too romantic, and anyway, this isn't about what I want."

"But it is. This date—it's for *you*. You needed—"

He takes a step toward me, then squeezes my arms in his big, warm hands. "Amelie, why won't you buy a dress?"

My throat closes up as I realize he's implying there's more to my hesitation than I've owned up to. "I told you. Martha has the one I wanted."

"But you *do* need a dress." His left brow quirks. "Are you sure that's the only reason?"

"Seriously, Ian? This is all about you trying to prove a point?"

"If I'm wrong, then . . ." He points to the shop with a flourish, then offers me a challenging look.

Unbelievable.

I glare at him and cross my arms. I exhale deeply, muttering, "Fine," then begin walking. I'm not sure what game he's playing, but I'll give credit where credit is due.

This really isn't romantic.

Ian relaxes into the white love seat, brushing some hair off his forehead as he folds his hands over his stomach. "So tell me, Amelie. What's your favorite color? Do you have any siblings? What's your zodiac sign?"

"Ugh." I keep scrolling through the dozen dresses our shop attendant, John, has put together for me based on my preferences. "Please, spare me."

"Fine. But I've got to tell you. No first-date questions, no third-date sex. You're making this unnecessarily hard on me."

"Dating an engaged woman is no easy task." I shoot a glare at him. "Especially when you trick her into wedding dress shopping."

"It really isn't. You wouldn't even let me buy flowers." He smiles, observing me in the usual unsettling way. I can't exactly figure out what that look means, but it squeezes something deep inside of me.

Eager to avoid his stare, I turn back to the white dresses and ask, "What's with the flowers? You bring them up all the time."

"Do I?"

"Yes. 'Tell Frank to buy you flowers' and 'Did Frank get you flowers?'" I shrug. "You always ask."

He grins, rubbing a hand on his chin, then shakes his head. "Flowers are the one thing people never get for themselves. They have no purpose except to bring joy to the person you give them to. To make them feel special, loved, and important." Crossing his legs, he sets his eyes on me. "It's one of those little things that aren't little at all."

He's right. Flowers are an unmistakable sign of appreciation. "Is that another one of your unpopular opinions?" I ask.

"My mom's, actually, but I agree. Flowers are the ultimate love gesture." I watch him, waiting for him to continue, and as he uncomfortably rubs both hands over his jeans, he smiles. "But what do I know, huh? I'm on a date with an engaged woman."

"A *friendly* date."

"Right. So how about this one?" He stands and studies the dress I'm currently looking at, then nods. "I like it. Those things are cute."

"Appliqués."

"Ah. That's what that is. Even after PFP, I wasn't sure I'd understood." He grabs the last one from the row, then shows it to me. "This one's even better, though. Better *applits*."

Before I can correct him, my eyes land on the dress in his hands. Long sleeves, a crystal-beaded waistband, and jeweled buttons down the illusion neckline. When I look up to see his self-satisfied grin, the breath is kicked out of my stomach. "Ian . . ."

Isn't that my—*Martha's* dress?

"If the first question to come out of those pretty red lips includes the name Martha, I will legitimately lose my mind." He points his index finger at me. "So choose your next words carefully."

I meet his glare with one of my own. He might not realize this, but what he's holding is currently someone else's wedding dress. Wondering how he got it out of Martha's claws isn't a stupid question.

Without staring directly at the dress, as if it'll cast a spell over me, I cross my arms. "All right. Who was crazy enough to give it to you?"

With a smile lighting up his face again, the whole shop looks brighter. He holds the dress against his chest and gently swings his hips. "I told the designer I've always dreamed of wearing this sleeve-something-shaped-something dress at my wedding, and she—"

"Ian," I scold.

"Fine. I was honestly trying to spare your feelings." He sets the dress down and comes a few steps closer. "When I told the stylist what had happened with the dress and your wedding, she sold it to me. Didn't need convincing or anything." He shrugs. "That's how *depressing* this whole wedding drama is."

"Depressing? How about a true show of friendship?"

He bites his lower lip, his eyes searching the ceiling as he considers my words. "Nope," he says as his blue eyes find mine again. "Just depressing."

"So what you're actually saying is that you stole this from Martha."

"No. I'm saying I paid for it."

"For a dress that wasn't yours."

"It's mine now that I paid for it."

I sigh, pressing my fingers to my forehead in frustration. I'm pretty sure Martha has no idea her dress isn't waiting for the next fitting anymore. Days before her wedding.

"Well, though I appreciate the thought, you have to give it back."

He snorts, dropping on the couch. "As if."

"As if?" I cross my arms. "Ian, you can't steal someone's wedding dress."

"Sounds like advice Martha could benefit from."

He holds my stare, the decided look in his eyes telling me he's ready to die on this hill. Knowing it's for my own good should sweeten the bitter pill, but it does not.

Of course I want my dress. Only knowing it's right next to me is enough to bring me to tears. I wish I could skedaddle to the back and put it on and then twirl in it and look at it for the rest of our date. But I can't. It's just too much hassle, and I've made up my mind already.

Rolling my shoulders back, I try to assume a power pose he'd be less likely to fight. "Really, Ian, this is so sweet of you, but—"

"Let me tell you the truth, Amelie." He crosses his legs, then hooks his arm behind the love seat. "I don't understand half this drama. I mean, so what if you have the same flowers? The same centerpieces or band or menus? You'll still make it yours, somehow, and it's not like the ceremonies will take place next to each other."

"But—"

He raises a hand. "But you say it's not an option, so fine. Not an option." He leans forward, then clasps his hands. "Let Martha have the rice paper menus and hire the Sound of Time and get the red roses bouquet. Like millions of people will have before and after her wedding."

I nod, knowing there's more to his point.

He stands, walks to the dress, picks it up, and walks back to me. "But this, Amelie, is one-of-a-kind. Made for you. You chose every single detail, and no other dress like it will exist before or after your wedding." He sets his jaw. "If she gets *everything else*, all the details that are so important to you, you get this one thing." He grabs my chin. "You get the *only* thing nobody else will ever have. It's *yours*."

His eyes hold mine, my heart beating so slowly, I wouldn't notice if it stopped. The amount of peace he can infuse into me with his presence alone is something out of this world. It's enough to make me hesitate instead of giving him the negative answer I know I have to deliver.

As silence settles and time stands still, his eyes leave mine and travel to my lips. The slow beats turn into loud, quick thumps in my ears, the shift so abrupt that it makes me flinch.

I should move away; I know I should. He looks like he's about to kiss me, and though I've been confident so far he'd never do it, I'm not at all certain right now. Not when he doesn't let go of my chin, his eyes remain on my mouth, and his breaths fan over my skin. This moment might be even more intense than a kiss, and I have no power in me to stop it.

"Unless," he whispers, his eyes still hooded and focused on my mouth, "unless you've reconsidered—"

"Okay," I interrupt him. I grab the dress, jerking my chin back to free it from his hold. "I—I'll think about it. The dress. I'll think about the dress."

He swallows, smiling mildly. His hands rest on his hips, and silently he studies me. Can he read the fear in my eyes? Because I'm terrified.

He's always made jokes. Flirted, given me his full attention, his endless kindness. But he said he didn't want a relationship and he knows I'm engaged. Things have always felt safe. Now they don't.

I finally recognize the way he looks at me. It's like that couple at the Quinns' wedding looked at each other. With the same intensity. The same drive. Like he's looking at everything he's ever wished to have.

I know he's going to say something, and it will inevitably cause a cascading series of events that will, one way or another, ruin my life.

John enters the room as he clears his throat. Neither of us turns to him, and instead we remain in the worst staring contest ever.

When John sets something on the table and walks away, Ian smiles at him, then goes back to studying my eyes. "Don't think about it. Wear *your* dress at *your* wedding and, most importantly, do what makes *you* happy. Humor me, Amelie." He points at the white coffee table between us, and with a glance, I notice John has brought us champagne . . . and cheese nachos. "I will always humor you."

28

Are We Friends?

"You know, someday you'll have to tell me how in the world you tracked down my dress, though I never said where it was, and convinced the shop to open at nine at night just so you could give me life advice."

"I'll tell you when you tell me the name of that damn bakery. That coffee cake—"

"Just shut up."

He chuckles, the laughter quickly dwindling as we get out of the car and walk toward my building.

"You'll have to let me reimburse you for it too," I add. We go through the gate and take the short pathway to the porch. I know for a fact how expensive that dress is, and it's got too many zeros to be a gift.

"It's my wedding gift to you."

I stop and give him a reprimanding look. "No, it is *not*."

"Early Christmas gift, then." He smirks, hooking his thumb into the pocket of his jeans. "I'm stupidly gorgeous, disarmingly funny, and disgustingly rich." Moving past me, he adds, "The whole package."

I sigh, following him to the door. "You forgot deceivingly humble."

"That too."

"I'm not comfortable with you giving me such an expensive gift, Ian."

"All right. You can pay me back." He halts at the door. "Drinks are on you on the next *friendly* date."

Thinking of the way he looked at me back at the bridal shop—of the way he looks at me in most moments—I stare down at the flagstone slabs of the patio. When I meet his gaze, there's a patient smile on his face, as if he doesn't mind my silence at all. As if he'd be okay with just turning around, walking to his car, and driving away, though we both know that's not *all* he wants, is it?

"Are we . . . friends, Ian?"

His lips part, his eyes roaming over my face for a few seconds before focusing on mine. "Yes. By my definition of it, we're friends."

"Let me guess. You've got an unpopular opinion about friendship."

He chuckles, taking a slow step forward. "I don't know if it's unpopular, but here it comes. A friend is someone who doesn't judge you. Who maybe can't make things better but will try and, if all else fails, will just sit in silence with you. Someone you can count on; someone who is happy when you are. A friend is someone who makes you laugh a little harder and smile a whole lot more." With another step, he stands before me. "You are that to me. Am I that to you?"

"Yes," I answer with no hesitation. "You are."

"Then we're friends."

I swallow; the word "friends" so inadequately describes me and Ian that I can't help but pout.

"You know what I think, Amelie?" he asks before taking a deep breath. "I think friendship is at the base of the best love stories." He smiles as he looks into the distance. "Maybe not all love stories start with friendship, but eventually the ones that last are the relationships in which your partner becomes your best friend too."

"I love that."

"Is Frank your best friend?"

Frank is probably the person who knows me best—or, rather, knew me best. Although objectively ridiculous, it feels as if Ian took that spot in only four months. But even if Frank were on the podium . . . no. I don't think I'd ever call him my best friend. After our engagement, I certainly wouldn't.

"He—he asked me to have an open relationship until the wedding," I confess.

I'm not sure why I'm coming clean now, but as soon as I do, I feel better. I always thought it would feel humiliating, but it's not. It's liberating. Cathartic. Now someone else knows, and I don't have to carry all this weight by myself.

Ian leans against the door, not nearly as surprised as I'd expected him to be. "Hmm."

"Ian?" I ask. Once he stares at me with a tight-lipped smile, my shoulders go weak. "You already knew."

"Well . . . I wasn't sure of it at first, but 'a paradigm shift'?" He smiles sadly. "You weren't as mysterious as you thought. Then, at the Quinns' wedding, you said he wanted to have some new experiences. That's when I knew."

Lip quivering, I look away. I might be overreacting, might be making no sense at all, but it feels like a betrayal. Ian knew all along. "So that's why you stuck around."

"What?"

I meet his gaze, my lips pressed tightly so that they won't tremble. "You were waiting for me to tell you so that you could—"

"Amelie," he says, stopping me. Resting a hand on my shoulder, he shakes his head. "Being your friend has been the best part of the last four months. Actually, scratch that: it's been the highlight of my life." He looks thoughtful, and I just know he's not done. "But don't ask me to tell you there isn't more. You know there is, and not only from my side."

"Why didn't you say anything before?"

He shrugs. "I was waiting for you to feel comfortable enough to tell me. We've always discussed pretty personal stuff, and you never said a word. I figured you didn't want to."

He's right. I didn't. And now I'm so relieved, I wish I'd told him before. "I guess . . . you've been my escape for the past four months," I say with a crooked smile. "I didn't really want to think about that when I was with you. And, well, I knew you'd have things to say."

"I've got a whole catalog of things to say—a list so long, it would have to come out in three volumes."

"Please, spare me," I say, raising my hand. "I know how pathetic this all is without your input."

"It's not pathetic, Amelie."

"Oh, but it is." I run a hand through my hair. "I let Martha walk all over me; I let my dad manipulate me; I let Frank blackmail me into this with the promise of a marriage."

"That's what he said?" His eyebrows knit together. "That he'd marry you only if you accepted an open relationship?"

Not in so many words, but close enough.

When I nod, he peers through the glass doors into the building, as if he's looking for Frank. Judging by his expression, it's not to congratulate him on his idea. "So he offered you what you wanted, what's most important to you—dangled it under your nose—then attached some absurd condition to it." He sighs loudly. "That's not manipulative at all."

"As I said, pathetic."

He turns to me, biting his lower lip as his blue-flecked eyes soften. "Why? Why did you agree to it?"

With a frown, I study his expression. It's a legitimate question. Why did I do it? Why did I take everyone's side but my own? "Because I loved my relationship with Frank and my friendship with Martha," I whisper. I think of all the years together, of how every single one of my memories involves the two of them. All my important moments, all the good and bad. "Because it all crashed at the same time, and I can't afford to lose everything."

"See, that doesn't sound pathetic to me. That sounds scary."

Well, it is. Or was. And as I look at him, I realize it's not that scary anymore, because even if everything else were to fall apart, I truly believe Ian would be there for me. He wouldn't let me down. "You're the only person in my life who's there unconditionally," I whisper. I take a step closer. "And I mean that literally. You haven't attached any conditions to our friendship. To us."

Smiling stiffly, he turns away, and a horrible weight settles on my stomach.

"Or not."

"No, Amelie, I—" He turns back to me and runs both hands over his face, the only noise coming from the buzzing overhead neon light. "The way I feel about you, I . . . I couldn't help it if I wanted to."

My muscles stiffen, the rest of his thought weighing on me even before he expresses it. "Just get to the 'but,' Ian."

He hesitates, his eyes scanning my face for a few moments. "If that's all you want me to be, Amelie, that's what I'll be. Your friend who has feelings for you."

My heartbeat accelerates as if it's knocking from inside my chest, asking me to open the door, asking me to let it free. I can't

say I'm surprised Ian has feelings for me, but it's the first time he's
said it openly.

"But I won't do it for him." He points at the door. "Because a
friend would tell you this isn't how it's supposed to be. A friend
would tell you there's nothing wrong with open relationships unless they're one-sided."

"Ian . . ."

He shakes his head. "My condition is that you do the scary
thing and break it off, Amelie. This sham of an engagement. My
condition is that you stop choosing someone who isn't choosing
you back."

Tears run down my cheeks, and I look downward in an attempt
to hide it. When his arms wrap tightly around me, I bury my face
in his sweater, grabbing it in my fists behind his back. I cry, and I
couldn't stop if I wanted to, but I don't want to either. It feels so
good to let go. To let part of it wash away with my tears in the comfort Ian provides.

"You do this one thing. This huge, terrifying, necessary thing,
and there will never be more conditions from me, Amelie. Never
again. I'll be in your life unconditionally."

I swallow against his chest, my throat sticking so much that I
can hardly breathe. Because it's undeniable: I'm considering it. I'm
considering his words with more than my heart. I'm thinking them
through, picturing possibilities, alternatives, consequences. My rational brain is being won over by my emotions, and I'm letting it.

What if I did break the engagement? What if I never saw Frank
again? Could I give up such a fundamental part of my life? Could I
do it for Ian, and, even more importantly, could I do it for myself?

"What happens then?" I sniffle against his chest as he drops
kisses on the top of my head. "If I break the engagement off . . .
what will I do?"

His chest heaves against me. "We'll figure it out together."

"Frank and I bought this apartment. How's that going to work? And how am I going to tell everyone the wedding is off? What will I say?" I restlessly shift against his chest, looking up at his face and begging for solutions. Begging for a magic fix. "How can I just turn my back on him? Everyone will hate me. Everyone will blame me and hate me."

"Amelie, we'll take it one step at a time."

"No, Ian, no," I wail as I push myself off his chest. "That's not enough. You can't tell me I should destroy everything—hurt every person in my life—and expect me to be okay not having a plan. What about us, huh? You say you have feelings for me, then you say if I want to, you'll be my friend." As anger mounts in my chest, I cross my arms. "But you never said you want to be with me, did you?"

His mouth opens but no sound comes out. His eyes are dewy, his forehead creased with worry, but he says nothing. And for the first time, Ian disappoints me too.

"Right. You've got plenty of answers when it comes to fixing my life, but what about yours?" I angrily wipe the tears off my face. "You don't want a girlfriend. You might have feelings for me, but you don't want me."

When he reaches forward, I take a step back.

"I want to be with you, Amelie. Of course I do."

"But?"

He shakes his head. "There is no 'but.'"

"But, Ian?" I insist. I know there's something. I can see the doubt in his eyes, the insecurity, the dread.

"But I can't promise you a wedding. A marriage." His eyes sweeten. "It's the one thing I can't do, and I know it's important to you, but you don't need a marriage to know I won't leave. I'll prove it to you by choosing you every day."

My eyes water again. "You're asking me to stop making sacrifices for others, to put myself first, to indulge in that 'Fuck it' attitude you have about everything so that I can start all over again with you."

"No." Gingerly, he steps closer and takes a gentle hold of my chin. "That's why I didn't make this about us." He slowly inhales and tucks some hair behind my ear. "Because it's not about that. It's about you. If Frank isn't the man you love, then you shouldn't be with him. And if getting married is so important to you, then . . ." His eyes half close, the shimmer in them telling me he's holding back tears.

". . . then I shouldn't be with you either."

For a while he says nothing. Just studies my face longingly. And for a while I wish he'd just close the distance between us and kiss me.

But the more he doesn't, the less I want him to, until my hand finds his and pushes it off my chin. "I should go."

"Amelie, wait."

"No, Ian. No." Tears spill down my cheeks uncontrollably, my nose so stuffy I can hardly breathe. And, God, it angers me because this might be the last time I see him, and I want to smell the fresh scent of clean clothes and man that's uniquely Ian. "You can't run after an engaged woman and be surprised that she wants to get married."

"I know, Amelie. I know. But I can't choose who I fall for, and marriage is just something I can't . . . I can't contemplate right now. Maybe one day—we could see if—"

"Just forget about it," I mumble.

"Amelie, I want to be with you. I have feelings for you. Does that not count for anything?" he asks, following me as I prepare to go inside my apartment. "Do you really want a wedding with a jerk who doesn't love you?"

"You came into my life and disrupted it for nothing, Ian," I insist as I fumble with my keys.

"Really? *I* disrupted your life?" He gives me a dry look. "Not your fiancé sleeping with other women? Not your best friend stealing your wedding?"

"No. You. Because when I met you, I started to see what the alternative was, and it made it impossible to accept anything less." Frustrated, I turn to him. "You say you don't know love. Well, news flash, Ian: My mom left. My dad is a huge asshole. I've had no other relationship apart from Frank my whole life—" I break off with a sob. "And then I met you. And it feels like . . . like you taught me what love is."

His eyes close, his throat working hard. "So did you."

"And now you're taking it away from me." I shake my head. "Dangling it in front of my eyes, then attaching some absurd condition for me to get it. That's what you said, isn't it?"

"Amelie, whatever happens between us has nothing to do with the fact that you're getting married to a man who doesn't love you. Who you don't love."

"It changes *everything*."

His fingers wrap around my arm, gently tugging me closer. There's a stern but loving look on his face, the look of someone who's not done fighting. Who's not done trying. But I'm so done. I'm exhausted, defeated, and lost, and the one person I thought was my light through it all is just as stuck in the darkness as I am.

We hug silently for a long time. My chest spasms against his, but as his fingers thread through my hair, I'm slowly soothed. Until his lips brush the side of my head, and his arms lower around my back. Then he kisses my cheek, once, twice, the soft contact sending shivers down my spine.

Before tonight, I never thought I'd consider being with another man but Frank. Not for sex, not for more. But now? Pressed against Ian's chest?

I pull back lightly, looking into his eyes. His lips are calling to me, and right now that's as far as I want to plan. I want to kiss him. I want to feel everything he said, everything I know is true.

Tilting my head up, I rest my hands on his chest and rise up onto my toes, then lean forward until his breath mixes with mine.

"What the hell?"

We both flinch, backing away from each other before our lips so much as graze, and turn to Martha. She's staring at me, wide-eyed, her face red and puffy. "Ma-Martha," I breathe, my heartbeat spiking as I take a step back. "What are you—"

"Who is this?" she asks, aggressively walking closer as she points her finger at him.

Ian offers her his hand. "Nice to—"

"Are you fucking kidding me, Amelie? Frank leaves for six months and you cheat on him?"

"We—Ian is just a friend who—" I stutter. "Don't make a scene. Frank knows." I notice the tissue in her hand. "Wait, what's going on? Why are *you* crying?"

She looks at Ian, her nostrils flaring, but her chin wobbles. "Trevor's mom passed away. And of course now Trevor wants to postpone the wedding."

Ian turns to me, eyes wide.

"Oh my God, M. What happened?"

"Don't you dare change the topic." She points at Ian and me. "You're here with another man, Amelie. You were about to kiss! What the hell has gotten into you?"

Great idea, Amelie, asking Frank to keep this arrangement quiet. Leave it to me to look like the cheater in this damn situation.

Ian moves his hand up. "Martha, I assure you, nothing's going on. Amelie and I—"

"Oh, you shut up!" she spits out. "What kind of man gets in between an engaged couple? Huh? Have you no respect?"

He smiles my way, unfazed by her screeching accusations. "Wait until she sees the wedding gift I got you. She'll be crazy about me then."

"What does he mean?"

"Just—" I groan, throwing Ian a glare. "Give us a second, M."

"Yeah, I'm not gonna do that." She crosses her arms, a challenging glare directed at Ian, who smirks down at her.

Grabbing his arm, I pull Ian back through the gate, but Martha follows us, muttering, "Like hell I'm giving you privacy." I'd like to strangle her, but I ignore her and hurriedly walk Ian to his car.

His eyes lock with mine as he opens the door, and after throwing a look at Martha, he focuses on me again. I know there's more he'd like to say, but his gaze tells me plenty. There's a plea, a promise, a future in it. "I'll call you. We can finish our conversation."

Martha interjects again. "No, you—"

"Just shut up for a minute!" I shout just as Ian screams, "Will you fuck off?"

I'm pretty sure I've never screamed at Martha this way, or so her shocked expression suggests as she takes a step back.

Taking a deep breath, I turn my attention back to Ian, to his beautiful smile, his kind eyes. To the little strands of hair over his forehead, the shapely jaw I felt against my ear a minute ago.

He can't call me because there's nothing else to say. Because there's something fundamentally incompatible between the two of us, and neither is willing to compromise.

Maybe if we'd met a few years back, things would have been different. But eight weeks away from my wedding, I can't do anything. Surely I can't do what he has suggested. I can't leave Frank, throw the last fifteen years to the wind. Not when I'm so close to the finish line, not after the four months of pure hell I've been through. And not when I'd do that for nothing at all. Soon it'll all be over, and things between Frank and me will slowly go back to the closest version of normalcy we'll be able to achieve.

Any alternative is madness.

So I shake my head in a silent yet deadly rejection.

Ian's shoulders slump, and the hurt in his face mirrors mine. He looks surprised, as if he held on to the belief I'd choose him until the very last moment, when I utterly shattered his heart. "Amelie, please, I—"

"No, Ian, no," I say, the words coming out in a choked-up voice. "You've made your decision and I've made mine."

For a few seconds he looks down with a slow nod, and when he lifts his head and his eyes look into mine once more, they're colder than ice. "Goodbye, beautiful."

29

Panty Proof

– TODAY –

In an irredeemably short black dress and coordinated knee-high socks, I walk down the stairs, headed toward the crowded bar. The chain of my necklace is long enough to be hidden by the dress, and my hand moves to it as it always does when I'm nervous. Knowing it's there makes me feel better.

I don't even know if Ian will be there, except he *has* to be. That's where we're most likely to meet. We haven't talked since breakfast, but I've seen the looks he's thrown at me. I'm here to prove what he said this morning is wrong, and he wants me to. I know he does. So . . . he'll be there, right?

I approach the hotel hall, but before I can turn to the bar, I hear Ella's voice. She's talking to the concierge with the usual scowl. Puffing out a breath, I turn my back on her just as she spots me. "Preston."

Oh, yay. Exactly what I need tonight.

I turn to Ella, who, arms crossed, struts to me. "I figured you should know something."

Shoulders stiffening, I try to convince myself that whatever she'll say now is a barefaced lie. That she's just trying to drive a wedge between Ian and me and that he's proved time and time again that he's deserving of my trust.

I'm scared senseless anyway as she finally opens her mouth in a snarl. "I *saw* you, Preston."

I pause, release a breath, and try to find the strength within me not to walk away. "You *saw* me? Saw me doing what? Where?"

"I saw you and Roberts."

My eyes dart left to right. Ian and I weren't exactly trying to sneak around, so—oh. She doesn't mean *Ian* Roberts.

She nods. "Yeah. At the Marguerite about four months ago? I saw you." Her smile turns smug. "On a date with Ian's *father*."

My heart hammers as I try to maintain a neutral expression. I know there's no point in denying it, as she'd never believe me, but that was *not* a date. Fuck me, I can't believe she was there. "So let me guess. Either I stay away from him or you'll tell him?"

With a scoff, she grabs her bag. "No, Amelie. I don't need to do anything at all, because Ian will never give you another chance. He might have sex with you, might look like he forgives you. But he won't." Stepping closer, she straightens her red dress. "But I want *you* to know that I know everything. And if Ian asks, I will speak."

She walks away, the noises in the room slowly fading away as my ears ring. Trying to shake the feeling off, I turn around and stare into the crowded bar.

Ian is there, standing with his mouth open wide and a hand to his chest, his gaze roaming up and down my body. His shoulders slowly fall, and he mouths something I can't hear from here, but it looks like "Fuck."

This conversation with Ella was not what I needed tonight, but I won't let it stop me. I'm on a mission.

Holding my chin up, I walk to him, stopping once I'm by his

side, next to the counter. "Hello," I say casually as I raise a hand to call the bartender.

"I'm pretty sure you mean 'God damn.'"

I chuckle, tossing a glance at him over my shoulder. His gaze is definitely south of my face, his chin tilted down and his mouth dumbly open. "Ian?"

"Hmm?"

"I think you dropped your eyes on my ass."

He waves me off, his throat working hard. "Keep them. They never want to stare at anything else anyway."

"In that case . . ." I wave to the bartender, who's serving someone to my right.

"Are you okay?" He places his hand lightly against the small of my back, his eyes scanning my face as if he can see Ella's words echoing in my mind. Of course he can sense that something's wrong.

"Mm-hmm."

When I keep my gaze lowered, he jerks his chin, then obnoxiously moves his face closer until his nose is an inch from mine. "Did the witch put a spell on you, Princess Amelie?"

"No, Prince Ian."

"What did you and Ella talk about?"

"Just chef stuff." The tip of his nose grazes mine. "You're kind of invading my space."

"I'm making up for all the time we lost when we were so, so far apart." He grins proudly, and I can't help smiling myself. "Am I making you uncomfortable?"

"A little."

"How about now?" he asks as he squishes my nose with his. "Better?"

"I swear your brain stopped developing too early."

"Closer?"

I giggle once his forehead presses against mine. "Stop trying to make me laugh. I'm not sad."

"You *look* sad, though." His forehead pushes mine until I'm forced to take a step back, and his arms tighten around me. "You know I can't have that."

"Stop it—Ian!" I shriek when he keeps pushing. "You come any closer and I'll kiss you again."

"You kiss me again and I'll fuck you right here, right now."

With my smile softening and a jolt of electricity striking my body, I lean back just enough to look into his eyes. I knew it. I knew he didn't give up on me. "I still owe you drinks from our friendly date. Can I buy you a glass of wine?"

His eyes dip to my lips as he nods. "It's about time."

I lean forward and gently press a kiss on him, his mouth responding to mine with the same slow, exploring pace. His hand bunches in my dress as our bodies press together, and once he lets out a lovely, low grunt, I lean back.

Phase one of the plan is complete.

We order a glass of Château Pape Clément 2017 for me and some type of beer for him, and once the bartender gives us our drinks, Ian's full attention is on me again. This is it. It's time.

Phase two.

Squaring my shoulders, I force myself to stare into his expectant eyes, exuding as much confidence as I can possibly muster. It feels like all eyes are on me, and I'm sure they're not, but my cheeks turn as red as the glass of wine I just ordered. It doesn't matter: What I have in mind is the perfect way to kick tonight off. I won't back down, won't overthink it. In fact, I hope the night will end with me being unable to think anything at all.

"So . . ." I press myself against him, his eyes rolling down my décolletage lasciviously.

"Yes, Amelie?"

I gently pinch his dark blue sweater. "Our outfits match to-night."

While he glances dubiously at my black dress, my hand meets his. His eyes widen slightly as they fixate on mine, and after a quick glance at his hand, he withdraws it and pushes it into his pocket, my blue panties tucked between his fingers.

"My favorite color," he mumbles.

Just as I entwine my fingers with his, Pamela walks over to us. "Hello, you two!" she says, a little louder than necessary. Then, probably noticing the tangible tension, she adds, "Is everything okay?"

Ian's mouth opens but he seems unable to answer, as no sound comes out. His eyes roll down my legs, then back to my face.

"Ian?" I whisper, unable to hide a pleased smile.

"Hmm." He clears his throat, takes a sip of his beer, then another. Finally, he acknowledges Pamela. "Everything's fine. I'm just a little warm."

With a series of loud complaints about the weather, Pamela drags me to her table, Ian following right behind. I can feel his presence, his eyes back to the only thing they want to stare at.

Pamela takes her place beside David and Lucille, chefs at a local restaurant, and before I can grab one of the remaining chairs, Ian holds it out for me. I sit down, and he does, too, his body angled toward me so much, it's almost as if there's no one else at our table.

His eyes study me hungrily as I exchange a few polite remarks with David and Lucille, waiting for my attention to return to him. As soon as it does, he points at me. "That's a—a very pretty dress," he swallows. "It's also *very* short."

I shrug, then whisper, "I thought you might need 'PFP': *panty for proof*."

There's a shimmer in his eyes that I don't know how to interpret: somewhere between angry and turned on. Then I think of his words when we discussed this specific fantasy of his.

I stare at your thighs, hoping to see underneath, terrified that someone else will. Unable to think about anything else, obsessing over how ready you are, how close, but unreachable.

Ian's beer is gone a minute after my panty-less entrance, but he semi-patiently waits for me to drink my wine. He's not too subtle about it, either, pushing my glass closer every time the chatter distracts me.

Not that I'm truly distracted. No, sir. I can feel his leg bouncing under the table, see his fingers tapping on his coaster. And I torture him, spreading my legs an inch wider every time he looks down, until the panic in his eyes is so jarring, I take pity on him and close them. Then I start again.

Our knees brush against each other, and as he slides nearer inch by inch, his hand casually grazes the part of my leg hidden by my dress. I have to keep myself from grinding against the chair. If he slid his finger a few inches up, he would find that spot slick.

I drink my last sip, and, like a spring, he jumps up and announces we're leaving. I think even the walls know what for. We walk upstairs, whispering words between kisses, but they're confused, slurred, distracted.

Once we're standing in front of the door to his room, he leans back and stares into my eyes. His knuckle trails along the shape of my jaw as he studies me hungrily. "What happens next?" he whispers. "Do I need to drop to my knees? Because I will. I'll beg if you want me to. You win. Please let me do unspeakable things to you."

I bite my lip to contain a grin, every single function in my body shutting off and a strange new awareness tingling through me. I'm drunk with power. Drunk with the idea of this man dying to touch me, craving me. No one's ever craved me before.

This man *needs* me.

He needs me, and he's perfect, and I definitely want to spend the night with him.

I could say that I should have figured it out sooner, but the truth is that I knew all along and did nothing about it. And *that* is my biggest regret.

That, and everything that happened since the last time he asked me to spend the night with him.

30

You're Mine, Amelie

– ONE WEEK TO AMELIE'S WEDDING –

I stumble past the door and slam it closed behind me. "Frank?" I shout as I drag myself through the corridor.

Tonight's conversation is still echoing in my ears. I spent the better part of an hour of my birthday-meets-bachelorette party hearing about how romantic it is to be engaged. How Trevor and Ryan can't keep their hands off Martha and Barb most of the time. How it's like they've gone back to their first year together.

Frank and I haven't slept together since before our engagement. I figured things would get better when he came back for Christmas, then I told myself we'd be okay once he moved back in, but neither thing has happened. Winter is almost over, the wedding is approaching, and still . . . nothing. He also forgot today's my birthday, but I'm much more concerned about marrying a man who doesn't love me or want me. The several bottles of wine the girls and I drank aren't helping either.

I enter the dark bedroom and climb on the bed. It's much easier when I'm sober, and I almost plummet to the floor twice before I squeeze Frank's shoulder. "Frank?"

"Hmm?"

"Wake up."

He opens his eyes and sucks a quick breath in. "What is it? Is everything okay?"

"Yeah. I just got back. We need to have sex."

His eyes squint even more. "What?"

I move my leg over until I'm sitting on top of him, then press my lips to his, sticking my tongue in his mouth.

"Hmm—wait. Wait, Ames."

"What is it?" I ask, reaching down for my dress and pulling it up. When it gets stuck over my face, he pulls it back down. "You're drunk. You know I don't like to have sex when—"

"It's fine, Frank. I'm your fiancée." I lean down, kissing him again, but his hands press on my chest until I'm lifted off him.

"Still, I don't think—"

"We haven't had sex in months," I say, slapping my thigh in frustration as I sit back on his legs. "*Months*, Frank."

"That's not true. We—we did it when . . ."

His eyes wander left and right as he thinks, and I'd like to tell him that if he struggles to remember how long ago it was, it was probably too long, but instead I say, "Seven months ago."

He sighs. "Okay, look, I'm sorry. And I swear I'll do better, but I've been away most of the time, Ames."

I nod, a lump forming in my throat. I know the drill. He's away, and when he's here, he's tired, stressed, busy. "The time to do better is over," I whisper. "We're getting married in a week, Frank. How can we do it when we're not even in a relationship anymore?"

He rubs his eyes, blinking again and again. "Do we need to discuss this at"—he presses on the screen of his phone—"two thirty in the morning?"

"Are you still attracted to me?" I ask.

When he drops back onto the pillow with a groan, I stifle one myself. It's like I'm going crazy. Am I the only one seeing all of this? All these signs of something being deeply wrong between us? Because Frank acts like it's all in my head. Like he's trying his best to keep up with my crazy mood shifts and unrealistic expectations. Does he not see how everything's different now?

"Jesus, Ames. Yes, I am."

"Then let's have sex," I insist.

"Tomorrow, okay?"

"No, no," I whine, a mountain of anxiety taking over my chest. I'm getting married in a week to a man who won't touch me. Who won't speak to me. Who doesn't love me. And I've given up the best man in the world—my best friend—for him. "Now. Please, Frank." I cling to his shirt, pleadingly staring into his eyes. "Fuck me."

His jaw tightens, and with a swift motion he pushes me to one side and stands. "Jesus Christ, Ames. Quit acting like a desperate drunk."

My limbs turn to stone as I land on the other side of the bed and I watch him turn the light on.

"You know I don't like it when you say shit like that. You're my fiancée. My wife, soon enough. Not a fucking whore." He fits into a pair of jeans he grabs from the side table, then fetches a shirt from the dresser, huffing and puffing his annoyance. "Two thirty in the morning, Ames. And I have a work call in five hours."

"I don't care about your work!" I shout as I step off the bed and follow him. "All I'm asking is fifteen minutes of your time, Frank. It's been seven months—seven!"

"Look at you!" he shouts back once we reach the corridor. He turns to me, the spiteful look in his eyes stabbing me like a knife. "Look at the way you're behaving! It's the middle of the night, and I'm *not* having this argument with you right now. Not when you're drunk and acting like a damn psycho."

He stalks to the door. Burning with hot rage, I continue to pursue him. "Where are you going?"

"I'm leaving."

"No you're not!"

"Fucking watch me," he barks.

"If you do, don't bother coming back," I say in a hushed breath. I am *done*.

If Frank's done, I'm done too.

He reaches the door, then stops and turns to me with a pained expression. He looks like he's about to say something apologetic, but then he just snarls, "Fuck this shit," and opens the door and slams it behind him.

I get back into bed and hug my knees, burying my face against them. My mind can't process coherent thoughts. I'm overtaken by nausea, my head thumping with pain and my heartbeat rising with each passing moment of silence.

Frank must have gone to his parents' place, a few blocks away.

As I sob, hugging my pillow, I try to wrap my head around it. Frank and I just broke up. It happened, and it was so anticlimactic, it almost doesn't feel real. You'd expect, after fifteen years, that we'd have a huge fight lasting for days. That we'd cry and scream for hours, throw plates and glasses at the wall or something.

But he just left. And now it's over.

Violent anger takes hold of me.

He *just* left. If that's what he wanted to do, then why not leave before? Why did he put me through the past six months if it was all meant to end like this anyway?

The ring around my finger feels heavy, a foreign object. Pulling at it with the other hand, I slide it off and set it on the nightstand, sniffling.

It doesn't feel any more real. It doesn't fill me with sadness, either, because I can't focus on a thought long enough. I dread the wedding I'll have to cancel, then think of our apartment: Who's going to keep it? I picture the way he fixes his glasses, and it makes my heart squeeze, then I imagine him talking about what *he* needs and want to rip my hair out.

It's too silent in here. Empty and silent and miserable.

Sitting up, I look at my phone on the nightstand. I shouldn't. It's been almost two months, so Ian probably moved on, but if I call and he has enough pity left in him to answer, it'll set him back. I shouldn't but, fuck, I want to.

I miss him so much. I think about him every day—hell, every damn minute. I haven't been able to delete a single message or image, hanging on to them with every pathetic shred of myself, scrolling through them whenever I get the time.

I miss him, and I'm drunk, and I'm throwing myself a pity party he's definitely invited to, so I scurry up and grab my phone. My fingers shake with adrenaline as I press his contact and the call button.

Beep.

It's late, so he must be asleep. But he's the one who always said, *If you text me, I'll wake up.* I guess that applies to phone calls too. Right?

Beep.

"Amelie?"

My breath catches in my throat. His voice is groggy, raspy, so he was definitely sleeping. And it immediately soothes me, my body relaxing against the cold wall.

"Amelie? Are you okay?"

"I'm okay," I whisper. I can barely talk with the way the thumps of my heart are making my whole body shake.

"You don't sound okay."

I walk to the bed and slowly sit, as if any sudden movement could break the balance of this reality in which I'm talking to Ian again. "It's my birthday. Well, it was until midnight."

Silence. Then: "Happy birthday."

My lips twitch with a smile that dies out in a second.

"Did you have a good day?"

"Yeah. The girls took me out for drinks."

"Just the girls? No Frank?"

I swallow. "Just the girls. It was also my bachelorette party."

"Sounds like it wasn't too fun."

"It was." I smile lightly at the memory of fluorescent drinks and penis-shaped cookies. "I just . . . Frank and I . . . we had a fight."

"What happened?"

"Nothing," I say, the tremble in my voice betraying me. "I was drunk, and he was sleeping. I woke him up, and—"

"And?"

"He—" I choke on the next words.

I hear the sound of a light switch. "Amelie? Did he hurt you? Did he do something you didn't consent to?"

A burst of laughter explodes past my lips. It's not funny, of course, that he's worried about something like that. But the truth is so far from it, it's almost comical.

"Don't laugh," he bellows. "I was about to vomit."

"Sorry," I say, looking down at the blue duvet. "It's . . . just the very opposite."

"Oh." He clears his voice. "He still won't . . . ?"

"No."

He mumbles something I don't understand, but before I can ask, he continues. "Are you sure he's not gay?"

"No, he's not gay. He's straight. Just not into me."

"The only straight people I know who wouldn't be into you are women."

I chuckle, my mouth filling with saliva as a sudden burst of nausea makes its way past my stomach and through my throat. Taking a deep breath, I let myself fall back on the bed and stare at the ceiling. "You know how long it's been since I've had sex, Ian?"

"No, Amelie."

"About seven months."

There's an "*Oof,*" then a few moments of silence. "You're climbing up the walls, aren't you?"

"I am. Especially because . . ." I think of the last time we had sex. "He . . . he mostly stopped trying."

"Mm-hmm. Can't say I'm too surprised." He sighs. "So you fake it?"

"Sometimes. When I don't, he tells me to finish myself." My lips pinch, the thought causing a new wave of rage to course through me. "Sometimes I masturbate, but it's not the same thing. It's not the orgasm but the intimacy I miss the most."

When I'm met by complete silence, I feel my cheeks flush.

"Sorry. TMI?"

"No, not too much information. It's not enough, actually." He clears his throat, and there's a little swooshing noise. I picture him lying down in his bed, the light on his nightstand on and a sleepy expression on his face. "I just . . . There's a lot I'd like to say to that. I won't, don't worry, but—"

"No, say it."

"Hmm . . . I can't."

"You can," I insist.

"Fine. I may have *occasionally*, once or twice, considered sleeping with you."

I can feel a smile curving my lips.

"And it's not the thought of what I'd get out of it that makes it an *interesting* scenario. It's what I'd do to you, how you'd respond, that makes it—" He clears his throat again. "Let's just say that knowing someone would use you for your body with no consideration for your needs and enjoyment is a fucking sin. A waste and a sin." With a sigh, he adds, "I'll leave it at that."

I open my mouth, though I'm not entirely sure what to say. I just want him to keep talking.

"Well, okay, I'll say one more thing. It's not fair that you should spend the rest of your life faking orgasms. Your fiancé should take care of your pleasure, among many other things."

Among many other things he doesn't do. That's what Ian thinks, and he's right. Frank is supposed to support me, to be there for me. And he's not. He's living his single life while I'm always alone. Except, once again, I'm not *really* alone. "If you're about to suggest I break up with him—" I start, but he quickly cuts me off.

"No, Amelie. I'm suggesting you get his ass back there, sit him down, and tell him you won't let him touch you ever again unless he considers your needs. I'm suggesting you tell your fiancé that if he doesn't pull his act together, he's going to lose you. And he won't manage to win you back." He lets out a disdainful *humph*. "It's inexplicable how he landed you in the first place."

"Maybe," I whisper. Right now, talking to Frank is the last thing I want to do. "Maybe tomorrow."

"It's your birthday, Amelie," Ian insists, and with a chuckle adds, "and you deserve a fucking orgasm."

My head feels light as the room spins around me, and for a second I smile up at the ceiling. Maybe at the absurdity of the situation. "You're right. I deserve an orgasm."

"Yes, you do," he insists.

Standing, I walk to my wardrobe, open my underwear-and-socks drawer, fish around, and grab my vibrator. Once I'm back on the bed, my heart is throbbing out of my chest. I'm not drunk enough to blame this on the alcohol: I think I just lost my mind.

Or, rather, I'm finally making sense.

"Do you think I could . . . do it?"

"Do what?"

"Make myself come."

Silence. I wait, my hand tightly wrapped against the small pink silicone bullet. If he says no, I'll die of embarrassment.

"You want to . . . now?"

"Yes," I breathe out.

"With me?"

"Yes."

"Here? On the phone?"

"Y-yes?"

"Oh. Yeah. Yeah, of course—" He sighs. "Wait, no, Amelie, you're drunk. Tomorrow—"

"I don't care about tomorrow."

"Right now. But Frank—"

"Please, Ian," I say in a low voice as I tighten my hold on the vibrator. "Don't think about Frank, or what happens tomorrow, or . . ." I let out a quick puff of air. "It's just you and me and right now. Tomorrow this will probably be a bad idea, but . . . right now, me and you? Is it a bad idea?"

"No. You and I are never a bad idea," he says in a husky voice that sends a wave of pressure down into my stomach. With a groan, he insists, "Amelie, don't tempt me. I don't have the strength to resist you."

"Is that you trying to change my mind?" I laugh. "Because the thought of being irresistible to you is more than a little hot."

"So is the thought of you masturbating. We're even."

"Ian . . ." I whisper.

"Don't say whatever you're about to say."

"I'm wet."

He groans, then sighs, then groans again for good measure.

"Your voice makes me wet. You make me—"

"Jesus Christ," he breathes. "Stop saying the word 'wet.'"

"How about 'drenched'?" I let my hand slide down my stomach. "I can check."

"Amelie," he whispers reverently. With a winning smile, I let my hand wander farther down, until his voice breaks through the silence again. "No, wait—wait, Amelie."

"Ian, I promise—"

"Listen to me," he says, cutting me off. "Feeling undesirable sucks. I understand you need someone to make you feel wanted. And I want you, Amelie. I want you so much, my cock hurts. I want you so much, my *everything* hurts. I want you so fucking much that when I end this call, I'll have some intense sex with my hand and come so hard my soul will leave my body." He barely pauses to breathe before saying, "But I also care about you. I care about you too much to disrupt your life. Not when you're drunk and emotionally spent. So I'll end the call now."

"Ian!" I blurt out as I sit up. "Wait! Frank—he left."

"What?"

"I just—I knew you'd have questions, and I'm . . ." I swallow. What's a classy way to say *horny, drunk, and depressed*? "I didn't want to talk about it."

"Wait. Wait, wait, wait. Hold on." I do, but he says nothing for a while. "You're single?"

"Yes," I whisper, though it still feels unreal. "I guess I am."

"You're single. Right now," he repeats.

"Yes."

There're a few seconds of silence. Maybe he thinks I'm lying and this is just a ruse to get what I want. Maybe the fact that I've been single for five minutes doesn't change anything.

"Spread your legs."

"I—what?" I ask, my heart jumping up in my throat.

"Spread your legs, Amelie. Tell me if you're drenched."

Fuck.

I lie back down, eyes wide and chest heaving. He didn't ask questions. He understood and . . . well, put my needs above his, because I'm sure he'd like to have about a million clarifications.

My hand slips under my panties, finding the pool of my arousal. I gasp lightly as the tip of my finger grazes my clit, then quickly release a breath. "Yes," I whisper. "I'm soaked."

"Fuck yeah, you are," he rasps. "Touch yourself, Amelie. I've dreamed of hearing you moan in my ear so many fucking times."

My breath hitches, my body arching over the bed as if his words are actually touching me. After sliding my underwear down my thighs, I turn the vibrator on, then slowly move it over my clit. "I wish you were here," I breathe.

"God, me too."

"I wish you were inside me."

He groans, and it's by far the most erotic noise I've ever heard. The thought that I did that to him and I'm not even there . . . I spread my legs wider, whining as my hips writhe against the vibrator.

"Fuck," he says in a coarse voice. "I want to be buried so deep inside you that there's not an inch of space between us— fucking you so hard, you can't kiss me back while you come all over me."

"Jesus Christ, Ian."

"TMI?"

"Not enough," I whimper, images of everything he just described dancing before my eyes. The feeling of fullness with him inside me, his eyes turning into slits as I clamp my legs around him, feel his hands gripping my hips.

"God, you sound spectacular."

So does he, with his raspy, breathy voice. With the way he's fanning quick and shallow breaths over the phone. I can picture them against my neck, against my inner thighs.

"Don't stop, Amelie," he encourages me. "Use your fingers and imagine they're mine. That I'm sucking your clit and fucking you with my hand."

"Oh, God." I do as he asked, letting the vibrator fall to the side. Tightening my hold on the phone, I begin thrusting two fingers inside me, my body squirming with every jolt of pleasure.

"That's it. Just like that."

"Ian?" I ask as I use my thumb to press my clit. I bet he'd be so much better at it.

"Yes, beautiful?"

"Are you doing it too?" I ask. Though I know the answer, I want to hear him say it.

"I almost came twice already."

I chuckle, tilting my head as if I'm cuddling up to him instead of a stupid phone.

"Your laugh is as good as your moans, Amelie."

"Tell me where you are, what you're doing, what you're wearing. Everything."

He exhales, then clears his voice. "I'm sitting on my bed, and I'm wearing black joggers. No shirt because I'm always warm at night. I'm touching myself as slowly as I possibly can without stopping, because I don't want to come before you do, and this is by far the most turned on I've ever been in my life." He lets out a shaky breath. "But I'm always up for a challenge."

"If I were there," I whisper, and before I even get the words out, he breathes harder, "I would lick the tip of your cock."

"Oh, fuck . . ."

"And I'd taste your precum."

"I'd smear your gorgeous lips with it."

"I—I would take all of you in my mouth," I continue, though with the rhythm of my fingers inside me and my thumb over my clit, my voice comes out all shaky.

"I'd push it all the way to the back of your throat and hold you there until you needed to breathe."

Pressure building in my stomach, I whimper. Ian's breathing turns even more erratic, and once he moans again, I grab my vibrator and push it against my clit. "Ian, Ian . . ."

"Oh, not my name," he mutters. "I can't take it, Amelie."

"I'm going to come. I'm gonna come so hard," I pant as my mind empties and my stomach fills.

"Picture me fucking you, Amelie. Hard and fast, stretching you. God, I *need* to fuck you."

"Yes, yes—I need you, Ian. I—" My eyes roll back, and my mouth opens, but no sound comes out. The pleasure is just so strong, it's like my whole body freezes for the most intense couple of seconds.

"Squeeze me inside you, Amelie. Come all over me," he gasps. "Let me hear you orgasm."

Something snaps, and I let out a loud string of pleas and obscene noises, every single working cell in my body lighting me up from the inside.

"Yes, Amelie, holy fuck—"

We both moan, call each other's names. It's so earth-shattering, it almost hurts as the vibrations hit my clit again and again, but I don't stop. I don't want this orgasm, this moment, to ever stop.

"You're mine, Amelie," he growls. I picture his cum gushing out and over his hands as he strokes his erection for me. "Your pleasure is mine. Your orgasms are mine. You're *all . . . fucking . . . mine.*"

My climax keeps rippling out; his too. Maybe it's the booze, but it feels longer than normal. Surely, it's a million times *better* than normal.

"You belong to me, Amelie. Only to me."

I close my eyes, focusing on the tingling warmth coursing through me at his claim. At feeling wanted and precious and someone worth fighting for.

Until out of my lips, again and again, comes the same word.

Yes. Yes. Yes.

31

Until It's Morning

Silence. Well, not silence, but breathing. My heartbeat is pulsating in every inch of my body, every cell of my skin. Drying the sweat off my forehead with the back of my hand, I swallow.

What did I do?

I glance at the phone, tight between my fingers, then burst into hysterical sobs as my stomach knots and my lungs struggle to fill with air.

"Amelie . . ." Ian says in a choked-up voice.

He can't say my name. Not after how he said it a minute ago; not after what we did. How do I come back from this? How could I have sex with another man twenty minutes after my breakup? How do I live with the fact that it was the best sex of my life?

"I'm such a horrible person," I cry.

"No, Amelie. You're not horrible." He sighs, his voice unrecognizable now that it's so sad and hollow. "You're lonely, exhausted, and a little drunk. None of that makes you horrible."

"I—my wedding was supposed to be in a week."

That's all I can think about. A week from today was supposed to be the happiest day of my life. I was going to stand in front of a crowd of people and tell Frank the reasons I love him, then promise to do so for the rest of my life.

And I had sex with Ian twenty minutes after our breakup.

"Do you *want* to get married to him, Amelie?"

I bring a hand to my face, sobs still shaking my lips. I thought I did. That all I wanted was to be the head chef for La Brasserie, that all I needed was to be Frank's wife. But now it feels like the only person I want is the one who won't have me the way I need him to.

"He doesn't need to know." His voice sinks lower. "You had a fight. You broke up. And besides, you were in an open relationship, so you've done nothing wrong."

I squeeze my eyes shut, my head pounding. Hearing his thin voice as he says those words might just break my heart. I know that I'll need to make some hard decisions, but all I can think about right now, at three thirty in the morning and drunk out of my mind, is that I'm hurting the best person I know. "Ian, I'm so sorry."

"I knew what I was doing," he says with a long sigh. "I knew you'd go back to him. Don't feel sorry for me, because I've done this to myself."

God. What am I doing? Ian doesn't deserve this—doesn't deserve to have me plummeting into his life and causing him pain.

I need to stay away from him. To let him live his life in peace. I should have never called.

With a harsher sob, I glance at my phone and hang up.

It immediately vibrates in my hand, his name blinking on the phone through the wobbly filter of my tears. When it stops, the screen lights up with a text.

Ian:
Amelie, pick up. Please.

He calls again. Again I sob. Again I don't answer.

> Please, I'm sorry. I fucked up.

How did *he* fuck up? Of all the people involved in this, he's the one who's *least* to blame.

> Answer the phone. I know we're done,
> but let me hear your voice one last time.

He's right. We're done. Getting married has been my dream for as long as I can remember, and being with Ian would mean giving that up. He hates weddings, hates marriage, and he'll never settle down. And what do I do? I go and fall for him.

The phone lights up with another call, and this time I pick up. If this is the last time, I want to hear his voice too.

He releases a deep breath as soon as I pick up. "I'm sorry. I'm sorry, Amelie. I should have said no, I know I should have, but—"

"It's not your fault, Ian."

"It is. You're obviously going through something. I shouldn't have said yes—I just . . ." He lets out a long exhale. "I have no self-control when it comes to you. I'm sorry."

"*I'm* sorry," I whisper. Tears keep raining down my cheeks, but I'm not sobbing anymore. I don't want that to be the last image of me he has. "I dragged you down in my mess."

"I knew I was playing with fire, Amelie. And besides, I'd let you burn me anytime."

There's a moment of silence in which it sinks in that this is a goodbye. In which he *doesn't* tell me that the mark I left will probably burn forever. And I *don't* tell him that I'll silently feel this way about him for the rest of my life.

It's a depleting, consuming silence.

"Give me tonight. Just tonight, before you go back to him."

"Tonight?" I ask, propping myself up against the headboard and grabbing a tissue from the nightstand to blow my nose.

He sighs. "Just for tonight, be mine. We've fucked it up anyway. But if I were there, and we had fucked it up in the right way, I'd be kissing you right now. I'd hold you between my arms, touch every bit of you, whisper words in your ear. I'd spend the night fucking it up some more and making you smile. And then I'd be gone in the morning. Let me do that."

"Ian, I—"

"Please, Amelie. Just one night—not even an entire night. Three hours, until it's morning. And then I swear you'll never hear from me again. I'll let you live your life."

My head throbs with the first signs of a hangover, and that's still not the most painful thing going on. Nor is the awareness that Frank and I broke up, although that's a close second. This is the last time I'll talk to Ian. Forever. A night with him is the least I can get.

"Yes," I whisper.

"Yes?"

"Yes," I repeat.

A breath of relief breaks through his lips. "Thank you." He pauses. "So . . . hmm . . . What did you and the girls do?"

I chuckle, drying the tears off my face, although some more follow. I tell him about my day, then he tells me about his. And then we fuck it up some more, superbly. We push the sadness, the sense of guilt down. And instead we spend our last three hours together chatting, laughing, telling each other loving, beautiful lies.

Until it's morning.

A gentle squeeze of my shoulder drags me away from a dreamless sleep. I blink a few times, waiting for the room to focus before my eyes, a knife carving the inside of my brain. When I see Frank offering me a glass of water, it all comes back to me.

The party, the fight, the night I spent with Ian. My hands pat the mattress until I find my phone, and when I turn the screen on, my heart sinks into my chest. Just like he promised, he's gone. I fell asleep with his words in my ear, and now the call is disconnected. No new messages.

"Are you feeling better?" Frank asks.

I nod, setting my phone down and grabbing the glass of water. I drink it all in small sips, more memories making heat spark all through my body. "You—you came back."

"Yes." He rubs his forehead, then sits next to me on the bed. "Yes, of course I did. Last night was . . ."

"I think we need to talk."

He nods, then slowly walks out of the bedroom. "I'll make coffee."

After I splash some cold water on my face and pull my hair back with some pins, I join him in the kitchen. There's a cup on the table, and he points at it as he takes a seat. His shoulders are tense, his forehead furrowed. I have to tell him what happened, and this will likely be the last conversation we have. The last coffee we share. The last time we sit in our kitchen together.

"I'm sorry about last night, Ames. I really am. But at two a.m., and after I've had a fucking long day . . ." He pushes his glasses up and sighs. "I really wasn't in the mood to discuss our sex life." Shaking his head, he continues, "And the way you threw yourself at me—"

"Yesterday was my birthday."

He blinks, and as he runs the numbers in his head, he closes his eyes. "Shit." His shoulders drop, and with an apologetic look, he takes my hand. "I can't believe I forgot. Why didn't you say anything? We would have gone out for dinner or something before the bachelorette party."

"It doesn't matter," I say with a whiff of apprehension. "That isn't what I want to talk about."

"No, Ames. Of course it matters. I should have—"

"Last night, when you left, I—" I cut him off as my heart skips a beat. Unable to meet his eyes, I focus on the dark brew inside my cup. "I was so angry. I felt lonely, and I needed to—I wanted to—"

Leaning backward, he studies me. "You're scaring me. What happened?"

"I . . ." God, I'm going to faint. "I was with Ian. We had—we . . ."

His hand leaves mine, and though I know I owe him the respect to look into his eyes while I tell him what happened, I still can't bring myself to do it. "Ian?" He shakes his head. "Doesn't he live in Mayfield?"

"Yes."

"So how—you invited him over?"

"I called him." He watches me with a confused expression. "We had . . . we—phone sex."

"Phone sex."

I nod. He remains still for a while, and I do, too, as I wait for his reaction. Then his lips curve into a smile and he bursts out laughing, immediately clamping his hand over his mouth when he sees the look of horror on my face. "Phone sex? What the hell does that mean? You—you listened to each other?"

"Y-yeah."

With his cup set on the table, he snorts derisively. His shoulders shake, his fingers pressing his eyes as chuckles bubble out of his lips despite the fact that he's obviously trying to hold them back.

I'm not sure how to react.

"Okay, well . . . I thought—" He suppresses his smile, his fingers scratching his head. "It's not like you had *sex* with him."

My eyes bug out. Not that I'd like to dig a deeper grave for myself, but I did. "I—phone sex is . . . sex. It's right there in the word."

"Yeah, but he never touched you. He didn't even see you."

So? That's not what sex is about. Seeing and touching. Okay, I guess those are a big part of it. But the point of sex is an emotional connection, and the point of me doing it with someone else is that I have none with Frank.

"Right. So you don't mind," I say, dramatically waving my hand. "No big deal."

"No, of course I mind. But . . . it's like you watched a porno. Less, actually. Like you listened to a guy jerking off." He bursts out laughing again. "I'm sorry, but it's so . . . pathetic. Why would he do that?"

He uses the cup to hide his next chuckle, and I don't know what to say. It's not pathetic that hearing me masturbate would turn him on enough to do it himself. It's not pathetic that what we did was the most intimate sex I've ever experienced. What's pathetic is the way he's reacting.

"I have feelings for him," I hear myself say. The words drag out of my lips, but as soon as I pronounce them, I know I wouldn't take them back even if I could. This is the most sensible thing I've said in the past six months, isn't it? I don't know why I tried to keep my feelings buried. Why I tried to deny them as strenuously as I did. To what end? It's so much easier to put it all out there. Now Frank can do with this information whatever he pleases.

He sets his cup down, all signs of amusement gone from his face. "What are you talking about?"

"You heard me. I have feelings for Ian."

We stare at each other, and for a second I hardly recognize him. His brows are taut, his jaw set, his lips twisted in a disgusted sneer. "Because he jerked off on a phone call?"

"No. Last night has nothing to do with it."

"Really? Because you might think he's interested in you, but he's only after one thing. And trust me, it isn't marriage."

I open my mouth to speak, then close it. Frank knows nothing about Ian, and I'd point that out if it weren't for the fact that he's dead right. Ian doesn't want a marriage, a wedding. He wants parties on Tuesdays and dates on Thursdays. Still, it has nothing to do with my feelings for him.

"Okay, fine." He rubs a hand over his beard, his glasses fogging up as if his anger is heating up his face. "You have a crush. We said our agreement stood as long as there was nothing emotional, so just stop talking to him."

Unfortunately, I'm one step ahead of him. My mind replays every moment after Ian and I had sex. The chatter, the unpopular opinions, the cute pickup lines he looked up and read to me. There won't be any more of that. Surely, there won't be any more of his groggy, post-orgasm voice calling me beautiful like that's my name. There won't be any more texts and calls and incessant flirting. No more Ian and Amelie.

"Ames? Did you hear what I said?"

"Hmm?"

"You *have* to stop talking to him."

With a distracted nod, I look out the window. "I know." I'm almost numb. All the anger I thought would come up during this conversation, all the built-up resentment and regret, they're not here. There's nearly nothing, yet it's the most overwhelmed I've ever felt. Like when a bomb explodes, and for a second there's just light and noise.

Then everything that exists is wiped away.

"Well, are you gonna?"

I meet Frank's gaze, furious from behind his glasses, and nod.

Releasing a breath, he shifts on his chair. His hand wipes his forehead, his eyes studying the table as he processes the news. He looks insulted rather than upset. "I can't believe this, Ames."

Scornful and bitter, his words burn into my brain. I know he didn't think this would happen, and, if possible, that pisses me off even more. "Why not?"

"What do you mean?"

"Did you not believe I'd sleep with another man?" I ask as I rest my chin on my fist.

"You didn't sleep with him."

"Yes, I fucking did," I snap. "And if he'd been here, I would have done it all the same but without the phone. With all the touching and seeing you're so fond of."

Through his lashes, he glares at me. "Listen, I get that you're pissed off, but—"

"But what, Frank?" I ask in a much more composed voice than I expect from myself. "Do you realize this is all your fault? All of this—do you understand it happened because of you?"

He frowns down at the table. "Right. Blame your *feelings* on me. I said we weren't supposed to have anything emotional, Ames."

I nod. "And I told you there was a risk it would happen."

He holds my gaze for a while, his jaw clenched and his lips compressed. Eventually he looks away and the silence stretches on, then some more. I don't know how long we sit there, contemplating our failures and regrets, reflecting on the past six months.

He clears his throat. "Well, I propose we end this whole open-relationship thing. The wedding is in a week anyway."

I'm somewhat taken by surprise, but the relief I expected to feel isn't there. I figured it would feel like completing a test, and it does, but with the awareness that I've failed. That *we* failed.

"Yesterday was your birthday and I broke up with you. I was a huge ass." He stands and holds on to my elbow, pulling me up. Once I'm standing in front of him, he wraps his arms around me, and I can't help but feel stiff against his chest. "We're fine, okay? Let's never talk about it again."

I stand there as he drops kiss after kiss on my cheek, too stunned to know what to say or think or do.

"How do you feel about eating out? We could call everyone and celebrate your birthday. And you'll have to excuse me for a couple of hours, because I'm going to go get you the most amazing present of your life."

When I smile weakly, he kisses the tip of my nose. "I love you, Ames."

"I . . ."

I'd let you burn me anytime.

"I love you too," I breathe out.

His fingers gently graze my cheek, then he takes a step back. "Okay. Give me two hours. I'll plan dinner, get your present, and be back with cake too." Pointing a finger at me, he grins. "You make a list of what we need to do for the wedding, take a shower, read. Just . . . relax. Today's your day."

"Okay," I whisper.

Satisfied, he nods and turns around, then faces me again before he can disappear into the corridor. "Really, stop talking to him, okay?"

Crossing my arms around my stomach, I nod. "I already told him we can't talk anymore."

"See? That's proof of what I'm saying." He inhales deeply. "Don't give it a second thought. It was just a stupid mistake."

Right. A stupid mistake.

32

More than One Night

Ian and I tumble into the room, an entangled mess of kisses and loud pants, but as soon as his fingers move to the short hem of my dress, then squeeze the highest point of my thighs, I flinch, my muscles turning rigid under his touch.

"Okay. Maybe we should stop right here," he says softly as his hands run up my sides. "And we could just keep all our clothes on and sit down—lie down, even—and kiss a little." His gaze bounces between my eyes and my lips, as if he's horny and afraid I'll bolt again.

"I'm just . . ." I rub my temple, the tension causing my head to hurt. I don't understand what's happening to me. Why every time I come close to having sex with the most perfect man to ever land in front of me, I end up freezing. "I think I'm panicking."

"That's a pretty safe bet. Care to elaborate on why, exactly?"

"Because—"

He nods, encouraging me to speak. "Because . . ."

"I'm afraid that it'll . . . suck."

His smile falls, a single chuckle shaking his chest. "Well, gee, thanks, Amelie."

"That's not what I mean, Ian. It has nothing to do with you."
I take his hand in mine. "After Frank, I just can't go through that
again. I spent fifteen years with a man I had boring, average sex
with, and I can't take a single more second being a complacent
body for someone else to use."

His jaw tightens, his shoulders tensing before he entangles his
fingers with mine. "I'm not Frank, Amelie. If we ever do have sex,
it'll be great. I wouldn't have it any other way. And besides, it's us.
Sex between us was great even when we weren't in the same room."

"But what if it's not about him—Frank?" I begin pacing back and
forth in front of the bed, my nerves getting the best of me, and I
wonder if I even stand a chance. Maybe I'm just too ruined.

"Then who?"

I look into his eyes, wondering if I should say it, only to come
to the quick conclusion that if there's anyone in the world I'd be
comfortable discussing this with, it's Ian. "What if it's me?"

His shoulders sag, and he shakes his head as a sad expression
takes over his features. "Amelie . . . no, of course not. It's not you."

"But what if it is? What if I just can't enjoy sex? What if I'm
frigid and dysfunctional and basic and just . . . broken?"

He slowly walks toward me. Without saying a word, he wraps
his arms around me, the weight of them pressing me against
his chest. It immediately soothes me, and, closing my eyes, I
lay my head against him and listen to his heartbeat through his
sweater.

"Amelie," he whispers, "even if that were true, if you liked only
basic sex or didn't like sex at all, it wouldn't mean you're broken.
You're perfect. But this has never been about you." He presses a
kiss next to my ear, then, in a soft voice, continues: "You want to
know what the problem is, beautiful? The problem is that you've
been used, ignored, and hurt. The problem is that you spent so

much time feeling you aren't enough, that you aren't worth loving and cherishing, that the people in your life actually made you believe it's the truth."

I close my eyes, his sweater in my fists as I hold him tighter.

"But it's not the truth." He kisses the same spot beside my ear over and over again. "And if it takes me the rest of my life to show you that, that's what I'll do. We'll have our one night together in twenty years, if that's how long it takes you to understand." He clears his voice. "I mean, I'm not *encouraging* us to wait two decades, but, you know . . ."

God, this man adores me. Reveres me. He's freaking smitten, one-night stand or not. Though I can't take another man ignoring my needs in the bedroom, being afraid Ian will be one of them is downright ridiculous.

Smiling against the soft cashmere, I nod. "You might not have to wait that long," I whisper as I look up, meeting his gaze.

He tucks some hair behind my ear. "Well, sex is off the table tonight. Let's take things slowly, and whenever you . . ."

I kiss the corner of his lips, my hands running along his chest and around his neck.

". . . feel like we should . . ."

I kiss him again, this time nipping his bottom lip with my teeth.

In a lower voice, he goes on, ". . . r-revisit the topic, then we can . . ."

At the next kiss, his hand grips my ass, pulling me closer, and mine travels underneath his sweater, feeling the corded muscles and smooth skin heave under my touch. "Ian, please, fuck me."

He groans, then takes my mouth with his, his fingers holding on to the small of my back tighter until my dress crumples up in his fist. "Can I?"

"Yeah." His mouth presses against my throat, little gasps coming out of me when his tongue traces down the side of my neck.

"Just to be clear: you're okay with me taking your dress off."

I purse my lips and, holding myself back, look into his dubious eyes. We definitely need to fix this before we do anything at all. "Ian, I know I've been acting a little crazy, but . . . please don't do that."

"Do what?"

"Don't treat me like I'll shatter if you do something wrong. Don't hold back or treat me differently or be delicate or—" When he wiggles his brows playfully, I chuckle. "No, I just mean—"

"I know what you mean," he whispers as he grips my hips. His teeth nibble my earlobe, a soft sigh escaping me at the light sting. "You're right. You're not fragile, Amelie." He steps forward until the backs of my knees touch the mattress. "You're starved."

I nod frantically as he looks down at my dress, eyes flaring, and once his lips crash against mine, his fingers tug on the fabric. We pause the kiss as he slides my dress over my head, and as the cold air hardens my nipples, I'm suddenly aware I'm completely naked except for the long socks. No bra, and he's still got my panties. I'm *naked*.

And shaved, thankfully.

"Amelie . . ." he softly sighs as his hand traces my chain all the way down between my breasts. "You're beautiful."

He leans forward, his lips pressing my shoulder, then my chest. His hot, wet mouth wraps around one of my nipples, and, clutching his hair, I let him lower me onto the bed.

As I grip the edge of the mattress, he kneels on the floor before me, his hands softly moving up my ankles, my shins, then my knees, pulling my socks off, first one, then the other, kissing both my thighs, and I'm pretty sure my heart is beating so fast that he can hear it from there. Can he also tell just how wet I am? Because I can feel it dripping down my thigh, probably onto his sheets.

Oh, God. Can one be *too* wet? Maybe that's what happens when you don't have sex for a long time. Will he think it's weird? Will he think it's disgusting?

His eyes shoot to my face. "Amelie."

"I—I'm fine."

"No you're not." He continues kissing my thighs, then softly biting before passing his warm, wet tongue on my sensitive skin. "How about, instead of lying, you voice your concerns?"

My ovaries dance the waltz. He *cares*. I don't know why I need to keep being reminded of it, but does it really matter? He gets it, and he's not here to use me, to take his orgasm and go. He wants me to enjoy it, and he won't continue until he makes sure I do. "I'm just afraid I'm a little too . . . *excited*," I explain as I quickly glance down.

His eyes follow mine as his hands stroke my outer thighs up to my hips. "Yeah?"

"Yeah," I say on a breath.

His throat works as he looks up at me. "Let me see." With his chest pounding under his sweater and his lips parted, he looks as tense as a bowstring. "Please," he continues in a deep, raspy voice, "spread your legs for me. I *need* to see how wet you are."

When I nod, his hands lightly tug my knees apart, and I let him. His eyes roll down, and, releasing a quick breath, his shoulders drop slightly. "God, yes. Look at you, dripping for me."

"Ian," I gasp as he sticks out his tongue and licks higher up my inner thigh. My eyes close, goose bumps breaking out on my skin and my fingers tightening in the sheets on either side of me. With his mouth so close to the mark and his hot breath fanning over my drenched skin, pressure builds up in my stomach as if he's doing much more than teasing me. "I—" I gasp at the contact of his stubble against my skin. "I need you."

"Hmm." His teeth pinch my flesh. "Show me where you want me." When I only stare at him, his fingers entangle with mine, and he brings them to the back of his head with a lascivious smile. "Show me, Amelie."

He pulls me to the edge of the mattress, and I'm splayed out in front of him, trembling as I guide him closer. Once his lips meet my slick skin, I moan, then moan louder as his tongue peeks out and sweeps through me, my body squirming. He smiles, then slides his hand up my thigh to grab my hip, his mouth wrapping around my clit and sucking.

"Oh—oh my God," I breathe, shifting forward to give him better access. Each of his strokes sends my hips bucking against his mouth, my eyes rolling to the back of my head, my mouth opening with needy whimpers. It's like my brain has been dipped in sugar and my body is turning liquid, until eventually I can't hold myself up any longer, and I fall back against the mattress.

He hooks my legs over his shoulders, flattening his tongue and lapping all the way across my slit. "Your taste." He inhales deeply. "God, you smell so fucking good."

"Ian," I murmur as I pull his hair to guide him closer. "Please."

"Don't rush me, Amelie." He teases my clit again and again. "I've waited a whole year. We're taking our time."

He rolls his tongue up and down leisurely, his fingers tightening around my hips every time my back arches and my feet press against his back.

"I'm—it's so good, so—" I swing my hips, rushing toward the orgasm Ian is keeping out of my reach. His tongue is sinful, jolting against my clit with erotic wet noises. It's so unfair, after how long I've waited, that the man who can definitely give me pleasure would decide to measure it out.

"Relax, beautiful." His tongue pushes and releases in quick

surges against my clit, my legs shaking against his shoulders as the sheets crumple in my fists. I need to find *something* to hold me anchored, but as my forehead glistens with sweat, and pressure builds in my stomach, I can feel my control being swept away. I can feel myself flying.

His finger pushes against me, then slides inside, thrusting in and out until he rubs a spot that makes my eyes cross. It's my undoing. My whines turn into begging, and, squeezing his head with my thighs, I go under. "Don't stop—don't do—" *Anything different* is what I meant to say, but an orgasm bursts through my body, my pussy clenching around his finger, against his mouth. My muscles tense up and relax in sweet, demolishing waves for so long it's like it'll never stop.

When it wears down, my whole body seems made of rubber. His hands stroke my thighs, his lips brushing my skin softly. Wiping my forehead, I look down at him. He's smiling—not smug, just pleased. And he should be.

"Watching you come is . . ." He shakes his head, a hungry expression on his face, then his mouth is dancing with mine again as he leans forward. "If I were keen to share, people would pay for a ticket to watch." Dragging his fingers up, he taps my bottom lip. Once my mouth is open, his fingers slide in, slick in my orgasm. I taste myself on him, my tongue swirling around his fingers as he exhales. "But this show is only for me, isn't it?"

I nod. I can still feel my climax tingling through me, my heart beating fast as he removes his fingers and I catch my breath. "You made me come."

"It wasn't that difficult either. Whoever failed before must have not spent more than two minutes trying."

"Ha-ha."

"I mean it," he says with a chuckle. "Look." He stands, then

Letizia Lorini

grips my ass and slides me across the bed. Once he kneels between my legs, I almost come all over again. He's so hot, all dressed in his blue sweater, with his jeans barely containing his erection, while I'm naked and undone in front of him.

"This is your favorite," he says. He leans down and presses his tongue against my clit, swiping through me and sucking the endless flow of pleasure. Once again his fingers grasp the backs of my thighs and his shoulders push my knees apart. "Oh—okay. You're right, that's my—"

He lets my legs go and pushes his finger inside as I jolt. "And this"—he rubs his finger again and again against the same spot until my hips jerk up and I cry out—"this is your G-spot, beautiful Amelie," he says with shallow breaths.

His mouth wraps around my clit again, and everything turns dark as my eyes close and my fingers bury themselves in his hair.

I catch my breath from my second orgasm of the night as I watch Ian, still dressed, still crouched between my legs. I've officially been doing sex all wrong until today.

"What are you doing?" I ask when the tickle of his lips turns into a light sting on my inner thigh. "You can't feed off humans without asking for consent, Dracula."

He lets go for a moment as he looks into my eyes. "I'm giving you a hickey."

"Why?" I giggle as he continues sucking, then I let my head drop. I guess he'll tell me once he's done.

Not even a minute later, he sets my legs down and lies on top of me, holding himself up on his elbow. "So that you'll have a mark from me. One only you can see."

His soft sweater presses against my hot skin as his erection rests on my waist, and I trail my hands down his firm body, then unbutton his jeans. "I'm sorry I made this so difficult," I whisper. I feel so silly now. Of course sex with Ian would be amazing. We've only just begun, and it's already the best sex I've ever had in my life.

Smiling, he kisses me. "Are you referring to the last few days, or the year before that?"

"I take the apology back."

He rises to his knees between my legs, hands clenched on the sides of his sweater. "Can I take this off, or will you freak out again?"

No, I need him to take his clothes off. I need to see his tattoos, trace them all with my tongue, bite those thick thighs and arms and those delicious pecs. I want his skin on mine, our sweat mixing, our breaths scorching each other's body.

I pull myself up and unzip his jeans. His sweater comes off, so I push him off the bed and pull his jeans down.

Fuck, this man. He's perfect. His diet of cheap snacks and fork-free meals works wonders on him, because as much as my eyes scan him all over, I can't find a spot that isn't toned and hard. Those arms—I want them moving me from one position to the other. I want his wide chest against mine as he presses me on the mattress; I want to hold on to his neck as he plunges inside me and I bite his shoulder to smother my cries.

When his lips move, I force my brain to reconnect. "What?"

"Ask me again." His eyes flicker as he touches his erection over his briefs. "Beg me, Amelie."

What—oh. I bring my hands to his perfect chest and move my mouth to his, our eyes on each other's. "Fuck me, Ian, please," I whisper.

He lets out a strangled noise as I'm settled onto the bed, his body trapping me under him. "Yes, Amelie."

Locking my arms behind his neck, I spread my legs wider to

make space for him, his hard cock rubbing against me from beneath a thin layer of cotton. Our conversation about dirty talk comes back to me. What was it he told me to say? "Use me as your dirty little fuck toy."

"Fuck, yes," he murmurs. His lips take mine, and he rolls us around until I'm on top of him. He sits up on the edge of the bed, mouth pressing on my neck and my chest reverently, like he's softly marking important spots on a treasure map. "I'll fuck you all night long, Amelie. I'll watch you take it from every angle and learn all the things that drive you crazy."

I whine as I rub myself against him, the friction creating a wet patch on his briefs. I can't even care. I crave him. At this very moment, I'd watch the world fall apart to feel him inside me. "Please, take them off."

He pulls his briefs down, my eyes catching a glimpse of his erection before he distracts me with a kiss, and the warm skin of his shaft presses against my core. "Let me grab the condoms," he says, pulling me up gently.

"No, I'm on the pill," I tell him. "And I've been tested after *him*." He nods. "What about you?"

"All clear on my side." He leans back a little, his eyes studying mine. "Are you sure you want to—"

"Yes."

"Okay." He softly blows a breath against my neck. "Lift your hips for me, beautiful," he whispers then, his lips only barely open. As I hold myself on his shoulders, the tip of his cock lines up against me, a soft sigh leaving me on contact. I clench around nothing, and as I push myself down, he stretches me deliciously with his erection. "Slow down: we're not in a rush."

"Speak for yourself," I say, my voice unsteady.

He smiles triumphantly as he grips my hips and holds me in

place. "I speak for you, too, tonight, Amelie." Then he lowers me, his jaw clenching as he groans. "Tonight, you do as I say. You'll savor every inch of my cock, every slow push, every filthy word I whisper in your ear. For as long as we both can take it."

I clamp around him as he fills me some more.

"Show me you understand," he says, letting go of my hips.

I fight every single one of my instincts telling me to hang on for dear life and shove myself down and toward pleasure, and instead gently lower myself a few inches.

"That's it." A breath trembles out of his lips as his eyelids flutter. "Good—more than good. Perfect. You're my perfect girl."

"I am," I whine as my head desperately bobs up and down.

"Yes, you are." He kisses me, his arm looped around my back as he lets me descend onto him a little more, then a little more until I'm sitting on his legs. He's crammed into me so deep, we might be fused as one now. "God, I knew you were made for me."

Stealing kisses, I move up and down, drenching him with my recent orgasms. He feels so fucking wonderful, there's quickly a familiar twist in my stomach. Looking into his eyes is the best part yet, because he loves it just as much as I do. His bottom lip disappears under his teeth, his jaw flexing as if he's struggling to patiently savor it just as much as I am.

His hands cup my ass, pushing and pulling along with my movements just as his face falls against the crook of my neck. He mumbles words against my skin, but I grasp only my name before he spreads loving kisses against my shoulder.

"I don't think one time will be enough," he says once he lifts his head again.

Whining, I nod. He won't find any argument here, because if I could, I'd stick to this very position, this very moment in time, forever. "More than once. All night long."

"More than one night," he whispers.

His eyes melt into mine as I squeeze him inside, his body flinching as he shoves me all the way down. It hits differently, maybe because I know I made him lose control, maybe because of what he said. It might not mean anything, of course. Yet it feels like it means something. It feels like it means everything, and everything is what I want.

His hands move to my forehead, gently pushing some hair away. Tightening my arms around his neck, I trace the shape of his jaw with my tongue, his skin pleasantly salty. I look down between us, at our bodies writhing together in a dance that builds up my pleasure slowly and surely. It's like climbing up step by step and getting higher by the second, not knowing when the release will hit.

"You're a fucking goddess, Amelie." His eyes burn deeply into mine—they're famished, the center of all his need, then his hot and warm mouth wraps around my nipple as his cheeks hollow out and he sucks.

"Ian!" I can feel it getting closer, the orgasm building up in my stomach with every new pump of his cock. "Ian, I—"

His hand slips between us, his finger rubbing my clit. "Come, beautiful Amelie. All over me. Don't hold back."

I don't think I could if I wanted to as my eyes cross and my stomach clenches. His fingers skillfully work me up, rubbing in a circular motion that's just the right speed, his thrusts maintaining the same delicious pace. When his lips find mine, I drown my moans against his mouth until it hits. Then, as everything melts down, I can't kiss him back anymore. Only arch my back and curl my toes and desperately call his name.

"Holy—" His breath hitches, his fingers digging into my hips. "I'm—I need to—can't—"

When I give him a crazed nod, his hands push me down and up, his hold so strong, he's probably bruised the skin of my hips. His eyes roll back as he moans, and it's the most delicious noise. Especially when he repeats my name, and I feel his orgasm release, hot and dense inside me, one gorgeous spill followed by another.

"So. *Fucking*. Perfect," he mumbles as his shoulders relax with the last of his stuttering thrusts. He kisses my cheek, my nose, the side of my head. Through it all, his eyes remain closed, his hands traveling up my spine and to the back of my hair, holding me in place. "Perfect and mine."

"Yes," I softly say as I rest my forehead against his.

"Holy shit, Amelie." His eyes open, sweet and blue and so full of affection, they overwhelm me in the best possible way. "I planned to do a lot more, you know."

"Did you?" I ask. My muscles are stiff, the sweat sticking to my skin, making me shiver as my body cools down.

"Mm-hmm." Tightening his hold on my hair, he grins with self-satisfaction. "I'm hardly discouraged, but I was planning to do more *before* needing some recovery time."

With a chuckle, I reach out for his face, but when I lean forward for a kiss, his hand keeps me in place, my hair lightly pulled back.

"Amelie," he says in a rush, his tongue wetting his lips. "The way you feel when you come with my cock deep inside you . . ." He leans forward to whisper in my ear. "You make me powerless. You own me."

My fingers squeeze his shoulders.

"Look what you did to me."

He gently pulls my hair until my face is tilted down; then, with his other hand, he maneuvers my hips up. His cock slides out, quickly followed by gushes of his cum. I whimper, the sight of it so erotic and filthy, I could start again this minute.

"You like that?" he asks in a breathy voice as more of his pleasure spills out of me. His fingers slide through my folds, all the way to my clit, and my body arches as I gasp. "You like it when I fill you up, beautiful?"

"Yes," I whimper.

"Good. I like it too." He smiles, then whispers, "How about I clean you up in the shower, then I throw you back on this bed and mess you up all over again?"

I nod, my heart drumming, and force myself not to ask him if cleaning up is really *that* necessary.

"Okay." He helps me up, pulling me close for a kiss, then a second one, then a third one that turns into a full make-out session. Slowly, we make our way into the bathroom, and once we're both in the small shower and under a jet of hot water, his hands rest on my back, mine on his chest. His hands cup my cheeks, my hands grasp his arms, and there's a soft look in his eyes that makes me shiver. His hair is darker, sticking to his forehead as it becomes wet, and in the warm fog, covered by droplets of water, he's as gorgeous as ever.

For a second, as he rubs his thumb on my wet skin and smiles, I think I hear him say it. Say that he loves me, that he treasures me, that he'll never let me go.

But he doesn't, and just as beautifully as it appeared, his smile tragically dies. "Amelie, I . . ."

My hands flinch away as my heart squeezes.

He's about to reject me. He'll say that though the sex was amazing—and it undoubtedly was for both of us—it can't happen again, and what he said about wanting it to be more than one night was just the result of his passion.

It'll break my heart. I knew it was a lie when I told him I could handle a night of casual sex with him, of course. But I figured something was better than nothing. And it was, except that now he'll . . .

"Hey, hey." His fingers graze my neck. With a gentle pull, our bodies stick together again and my forehead drops against his perfect pecs as tears run down my face and mix with the water. It's not fair that I'd start crying, that I'd make him feel guilty for doing what he said he would and giving me what he promised. But I can't stop.

The thought that this will never happen again is the final blow—the blow that has my spark fading into nothingness. It's the final confirmation that Ian is another thing I've lost.

"Why are you crying, beautiful?"

"Because you're about to dump me," I whisper.

His arms tighten around me, his lips planting kisses on the top of my head. "No, Amelie. No dumping, I promise."

Daring to look up at his face, I see the sincerity of his words, the gravity of his gaze. Maybe he's not about to dump me, but he has something to say. I can see it. "Then what is it?" I breathe.

He swallows, doubt moving through his eyes. As if he's considering whether he truly should say whatever is on his mind. In a second, my fear ripples, my mind zeroing on the one, most terrifying possibility.

What if he asks about my restaurant? What if he figures out there's a secret I've been keeping from him, and it involves his father?

"I think . . . I think I need to know about Frank. I need to know what happened."

Oh. Frank. That's it—he just wants to know about my ex. I let out a deep sigh. Though it's not exactly my favorite topic, he deserves to get the full story, and I'm just so relieved I get to keep my secret buried for another day. If I can help it, I'll hide it forever.

When I look up at the dark blue spots in his eyes, they look like deep oceans surrounded by shallow waters. "All right, so the last time you and I talked—"

"Please, spare me the painful recap. Just tell me what happened after."

"That's when everything went down," I explain as the water trickles down our bodies and steam fills the room. "On the day of my wedding."

33

It Doesn't End with a Wedding

– THE DAY OF AMELIE'S WEDDING –

The hairdresser smiles at the mirror, and I return her joyful expression before averting my eyes. My stomach is a tangled mess of emotions, and since this morning I've held myself back from gagging twice already.

"We're almost done," she says, to which I distractedly nod. It's the first moment I'm sort of alone since the day started and I was hurried out of the apartment and into a cab by Frank's mom. She's so nervous, it almost feels like she's the one getting married in three hours.

"Your dress is beautiful," the hairdresser says. I look up at the reflection of her kind eyes in the mirror, and she points at it. "I saw it hanging."

"Thank you," I breathe as I throw a look at the champagne princess gown. My backup dress. My voice is thin, barely audible, but she seems satisfied with my answer as she curls a lock of hair with the straightener.

"Are you sure you don't want me to add some extensions?"

"No, only some curls."

There's a knock at the door and, without waiting for a greeting,

Martha and Barb walk into the room. They shriek as my eyes meet theirs, and my heart palpitates. They're both beautiful in their short, light blue dresses, but seeing those outfits only reminds me that this is happening. This is real. It's the day of my wedding.

"How's the bride doing?" Barb asks, dropping a kiss on my cheek.

"A little nervous, honestly."

"That's perfectly fine. I freaked out before my wedding. Remember?" she says.

I nod, but I can't. She was brimming with excitement, counting down the seconds until she could walk down the aisle in her dress. She wasn't fighting against her breakfast like I am right now.

"Where's the photographer? Shouldn't he be taking pictures?" Martha asks, her head bobbing to either side of the room.

"No, I think he took a billion. He was starting to get on my nerves."

"Don't be silly. You need pictures of you in the dress." Throwing a disgruntled look at it, she gives me a tight-lipped smile. "Then maybe after the wedding you can explain why you went through the trouble of *stealing* my dress and you won't even wear it."

She leaves the room as I sigh, and Barb takes a seat next to me, then passes me a flute of champagne. "Happy wedding day."

"Thank you."

Her smile wavers. "Are you good?"

"I don't know." I swallow, my throat as dry as dust. Time is running out and I don't know what to do, who can help me climb out of the spiral of panic I'm losing myself to. "What if I'm not sure? What if this is a mistake?"

She shakes her head. "No, of course not. You and Frank love each other so much. It's jitters."

"But what if it isn't?" I ask, my voice cracking. "Since we got engaged, things with Frank have changed, Barb. And then . . . I got close to Ian, and now I don't know if this is what I want anymore."

Her lips part in shock. "Ian? Who's Ian?"

"And this—today wasn't supposed to be like this. Here, with the wrong dress, the wrong flowers, the wrong—"

"Here we are!" Martha announces, reappearing with the photographer. Both the hairdresser and Barb are wide-eyed, but when I clear my throat and smile, they follow my lead, pretending nothing happened.

"It's nerves," Barb whispers, her eyes fixed on mine until I nod.

She nods, too, but I don't think the makeup artist covered my pale skin very well, because her eyes scout my face. Maybe she can see the dark circles around my eyes, my sunken cheeks. I haven't slept properly in weeks.

Why is it so fucking warm in here? It's only the first week of spring.

The photographer instructs me to look in one direction and try out another pose as the hairdresser completes her work. Then it's time to fit into the dress. It takes two people and a whole lot of swearing, but in under half an hour my shoes, gown, and veil are on. Martha and Barb talk around me. They say how beautiful the location is, comment on the guests who have arrived and their outfits, and speak of how they're looking forward to the lunch, since my dad prepared it.

Their voices don't reach me. They echo, like I'm wrapped in a plastic bubble, isolated. Instead, one thought torments me, over and over again.

I'm making a mistake.

I can keep pretending I don't know, that everything is fine, but it won't change the truth. Things went to shit a long time ago, and I've ignored all the signs.

I almost want to hit myself. Not wanting to let go at first made sense. It's almost excusable. But how did I get here? How did I get to the day of my wedding, knowing it'll end in divorce? There's no way I can go through with this. I need help. I need something—*someone*. Anyone.

My phone beeps, the vibration making it rattle against the table.

It can't be, can it?

My fingers tremble so much, I struggle to grab the phone, and when I check the notifications, I find the simplest and most complicated message I've ever received in my life.

PFP.

It's Ian. I don't have his number saved anymore, but the text dispels any doubts. Does he seriously want me to send him a picture? He must know it's the day of my wedding. Is he reaching out to check whether I'm actually going through with it?

I'd say I can't possibly be so cruel as to actually send a selfie back, but, knowing Ian, this might well be his way of getting over me. Nothing less sexy than a bride, after all.

I point the phone at the mirror, then snap a picture. This time around, I don't force a smile on my face. I don't pinch my cheeks or straighten my hair. It's always been pointless, and it'd make even less sense today.

Holding the phone in one hand, I stare back into the mirror at my champagne-colored princess wedding dress. At the laced top, the draped gown. At my long veil and flawless makeup. It's all wrong. Everything's so wrong.

Maybe Ian will see my text in time. He always did. Maybe he'll text back and tell me the solution to the mess I'm in. I'm supposed to get married in two hours, and I'm floundering.

I hate this dress, this stuffy villa. Even the menu isn't what I want, but there was no discussion with my dad. Nothing's right, and I'd be okay with it if I were sure about the man I chose to marry, but I'm not.

"Your phone." Martha turns to the mirror, her eyes meeting mine.

"What?"

"Isn't that your phone?" she repeats.

I look down at the screen just as my ears stop buzzing and hear the ringtone: Ian's number blinking on the screen. He's calling me. Ian is calling me.

A wave of adrenaline hits me as I turn to my friends. "I need to take this. Do you mind?"

"Who is it?" Martha asks.

My eyes meet Barb's, whose brows rise questioningly.

"What's going on?" Martha asks as she turns to Barb, me, then back to Barb. "Somebody speak, please."

"I need to answer," I insist. I had no plans of talking to him today, but now that he's calling, it feels imperative that I do. Like my life depends on it, and it probably does.

Martha stands, motioning toward my phone. "It's Ian, isn't it? Friends, my ass. I knew it. I knew you two were up to no good."

"Please go," I say, and when she doesn't budge, I try to walk around her. "Respect my wishes for once. Just this time, care about what someone else wants instead of yourself."

She keeps stepping left and right to block my access to the door. "Frank is my fiancé's best friend, Ames," she hisses.

Placing a hand on my chest, I shout, "I am *your* best friend!"

She crosses her arms, her head shaking stiffly, and as the phone stops ringing, I sigh.

"Get out of my way." Moving around her, I leave the room and walk through the corridor.

"Ames—Ames, stop! *What* are you doing?"

"You don't know the whole story, M." I turn right, the corridor extending in every direction like a damn maze with ugly beige wallpaper.

She hurries after me and grabs my arm, and once I shake her off, she groans. "It doesn't matter, Ames! You're getting married in a few hours. What in the world—"

A bathroom. God, I've never been happier to see one. I open the door, then quickly close it behind me before Martha can enter. Once the door is locked, I ignore her thumping against it and grab my phone.

My fingers press on the screen, and after two wrong attempts at inserting the PIN, I tap on his contact.

Beep.

Beep.

I swallow, holding my breath as Martha shouts that I'm an idiot before finally leaving. This is definitely it. If he doesn't pick up, then I shouldn't have called back to begin with.

Beep.

My arm slowly settles down, nausea filling my mouth with saliva as a sheen of cold sweat covers my forehead. Leaning against the sink, I look down at the phone, which is still beeping, but the call remains unanswered.

It feels like the most effort I've ever put into something, but slowly my thumb presses on the screen and ends the call.

He didn't answer.

I remain in the same position for a while, just existing. I'm not even sure I'm thinking; rather, there's a thick smog of confusion clouding my rational brain.

A firm knock comes from the other side of the door, and the thought of letting my sadness and anger explode all over Martha or Barb sounds like as good an idea as any. I take the few steps, the weight of the dress only more constricting with each awkward stride.

"What?" I shout as I open the door, immediately freezing when my eyes meet a set of blue ones that are comforting and familiar yet kick the breath out of me. "What—Ian," I whisper as he swallows. His usually scruffy hair is just messy today, and though he's wearing a white cotton shirt, it's wrinkled and unbuttoned at the top of his chest. There are dark purple hues around his eyes, and even his posture seems off.

"Amelie," he whispers. He looks relieved for half a second, then his expression turns neutral again. "Don't worry, nobody saw me." He turns around to double-check, then turns back to me. "Can I come in?"

Unable to process any sound, I step back.

Ian is here, and he should definitely not be here, and there's a sharp pain in my chest just when I feel like I can breathe for the first time in a while.

Once he enters and closes the bathroom door behind him, I'm still at a loss for words. Why is he here?

"You never gave me the name of that bakery," he says with a half smile.

"What?"

"The bakery? The one that took care of Barb's nuptial cake?"

Oh. My brain is spinning around so fast, it takes me a few seconds to understand he's joking, and by the time I do, there's no point in smiling, because his chest is heaving and there's a wrinkle between his eyebrows that tells me even Ian knows the time to play around is over.

"I couldn't sleep. I was—" He rubs his forehead. "So I just drove here."

My lips quiver and, feeling my throat prickle, I nod, not even attempting to speak.

"And I sat outside, in my car, for . . ." Bringing a hand to the back of his head, he sighs. "For a long time. I thought—I really wanted to come in and find you." He sighs again. "I know I shouldn't be here. I promised I'd let you live your life. And I really tried."

A tear moves past my defenses and runs down my cheek.

"But I couldn't just sit there, and then I saw your picture, and you looked—" He breaks off and points at me, shaking his head. "You look . . . horrible."

"Thanks?" I whisper as I look down.

"No, not . . . ugly." He reaches out but his hand drops before it touches my cheek and tightens into a fist at his side. "Just . . . your face. Your expression. I had to come in."

I nod, and his shoulders relax as if a huge weight has been removed from them. Maybe he was afraid I'd be upset he's here, but I'm not. I'm shocked, afraid, hopeful. But I'm not angry.

"You're not wearing your dress," he says, looking down at my gown.

Uncomfortably rubbing my arm, I follow his gaze. "No. It didn't feel right."

"Is that the only thing that doesn't feel right?"

There's a moment of silence. "He's been better," I say, my words soaked in self-doubt. "We ended that whole open-relationship thing, and he's been . . . present and sweet and—"

"It's too late."

I shake my head quickly, my chest heaving. "But what if it's not? We have the rest of our lives ahead of us and—"

"It's too late because you're in love with me, Amelie."

My heart stills. My everything follows. It's like my muscles have turned stale, stiff, as if I were a mannequin and not a real person. This isn't what I need to hear right now. "Please, don't," I whisper.

"I drove here not even knowing if I'd say this. If I'd have the chance to see you, if you'd listen," he says. The corners of his lips bend downward, and there's so much hurt in his face that it's hard to look at. "Now you're here, so please let me say it."

"I can't hear it, Ian." I take a step back and I hold up my hands, palms out, as if they'll somehow hold him back. "You can't say what you're about to say two hours from my wedding."

"Don't marry him."

A sob breaks the silence that follows, and though I cup my mouth, more sobs power through.

"Don't marry a man who doesn't love you." He comes closer, his fingers finding my own as he rests his forehead on mine. "Don't marry a man you don't love. And please, I beg you, don't choose him over me."

"Ian—" Another violent sob shakes me, and as I look at him through a veil of tears, I see that, through his closed eyes, he's crying too.

"I told you I don't know much about love, Amelie, and that's true. But I've learned a lot." His smell soothes me a little as he breathes against my lips. "Like how, when you'd do anything for someone, when their smile fuels your very soul, that's probably love."

His hand cups the back of my neck, our foreheads still pressed together as our quick breaths mix. "I wondered when exactly it started. If all of it, all along, was love. And I realized, since I met you, you never left my mind." He sniffles. "And the more I tried to ignore my feelings for you, the more they grew."

"Please," I beg as makeup stains my face.

"I lost you, Amelie. You've never been mine, but I lost you

already. And I'm here to get you back, because if I don't, it'll break my heart."

"Stop, Ian—"

"Please don't break my heart, Amelie."

My legs give out, the pain too intense to bear. I just want to fall onto the floor of this bathroom and cry until this is all over. Until there's no wedding, no Frank, no Ian, no Amelie either. Until the world has moved past us and we're nothing but a speck in history. Until there's no more thinking or feeling, no more love or heartache. No more anything.

But Ian's arms hold me up against his chest, and I feel safer than I've ever felt before. I can't help but think that if we'd met in another life, we would have really been something. We would have been *it*.

But love needs the right timing.

"You have to let me go," I whisper. I don't just mean the way he's holding me, and I think he knows, because after making sure I can stand on my own, he takes a step back and turns around, his hands running over his face. "Ian, I—I'm about to get married, and—"

"You texted me back, Amelie." He whips around. His eyes are glossy, and there's a pink hue over his cheeks. "Why did you do it, then, huh?"

"Because—"

When I halt, he shrugs. "Because what?"

"Because I'm panicking, okay?" I bring both hands to my face, wiping my tears and probably making more of a mess of my makeup. "I'm panicking and I needed to hear your voice and talk to you because—because you're my best friend," I whine.

"Your best friend." A bitter chuckle rolls out of his lips. "Really? Give me a break, Amelie."

"But you are," I insist. "Aren't you? You said you'd be my friend, you said you'd—"

"We're not *just* friends. We'll never be just friends, and that's why you dumped me after our *friendly* date." His jaw sets. "Because you know that too."

"Don't say that. I didn't dump you, Ian."

"That's not the point," he says with a groan.

"I didn't dump you, I—"

"That's not the point!" he shouts. Taking a deep breath, he runs his fingers through his hair. Then he shoves his hands into his pockets. "You can't tell me you don't want me, Amelie. I know you do."

My head is pounding, my heart following the quick rhythm.

He's right, of course. I do want him. Just being locked in this small bathroom with him, breathing the same air, is intoxicating. Since my birthday, I've thought about our night together constantly. About all he said, about his voice and his moans and his gasps of pleasure. About the sweet words that followed.

"I—" My fists clench. "It doesn't matter, Ian. We want different things, and just because I have a crush, it doesn't mean—"

"A crush?"

As his eyes narrow, my shoulders sag. "No. You know what I mean."

"Yeah, I *do* know what you mean." He looks out the window, his fists clenched. "I just don't know if you're lying to yourself or if I . . ." He swallows. ". . . if I really do know nothing about love."

I close my eyes. The need to tell him he's much more than a crush is fighting with my awareness that if I decide that's the truth, then I'm welcoming more heartbreak. Because there is only one truth and one alone: Ian can't give me the thing I want the most. He can't promise me forever. He won't marry me.

God, what am I doing? Why am I even considering this? I can't walk out of my own wedding. I can't leave Frank at the altar and run away with Ian. I can't let my father wait to walk me down the aisle. I can't let the whole world know just how badly I fucked up.

"I'm begging you," he pleads. He doesn't even look into my eyes, and I can't tell if it's fear or shame over the fact that he's pleading. "Call it off, Amelie."

"Ian, Frank is—"

"Fuck Frank."

"Every person I know and love is here. I—"

"Fuck everyone else, Amelie," he insists as he clasps me by my forearms. His eyes burn into mine as he speaks slowly. "Stop thinking of the way you're *supposed* to feel. Just feel."

"I—I . . ."

His hold on my forearms lightens, almost as if he knows what I'll say before I do.

"I can't, Ian. You don't want me, not the way I need you to."

His jaw twitches as he looks down at the floor. "Is marriage so important to you that you'd choose to be his unhappy wife over being my happy girlfriend?"

"That's unfair," I say, my eyes fighting against the weight of my brows. "You know marriage has always been my dream. You said I shouldn't be with you."

"Choose me unconditionally," he says. His lips are almost on mine, and even amid all this madness, it's difficult not to lift my face to his and kiss him. "Choose me unconditionally, and I will choose you unconditionally too."

When I say nothing, only whimpers and sobs coming out of my lips, he straightens, as if he's found his answer in my hesitation. "Okay. That's it—that's . . . enough." Tears roll down his cheeks as he blinks. "I'm leaving."

He walks past me, and my hand clings to his shirt, my fingers gripping the soft fabric even as he gently tries to shake me off. But I can't let him go. This can't be the last memory I have of him—the one that'll burn into my mind forever. "Please, Ian, wait."

"No, Amelie." He pulls his arm closer to his body, freeing himself from my hold. "We're done. *I'm* done. Please don't contact me anymore."

I stare at the back of his head, as he hasn't turned to speak, but his voice is shaking hard enough that I know he's crying.

I'm not. What I feel at this moment, in this very instant, goes far beyond pain. Beyond guilt and regret and confusion. It's as eradicating as death, but without the peace that comes afterward. Just darkness.

"I'm sorry," I say.

He turns around, and the look in his eyes terrifies me. Not because it's in any way menacing but because it's empty. Just shallow and final and dark. "Goodbye, Amelie."

I stare at the door but my feet are frozen on the spot, my body reaching an uncomfortably low temperature as my stomach clenches again and again, until I turn to the toilet just in time to vomit breakfast. Looks like I lost that fight. Tears roll down my cheeks as I grasp the cold porcelain, my throat burning and my head thumping with pain. Then there's a knock at the door.

Oh my God.

Did he come back? Please let that be him.

"Ames?" Barb calls. "Can I come in? What's going on?"

My shoulders slump as I rake the back of my hand over my mouth. Nausea still makes me feel like I'm on the deck of a boat, but the gagging has stopped, so I tentatively stand and flush.

Is marriage so important to you that you'd choose to be his unhappy wife over being my happy girlfriend?

His words echo in my mind over and over again in the same broken, distressed voice he used to pronounce them as my eyes find my reflection in the mirror. My skin is gray despite the makeup, and clumps of black mascara are gluing my eyelashes together. My lipstick is smudged and my hair is flattening out already. I'm gross and sickly, my cheekbones sticking out and my dress hardly fitting me right. The lack of sleep, the stress, the heartache—I can almost see the scars each has left on my pale skin over the past six months.

For a moment, in the silence of the bathroom apart from my ragged breathing, I forget about Ian and Frank. About everyone else too. I look at a reflection in the mirror I don't recognize, and her eyes are asking me a single question.

Why are you doing this to me?

It's maybe the biggest blow yet, how I've let myself down. At the moment, it feels unforgivable. But if there's a path to forgiveness, I know what the first step is.

I have to call this wedding off.

I have to go after Ian and tell him the truth. That I have feelings for him, too, that I think I've always had them, ever since Barb's wedding, when he sat down at my table and then danced with me. That I've tried to hold my feelings back, then tried to keep him out of my life so that at the very least my feelings for him would go away. But they haven't, and it feels like they never will. Like I don't want them to.

Just as Barb knocks again, a jolt of adrenaline pushes me to the door. Fumbling for the handle, I pull it open.

Barb looks me up and down in shock. "Ames, why did a guy just come out of this bathroom and throw this in the bin?"

Looking at the small black box she's holding, I extend my

hand. As she sets it on my palm, my heart wrenches painfully. It can't possibly be anything but a ring, and the awareness of it almost floors me.

I made a mistake. Worse, I made the one mistake I'll regret for the rest of my life.

I know it for a fact, and it's not the awareness that if I had chosen him unconditionally, he would have done the same. He would have proposed. It's realizing how close it all is to meaningless right now. I've wanted to get married for so long, I've dreamed of this day so much, and all I can think about right now are Ian's words.

I'd much rather be his girlfriend than anyone else's wife.

"Are you . . ." She swallows. "Ames, I—maybe you shouldn't get married."

"One step ahead of you." I walk past her with the sharp corners of the black box digging into my hand. At this point I've already messed everything up irreversibly. The only thing I can do is explain it all to Frank, then call Ian and beg him to listen.

I step back out through the endless corridors of this horrible villa until I find Trevor and Martha talking by one of the many identical doors. "Hey," I say, and as their eyes land on me, they both gasp. Right. I look like I just escaped a psych ward in a horror movie. "Where's Frank's room?"

They exchange a look, then Martha clears her throat. "It's this one, but, Ames—"

I yank the door open and stride inside. I really don't have time for her right now, but she's someone I'll deal with later. "Frank?" I call out, Martha following close behind me. "M, please, Frank and I need to talk in private."

She presses her lips together, then walks to his desk. As she strides back to me, she holds out a paper, her eyes stuck to it as if she's specifically avoiding my gaze. With my heart beating as if I've just run a whole marathon, I grab it, skimming the words written on it and knowing they won't be good.

I'm sorry. I can't.

Martha squeezes my arm when I look in her eyes for an explanation. "He . . ." She trails off. "Frank's gone."

LES DESSERTS

34

You Texted?

– TODAY –

"'I'm sorry. I can't'?" Ian asks as his hand travels up and down my side, his forearm on my back, squishing me against his naked chest.

I nod, my fingers playing with the short, light hairs sprinkled across his pecs. He listened to the first part of my story during the shower, then we moved back to the bed to do some more of that not-talking from before. It was glorious.

"That's what the note said."

"Shit. What does that mean?"

I shrug, tracing the tattoos of little triangles that circle the midpoint of his forearm. "I never asked. But my guess is . . . 'Sorry, I can't marry you.'"

He clicks his tongue, then presses his mouth to my sweaty forehead over and over. "He couldn't make up his mind about it before?"

Beaming so hard, I'm pretty sure I'm irreparably straining my cheeks, I look up at him and greet his lips with mine. "It's fine, Ian."

"No, it's not *fine*. He put you through hell for six months, Amelie, only to leave you at the altar?" His jaw clenches. "And me? You know what I've been through since the day of your wedding, all because of that asshole?"

Feeling his muscles tensing under my touch, I hoist myself up and hold the blanket around me. I know it's far from *fine*, but at this moment I couldn't care less. Ian's lying in all his naked glory, half sculpture, half man, and that's really all I intend to focus on for the foreseeable future. "It wasn't his fault—well, not only. *I* hurt you."

"Hmm." He hooks a finger in the blanket, then pulls until it falls down, leaving my body bare. "I know exactly how you can ask for forgiveness."

"You don't say."

"It involves a lot of begging."

I chuckle as he rises to a seating position and pins me down on the mattress.

"Lots of you on your knees."

I breathe out sharply, then his lips are on mine, my hands pulling his hair and tracing his sturdy shoulders. I'd do close to anything for another chance with this man, but what he's talking about, I'd do any day, anytime, for nothing at all.

"Then what happened?" His hand lingers over my ribs. "Martha dragged him back by his hair?"

"What do you mean?"

He leans back to look into my eyes. "Well, how did you end up getting married? When did you divorce?"

"What—" I shake my head. "What makes you think we got married?"

"You didn't?"

"I haven't spoken to him since. In fact, I believe the last words we said to each other were 'Where the fuck are the keys?' as we left for the wedding."

His body stiffens over mine, his brows furrowing deeply. "You didn't get married?"

"No. I told you: he was gone, and either way, I was going to tell him I wanted to call it off to be with you." I put my hand on his cheek, wanting him to go back to his usual self. "Took me long enough, but I got there."

"You—" He searches my eyes. "You chose me?"

I nod. "I chose you unconditionally, and I'll never change my mind."

His eyes close for a moment, the tension leaving his body as he kisses me. I get it. Ella didn't choose him when it came to it, and he thought I didn't either. But I did, and it's a decision I will never regret.

When he opens his eyes again, he settles next to me, his hand worriedly rubbing his jaw as he avoids looking at me. "But if you . . . if you never got married and wanted to be with me, then . . . why didn't you?"

"Well, I didn't know where to find you, Ian." I offer him a sad grin. "I thought of hiring a PI, but it felt a little stalker-y. And I came to Mayfield to spend the day a few times, and I might have walked around the city looking for you like a pathetic—"

His stern voice cuts me off. "Amelie, you could have just called."

"Right. I didn't think about that," I say with a playful smile that dies immediately when I notice his frown. "Ian, I . . ." I grab my phone from the nightstand, the chain of my necklace shifting and causing me to shiver against the cold metal. I settle next to him, then find our text conversation and show it to him. "I called. I texted. But you don't receive any of it if you block someone's number."

He gazes at the screen, his lips parted. Slowly, his thumb scrolls down, reading the slew of texts I sent him, dating back six months. "You texted."

"Of course I did."

His hand moves to his mouth, his eyes wide-open as he scrolls more and more. "You texted me pickup lines."

"Every day for six months—except for one Saturday when I ran a fever so high, I didn't text you because I could see you in the room with me." As he keeps scrolling, I stroke his soft, gorgeous hair. "And I called, too, every once in a while. Just to check if I was still blocked."

His eyebrows rise higher and higher as he goes through the texts, as if he's not even listening to me. He smiles, then chuckles at one of the pickup lines—I'll have to ask which one it is—and shakes his head, until eventually he sets the phone down. "Amelie, I never blocked you."

"Hmm . . . yeah, you did. See how there's no checkmark next to the text? That means I'm blocked. And if I call you, it goes straight to voicemail. Another sign I've been blocked." At his questioning look, I shrug. "I might have done some research."

"Why would I block you?" He shakes his head, then hops off the bed as he points at my phone. "Do you have the right number?"

Frustrated, I sigh. Yes, I have the right number. Does he really think I'd spend months texting him pickup lines, hoping he'd decide to talk to me, without being sure?

Once he's back on the bed, I show him his contact. His lips purse, so I know it's just fine. With a dubious shake of his head, he quickly taps on his phone, and eventually he lets out a puff of air. "You—you're blocked."

"Mm-hmm."

"I don't remember blocking you."

Well, that's weird. It's not exactly something you forget. Racking my brain, I think of a possible explanation, and judging by his pensive expression as he unblocks me, he must be doing the same. "I called you a few hours after you left the wedding, once I had dealt with the guests, and I was already blocked." Tracing the curve of his neck with my hand, I sigh. "You weren't really looking like yourself that day. That's probably it."

He nods, his forehead furrowed in confusion. "Yeah, I guess. I can hardly remember driving back home. Then I got so drunk,

I . . . that's probably when I did it." He sets his phone down, then quickly grabs it again. He taps on it a few times, and when my phone beeps with a text, he releases a deep breath. "Just checking."

With a smile, I move both phones out of the way and nestle against his chest. He looks so sad, I almost wish I didn't tell him. "It's okay, Ian. We're here now."

"But if it wasn't for the ICCE, we wouldn't be here. You would have moved on eventually, and tonight would have never happened."

I pull him closer until his arms lock around me. "You don't know that. Maybe fate would have brought us together some other way."

"Fate?"

I nod. "Fate. Destiny."

Nose buried in my hair, he inhales deeply, and I can't help a huge smile from taking over my face. Then he says, "Maybe fate brought us here, but I've worked pretty hard for everything else that happened, and I'd like some recognition."

My heart is filled with such happiness, it might just burst. After all that's happened, I never thought we'd be here, but we are.

For the moment I choose to ignore the prickly feeling at the base of my throat, the question echoing through my mind over and over again.

This thing between us—does it have an expiration date?

———————————

"You can use store-bought beef stock for making your espagnole, but use a low-sodium or unsalted stock. You don't want to concentrate the saltiness, especially if you plan to use the sauce to make another one you'll also reduce. Season at the end instead."

I glance at the nodding faces and strain the sauce, showing the audience how smooth it is as it falls into the bowl.

"And—"

The door opens, and Ian pokes his head inside. "Hi," he says, his eyes landing on me. "Can I steal you for a minute?"

"Of course."

Barb takes my place as I leave the room, and once the door is closed behind me, Ian's lips are glued to mine. The taste of coffee and Ian is so good, they should make a candy out of it. "Is everything okay?" I ask when he lets me lean back a little. Not that I mind the interruption. I wasn't that invested in the lecture to start with; who would be, when there's a man like Ian I could be with instead?

He tugs at my hand as he walks toward the hall of the hotel. "Everything's okay," he says. He keeps strutting away and dragging me along. "But everything will be even better when I bottom out inside you."

Oh. My stomach clenches, my body flushing so fast and hard, I might just spontaneously combust. "We'll have to use your room," I say, the thought of contradicting him not even on my radar. "My keys are in my bag—back there," I say, pointing to the room I just came out of.

He shakes his head, then turns right at the hall. "My room's too far." After one last step, he opens the door to the conference room he dragged me to on our first day here and pulls me in. It's the same as it was a week ago, except the white neon lights are on today and, judging by the scattered chairs around the room, it's recently been used.

As soon as the door closes, Ian takes me in his arms, and I realize everything that counts is different than it was that first day. His teeth nibble my lower lip, his hands roaming under my skirt and grabbing a handful of everything as his breath fans over my lips.

"Ian, this door doesn't lock."

He smirks, trapping me against the wall with his forearm on either side of me. "I know."

He *knows.*

My chest slowly falls, my lips parting with a needy little whimper as he hooks a finger under the strap of my top and lets it fall down my arm. "Does it turn you on?" My chin dips as he nips the skin of my chest. "Knowing that anyone could walk in and find me fucking you against the wall?"

"Yes," I say. It comes out all breathy, needy. Not subtle at all. And I'd be embarrassed, except I'm with Ian, and he appreciates my eagerness. There's even more in his fumbled movements.

His lips press to my collarbone, my body arching against his as his hands squeeze my ass. Every time he touches me, he leaves indelible marks I'd like to show off like tattoos.

"Hmm." His hands work on his jeans, and once his cock is out of his briefs, hard and ready, he holds his hand out. "Be a good girl and give me your panties again."

Shakily breathing out, I throw a look at the door and slide my panties down my legs. I give them to Ian, and once they're pocketed, he grabs my hips and picks me up. "What if someone comes?" I ask as my legs wrap around his ass.

"Oh, someone's coming all right."

His shaft presses against me, sinking in with little effort, and I gasp, my head gently resting against the wall.

"If you knew how many times I pictured you like this." He pulls back and rams back inside, my eyes fluttering as I get lost on the dangerous mix of sensations coming from his hands on my ass and his lips on my chest. "Pressed against the wall, dripping on me."

"Ian, please," I whine, quickly silenced by his lips.

"If I were you, I'd keep it down." His rocking movements fall into a steady rhythm that leaves me breathless. "That is, if you don't want to get caught begging for more of my cock."

Heat envelops my whole body, fear mixing with something

that feels like excitement but can't possibly be that. I swallow the next of my moans as my fingers dig into his shoulders; it's the most self-control I've ever exercised in my life.

"That's my girl." His nose dips into my hair before he kisses the side of my neck. "I love every single noise that comes out of those lips, but they're only mine to hear."

Oh, God, I can't. I push my mouth to his, hoping it'll stop him from saying the hottest, filthiest things anyone's ever said to me when I can't freely express my approval. But it's not enough, and every time he's crammed inside me, I can hardly smother my whimpers. In fact, I don't even want to. Let someone catch us. Who cares?

"More, Ian," I manage before I drop my forehead to his shoulder. "Fuck me harder."

"As hard as you want it, beautiful." He slides out and safely returns my feet to the floor, then spins me around. "Hands on the wall."

With my dress pulled up, he presses his erection against my ass. It makes shivers rain down my body, every one of my nerves tense with anticipation. "Fuck me, *please*," I beg as he rolls his shaft over my clit, his hips grinding on my ass.

"Well, I can't say no to you, can I?" He's inside me again, his fingers wrapping around my throat and holding me up when my arms give out. His lips graze the top of my back as he backs up and thrusts hard inside me. "You've ruined me, beautiful. You'll have to let me fuck you forever now."

"Forever," I choke out. Since yesterday, this is the only reference he's made to this—us—being something beyond a few days' thing, but my obsessive worry about the future will have to wait until my brain can function. "You feel so good, so good, so good," I chant, my voice getting increasingly loud.

"You feel like a fucking dream I don't want to wake up from, Amelie."

As he speeds up, his hips slapping against my ass and his fingers like a necklace around my neck, the talking subsides in favor of moaning, grunting, and swearing. All the sounds echo in the empty conference room, my hands sliding down the wall once I start sweating.

"Shh," he says sweetly when a loud grunt escapes me. "I'm not going to stop if someone comes in, Amelie. They'll watch you fall apart on my cock."

"More, Ian, more." My voice is raspy as my hand flies behind me and I tug at his shirt, uselessly trying to pull him closer.

"Will you keep it down?"

"Yes, please, I promise," I cry out, which I realize isn't convincing at all.

His hand abandons my throat, running through my hair until he wraps the strands around his fist, then pulls my hips back. "Fine." Once I'm basically folded in front of him, he thrusts again. I can feel him better now, opening me up and breaking me down. My next moan is so loud that, letting my hair go, he puts his hand over my mouth. With a breathy, faltering voice, he says, "Gee, beautiful. Your word's worth nothing, huh?"

I mumble confused words against his hand, my body slamming back and forth to meet his.

"You're so pretty like this," he huffs as his hands move across my back. He grips my hips, and when his hold tightens, I could die from that alone. From knowing fucking me with little restraint is what he wants.

"Yes, Amelie, come," he gasps, and, pumping slower inside me, he lets out a low grunt. "Just like that, beautiful."

My orgasm explodes around him as he hits the same spot

over and over again, and with his thrusts faltering, he gushes out his pleasure and pulls me up.

My body shudders as his mouth rests on my shoulder, his hot breath making that spot his as he rides the last wave of his orgasm.

For a few seconds, nothing happens. We stand against the wall, sweat dripping down both of us and our orgasms still tingling, electrifying the air. But his hands don't rest for too long before he starts rubbing them over my ribs, then my thighs, tracing my body like a map. He kisses the back of my head, my neck, and once he slides out and turns me around, he takes my lips with his.

"I can't go one day without being inside you now. Do you understand?" he whispers, his words slurred and only half pronounced. "I'm done for, Amelie."

I hook my arms around his neck, his warm breath mixing with mine and my heart skipping a beat. He said it again. Maybe he *really* means it. Maybe he's forgiven me.

Once we clean up and walk out, we're entrapped in a cloud of giggles, kisses, and whispered words I really hope nobody else hears. But to be honest, I'm too busy being disgustingly happy to actually check. On top of that, walking is challenging as Ian grabs me from behind and forces me to move with my back against his chest as he kisses the side of my face.

We tumble into the hallway, our bodies still together as I shriek and tell him to let me go, though that's the very last thing I want. We're back to being us, finally, though it's even better now because there's no distance, no phones, and no Frank. Just us. As for the seed of fear planted deep in my soul, I'm trying as hard as I can not to let it sprout. Trying even harder not to think of Ella's words.

It feels as if this is more than just a few days' worth of adventure. But he hasn't flat out said it. He hasn't spoken of logistics, of what kind of future he envisions for us, if any.

"Let's grab lunch?" he whispers into my ear as we move in front of the counter. The receptionist glares at us as his arms wrap around my stomach, holding me to his chest. "Or I could just eat you."

"Your diet appalls me."

"Then I'll eat some food," he says, dropping kisses onto my shoulder. "And you can eat my co—"

"Ian."

We both turn to the right, and standing in front of the revolving doors are two men. I'm not sure which one I recognize first. If it's my dad, standing to the right with his nostrils flared and the face of someone who's just been stabbed in the back, or the one who called Ian's name. *He's* sucked away all the light in the room, as if he's acting like a black hole where all my joy goes to die.

William Roberts.

"Dad?" Ian asks with a jovial voice. Immediately, his body stiffens behind mine, and once I check his expression, I notice his glare is directed at my dad. It's probably for the best, because judging by William Roberts's expression, he definitely didn't expect me to be here, just as I didn't expect him.

"Get your hands off my daughter *right now*," my dad demands.

Ian scoffs, leaning closer to me. "I really was onto something when I said your dad's stuck in 1968." Then, with a smirk, he turns to my father. "Mr. Preston, I will get my hands off your daughter as soon as she asks me to, and not one second before that."

There's such tension in the room, it's almost hard to breathe, the air warm and dense despite the AC. Though I have lots to add to that conversation, I can't utter a single word, because all I can see is William Roberts.

Panic makes me freeze. I knew I was bound to meet this man

again, especially if things between Ian and me turned out to be more than a few days of adventure, but I expected I'd have some sort of notice—some time to prepare. Or maybe I just lied to myself about ever being ready for this moment. Either way, it looks like it's time to face the music.

"Let the kids be, Hammond," William says, waving my father off. His voice is deep and cold, making shivers run along my arms and neck. Next to my dad, he looks taller, fitter, and younger. Surely, he looks handsome in his fitted suit. He approaches us, and I almost want to shy away, almost want to run and hide somewhere in this hotel until it feels like I can breathe again.

Once he reaches us, he quickly hugs his son, glancing at me from over his shoulder with a predatory look in his eyes that makes my skin itch. Whatever shock he must have felt on seeing me is long gone and has been replaced by his usual scheming expression.

"Dad," Ian says as they break away. "This is, uh—"

His eyes jump from his father to me until William comes to his aid. "Amelie Preston?"

"Yeah, thanks." Ian rolls his eyes. "She's the woman I told you about. She's . . . from the past year?"

"Oh. *Ooooh*," William says in surprise as his eyes bob from his son to me. "Of course." Squeezing Ian's shoulder, he asks, "She's not engaged this time around, is she?"

My stomach drops. He *knew*? William knew all along about his son and me?

"Dad," Ian scolds with a smile. "She's single. Or, er—" He takes his hand in mine. "Well, we haven't—we're not—" With a sigh, he focuses on his dad again. "Jesus, thanks a lot."

His dad chuckles, throwing amused glances at me. Somehow, I know he's not laughing about the awkward position he's put his son in. He's probably remembering that night, four months ago.

Is it now when he'll say something? When he'll ruin this thing between his son and me? Is this the moment in which he'll deliver the final hit that'll leave me in a bloody mess on the floor?

"I didn't mean to put you on the spot. Forgive me." He turns to my father, who's watching from the sidelines. "We're here for the concluding seminar."

"And if I'd known you'd show up, I would have never accepted," my dad manages through gritted teeth.

"Enough with this, will you, Hammond?" William's cold eyes focus on mine. "Especially now that we're all family."

"Holy—Dad! We're just—" With his shoulders straight, he says, "Do you fucking mind?"

"Sorry, sorry."

Ian's eyes narrow, then a quick puff of air comes out of his lips. He throws a glance at me and, noticing my "anything but happy" expression, looks away.

Involuntarily, I take a step backward. *Family*, this demon said. I can't be family. I can't be around him at all. I'll do anything in my power to be with Ian, but I don't think I can accept this man. That I can pretend nothing ever happened.

"Oh, so rude of me." William walks toward me, and my whole world crystallizes as I await the fall of the hammer that will smash it to pieces. He holds out his hand and with a smile says, "Wonderful to meet you, Amelie."

35

Wonderful to Meet You

– TWO MONTHS AFTER AMELIE'S WEDDING –

The spring sun shines bright in the sky, warming up my cheeks and forcing me to squint as I walk to my bike. With my helmet on, I ride through the city center, the wind a pleasant distraction from today's heat. They say summer will be brutally warm this year.

The air smells like salt and the sea, and the window-lined single-story construction site that's become familiar in the last two months takes up the view. The wide doors are open, and men in tank tops walk in and out as they move heavy appliances.

And right at the top, though it's still covered in a thick tarp, sits the logo of Amelie's Bistro. My restaurant.

"Good afternoon," I say as I hop off my bike and enter the empty space. I've ordered tables and chairs, but they won't be here until next week. On top of that, I have to finish up my new menu and get it printed, and—well, a million other things.

"You got some mail," one of the workers says in response as he points at the newly installed counter.

"My first mail delivery?" I bite my lips, a flicker of excitement coursing through me. I grab the thin pile and frown at the first three papers: takeout menus from nearby restaurants. The last one is a letter, though, sent from the International Cooking and Culture Expo. Interest piqued, I quickly rip the paper open and grab the invitation inside. Apparently, they want me to be one of their speakers at this year's conference in September.

After mentally confirming that it doesn't conflict with Martha's wedding, I smile. Maybe they heard about Amelie's Bistro. Either way, it's an honor. And they say I can bring a sous, so Barb could come too. She'll be about six months pregnant by then.

I look around, a smile spreading across my face.

Today's a good day.

Some workers are painting the walls with the baby-powder white I chose, while others are moving out the old equipment from the kitchen, when my phone beeps. At this point I've stopped jumping every time it does, but the hope that it's Ian still slithers its way into my brain.

It's much more likely Barb checking in on me. She's been doing that a lot, and she's been the only one who has, seeing as Martha blames me and Ian for Frank leaving me at the altar.

With a sigh, I take the phone out, my heart pausing when I see a Twitter notification. Since I quit my job at La Brasserie, my dad has taken over the feud, but the public interest has steadily decreased. Still, I'd be lying if I said I didn't spend more than a fair share of time picturing what I would have answered to the Marguerite's tweets if it were still my job.

I press on the bubble and, staring at their latest tweet, my jaw falls open.

Shit. They know: whoever this is, they figured out there's been a change in the chain of command at La Brasserie. They know it's not me answering their tweets anymore, and I must really be starved for affection, because it warms my heart that there's someone out there who *noticed*. Who, in the most fucked-up way ever, cares.

Wishing once again that I could answer, I open my chat with Ian, the screen exclusively filled with my own bubbles no matter how much I scroll. Every day I hope the message I send is the one that'll be checkmarked. The first one he actually receives.

After thinking for a few seconds, I tap:

> **Amelie:**
> I'd take you to the movies, but they
> won't let me bring my own snack.

Better than yesterday's Do you have a map? Because I got lost in your eyes.

My breath catches once I hit "send," and when no checkmark appears, my shoulders drop and I put the phone away. Maybe tomorrow.

"So it's true. Amelie Preston is opening a restaurant."

I turn around and notice a man standing at the entrance. His black suit almost takes up the whole space, and against the bright rays of sun streaming in, he looks like the epicenter of all that's dark.

"Hello?" I say, not sure who he is or why he knows my name. "Do we know each other?"

He takes a step inside, and then another. The third step is when I recognize him. We've never met in person, but I've heard, read, and talked about this man more often than I care to admit.

"Not yet," he says as he keeps advancing toward me, his pace slow as his dark eyes roam my barren walls and freshly painted ceiling. "But I'm hoping we'll get to know each other better."

Yeah, I don't see that happening.

He halts in front of me and holds out his hand. "William Roberts. Wonderful to meet you."

William Roberts is in my restaurant.

Why? I'm not sure.

Some strands of his hair are turning gray, but most retain their dark brown, almost black color. His eyes are a shade lighter but not by much, and he has a trimmed beard. By all accounts, he's handsome. I knew that already; I've seen him online or in magazines. But now that he's here, I realize he's magnetic, intimidating. It's not even that he's overly tall or strongly built, which he is. It's his attitude.

"Here's your coffee," I say, offering him a cup.

He graciously accepts it, then points out to the sea. "Gorgeous view. If you look that way, you can see the outermost point of land."

I follow the direction of his finger and nod. For all the smack our restaurants talked about each other over the last year, he seems nice enough. "Yeah. This comes second."

"Still takes the podium." He grins, then sips his coffee. "I've been looking forward to meeting you for a while, Amelie. Hammond has kept you locked in his kitchen, far away from the public."

Because he doesn't think I'm ready or worthy of any attention, and though technically the enemy of my enemy is my friend, I'm not sure it applies to this situation. "I've been focusing on cooking." I offer him a light shrug. "I'm not really interested in the public part of my father's career."

"I can understand that."

I wait for him to get to whatever he's here to say, but he just keeps studying me with a look I can't quite decipher. It's somewhat intrusive. "So . . . um, how can I help you, Mr. Roberts?"

"Please call me William."

I offer him a light nod.

"I just figured introductions were in order." He slips a hand into his pocket. "And congratulations too."

"Thanks." Still doesn't explain why he's here. An email would have sufficed.

"And what better chance to start off on the right foot?" He takes a sip of coffee, not once breaking eye contact with me over the rim of his cup. "In fact, we should celebrate your new venture. How would you feel about escorting me to dinner tomorrow night?"

"Dinner?" A nervous giggle escapes me, and I try to hide it by looking at the blue waves crashing against the rocks beneath us. "I—if you're here as part of some espionage ploy, I'm sorry to disappoint you, William—"

"Espionage!" He huffs out a laugh, then looks down at his coffee, a shy smile on his lips that doesn't match anything else about him. "Look, Amelie, I know you're an extraordinary cook. With this restaurant, you'll do great things. It's in my best interest to have you on my side."

"Or we could just not have sides."

He chuckles. "I agree. This silly little crusade Hammond is fighting against me is getting old. I have nothing but respect for your father and his restaurant."

Cocking my brow, I give him a "Who are you kidding?" look. I'm not one to often defend my father, but I also wasn't born yesterday. "You defined my father and La Brasserie as 'pretentious, overpriced—'"

"'—leftovers from the past,' yes." He thoughtfully rubs his jaw. "I believe it was during an interview with *Yum* magazine."

Yes, it was.

As if brushing the thought away, he focuses on me again. "And if I'm not mistaken, you suggested that my restaurant offers a low-quality imitation of your father's work."

Right before the journalist asked if I was afraid of William Roberts.

"You also said you'd only be afraid of me if I came after you with one of the items on our menu and asked you to eat it."

Pressing my lips together, I try not to let out a laugh. I can't say I don't believe those things, but telling them to the man's face—especially when he's being so polite—must be torture for something I've done in a previous life.

"It's all in the past," he says, straightening his tie. "That's precisely why I'd like to invite you out for dinner. Now that you're opening your own restaurant, maybe we could bury the hatchet." Leaning forward with a sly smile, he winks. "What do you think, Amelie?"

That it's ridiculous. That there's nothing he could say to make me change his mind about him. But I guess the less I need to concern myself with William Roberts, the better, and if having dinner together will get me off his radar, then subjecting myself to his company is what I'll do.

"Considering you're no longer a chef of La Brasserie, is it safe to assume you and Hammond had a disagreement?" he asks in a suggestive tone.

"You could say that," I mutter as I think of when I told him I'd open my own restaurant. All he said was "Congratulations."

"Then let me add that your dining with me would be a great 'Fuck you' to your old man too."

I laugh, watching as his eyes lighten up and his head tilts to the side—the same expression as a connoisseur savoring a sip of a fabulous wine. Though he's joking, I fight even harder to find a good reason to say no.

Only more reasons to accept.

"Yes. Okay." Pushing myself off the railing, I smile. "Let's bury the hatchet."

36

Buffet of Betrayal

– TODAY –

I rush up the stairs. Unsurprisingly, Ian follows. That's it. I'm pretty sure his dad is the devil himself—a handsome Hollywood version of the devil with too much savoir faire and not a shred of conscience.

"Amelie?"

No. I can't talk to Ian. Not before I understand. Roberts definitely knows about my past with his son, but did he know at the time he came to my restaurant? And if so, what sort of sick game is he playing?

"You know me well enough to have gathered that I won't let this go," he says, following me through the corridor. "So how about you stop running away and tell me what's going on?"

Fuck, fuck, fuck. My heart is beating so fast, it's hard to walk in a straight line. He can't know what happened between his father and me. I've known it since the moment I figured out Ian was actually Ian Roberts. This is something I'll have to bring to the grave. More than that, I'll have to actively work for him to never *ever* find out.

I need to pull my shit together and protect him, the way he's always protected me. I won't let him lose his father after he's lost his mother already.

"Really?" Ian asks as I halt by the door, then grab my key. "You need more proof of my persistence?"

"I don't know what you want me to say." I attempt a smile, but it's obvious he doesn't buy it for a second. Opening the door, I enter the room, where Barb is packing up.

"Hey!" she says cheerfully, then, noticing the expression on my face, her smile falls. "What's up?"

I throw her a desperate look just as Ian comes to stand in front of me, and, catching on to my silent plea for help, she addresses him. "Oh, Ian, do you mind? I need to take a shower and—"

"Sorry, Barb, but yes. I mind." He gives her an apologetic smile, then turns to me again. "What's going on, beautiful?"

Fine. There's no escaping this. Turning to Barb, I ask, "Can you give us a minute?"

"Of course. I'll shower later. I'm kind of hungry anyway." She moves past us and, with a questioning look at me, leaves the room.

Once she's gone, I focus on Ian. He's done so much to keep me sane. To protect me, to make me feel special and loved.

If it's the last thing I do, I'll protect him from this.

"So what's going on?" he asks, his forehead creased. "Why did you look so uncomfortable with my dad?"

You can do this, Amelie.

Casually shrugging, I move past him and go to the kettle. "You know. I've said things about your dad, your restaurant. And my father—he hates him."

"That's it?" he asks as he comes to stand next to me. His eyes scout my face, probably looking for signs I'm lying. "Is that why you were being weird?"

"It's just . . . complicated."

His fingers wrap around my wrist when I move to grab the bottled water on the nightstand. "Amelie?" he asks, his shoulders squared and his brow low and determined. "I know we haven't really . . . talked. About us and what happens after tomorrow. But . . ."

Shaking my head, I walk back to him and set the kettle down. "No, your father has nothing to do with us. I understand that, I promise."

"Do you? Because it doesn't look like it."

Great. Now, instead of suspecting there's something more than what meets the eye, he thinks I don't want to be with him because of his dad. I swear to God, I'm the worst liar in the world.

Running my hands along his arms, I look up at Ian's gorgeous face. At his high cheekbones and the perfect curve of his lips. At the long lashes encircling his eyes, the freckle on his forehead. He's my perfect.

"Look, I know our families haven't always—"

My lips crash on his, my fingers desperately gripping his hair when he leans back a little. I wrap my other arm around him, and in a second his shoulders relax, his mouth responding to mine as he pulls me closer, then holds me in place.

It makes it better. It reminds me of who I'm doing this for. Us.

"Hmm—*melie*," he mumbles, but without giving him an inch of space, I pull him to me and step back until we reach the bed, where my fingers fumble with the button of his jeans. "Amelie, wait."

"I *need* you," I whisper as he keeps his face just out of reach. His eyes dart to my lips, and after a second of hesitation, he kisses me, his tongue swiping mine as we lie in bed.

Rising to his knees, Ian grasps the sides of my top and pulls it over my head. I do the same with his shirt, the intricate black tattoos on his arms distracting me and slowing my movements.

I lean forward to whisper in his ear, "I want you in my mouth."

He releases a shuddering breath, then kisses my shoulder. "That can absolutely be arranged." The sting of his teeth biting my neck fades away as he licks the same spot. "Get on your knees, beautiful."

Eagerly, I kneel on the red-carpeted floor. He unbuttons his jeans, his eyes studying mine, then takes his cock out with a breath of relief. I can feel the warmth coming off it, and my mouth pools with saliva at the thought of giving him pleasure this way. Of seeing him lose control because of me.

Once my mouth closes around him, he groans, his muscles contracting as all restraint fades from his face.

Unpopular opinion? It's better than an orgasm.

My eyes open, the alarm of my phone deafening me from the bedside table. I lunge for it, then confusedly look for the snooze button, until I realize it's not the alarm but a phone call. Ian.

Turning to the side, I see he's not where he should be, and I'm immediately struck with panic. After Ian and I had dinner with Barb, we slept together in his room last night, so where is he?

"Hello," I say grouchily before clearing my throat.

"Good morning."

"Good morning." I pull the sheet around me, then step on the fluffy floor. His tone's definitely off, and it immediately sends me spiraling. Walking to the chair, I find my clothes—which last night were thrown everywhere around the room—neatly folded. "Where are you? What's going on?"

There's a long sigh. "We need to talk."

Holding the phone between my shoulder and my ear, I step into my panties, tugging them up clumsily. My throat closes up, and I have a feeling I'll want to be dressed for the next part of this. "Ian? Are you dumping me by phone?"

"Dumping you?" he scoffs. "No. Why would I dump you?"

"You said, 'We need to talk,'" I scold as I maneuver myself into my shorts and hop on one foot to pull the legs up. "That's the universal code for 'I'm about to break up with you.'"

"Okay. And what do I say if we need to talk?"

Once my shorts are buttoned up, I sigh. "I don't know. You . . . you just say what you need to say."

"Fine. So can we discuss—"

"Where are you?" I ask as I grab my T-shirt.

"I . . . I'm somewhere safe. Seriously, Amelie, we—"

"Somewhere safe? Safe from what?"

"From you?" He laughs. "You keep jumping on me every time I try to talk to you, and I'd be thrilled if I wasn't pretty sure you're trying to avoid this conversation. And you keep doing that thing with your voice and, holy fuck, you have me in a choke hold every time."

On my way to the restroom, I stop. "Which thing with my voice?"

"That thing. You know. 'I *need* you.'"

"What? I use emphasis?"

"No, not emphasis." There are birds chirping in the background, so he must be outside. "Your voice gets all raspy and low. And you bite your bottom lip. I just want to pull it free and then push my thumb in there and feel you suck—you're doing it again!"

"I'm not even speaking, Ian," I say as I enter the bathroom. "Where are you? I'll come to you."

"Patio. But no sex, Amelie. Not for . . . ten to fifteen minutes. Twenty, maybe. Until we've talked."

"I'll even give you half an hour."

"All right. I'll get you a coffee."

"See you soon."

———————

"Hi," I say as I step onto the patio.

Ian, sitting with his back to me, turns around, sunglasses on and a wide smile on his lips as he takes me in. "Good morning, beautiful."

I move closer, lean forward, then stop. Studying his face, I narrow my eyes. "Can I kiss you?"

"Yes. No. Wait—" He puts his hand behind my head and pulls me closer, then stops before my lips are on his and cocks an eyebrow. "No tongue. I don't trust you."

As I giggle, he presses his lips to mine, his tongue swiping past and finding my own. The hypocrite. His fingertips rub my scalp as my arms loop around his neck, and with a low moan he pulls me onto his lap.

"You're doing it again," he whispers as he rests his forehead on mine. Quick breaths burst out of his lips, his shaft hardening under my ass.

He must realize I'm doing nothing at all.

"Sorry," I say as I gently kiss his cheek, then stand. I grab the cup on the table, then take a long sip as I sit down. "Did you have breakfast already?" I ask when I notice only one plate of food.

"Yeah. I met my dad."

Oh, shit. I nod with fake enthusiasm, then tone it down when I end up nodding like a bubblehead doll. "Great. Great. How—how is he?" Which is to say, did he finally grow horns?

"He also isn't giving me the full story." Ian's arms are crossed over his chest, and with a reassuring smile, he asks, "Will you?"

"Ian, I promise, there's nothing to say," I repeat for the millionth time since yesterday. No matter how much I insist, he won't believe me. Turns out that him knowing me so well is a real inconvenience.

"Really?"

"Really."

He sighs loudly, nodding as he turns to the large daisy field beside us. "Fine," he says, holding his hand out for me. "Today's the last day. ICCE will be over tonight."

I entangle my finger with his. "Martha's wedding is tomorrow."

"And you still haven't invited me." His eyes narrow, and then he squeezes my hand tighter. "And then . . . then I'll be back in Mayfield, and you'll be in Creswell."

I nod, my heart beating out of my chest.

"Well, I don't know about you, but I don't think I'm physically able to let you go," he says matter-of-factly. "I know we agreed to one night only, but seeing as you didn't relent with your texts despite my lack of response, I assume you'd also be okay with—"

I'm too befuddled to manage the mechanics of speaking, so I nod dumbly.

"Yeah?" He smiles. "Good. I'm not exactly sure what's the best move here. It both feels as if I'm coming off way too strong and not strong enough. Like you're a stranger and . . . well, my soulmate, all at once."

Did he say . . . soulmate?

"See, I probably shouldn't have said that." He rubs his jaw, then sighs deeply. "Amelie, I'm not here to see how it goes. I don't want to play it cool, and keep you on your toes, and tactically think about whether I should text you, and wonder when it's the right time to tell you how I feel or if I should wait for you to do it first." One side of his lips pulls up. "I want all the cards on the table. I want to show you my hand, and I want to be as transparent as I possibly can. If that's okay with you."

I know I need to get some words out, but, God, is it difficult. Of course it's okay with me. It's more than okay. I don't want to pretend I'm not desperately in love with him; I've lied to myself and him about it already for months. I want him to show me his hand, and I want to show him mine, and I want to pick this back up exactly where we left it.

It's Ian.

He's my soulmate.

"I'd rather be your girlfriend than anyone else's wife" is all I can say. I get his feeling, his fear of coming off too strong, but the words fall naturally out of my lips. It would be pointless to deny it when it's all I've been wanting to tell him for the past six months.

His fingers entwine with mine, a full smile taking over his whole face. "I'd rather be your husband than be single ever again."

I can't help the tears welling up in my eyes. *Husband.* That word—the whole concept of marriage—is no longer my dream. Not the way it was before, at least. But knowing he'd do it for me means more than words can express.

"So . . . do you want to go back to texts and calls and phone sex? Because I don't." His fingers rub mine. "Not after having you with me for a whole week."

"No, of course I don't want that."

"Hmm. So we'll have to decide. Creswell or Mayfield."

Oh, hell no. I want nothing to do with his father. "I don't— I don't think I—"

"Huh." He taps his chin. "See, you're looking as green as a vegetable, Amelie."

"Ian, I don't know what you're after." I cross my arms. "There's nothing to say. I know your dad is the most important person in your life, but it'll take me a minute. I was taught to hate him and . . . there's a lot of history."

"In the spirit of this 'all cards on the table' policy . . . is there any chapter I've missed?"

When I glare, he raises both hands in defeat. "Fine. Well, I really hope you'll try. I know things have been said and done during the years, but you're right. My dad's really important to me."

"I know. I'll work on it."

His head tilts, and, taking his sunglasses off, he levels his warm azure stare on me. "All right." Throwing his sunglasses onto the table, he motions at me to move closer, and as soon as I'm within reach, he pulls me onto his lap. "But just so we're clear. My dad isn't the most important person in my life, Amelie." He presses a soft kiss on my lips. "You are."

Dinner with the Enemy

Large metal rings hang from the ceiling next to blue, white, and red ribbons that gently flap as the breeze from outside makes its way in. Closing the door, I study the empty high tables, the tablets placed on each, the colorful theater masks hanging on the walls. Now that it's empty, the Marguerite has lost all its usual festive atmosphere, and instead reminds me of an abandoned amusement park.

It's bigger than what it looks like on TV or in magazines. And though it smells somewhat similar to La Brasserie, there's something that's just a little bit different and has me scrunching my nose. Maybe it's what bad taste smells like.

"Hello?" I call, taking a reluctant step forward. I must say, when I suggested we come here for dinner, mostly pushed by a morbid curiosity, I didn't expect the restaurant to be closed.

"Amelie." William enters the dining room through the swinging doors of the kitchen, a warm smile on his face as he cheerfully walks toward me. In his gray suit, he looks even better than he did yesterday, and I'm suddenly self-conscious about my unimpressive jeans and shirt.

Ian didn't receive today's pickup line either. "Are you French? Because Eiffel for you." It was stupid anyway.

I guess I should give up, but he didn't when we met, and I won't now, even if we're strangers again.

"Come. The chef is cooking a special dinner for us." William gestures to me to follow, and we stop in front of the only set table in the room, the one right under the large upside-down candelabra hanging from the ceiling. With two lit red candles, colorful plates on white linen, and light pop music coming out of the speakers, this place couldn't be more different from La Brasserie. "What do you think?"

"Hmm?"

He gestures toward the decor as he pulls my chair out for me. "About the restaurant. It's your first time here, isn't it?"

"Oh, yeah." He pushes my chair in after I sit, then settles down in front of me as he unbuttons the cuffs of his jacket. "It's really gorgeous."

And a little flamboyant.

"I'm afraid I can't take the credit for it. My wife did most of the design."

"Your wife?" I search my brain for any piece of information I have about this man. I know he has a son who's not a chef. A wife, though? I don't remember anything about a wife. "You're married?"

"I was, a long time ago." He smiles stiffly. "Marguerite."

"French?"

"Parisienne." Clearing his throat and resting his forearms on the table, he smiles wider. "She was the family's French cuisine fanatic. She's no longer with us, I'm afraid."

I immediately feel more confident in my decision. To this day, all I've known about William Roberts has been about his mediocre cuisine and more than awful attitude. Now he's a man who's lost his wife, and I can sympathize with him a little more. "Sorry for your loss."

"Thank you, Amelie."

Two waiters come out of the kitchen, and instead of the stuffy tuxes my father's staff wears, they're in black T-shirts with the Marguerite's logo and red jeans.

Also flamboyant.

They set two wooden trays on either side of us—on one, a selection of French cheeses and charcuterie, and on the other, a sampling of appetizers that's fairly familiar. Pissaladière, smoked salmon canapés, *socca*, and more well-presented delicacies in small portions.

With one quick look, I can tell this isn't going to be a good meal, but I smile and force a "Wow" out.

"Please dig in. I'm dying to know your opinion."

He's really not.

I grab one of everything and set it on my plate, slowly making my way through the amuse-bouches. They're anything but amusing, though, and if there's one thing I hate, it's forcing down bad food. "Delicious," I comment after a bite of the canapé.

"Oh, Amelie, I can't see you suffer like that." He laughs, dabbing a napkin over his lips. "Please don't eat whatever it is you don't like."

When my apologetic look meets his, he scoffs. "Nothing?" Shoulders sinking, he points at the board on his right. "Not even the cheese? You know we just cut it, right?"

I study his expectant expression and, deciding he's definitely more of a good sport than my dad, I point at the salmon. "See the dark coloration there? It's because it's frozen. Fresh salmon has an even, lighter color. And the socca . . . it's dry. As for the canapés, you should tell your chef they were done about two minutes before they actually served them, and the pissaladière is . . . basically a pizza. The dough should be about this much thinner." I show him my thumb and forefinger almost touching. He mostly looks entertained, so I turn to the cubes of cheese. "As for this . . . that's not how you cut cheese. It should be in slices."

"Huh." His brow furrows as he studies the food around him.

"Sorry. I'm pretty sure that's not how one is supposed to bury the hatchet."

Laughing, he shakes his head. "No, no. I asked. Or, er, well, I didn't. But I wanted to know, and if you weren't about to open your own restaurant, I'd hire you." He throws a look at the door leading to the kitchen. "I've been waiting for an excuse to get rid of my current head chef."

I force out a laugh. One would think mediocre cooking skills would be enough to fire a chef.

"I must admit I'm somewhat curious," William says, taking a bite of a canapé. "What happened between Amelie Preston and her father to cause such a deep rupture?"

Throwing a look at him over the light of the candle between us, I shrug. Though I don't intend to fight my dad's war, I'm certainly not fighting William's either. "No rupture. It was just time for me to move on."

"That easy?"

"That easy," I confirm. It surely was that easy for my dad, since he barely reacted to the news.

He tilts his head, then takes a sip of red wine, his eyes burning into mine until he sets it down. "And when will the grand opening be?"

"The date isn't set yet," I lie. I think he knows, because he continues eating with a smug smile as he observes me.

"And your menu? What do you plan to—"

"William," I say, offering a smile to balance out my rude

interruption. "We both know I'll either lie or refuse to share any detail about my upcoming venture."

"Fair enough." He gestures to the waiter, who comes closer and begins removing the appetizers from the table. "So you won't tell me anything about your restaurant."

"I will not."

"And you won't tell me what happened with your father."

"Definitely not."

He raises both hands in defeat. "All right, Amelie. Tell me about you. Who's Amelie Preston, besides her father's daughter and a soon-to-be restaurateur?"

The question nearly sends me reeling.

For the longest time, I've been Frank's girlfriend. I've been one of La Brasserie's chefs. Martha's best friend. Then Ian became a huge part of me until he wasn't anymore. Now, I don't know who I am.

I guess I'm Amelie, sharing dinner with someone I probably should avoid at all costs.

Amelie who was left at the altar.

Amelie whose father let her go without batting an eye.

Amelie who made the wrong decision.

"I—I need to use the restroom," I say, moving my chair back and rising.

William sets his napkin down and, with a nod, points behind him. "Second door to the—"

I glance at him, but his eyes aren't on my face. They're just a touch south of it—enough to immediately cause me to panic, thinking I might be flashing him with a nip slip. But when I look down, ready to cover up, I notice the long silver chain I keep around my neck has escaped from underneath my shirt, and what William sees is an engagement ring.

Yellow topaz tear-shaped stones around a central white diamond on a thick gold band. Like a yellow daisy.

The ring that Ian *almost* gave me.

I slide it back under my shirt and offer him a circumstantial smile. For a few seconds, his eyes roam left and right, his lips parted. God, how pathetic. He must know I'm not married, because he's utterly shocked. I clear my throat. "Second door to the . . ."

"Left. To the left."

Politely, I nod and walk away, cursing myself in every French and English word that can be used for the occasion. I enter the bathroom, taking stock of its black-and-gold marble sinks, rendering it just as eccentric as everything else. I step in front of the mirror, throwing a disgruntled look at my flushed cheeks and sunken eyes. Even with makeup, I've been able to cover only part of the misery I've been through in the last eight months. And this heat isn't helping either.

After splashing some water on my wrists and dabbing a tissue over my face to dry up the thin layer of sweat covering it, I leave the bathroom and make my way back to the table. William smiles, but something's definitely off, and though I certainly don't owe him an explanation, I'd rather say something now than be surprised by his question later.

"I'm not married," I say as I avoid his gaze. "Just . . . just in case you were wondering."

"You're not?"

This time I focus on his dark eyes and shake my head.

"Why aren't you—" He breaks off, then rubs his chin. "I mean, if you're not married, then are you . . . engaged?"

Well, if it isn't my favorite topic of conversation. "Hmm . . . I was engaged for a while, but things didn't work out."

"Why not?"

Lord, he will not let this go, will he? And after refusing to share any details about my restaurant or my father, then freaking out at his next question, I feel weird telling him to mind his own business. "We broke up."

"What happened?"

Clearing my throat, I meet his gaze. Why is he being so damn invasive? I'm obviously being vague on purpose. "William, I'm afraid there's been some sort of misunderstanding. I've agreed to have dinner with you because I'd love to—what was it you said?" I ask, not giving him time to answer. "Hash out our differences. Start fresh. But whether I'm married, or engaged, or one of eight sister wives, should be of no interest to you." Taking a deep breath, I square my shoulders. "We're not friends, and you're making me uncomfortable."

He seems to remember himself, and as the waiters set a plate of salmon and another of entrecôte on the table, he rubs his hands together and studies me with an apologetic smile. "You're right. I'm so sorry. I guess . . . you're wearing a ring around your neck and . . . it's peculiar."

I stab my salmon, my annoyance growing with his insistence. I refuse to acknowledge it, though. I've given him all the answers he needs.

"So did you leave him? Or did he leave you?"

God! Why does he keep insisting?

I set my fork down, knowing there's one answer that will get him to drop the topic immediately. "He left me at the altar, okay? We were having problems for a while, and I tried really hard to fix them, but it didn't work out."

"Hmm. So sorry to hear." His gaze narrows as he cuts a piece of his steak, his charming demeanor now only a distant memory. He looks . . . annoyed, for some reason. "Are you still in love with him? Is that why you're wearing that ring?"

"I'm not in love with anyone," I mutter through gritted teeth. It's a lie, of course, but there's no way I'm telling him the ring I wear around my neck is from another guy. The guy I should have ended up with.

Blowing out an annoyed breath, I try to compose myself. "If this is what you'll want to talk about for the rest of our dinner, then I think we should end it right now."

He distractedly nods, his jaw clenched. Quickly, he grabs his phone, throws it a look, then turns to me. "I'm sorry, Amelie, but it looks like we'll indeed need to call it a night. Something came up that has to be taken care of right now."

With my fork and knife still in hand, I study his expression. He's clearly not joking, but this makes no sense. The guy came to my restaurant to ask me to bury the hatchet, then questioned me about Frank, and now he's getting rid of me? "What—"

He stands. "Thank you so much for coming. Do you know how you're getting back home?"

"Y-yes." I stand, too, just as he motions to the waiters to come over. They take away our plates of nearly untouched food, and once I grab my bag, William walks me to the door in complete silence. The tension is so palpable, it can't possibly be because of the ring. Because of my personal life. Is he annoyed because I didn't answer all his questions? Because I dared to defy him? Maybe my dad was right all along, and he's just an arrogant douchebag.

We reach the entrance of the restaurant, and when I throw a questioning look at him, he smiles politely. "Apologies for cutting our evening short. You'll hear from me sooner than you expect."

I open my mouth to say something, but I'm possibly less interested in all of this than he is, so I just nod, plenty aware that I won't hear from him at all. Thank God.

I guess the hatchet remains anything but buried.

38

The Truth Isn't Yum

– TODAY –

Leaving Barb in the room, I walk downstairs. Ian has a couple of hours of work to do, and I miss him. I miss him so much, it makes me wonder what exactly awaits me after tomorrow, once the ICCE is over and we go back to our hometowns. We haven't properly discussed it besides his brief attempt at making me spill the truth about his dad, but we'll need to make some decisions, possibly a compromise or two, sooner than later.

I walk through the hall, filled to the brim with people, then along the small corridor and into the kitchen, immediately halting as I notice wide shoulders, dark hair, an even darker aura around him. William *fucking* Roberts.

He turns around, his brows slightly rising as he takes me in. "Amelie."

"I'm just—" I take a step back. "I'll come back later."

"Please, come in. We're bound to have a conversation anyway, don't you think?"

Are we? Can't we just never talk? Never look at each other again? Can't we simply pretend the other doesn't exist and go about our lives?

No, we can't. Because of Ian. And though I hate this man, I love Ian more.

Hyperaware of the danger, I make my way to the kettle, urging my legs to cooperate. Once I've poured my tea, I lean my back against the counter and turn to William.

He's cooking something—fish, by the look of it. And badly, by the smell of it. "Just making one of my specialties for Julia Banks. Have you met her? Lovely English chef."

The muscles of his back and arms strain against his dark shirt as he whips the pan back and forth. God, the flame's so high, he's basically murdering that piece of salmon. When he turns to me, I shake my head.

"She's a big fan of my *saumon*."

"Probably because the burned bits cover most of the actual taste."

With a chuckle, he turns to me. "Hmm. It looks like my son didn't change your mind about our restaurant, then." He turns the stove off and sets the salmon on a plate, then adds asparagus and roasted fingerling potatoes. He mirrors my position on the other side of the island, arms crossed and a friendly expression that quickly disappears. "So, what are we going to do about this?"

God, the audacity of this man. He speaks as if we're part of the same team, as if we're "together" in this. We're not. We're as against each other as one could be.

"Nothing?" He nods. "Well, I'd much rather have you out of Ian's life. You certainly don't deserve him, since you didn't choose him when given the chance."

"And *you* deserve him?"

He smiles. "I'm his father."

"Parents need to deserve their children too."

He steps forward, his arms uncrossing as he studies me with

interest. "Your mom. She left you, didn't she?" When I say nothing, he nods. "Right. And I can't imagine growing up with Hammond was that much fun."

"What's your point, William?" I ask, barely containing a hiss.

"Your mother abandoned you. Your father is—well, Le Dictateur, and your fiancé left you the day of your wedding." His sharklike eyes run over me, scanning me so deeply, it's almost as if he can see under my skin. "You're damaged. Insecure, broken. That's probably why you were unable to accept my son's love when it most mattered." I flinch, but he continues as if he's not even talking to me. "Do you have any idea how badly you broke his heart? You'll hurt him again, Amelie, and after his mother, then that wretched woman he made me hire, then you, he's been through enough."

I look down at the metal counter with a sigh. God, do I wish this man were just evil. Plain evil. If he were, I would have told Ian everything the moment I figured out who his father was. But he's not. He cares about his son greatly. He'd do anything for Ian, and I'm sure from where he's standing his actions are more than justified. His son got his heart broken by Ella, then lost his mom right after that. And then I did what I did.

"I have no intention of hurting Ian. But I know you think I will anyway, and hell, I might. I can't see the future." When his jaw sets, I tuck some hair behind my ear and whisper, "But he's not weak. He's not this broken, defenseless person you make him out to be. He doesn't need you to fight his battles, and if he knew *how* you do it, he'd be appalled. Because your son is good."

"I agree." He lightly taps his hand on the counter. "And because he's so good, he deserves someone who chooses him from the get-go. So you'll break it off. He'll find someone better, and—"

"William," I interrupt. I straighten, then calmly study his cold smile. "I won't leave Ian's life. There's nothing you can do, nothing you can threaten me with that would make me go away. In fact, I'm only willing to lie about what happened between you and me because I don't want your son to lose you. That is as far as I'll go to accommodate you. For him. Only for him."

"He'll never marry you," he taunts. "Especially not after the number you did on him. He's done with all that, Amelie."

"I don't care."

A grim shadow passes over his face. "Really? And what happens five years from now, when all your friends are married and you want to wear a pretty white dress?"

"Your son gave me the perfect dress already," I say as I slowly stir my tea. "I'll just wear it for him."

"Amelie—"

"I thought I smelled rat," comes from the kitchen entrance. Both William and I turn around, and my father slowly makes his way to us, his glare not focused on me for once. "I should have known it was the work of a Roberts in the kitchen."

Barely holding back a chuckle, I glance at the honey-brown liquid in my mug.

"Hammond," William says, returning to his piece of salmon. "Aren't you a little too old for these games?"

"*Bien sûr.* Amelie?"

"What, you want me to roast him?" I ask with a sly smile. "He'd probably end up burning that too."

William comes closer, the smell of his cologne nauseating, especially together with the fish he's holding. "Did you tell your father about our dinner, Amelie?"

Holy fuck. I feel my dad's wide eyes scan the side of my face and, gripping my mug tighter, I prepare for his face to turn red and his voice to sharpen as he scolds me.

"If you touched my daughter—"

"*Dad*," I squeal. "A *professional* dinner is what he means." If it's in the celestial plan that I should die of a stroke, I can't think of a better moment. Unfortunately, nothing happens as my face reaches the temperature of burning briquettes. "And anyway, if he did touch me, you'd know, because I would have scrubbed myself raw." I turn around. "Now, if you'll excuse me—"

My phone beeps and, after taking it out of my pocket, I glance at the screen.

Ian:
Come to my room, beautiful?

Saved by Ian again.

Releasing a pent-up breath, I set my tea down and leave the kitchen. I don't feel like Earl Grey now anyway; maybe whiskey. Whatever solution Ian and I settle on for our future, it'll have to be far away from his father, or I'll end up giving myself an ulcer.

Pushing the thought to a remote corner of my brain, I climb the stairs and glance down at my phone. The two hours he needed to take care of work might just be worth seeing his name on my screen again.

God, how I've missed it.

The hotel is as busy as always, even more so today, with the guest lecture William Roberts and my father will bestow upon us in half an hour. Maybe there's a way I can avoid it altogether without Ian getting suspicious.

When I knock on his door, he shouts that it's open, so I quickly make my way in. He's sitting on the armchair by the window, his eyes hard as he studies me with a less than pleased expression.

My heart skips a beat.

"Hey . . ." I tentatively step forward, stopping after a couple of steps. "What's up?"

"What happened between you and my father, Amelie?"

I swallow, bile rising up my throat as I try to keep a blank expression on my face. He caught us. He knows what's going on, and now he'll lose everything. His father, his restaurant, and eventually me.

"Nothing," I whisper as I sit on the bed. "Wh-why do you ask?"

"You know my father. You've met him before today." He stands, then walks up to me. He's the most serious I've ever seen him, though also strangely calm, while there's sweat running down my back and a whole herd of horses in my chest. "Do you really think I haven't noticed how distressed you were when you met him? Not hateful, not angry, not hostile. You were afraid—more than that, you were terrified."

"No, Ian—" I attempt, but he raises his hand.

"Spare me." His neutral expression shifts to anger. "You were terrified. As you were after talking to Ella. And as you are every time I ask you about your restaurant's failure."

My head spins, and he turns away as he walks to his open suitcase on the luggage rack. He grabs something out of it, and when he drops it on the desk, my heart stops.

Yum magazine. The glossy cover with a picture of me and my restaurant stares back at me, familiar and disturbing, as heat creeps up my neck and cheeks.

"I asked Ella for her copy." He crosses his arms and stares at me for a few seconds. "Imagine my surprise when she mentioned she cooked dinner for you and my father about four months ago."

Oh, fuck.

My heart beats out of my chest, sweat dampening my upper lip as my hands shake. I've seen Ian upset before, but I'm not sure I'll be able to deal with the shitstorm that's about to hit me.

I stand, the muscles of my legs shaking with adrenaline and fear, and go to him. Grabbing hold of his arm, I whisper, "Ian, whatever she said—nothing happened, okay?"

"Nothing?" he asks.

"*Nothing,*" I repeat slowly, staring deep into his eyes. It looks like the dinner is all he's aware of, and if I keep it that way, then my deal with William stands. I can still protect Ian. "He wanted to bury the hatchet. We had dinner. That's it."

"Are you sure *nothing* happened?" he asks, and this time uncertainty makes my head spin. He knows more than what he's telling me—but how?

Stepping to the side, he grabs the magazine and sits down. He scrolls through the pages, then folds it and clears his voice. "'Amelie Preston, daughter of Hammond Preston, has failed in her first business venture. The thirty-year-old woman, who's been working for her father, arguably the biggest chef of fine French cuisine in the country, is now closing down Amelie's Bistro after merely two months of activity.'"

"Ian . . ." I whisper, my fingers trembling as I grip the desk.

"You're right. We don't need the introduction. We know who you are." He hums, his eyes scrolling through the lines of text. "'Her opening was pushed four times, costing her most of her bookings. According to various sources, her restaurant didn't get approved for a liquor license, then was given an insufficient grade by health inspectors.'"

I press my lips together tightly, the humiliation still making me feel like I'm being roasted on high flames.

"Curious, don't you think?" he asks. "You're not a newbie. I'm sure you've cleaned a kitchen a billion times before. You must have seen plenty of inspections too. Even weirder that you were denied a liquor license."

God, I'm going to faint.

"'Amelie finally managed to open her restaurant a month after she originally intended to,'" Ian keeps reading. "'More than a few of us were surprised when the previous member of La Brasserie's successful kitchen got bombed with negative reviews, bringing her Yelp score to 1.8.'"

Once Ian sets the magazine down on his thigh, I sit on the edge of the bed, my hands on my lap as my eyes burn a hole in the floor. No point in trying to lie more, not until I know for a fact how much of this he's put together.

"1.8, Amelie. I'm pretty sure Burgerman scores higher than that," he says. When I say nothing, he resumes reading. "'The critics' opinion didn't go much better, with four different insufficient scores across the board.'"

He throws me a dubious look, then continues reading. "'And proving herself unprepared for all that running a restaurant entails, her lack of marketing skills and inability to promote her new restaurant quickly sank her, resulting in an embarrassing ordeal for the pristine line of Preston chefs.'"

He snaps the magazine closed, then sets his consuming gaze on me. "Then the article goes on to speak poorly of your personal life. Which, if you ask me, they deserve to be sued for. Being left at the altar hardly has anything to do with your skills as a chef. But anyway . . ." He takes his phone out of his pocket. "Guess what? My dad's real close with the director of *Yum* magazine, so I called him. I asked who the critics were, and he could only remember two. Interesting fact?"

Let me guess. They're friends of his father.

He nods as if he's read my mind. "And you know what else? Danny—that's my dad's friend at *Yum* magazine—said he remembered the article, because when they do these kinds of stories, they always gather comments from people who've eaten at the restaurants to back up their articles." His face softens as he lightly smiles. "Congratulations, Amelie. Not one single person who they

reached out to had anything bad to say about you. They had the
meal of their lives at Amelie's Bistro."

A sob shakes my shoulders, then another, and another, until
I'm gasping for air and drowning in tears. My chest clenches painfully at every new memory crowding my mind. At the panic that
rose inside me when the first reviews came, at the sleepless nights
spent hoping it was all just a bad dream and not me crashing
against a wall at full speed without the power to stop it.

The weight on the bed shifts, and Ian's lips trail along the side
of my head, one of his hands touching my cheek and the other
one pressing me against him. He holds me there, in that same position, until I cry all my pain out, until my wails turn into soft
whimpers, my face so bloated I can barely see and a persistent pain
settling in my temples.

"If, when you say 'nothing happened,' you mean you didn't kiss
him, sleep with him, use my father as a rebound after Frank, I believe you," Ian eventually says as he hands me a tissue. "But it's
time to tell me the truth, Amelie, because something definitely
happened."

39

Walk Away

I lock the door of Amelie's Bistro and sigh. Glancing at the insignia, at the barren walls, the dirty floors, I almost want to cry. But I have no strength for that either.

William Roberts won.

I never thought I'd say that sentence out loud. Letting Roberts win is the very last thing I thought I'd ever allow myself to do, but I have no more ammunition, no more drive.

He turned my dream into a nightmare—into what has me sobbing into my pillow until I finally fall asleep.

I should have gone to my father, but I couldn't stand the idea of disappointing him yet again. I couldn't imagine how I'd ask, what he'd say, the judgmental expression on his face when I'd tell him about my failures.

So I didn't. I let it all unfold before my eyes, at first wondering if it was really my fault. If the bad reviews and the logistical and bureaucratic mistakes were really my own shortcomings. Until it became plenty clear they were not.

What I don't know is why. Why he's done all of this. Was he afraid I'd be his competition? Was it because of my father? Maybe this was the reason he invited me to dinner. Or why he interrupted our date?

My foot hits a box at the entrance. I lean down and grab it, and once the For Rent sign is on the ground, I sit on the last chair left by the deck. The sea looks calm today, like an endless mirror of the sky. Funny, because in some ways it resembles the way I feel inside. Serene.

I'm done. I lost, and I accept it. Giving up feels liberating.

I rip the box open. I'm not supposed to receive mail here anymore, but I'm sure it'll keep happening for a while. Fishing inside, I find a magazine. I pull it out a little, recognizing the name on top. *Yum* magazine. It's a monthly magazine consisting mostly of fluff about restaurants and cuisine, but it often leans into gossip a little too much for my taste, so I never bother reading it.

It's also not free, so I don't see why I'm getting a copy.

I check the sender, but the field is empty, so with a sigh I pull the magazine out, and the first thing that catches my eye is the red sticky note on top. The black ink used on it feels darker than dark even before I read the words written with it.

"Nothing personal, Amelie. William Roberts."

Behind it, on the cover of *Yum* magazine, there's me. My picture. It's the first one that shows up if you write my name and surname online. I'm wearing La Brasserie's black chef's coat and smiling with my arms crossed. Next to the huge picture, there are several bubbles encasing shots of my restaurant, and a blue, white, and red title that reads: "The French Disappointment."

With my hands almost numb as my heartbeat skyrockets, I turn page after page until I'm greeted by the same picture of myself. My eyes scroll through the lines, grasping words here and there but not really retaining much. "The face of nepotism" and

"Just a byproduct of her father's success" are what stand out the most. By the time I get to the end, I know what the gist is, but I couldn't quote a single sentence if I tried.

I read it and read it and read it again to no avail until I can't feel a thing besides cold from the strong gusts of wind that have picked up in the last minutes. I can't feel angry or defeated anymore. I just grieve everything I lost silently, like a funeral hymn echoing in my mind.

Setting the magazine down, I close my eyes, and I breathe.

How long will it take for my father to see it? How long until Barb does? Will it get to Frank or Martha too? How big will it become? Maybe it'll find its way to Ian.

My phone beeps, and these days, every time it does, I dread it. It's either someone asking for money or Martha complaining about wedding planning, which she started again a few months back. I don't know when it happened, but at some point I started hating my life, and I still can't get out of this slump.

I guess it started when I met Ian. When he showed me what else is out there.

If he were here, he'd know what to do—how to get rid of William Roberts. He'd tell me encouraging, lovely words that would push me to try one more time to think of a new solution.

But I'm out. Out of will, out of money, out of ideas. William Roberts destroyed my restaurant and my reputation, and I don't know how to recover, nor do I truly want to. I'll just find another job, one that doesn't involve cooking. And I'll be my own chef in my free time.

With a sigh, I grab my phone. It's Martha.

Martha:
Call me sometime today?

I'm not exactly in the mood to talk, but it might be about Barb's pregnancy, so I can't exactly ignore her. Bringing the phone to my ear, I listen for the beeps.

"Hey, Ames."

"Hey. Is everything okay?"

"Where are you?"

"At the restaurant. I had to clean up before the new tenants come in."

Silence. I hear noises in the background, then she clears her throat. "Oh, maybe we should talk some other time."

"Tell me whatever you need to say, Martha," I say, stiffening on the chair.

We've been fighting a lot lately. And I don't mean fighting like in the last year, where she does whatever she wants and I just take it while resentment brews under the surface. No. It's been some proper fighting, with screaming and accusations and anger. Since I opted out of telling her about Frank's arrangement in the end, she continues to blame me and Ian for the breakup, and I let her. Because I don't care about her opinion and it's less humiliating than the truth anyway.

"It's just . . . I was wondering . . ."

Oh my God, I've got no patience left for this. "What?"

"You know the wedding is in twenty days, and . . ."

As she stutters incomprehensible words, my brain tries to guess what exactly she's asking for. I haven't got a clue.

". . . Frank will be there."

"Mm-hmm." I bite my bottom lip, trying to push down the anxiety I feel at the idea of seeing him again. I already knew he would be, so there must be more to this call. "And?"

"And I was thinking maybe you could . . . talk? Before then?"

I remain silent.

"I know what he did was fucked-up, Ames, leaving you at the altar like that. But you can't blame him. Not after you had an *affair*—"

"No."

Martha says nothing for a few seconds, and I can't help the smile that forms on my lips. *No.* What a beautiful word that is.

"Really, Ames? You're just going to let him go without even fighting?"

"Really." I settle in the chair and tilt my head back, enjoying the warmth of the sun on my face. "I don't want to fight for Frank. Nor do I want to marry him."

"Ames, this is ridiculous. Look at your life for a moment. You can't tell me you're better off now, and it doesn't look like Ian stuck around—"

"Martha, I said no. And you have to respect it. I don't need to explain myself, and I don't have to give you my reasons." Grinning wider than I ever have, I continue: "No means *no.*"

She grumbles something that sounds like "Unbelievable." And it *is* unbelievable. It's unbelievable that I've waited so long to say no. *No, Martha, you can't have everything you want with zero regard for anyone else. No, Frank, I won't marry you when you obviously don't love me. No, Dad, I will not be a pawn in your sick games.*

So easy. How in the world it took me so long to get it is beyond me.

"Fine. If you're gonna be unreasonable, do what you want. But you'll end up alone."

"Is that so?" I ask.

"Yes. Since that Ian guy, I swear you're unbearable," she spits out. "And it's not enough that he ruined your relationship. Now you're going to let him come between our friendship too."

My fist clenches on my thigh. I couldn't care less about her opinions, but she should watch her poisonous mouth before she says a word about Ian. "He's the best thing that's ever happened to me, Martha. And I let you, Frank, and mostly myself ruin it. But I can at least take solace in the fact that the past year wasn't for nothing, because I won't let you or anyone else walk over me. If that means ruining our friendship"—I shrug—"well, so be it."

"Fine, Ames. Maybe when there's nobody left, you'll change your mind."

Happier than ever with my decision, I look at the colorful sails in the distance. "Yeah, maybe."

"Bye."

Once she hangs up, I glance at the glass construction one last time, step onto the creaking planks of the deck, and take hold of the slick metal handrail. I breathe in the salt, the sea, the summer.

It's time to walk away.

Though no one said I couldn't do it on my own terms.

I throw my bag on the table, deciding I'll be back for it later. But first, there's something I've been wanting to do since the first time I saw this place. This is my last chance before the temperature drops— and, more importantly, it's my last chance before I give up this place.

Gripping the handrail, I lift one leg over it, then the other, and step on the narrow edge. My heart tumbles as I look down at the water. It can't be more than fifty feet away, and the beach is a short swim from here. Still, jumping into the unknown is scary. Doing it alone even more so.

But it's what I need.

I take a deep breath, the toes of my shoes suspended over the void, then close my eyes. As I let go of the rail, I leap forward and let myself fall.

40

Cease the Activity

"I'm sorry I didn't tell you before, I just . . . I know you won't be able to look past this, and you're so close to your dad. I just . . ."

Still no movement except for his chest heaving, so at least I know he's breathing. But his eyes are still slits focused on the carpet. His fists are still clenched on his thighs, and there's not a hint of the good, patient man I know left in him. He's furious. Is he mad at me too? Is he planning a murder? I have no idea.

"He blocked your number on my phone," he hisses after a while. Before I can ask how he figured it out, he forges on. "He drove with me to your wedding, and the whole time he kept trying to dissuade me. Said it was a mistake, that I would end up getting hurt. When I called and you didn't answer, I left my phone in the car and came in."

My mouth hangs open, a fresh wave of rage taking over my brain. Of course it was him. I should have realized it before. He's gone to such extremes to protect his son from me that blocking my number is really the tamest of his interferences.

"How did he know?"

"What?" I ask.

"That you were you. I told him about us, but I never mentioned your name. He's been known to overshare during interviews, and with you being engaged I was very careful. So how did he figure it out?"

I shake my head, thinking of the day of my wedding. "After I missed your call, I called you back immediately. He must have seen my contact and—" Even before I finish my sentence, I remember the screenshot Ian sent me the night we met. "Beautiful" with a red heart. He didn't use my name to save my contact. So maybe . . . maybe it was during that night at the Marguerite. He *did* flip out at some point, but why?

My eyes widen as it comes back to me. "He saw the ring. Your— the ring he got for your mom." I pull it out of my shirt and show it to him. "And midway through our dinner, after seeing it, he kicked me out."

He exhales deeply, as if the information only fuels his anger. We've been sitting here a while, so I'm pretty sure William and my father are already giving their lecture, and missing it might be the one perk of this whole situation. But then again, if Ian breaks up with me now, everything else will pretty much disappear in comparison.

He might, right? Sure, he said I'm the most important person in his life, and with everything that he's given and shown me over the last year, I believe him. But William is his dad. I guess there is a chance that, despite his actions, Ian will choose him.

Or maybe he won't. Maybe he'll find a way to forgive his dad and be with me, and I won't need to pretend I like William for the rest of my life.

Maybe. But not knowing is killing me.

"Do you want to—"

He leaps to his feet and, without a word, strides out of the room in a fury. If I'm to guess, looking for his dad, and if I'm to be even more specific with my guess, to strangle him.

"Ian!" I barge out of the room and along the corridor after him. "Ian, wait. They're giving the seminar. The whole world is there. TV. Newspapers. Don't make a scene right now or you'll sink your mom's restaurant. Please."

He ignores me, his bloodshot eyes focused on the goal, and rushes down the stairs. My begging does nothing to slow him down, and once we arrive at the hotel hall, I step in front of him and reach for both his arms.

"Ian, please wait."

"Amelie, let me go."

"I know you're angry, but—"

"*Angry?*" His eyes meet mine, and I know *angry* doesn't adequately describe his emotional state. Maybe . . . *murderous*. "I'm way past angry, trust me. My father ruined your life. He killed your reputation. He *knew* you weren't married—that you were wearing my ring, even—and didn't say a word to me. He let me suffer for months, thinking you were married to that asshole."

"I know, but your restaurant! Your mom's restaurant!"

"Do you think my mom would have wanted this? That she would have approved of it? If she'd known all of this would happen, she would have burned the Marguerite down herself." He walks past me and toward the largest conference room. "Now watch *me* burn it to the ground."

Panic strangles me as he opens the doors to the conference room, and a few interested eyes meet mine because of the commotion. William is on the small stage, talking into a microphone about market trends, and my dad is scowling behind him.

With the glances I steal at the audience, I notice three of the well-known critics who reviewed my restaurant, journalists from

Yum magazine with their cameras rolling, head chefs and owners of some of the biggest restaurants in the country. There must be hundreds of people in here, and among them most of those who count in the industry.

"*Ian*," I whisper-scream. "*Ian, wait.*"

But he doesn't, instead hopping onto the stage without a pause until he's facing William. His father looks confused for about a second; then his son's clenched fist crashes into his nose and he falls back with a loud thump.

The collective gasp is as deafening as the one people had for me when I announced my wedding wasn't going to happen—and, if possible, just as painful.

Ian reaches down, grabbing his father by the collar of his suit. I rush onto the stage, and my father steps in front of me to keep me away from the commotion. "Ian," I beg as I try to get past his imposing figure.

William's face is smeared with blood, his hands clinging to his son's shirt as Ian pulls him up. There's a confused look in his eyes, which I'm sure is only the result of the punch he took, because he *must* know what this is about.

"What did you do to her?" Some people have stormed the stage in order to separate the two of them, but Ian has lost all control and is close to growling as he tries to free himself from the arms that are holding him back. "You ruined her life. For what, huh? What was your goal? Revenge?"

William's eyes slowly refocus on his son as someone hands him a tissue and someone else calls for water. Everyone in the room is talking, moving, speculating. All of it in front of cameras and journalists. This is a damned disaster. A clusterfuck of epic proportions.

"She . . ." William moves toward his son as he dabs his bloody nose with a grimace. "She hurt you, Ian, and—"

"She *hurt* me?" Ian lunges at him again, but the people standing between them keep him back. "You don't know her. Don't know shit about what she went through."

"It doesn't matter," William insists.

"No, you're right. It doesn't. Whatever she's done to me will never justify what you did to her."

William shakes his head, copious amounts of blood spilling from his nose to his trembling lips. "I wanted to make sure you'd never have to see her again, and I knew if she stayed in our shared business, you eventually would."

"All I've wanted for months was to see her again!" Ian shouts.

God, I want to reach him. I want to hug him and make it all better. If I can't, I want to at least be there for him, hugging him in silence as he cries out all the tears I'm sure he's holding back.

"Let's talk about this in private," William says, gesturing toward the door.

"Why?" Ian tries to take a step forward. When the middle-aged man in front of him holds a hand to his chest, Ian spreads his arms. "What's there to keep secret? You don't think everyone should know the truth?"

With his dark eyes narrowing, William removes the tissue from under his nose. "Think about your mother's restaurant before you do anything you'll regret, Ian. Especially for some meaningless girl."

"*Meaningless*," Ian grinds out. "You think I care about the Marguerite more than I care about Amelie? I love—" He turns around, looking for me. When his eyes meet mine across the crowd of people on the stage, they soften. "I love you, Amelie."

My lips tremble for a second, tears falling down my cheeks as soon as I blink. "I know," I whisper. "I love you too."

He smiles for just as long, his blue eyes even bluer now that they're coated in tears. I'm not sure if it's pain over what happened, anger at his father, or happiness at hearing my words—though probably it's a mix of all three.

Focusing back on William, he continues, "You know what the restaurant means to me. It's all we have left of Mom." His voice breaks, but he shakes his head as if telling himself he's not allowed to break down. "But I love Amelie more than anything else. She's alive; she's here. She has emotions and feelings and dreams, and you squashed them all, you fucking psychopath."

William's jaw sets as he wipes his mouth with the back of his hand. He looks around the room, then turns to his son again. "Ian, you are good. Too good. These women almost killed you with how much they hurt you. And then I find out a Preston broke your heart? I wasn't going to stand by and—"

"I don't care!" Ian shouts. "You were all I had left, for fuck's sake." With one quick twist of his upper body, he frees himself of the men's hold. "I'm good. I'm not going to hit him again."

He turns to the crowd, pulling down his sweater, which has run up his chest in all the commotion. Dragging a shaky hand through his hair, he inhales, then steps up to the microphone. "Hello, everyone. Sorry to interrupt your seminar."

"*Ian!*" I shriek.

What his father did is illegal. Unethical. It's the death of the Roberts name and their restaurant. He can't tell the whole world.

"Most of you know about the *idiotic* feud between the Robertses and Prestons. Well, it ends today. I have not one single issue with Hammond Preston's professional life and the way he runs his business."

"Ian, stop," William insists, but when he tries to reach his son, he's held back.

"Most of you also know about Amelie Preston's recently failed venture, thanks to *Yum* magazine." He trains his glare on the journalists and cameramen whose devices bear the magazine's logo. "With their display of unethical journalism and media bullying, they made sure her professional *and* personal life were dragged through the mud."

The murmurs in the room grow, and, feeling all eyes on me, I move behind my dad a little. Probably not the best place to look for protection, but here we are.

"What you don't know is that my father is responsible for her failure," Ian continues. "That he used his contacts in the world of fine cuisine to sink her business. And that this industry is permeated by nepotism, corruption, sexism, and all sorts of exhausting shit." He shakes his head. "Maybe you do know but you don't care."

The room is now uncomfortably silent, the occasional squeaking of chairs the only interruption.

"Anyway, I'm done with it. I'm done with all of you, with butter and disgusting fucking cheese, and most of all"—he turns to his father—"I'm done with William Roberts."

He faces me for just a second, and I wish there weren't as much pain in his eyes as I see. That I could take some of it away. Then he turns his attention to the silent audience again and takes a deep breath. "The Marguerite is, from today onward, closed."

My jaw drops, and it's safe to say the same thing happens to most of the other people in the room. Did he just say he's closing down the restaurant? Given how upset he is, I'm sure he doesn't want to work with his father—or see him, for that matter—but can't we find another solution? Take a moment to think about it?

The room explodes in a cacophony of voices as Ian abandons the microphone and, without one single glance at his father, comes over to me. As the audience members talk excitedly among themselves, the journalists in the room start shouting questions about our relationship and ask for proof of what Ian just revealed. William repeats Ian's name. My father launches into one of his monologues of French insults. And through it all, Ian drapes his arms around me.

It's like nothing else exists beyond our hug, and if something did, Ian wouldn't notice. His face sinks into the crook of my neck, his body shaking against mine, and I'm not sure if he wants to comfort me or needs comforting himself, but I hold him as tightly as I possibly can, not wanting to ever let go.

"I love you," he whispers. "Let's leave Mayfield and Creswell. Your father and mine. The restaurants. Let's leave it all behind together and start over somewhere else."

"Yes," I answer without hesitating. I don't need to think about it, don't need to consider it or wonder or worry. It's the easiest yes of my life.

Ian leans back, kisses my lips, then lets me go, the hauntingly sad expression still on his face. "Let's get out of here."

———————

"Fucking hell, this baby better be cute," Barb says, shutting the door of the cab. "I can't believe I missed a literal smackdown because of a headache."

The Kent Farm stands before me, the endless fields on my left and right as familiar as they are painful. Stepping on the gravel, I straighten my forest-green dress. "It was quite the show. Of course, not if you're involved in it."

"What happened then?"

We approach the entrance of the venue. "Ian wanted us to leave, but you were still there, and with Martha's wedding today . . ."

"So where is he?"

"I don't know." He said he needed to go and that he'd call me, but he hasn't yet. He sent a text last night saying that he loves me and that he was settling things with his lawyer and dealing with sponsors and journalists and curious friends. The web's already filled with articles, and people keep contacting me to hear my side of it, to give an interview or make a statement. It's even bigger than the *Yum* magazine ordeal.

Once again, my life's on everybody's lips, and I'm loving it as much as the first time: not at all.

"I asked him to come today, but I'm not sure he will. He didn't answer, and if you knew him, you'd know that's concerning at best."

"He can't be in a good place right now."

No, he's most definitely not. His dad and his business—that's what he lost yesterday. And with that, he lost his best friend, his job, his reputation, his mom's dream. Wherever he is and whatever he's doing, he can't possibly be doing well, and as soon as my responsibilities today are dealt with, I'll be by his side. I'll pick up the pieces one by one and put him back together.

"And how are you dealing with all of it?" My eyes meet Barb's compassionate gaze as she pats my back. "It can't be easy for you either. All of that plus all of"—she looks around—"this."

I smile, delighting in the Kent Farm, which I dreamed would be my own wedding location for the longest time. "I'm surprisingly fine. If anything, last year taught me to deal with high stress levels."

"Yeah, I bet."

With a chuckle, we enter the barn. The location is mostly empty, apart from the people working here, setting up the bar and bringing flowers to the other side of the property.

"There you are," Martha says, coming out of a corridor to our right. She's still in her regular clothes, no makeup, her blond hair in a messy bun. The wedding won't happen for hours, but shouldn't she be getting ready? "How was the trip?"

Barb and I exchange a look as Martha distractedly fidgets with her engagement ring, her eyes moving around the room behind us.

"It was . . . good. Are you okay?" I ask.

"Yeah. No. Yeah." She smiles briefly, then gently rests her hand on mine. "A coworker sent me an article about you and your restaurant. It's insane—everything that man did. Will you be okay?"

All right, something's definitely wrong. It's Martha's wedding day, she's had a full thirty seconds with us, and she's still not talking about herself.

This is freaky. I hate it.

"Yeah, I'll be fine. Where's Trev?"

"Somewhere around here. I don't know."

"And the makeup artist? The photographer? The hairdresser?" Barb asks, her eyebrows knitting together.

"Yeah, yeah. They're here." Martha's eyes meet mine. "I wanted to talk to you before we start with all the wedding craziness."

"Sure," I say, tentatively. Barb says she'll go outside and call Ryan, and once she's gone, Martha and I settle at a small table by the side of the room. "What's up?"

Biting her lower lip, she looks down at the table. Her foot taps against the floor, nervous energy bouncing off her as she hesitates. "So there's a lot I need to cover, but . . ."

My muscles stiffen, my mood worsening by the second. "What happened?"

She rubs the side of her neck, her green eyes lowering. "Nothing . . . well, not nothing. I just . . . Look, this isn't the wedding I want, okay?" She drags a hand over her face. "You know I've always dreamed of something much different. But . . . but then Trev's mom . . ."

"Trev's mom?"

"Yeah," she whispers. "I know she's dead, and she's my fiancé's mom, but that woman was an absolute bitch."

"Martha, I'm not following. What does Trev's mom have to do with anything?"

"She wasn't okay with my Vegas-inspired wedding. With upside-down keg drinking and Jell-O shots and fireworks. 'It's not classy,' she said." Her lips twist, her eyes rolling. "As if her son were the king of England or something. She loved your taste, and I wanted to impress her, and . . . and I fucked up."

Oh. Well, that makes much more sense than Martha in a white wedding dress, for sure.

Releasing a breath, I ask, "Why didn't you tell me?"

"Because!" Her head drops forward but she quickly pulls herself back up straight. "I was embarrassed. Plus, it's not like it changes anything. What I was doing was so fucked-up. I just couldn't take her constant nagging, and one day she asked to see your location, and . . ." She shrugs. "And after that, it all got out of control. She stopped with her constant criticism, and I let it . . . happen."

I nod, her visible discomfort filling me with sadness. I guess I should have figured something was wrong, because although she's definitely self-centered and overbearing, she's never been mean. During the last year? She was evil.

"Anyway, I know it's not that great of an apology. The truth is there isn't much to excuse myself with. I behaved like shit, and I hurt you." She presses her lips together tightly, blinking again and again. "Since finding out about what you were going through with Frank, I can't stop thinking about the fact that I put you through all that while you were struggling. Then the restaurant happened, and I . . ." She pulls her hair up. "And I had no idea! I should have noticed, Ames. I should have said something. I should have—"

"Martha," I say, pulling her fingers apart when she clenches her hands together. "I appreciate your apology. I understand better than anyone what the pressure and stress of planning a wedding can do to your head."

"Yeah, it can definitely do a number." She chuckles bitterly. "It's kind of ironic, though. I stole your wedding, and we both end up with weddings we hate."

"Why didn't you plan something else after Trev's mom passed?" I ask. It hurts to think she hates her wedding. I know it could have been me, but it wasn't, and the thought of settling for less than what I want seems unrealistic today.

"Because most of the deposits were already paid. They let us change the date because of the circumstances, but we would have lost too much money if we'd just withdrawn."

Thinking of all the money I lost with my non-wedding, I nod. "I'm sorry, M."

"Don't be. I'm not getting married today."

My jaw drops. "Come again?"

"I'm not getting married." She stands, and with the same fidgety attitude she looks to the right. "This wedding has always been yours, and it wouldn't feel right."

If someone's making a study on runaway brides, I'd like to see the numbers. It can't be as common as it is in our happy little group. "Okay, but . . . does Trev know? Are you guys okay? What about the guests? Have they been informed, or—"

"Yeah, yeah," she says distractedly. Trevor comes out of the side corridor, then gestures to her to come. Holding my arm, she pulls me to my feet and begins walking. "Let's go."

"What? Where?" I ask. If the wedding isn't happening and she's okay, I kind of have somewhere else to be right now. Which is wherever Ian is.

"I need help packing all the makeup and the dress and the shoes and—" She reaches a door, then opens it and smiles. "I know this doesn't make up for everything, but I hope it's a start." She throws herself at me and squeezes me, and after a kiss on my cheek, she gently pushes me forward. As I turn to what looks like the bridal room, my breath catches. It's filled—filled with flowers. I'm no expert, but they look like daisies, and there must be hundreds of them. Beautiful, long-stemmed yellow daisies in transparent vases scattered all around the room, the scent of spring and grass so intense, I can almost taste it.

And standing in the middle of the room . . . "Ian," I whisper as I take a step closer. God almighty, I might faint. He looks perfect in a linen jacket and pants, with a crisp off-white cotton shirt and a dark green tie. His hair is styled back, his beard freshly groomed, his smile still the most beautiful thing about him. That, and the tattoos I can't see right now. "What are you doing here?"

His grin looks genuine. I don't know how it could be with what happened yesterday, but he looks excited, and it's like a balm on burned flesh: soothing and fresh, and boy, do I want to kiss him. "Hi, beautiful."

I turn to Martha, who disappears into the corridor with a giggle. I look around the room again, then walk toward Ian. "What's . . . what's all this?" When I reach him, my lips find his for a kiss. Then another. And another. "God, I've missed you."

"So have I." He presses his nose to my forehead and breathes in. "Sorry I vanished like that."

"It's completely fine." My hands snake over his shoulders, and with my arms on each side of his neck, I look down at his linen suit. "How are you doing?"

"I'm . . ." His hands rub my arms. ". . . working on it, I guess. But if it's okay with you, I don't want to talk about my father right now."

"Taboo topic?"

He chuckles. "Just for a minute or two." Leaning backward enough so that he can look into my eyes, he whispers, "Amelie, you have something of mine."

When his eyes dart to my chest, my fingers close around the ring hanging under my dress. His eyes follow the movement, and with a devastatingly gorgeous smile he whispers, "May I?"

All I can do is nod. He reaches out and fumbles with the clasp of my necklace, unable to see what he's doing as he looks into my eyes, his face only a few inches from mine. The smell of his after-shave is so comforting, I could just melt against him, and that's even truer as he withdraws his arms, having successfully unfas-tened the necklace, and sweetly kisses my cheek.

My hands shake as he leans back and his fingers lace with mine, his mom's ring in his hands. I'm not exactly sure what's going on, but he might be proposing. *Ian. Proposing.*

He slides the ring off the thin chain, then inhales, holding it between his thumb and index finger. "All right. Look, I know this ring is horrifying, but I'll get you another one. A normal one. Whatever you want."

Shaking my head, I look down at the ring that's been my only connection to Ian for so long. "Unpopular opinion. I love your mom's ring. Yes, it's a little . . ." I study the white diamond sitting at the center. "It's peculiar. But it's your mom's. It reminds me of her; it reminds me to be more like her."

"More of a 'Fuck it' attitude?"

"Yeah, fuck it."

He brings my hand to his lips. He kisses my knuckles, then the top of my hand, and smiles. "Amelie, I should have proposed to you at Barbara's wedding." He shakes his head. "I lost so much time with all my nonsense about marriage. My mom was right."

A smile curves my lips. "Well, we'd just met back then, and I was engaged to someone else. I *probably* would have said no."

"Then I should have proposed to you when you texted me for the first time. Or when you called me by mistake. Or when we checked out the band at the Quinns' wedding. Or at that bridal shop." He exhales deeply. "I should have proposed to you every time I talked to you until you said yes."

"Yeah," I agree, brushing a lock of his hair off his forehead. "It's definitely in line with your style."

Huffing out a laugh, he looks down at the floor. "I'm not sure how— Do I get down on one knee? Or is that—"

"No, you're fine."

"So do I just . . . ask?"

"I think you should have planned this before."

He nods, looking left and right. "You're probably right. Wait." He reaches over and grabs some daisies out of one of the vases. He shakes them up and down, getting rid of most of the water dripping from the stems, then offers them to me. "I've been trying to give you flowers for a while."

"You gave me a flower the night we met," I say as I accept them from him.

"I want to give you flowers every day."

Ignoring the drops falling on my shoes, I bring them to my nose, inhaling the scent of spring. It makes my heart flutter, goose bumps taking over most of my skin as a single tear rolls down his cheek. This moment—all the moments that will come after this one—they make it all worth it. William Roberts, my restaurant, my father, Martha, Frank . . . I'd do it all over again. I'd take any path, no matter how painful, as long as it brought me here. To Ian.

For a brief but thoughtful moment, Ian looks around the room, taking in all the daisies, then turns to me, a dazzling smile lighting up his face. "Amelie, will you come to my wedding?" Before I can tell him I'm pretty sure that's not how he's supposed to ask, he wiggles his eyebrows suggestively. "Because I'm definitely going to need a bride."

My hand covers my mouth, joy exploding out of me like tiny fireworks.

That is the cheesiest pickup line in the world.

41

Fifty Percent Mine

– TODAY –

I clutch my chest, my heart is beating so fast: it feels like there's a whole engine working in there. "Ian, this is lovely. Really, it's just . . . I love it. And I love you for it."

Lowering the hand holding the ring, he takes a step back. "Holy fuck. There's a 'but,' isn't there?"

After a second of hesitation, I nod. "Just a tiny one."

"Jesus," he groans. "I can't catch a break with these engagements, can I?"

"No, no. It's just . . . what's the rush?" I study his eyes. "Why propose today, after . . ." His smile wavers, so I know he's thinking of yesterday too. "And at Martha's wedding?"

With a short-lived chuckle, he shakes his head. "This isn't Martha's wedding."

"Yeah, I know, but—"

"Didn't you notice what I'm wearing?"

Of course I did. It's weirdly similar to the outfit I planned for Frank to wear at our wedding—which then turned into the outfit the groom is supposed to be wearing today. "You look insanely great."

He looks down and considers what I'm wearing. "Thanks. You should change."

"Ouch."

He's happy and unbothered as he points to the right, where, hanging from the handle of a large white wardrobe, there's a wedding dress.

My wedding dress.

"I called Martha yesterday. I expected it would take a while to explain what a terrible friend she's been to you, but I'd barely even opened my mouth when she started bawling." He tucks some hair behind my ear. "She really missed you."

"I missed her too," I whisper.

"I know." His smile widens. "She helped me figure out who to invite from your old guest list, then I had to find the damn dress and a suit similar to Trev's, because that's one skinny man and I couldn't fit in his. Oh, and invite people myself. Honestly, without her, Ryan, and Trevor, I wouldn't have pulled this off."

My heart almost bursts. After feeling so lonely for so long, knowing that all these people I love have come together for me is enough for a lifetime of happiness. "You—you want to get married . . . *today*?"

He nods, his blue eyes flickering with excitement. "I get it now." He pecks my head. "I've seen your perfect wedding, and it *is* perfect. The white ranunculus and floating candle centerpieces and the white theme. They're perfect. And you deserve the perfect wedding, Amelie."

Cupping my mouth, I bury my face in his chest. He's wrong. So wrong. I deserve the perfect husband, and that's Ian. Nothing else matters now. The flowers, the photographer, and the music are just the backdrop. My perfect wedding is with Ian.

Tears roll down my cheeks, his fingers rubbing the top of my head. Though *yes* is the word he wants to hear, as I grasp my arms around his neck, I mutter an apology. He deserves it. He's been loving me from day one, and it took me a year to get here.

"'Sorry'?" He leans back a little so he can look at me, a worried look in his eyes. "As in 'Sorry, I'll pass'?"

"I can't wait another minute," I say. "Please marry me."

"Yes? Are you saying yes?"

I nod frantically, his eyes closing as he laughs nervously. "I'm saying fuck yes."

"Fuck yes," he repeats, his lips meeting mine. He kisses me, his tongue swiping against mine over and over again, then abruptly stops. "Are you sure? Is this really what you want? I need to know for sure before I tell you everything else."

"I'm one hundred percent—wait. 'Everything else'?"

He nods. "Before I do, I need to know that, regardless of everything else, you'd marry me today, right here, right now." He raises my chin with two fingers. "Would you, Amelie?"

My stomach twists, an ominous feeling settling in my chest. Ian can certainly act like a complete lunatic when he wants to, and the timing of it is too casual not to involve his father. I just know Ian came up with something crazy. "What did you do?"

He shakes his head. "First, your answer." He gives me a little smirk. "I need to know that what I'll say next won't send you on a self-sacrificing journey. That, regardless of what comes next, you'll marry me."

I extend my hand, spacing my fingers enough that he can fit the ring. Whatever Ian's done, I'd make any sacrifice for him any day precisely because he wouldn't want me to. And if this sacrifice includes marrying him, I don't need any more context. I will. "Yes."

With a radiant smile, he steps closer and holds my hand in his, and, cold against my skin, the metal slides along my finger until it's secure. It's a little heavy and definitely vintage, but it feels like an extension of myself, now that it's on. "It's perfect."

"I think so too."

My own smile wavers, and, lowering my hand, I look at Ian. He's serious, which is never much of a good sign. "So . . . what's 'everything else'?"

"Right." He scratches his forehead. "You heard what I announced yesterday. I imagine you have lots to say about it."

About him deciding to close down the Marguerite? Yes, lots. That he doesn't need to rush into making a decision, and that we can work out a solution together. That if he wants to keep it open, to forgive his father, I'll never resent him for it. And that the world won't miss Ella's delicacies, though that's not as necessary. Shrugging, I settle on "Are you sure that's what makes you happy?"

Running a hand over his face, he looks down at the floor. His expression is similar to the one he wore yesterday, something between anger and fear. It might be defeat. "Amelie, my mom had this dream of a restaurant for us, her family. She kept telling me how one day I'd find this woman and she would work at the restaurant with all of us, and Brie would taste like cotton candy and . . ." He gestures wildly.

"She didn't envision the possibility that you'd marry outside the restaurant world?"

"That's what *I* said: What if I fall in love with an astrophysicist or something?" He rolls his eyes. "But I didn't. I'm marrying a chef. How can it get more perfect than that?"

When his smile fades and turns into a grimace, I squeeze his hand, and he squeezes mine back.

"But it's all ruined now, isn't it? I know you wouldn't have

worked at the Marguerite anyway, but our restaurant was supposed to be for our family. One day, for our kids, assuming you
want kids."

"I . . . don't think so."

"That's fine." He waves the thought off as if it doesn't matter,
and I'm once again mesmerized at how his brain works. Fast and
chaotic and just inherently good. "The point is it was supposed to
be something good. Somewhere safe. And to me it was the place
that represented all her joy. All her positivity and love." Tearing
up, he shakes his head. "My dad took that away."

"I'm so sorry, Ian."

"Me too. I really thought . . . I thought he was a better man.
I hope one day he will be, but until then I can't have him in my
life. I just can't." He clears his throat, as if he's decided he's done
with sadness. I'm afraid that won't be the case. "It's time for new
dreams anyway, don't you think?"

As his arms wrap around me, I rest my ear against his chest.
"New dreams?"

"A restaurant by the beach, maybe? One where people feel at
home?" Whispering, he continues, "One with no sticky, smelly
French cheese?"

"Maybe one where food is mostly eaten with your hands."

"Really?" His jaw drops. "And no vegetables and no water?"

"No, Ian. We'd still need people over the age of four to come in."

He nods. "Fair enough. We can figure it out on our honeymoon.
But the point is . . ." He turns serious again. "I spoke to my lawyer.
It turns out when you *only* own fifty percent of a restaurant, you
can't dispose of it as you please."

Our conversation about his mother's will comes back to me.
"You need to get married to access your inheritance and sell the
restaurant."

He nods but says nothing.

I inhale. Then blink. Then exhale as the idea fully settles.

I expect it to come all crashing down on me. All my fear of rejection and my abandonment issues and all the billion problems I can thank my parents for. I wait for the paranoia to take over my brain. To tell me that he's rushing it because he needs to and not because he wants me to have a perfect wedding. That he wouldn't get married at all if it weren't for the restaurant. But there's only a thrilled excitement coursing through my veins. Only a huge *YES* tattooed on my heart. Ian's proven more than once that he'd do anything for me. Most recently yesterday.

If he says he wants to marry me, I have no doubt that's the truth.

"Okay."

"Okay?" he asks. "You don't . . . have questions or need me to—"

"No. I only ask that you take some time to think about the Marguerite. You're angry and hurt, and I don't want you to rush into any decision."

"Sounds fair." His smile widens. "So, are we really doing this?"

"I think so," I say. With an exhilarated giggle, I wrap my arms around him as his own arms circle my waist and pull me to him.

We stand like that, embracing, for a long moment before he gently pulls away, raises my hand, and kisses my new engagement ring. "Let's go get married, Amelie."

———

"Well, isn't this a whole different picture from last time," Barb says, entering the room. Martha sobs—that's all she's been doing for the past half hour—and though I can't because of the makeup, I feel a new wave of overwhelming emotion every time she sniffles.

Turning to look over my shoulder at Barb, I smile as she puts a hand to her mouth and screeches a loud "Oh my God." Her eyes close, and waving her hand frantically, she turns around.

"I can't. I cannot, Ames—I can't."

I know. It's perfect. My beautiful dress, with the floral lace appliqués I love so much, the illusion plunge bodice, and a soft skirt that follows all my movements. My light nude makeup, my hair, curled at the tip.

My smile. The light in my eyes. And the jitters in my belly? Those are amazing too. They're the expectant kind that bubble up your throat and explode out of you with giggles. The ones that make you warm, that can't keep you still or steady. The ones that make you shake with adrenaline and not fear, the ones that make your stomach shut because food is no longer your sustenance, not when you've got those jitters. They only feed themselves, turning you into a giddy, fluttery, warm burst of happiness.

Everything's perfect, but I'd rather take a little less perfect if it meant I get to marry Ian sooner.

"How's Ian doing?"

Barb comes to stand beside me and holds out a glass of champagne. "He's with Trevor and Ryan, and I honestly think if he tried to bail, those two would pin him to the ground and force him to marry you at gunpoint. But it's hardly necessary. Your fiancé keeps tearing up. I think he can't believe his luck."

I accept the glass and notice that in her other hand, Barb has a small bowl of cheese nachos. Biting my lower lip, I grab both. "I can't believe mine."

Martha perks up on the couch beside me. "He's so hot, Ames."

Barb turns to her with a gasp. "And you haven't seen his tattoos."

"Tattoos?"

"*Bold and black, all over his arms!*" Barb shrieks. "I hope he does his legs next."

Snorting into the glass, I throw a look at the hairdresser, who smiles down at me before curling another lock of my hair. "Guys," I scold as I watch them through the mirror. "It's my future husband you're talking about." Setting the glass down, I sigh. "Plus, he's more than hot. He's sensitive, smart, talented, hilarious."

"He really is," Barb agrees.

There're a few seconds of appreciative silence, then Martha throws her head back. "And he's *sooooo* hot."

"Wait until you see the tattoos!" Barb explodes.

"And his ass! It's sculpted!"

"Martha!" I click my tongue. "Don't objectify my husband."

"I'll stop once he's your husband."

When I mock-glare at her, Martha raises her hands in defeat, and Barb claps her hands. "Oh, you guys. I've missed the two of you bickering."

"We did too," Martha says.

It's weird. It does feel like we've missed a huge chunk of each other's lives, but also like we're back to being us. Maybe it's because of the happiness goggles I'm wearing at the moment, but for the first time in a year it's like everything is back to what it's supposed to be. Like I've reached the destination I was always supposed to get to.

Barb shifts on the couch, turning to me. "So about today . . ."

"Yes. We need to talk pictures," Martha interjects. "With the photographer, I planned—"

She's interrupted by a knock. Chugging the champagne, Martha stands, walks across the room, and opens the door. Her body straightens, and although she's facing away from us, I can imagine her eyes widening. "Hello."

Oh, God. What now? If William Roberts enters the room, I might just set this farm on fire.

"Hello, Martha. Is Amelie in here?"

"Dad?" I call.

Shit. Just how sad is it that I completely forgot about my dad? I didn't think of calling him, of letting him know about my wedding today. Sure, it's been a whirlwind of emotions, but that's my *dad*.

With my happiness slightly dampened, I gesture to the hairdresser to give me a second and stand just as he walks in.

He turns to me, his eyes scanning my dress, and I squirm a little on the spot. Though I wish I could say I don't crave his approval, I don't think I'll ever truly stop. I don't let it crush me when I don't get it, but I still can't help but want it.

"Wow, Amelie." He looks up at me, his stern expression just a little less daunting. "You look . . ." Glancing at Martha and Barb, he clears his voice. "We need to talk about a couple of things."

Okay, maybe it still *does* crush me a little.

With sympathetic glances, Martha and Barb leave the room, followed by the hairdresser. My dad waits for the door to close, then ackwardly rubs his hands together. "So . . . Ian Roberts."

I almost feel bad for him. He's far from perfect, but his daughter marrying a Roberts is probably his worst nightmare. "Yeah, Dad. He's—"

"He's a good man." He quickly looks away. "A man deeply in love."

I swallow, trying not to let my emotions show. Though he hasn't explicitly said it, I think this is his way to let me know he approves, making it the first time he approves of anything I've done. "Yeah, he—he is."

"The thing I wanted to talk to you about . . . I . . ." His hand scratches a spot over his ear as he stares down at the floor uncomfortably. "The head chef position is yours if you want it," he eventually says with a frown.

Wow.

How can I say no to such an appealing offer? It's like he's doing me a favor—like he feels forced to give me something to make me happy.

I take a step forward, the dress flowing with my movement, then ponder how to phrase what I need to get out, but I don't think there's a good way, nor do I see a scenario in which this doesn't end in a screaming match. "I . . ." Biting my lower lip, I look up into his eyes. "I'm sorry, Dad, but I don't want it."

He remains still for the longest time, then cracks a smile. I figure it's a cruel grin, but when he finally looks into my eyes, he nods. "Good."

"Good?"

"Yes, good, Amelie." He crosses his arms. "You've always wanted me to tell you you'd be as good a head chef of La Brasserie as I am. That you're as good a cook as I am." He shakes his head firmly. "But you're not."

If there's a hell, that's where he's directed. How can he say this two minutes before my wedding? "Okay, Dad, I—"

"You don't have forty years of experience, for one."

"You know I've never claimed that. Of course I lack your experience."

"Okay, okay," he says, catching on to my annoyed tone. "Compared to me, at your age? You're not as good, Amelie, because you're not enamored with French cuisine. You'd be a great head chef for La Brasserie. You're talented and hardworking. But as good as me? No. You'd never be as good as me."

Ian punched his father yesterday. I could punch mine today. What's the worst that could happen?

"Are you listening to me?"

I nod, lips pressed tight.

"I taught you everything I knew, Amelie. You had raw talent, and I showed you the way. I made you the chef you are today."

He's right: I owe my career to him, and not because of his connections or his restaurant but because of his teaching and his recipes.

"I could see this is what you wanted to do. Cooking. And it filled me with incredible pride, so I fed that part of you. I tried to guide you, to inspire you. And though cooking is my passion, you are my daughter, Amelie. La Brasserie and my work were always for you."

My throat clenches violently, but I nod again.

"You'll be as good a chef as me when you find *your* way." He shrugs. "I hoped it'd be my way, but it isn't. You'll always have La Brasserie to fall back on should you need it." He looks away. "Whatever you end up cooking, I'll be your harshest critic, because that's how you'll rise to the top. But for what it's worth, I think once you do what makes you passionate, you'll be a *better* cook than me." He holds his chin up. "You had a better teacher than I did."

I smile, my lips quivering as I try to hold back tears. He's just given me the bare minimum a parent should give their kid—reassurance and approval—yet it feels like one of those long, warm hugs that are meant to make you feel loved. Why is he being this affectionate for the first time when I'm refusing his life's work?

"As for William Roberts and Amelie's Bistro, I—"

"I really don't want to hear that name again, especially today," I say, cutting him off. "What's done is done."

"Fair enough." He adjusts the pants of his suit. "Ian came to talk to me yesterday. He explained what's going on. The reason for marrying you out of the blue."

Uncomfortable with the implication, I look down at my gown. "It's not about the money, Dad."

"That's what he said," he says, and as my eyes meet his, he continues. "He said you've been in love with each other for a long time. That you've been friends, but he's always known you'd be the one." He walks closer still. "Did you know I met him before?"

Trying to stifle a chuckle, I think of that first night at the conference when Ian told me not so kindly that he understood why I was "like that." "He's mentioned it, yes."

"I like him." He nods. "I can see why you do."

"I love him."

"Quite an upgrade from your previous choice." He kisses my cheek, patting my shoulder, then quickly moves back. "You look *magnifique*, Amelie. Your mother will be extremely upset she missed this, and for that I'm thankful."

As I hold back a laugh, he walks away. I do wish my mom were here, but she hasn't been a constant in my life for years. My dad has, for better and for worse, and I'm happy he won't miss my wedding.

"Dad?" I call as he opens the door. When he turns to me, I bite my lower lip. I do feel a pinch of guilt. He's an old-fashioned man, and he probably expected to be asked for his opinion. "I'm sorry we didn't talk to you before today. Do we have your blessing?"

He clears his throat. "As I told Ian when he asked, you don't need it. The choice is yours." He clears his throat. "But if I can make a small request . . ." He grimaces. "Please, keep your surname, Amelie."

42

It Ends with a Wedding

– TODAY –

"Okay, Ames. You ready?" Martha asks. With my heart thumping in my ears, I nod. Just now it occurs to me that when the barn doors open, I'll have to walk down the aisle with everyone's eyes on me. How did I not realize it before? I'll totally trip on this dress and fall face-first on the grass. People will have to leave their chairs to help me up. I'll probably squish my bouquet in the process.

And of course, because this was sprung on me at the last minute, I didn't prepare any vows. And the whole formula you need to say: I would have repeated it a little in my head last night if I knew I'd be getting married today. I know the officiant will tell us the exact words, but what if I forget the next ones halfway through? And who goes first? Is it me or him?

"You're so pretty," a young girl in a green dress says. She's holding a basket, so I assume she's the flower girl, but I've never seen her before.

"Oh, th-thanks."

"Ames?" Barb grips my elbow. "Are you all right?"

I am. Of course I am. I can't believe I'm saying this, but I kind of wish the wedding were over already so I could just be married to Ian. That part I'm not struggling with. "Just nerves."

"Okay. Take a minute," Martha says.

I nod, breathing through my nose. I could use a minute, and brides are always late anyway.

But the child keeps asking me questions. "Is the dress heavy?" and "Why didn't you buy it in pink?" and "Is your boyfriend blond?" I normally don't know how to approach kids, but this one I'd gladly shoo away like a stray dog.

"Where—where's Ian?" I ask as I ignore the latest onslaught of questions.

"At the altar." Barb exchanges a worried look with Martha. "That's where the groom usually is. What's going on, Ames? Are you—"

"Can you get him?"

She nods, squeezing my hand, then walks out the door. The music begins before stopping abruptly as the band realizes the bride isn't following. A couple of minutes later, Barb is back, followed by my beautiful fiancé with his eyes closed.

"Hey," he says as Barb positions him in front of me. I've seen him in his suit already, but it hits me all over again just how handsome he is. His hands find my arms and he smiles. "Are you ditching this wedding too?"

"No," I rush to say. "Did I worry you?"

He tilts his head. "I'm waiting to see where this goes."

Barb and Martha walk away, giving us some space, and, to my relief, they take the chatty girl with them.

"Sorry," I say as soon as we're alone. "I guess I just . . . panicked a little. I wanted to see you." I smile, though he can't see me. "You can open your eyes. You've seen the dress plenty already."

"You panicked?" His fingers locate mine as he keeps his eyes closed. "If you're rethinking it, we can take our time and—"

"I'm not. I'm just . . . I never realized how daunting it is to walk down the aisle. And with a long dress too. Plus, I don't have vows and I don't remember who says them first and—wait, at what point do we sign? Trev is religious. There isn't a priest at the altar, is there? Because—"

"*Ooookay*," he interrupts as his fingers squeeze tighter. "You're definitely panicking. I thought you loved weddings."

"I thought so too."

He leans forward and gives me a peck on my cheek, then my lips. With a smile, he whispers, "First of all, it'd be hilarious if you tripped. Not immediately, but eventually. Plus, it can't get any worse than being naked, covered in butter, and—oops. Taboo topic. Moving on."

"I don't even know why I'm marrying you," I mutter.

He raises one finger. "Gorgeous." Two fingers. "Rich." Three fingers. "Trembling orgasms."

When I swat his arm, he drapes it around me and exhales softly. "You know, if your dad walked you down the aisle, the whole tripping scenario would be much less likely. I'm sure he'd be happy to hold you up."

Maybe, but I don't want him to. Though I'm glad he's here today, and his words meant a lot to me, it took him thirty years to say them, and it stings. I'd be happy to give him a chance to fix our relationship, but one moment doesn't change everything that happened before, unfortunately.

"Would *you* walk with me?" I ask.

"Me?" His eyebrows rise. "Don't you want me to wait at the altar? Watch my expression when I see you? It goes like this." His face contorts into a half frown and half smile, and with a fake sob he brings a fist to his lips and shakes his head.

"You're the worst."

"I'm just saying, I feel lucky every time I look at you, and though you look gorgeous in that dress, you look just as good in your *I'm not as think as you drunk I am* T-shirt. Or naked."

Holding a hand on his cheek, I smile. God, I love this absurd man. He's always happy, always positive and up for everything.

Except dairy.

"Not that I don't love the whole staged performance you have planned, but I think I'd rather have you walk down the aisle with me." I stand on my tiptoes and kiss his lips, resting my hands on his shoulders. "Open your eyes, Ian."

He does, the light and dark blues warming up my heart and soothing my nerves all at once. "Hi."

"Hello."

When I step back, his eyes roll down my body. He presses his lips tightly together, blinks, then blinks again. "Fuck, Amelie. You . . ."

Are his eyes dewy?

"Beautiful Amelie." He points at the bouquet. "What happened to your red roses?"

"Unpopular opinion: yellow daisies are much more beautiful."

"Agreed." With a nostalgic smile, he holds out his hand to me. "Ready?"

Taking it in mine, I nod, a roaring waterfall of feelings in my chest. "Fuck yeah."

Maybe some people actually listen to what the officiant is saying, but I'm not one of them. I'm thinking about a million things, and even if I were paying attention, all I can hear is my heart beating annoyingly in my ears.

The view isn't bad either. Ian's in front of me, our hands

together since we walked down the aisle. I didn't know the perfect wedding included storming in with your future husband, barely giving the band time to catch up, but I'm sure of it now. It should be a standard part of any ceremony.

The wedding is beautiful, and I'm sure if I bothered checking I'd find all the things I've always wanted. But I'm too busy looking at the one thing I want: my soon-to-be husband. He's not listening, either, I can tell. He's smiling like a hopeless fool, looking gorgeous in his linen suit as if it's a second skin.

When the officiant waves her hand between us, we both turn to look at her smiling face as the guests chuckle. "I think the two of you are on your honeymoon already."

I smile, grateful I'm wearing a ton of makeup when heat moves up my cheeks. "Sorry."

"Have you prepared your own vows?"

"Oh." I meet Ian's gaze, and when he gives me a "Let's wing it?" shrug, I nod. "Yes, sort of."

"Ian, the floor is yours."

Widening his eyes, he huffs out a breath. "We know who goes first, I guess."

His mouth opens, his shoulders rising and falling quickly. He swallows, then opens his mouth again and shakes his head, an amused smile bending his lips, as if he's surprised nothing's coming out.

"I can go first," I offer.

"No, no, I—"

"Really, I can go first."

He nods, his shoulders relaxing as the guests laugh again.

"I . . ." My mind's completely empty. Not one single thing. I think we might be here all day. "I'm not . . . great at making choices, but you, Ian, are the one choice I know for a fact I won't regret."

He nods, bringing a finger to his left eye.

"I have no doubt I'll choose you every day. I'll choose us over and over again. I'll choose to love you and trust you and grow with you." With a smile, I squeeze his hand in mine. "Whether or not we're here because we're destined for one another—if fate brought us together—has nothing to do with it. From today on, I *choose* you. And I'll do it in every big and small moment, in any world and any lifetime. You're my most certain choice."

I kiss him, and as I lean back, Ian smiles. After hesitating for a while more, he shakes his head. "Wow. That's a tough act to follow."

Gentle spurts of laughter come from the crowd as he hesitates.

"There's no word that feels just right. They're all . . . not permanent enough." Looking down for a few seconds, he clears his voice; then he stares deeply into my eyes as if we don't have any audience at all. "I wasn't looking for anything when I found you. I liked you and I wanted you, but I didn't want love." He shakes his head. "I fell for you without noticing, because it didn't feel like falling; it felt like standing. So fucking high." He inhales sharply with a hiss, looking embarrassed and throwing a look at the officiant. "Oh, shit—sorry. And sorry again."

When the woman waves him off, he turns to me. "You became my best friend, and my home, and my safe place, and at the same time my craziest adventure. Until at some point you weren't just *in* my life: you were all of it."

I swallow a sob. The feelings he is expressing are so familiar, it's like he plucked them out of my brain.

"Today I vow to you, Amelie, that I'll let you listen to Beyoncé whenever you want, though she's definitely overrated. That the best years of our life aren't your twenties. They're yet to come, and we'll spend them together. That I'll never pronounce another Q-word ever again if that's what you want. That I'll take you on road trips, and if Christmas is your favorite holiday, then I'll make it memorable every single year." He grins widely. "I vow to always make sure your champagne comes with cheese nachos, to always talk during a movie, and to come up with the cheesiest pickup lines your heart can take." He steps closer, holding both of my hands in his. "I promise to buy you flowers and to always value your opinions, popular or unpopular."

I almost expect the guests to stand up and clap, but when there are only sniffles and sobs, I cover his lips with mine. "I love you and also I hate you for being so good at this," I say in a choked-up voice. I can't imagine the state of my makeup right now. Waterproof's one thing, but *Ianproof* is another.

"Yeah?" he whispers. "Now can you please be my wife?"

"Yes."

The officiant continues with the ceremony, and besides speaking when I'm asked to, then signing, then kissing, it all blurs together. We walk back up the aisle as husband and wife, then we dance and we eat and we talk to the guests who managed to be here despite the late notice. There are plenty of empty tables, our dance is to the notes of a song neither of us knows, and Ian eats only one of the several dishes planned for dinner, yet it's as perfect as it can get.

I know, because by the time most of the guests have left and I'm dance-napping on my husband's shoulder, there's a peaceful smile on my face. The smile of someone who has found their happy place.

"What about our honeymoon?"

"Hmm?"

He kisses my forehead, then pushes some hair off my cheek. "Our honeymoon? Are we jumping on Martha and Trevor's?"

"No, they're going. They got time off work, so they'll do the honeymoon first and the wedding later."

"Another wedding, huh?"

"Yep. But judging on what she has planned, you won't even notice it's one."

He kisses my nose, runs his hands over my back, holds me as close and tight as he possibly can. "So what's next for us?"

"Good question." We're starting over, and it's not scary as long as it's with Ian, but the possibilities are limitless. All I know is that I'll never have to live another day without talking to him. Another day sending him pickup lines and waiting for an answer back. And for now, that's enough.

Which reminds me: "Which was the line that made you smile?"

"Excuse me?"

I look up into my husband's kind blue eyes. "The pickup lines I texted you when I was blocked on your phone? There was one that made you smile."

"They all made me smile."

"But one made you smile *more*," I insist.

His eyes narrow for a moment, and once it hits him, his eyes widen. "Oh, right." He kisses my jaw, then my cheek, my nose, my lips. "Know what's on the menu?"

As he flashes the brightest smile at me, my heart flutters.

I *do* know what's on the menu.

"Me 'n' u."

43

Epilogue: Welcome to Roseberg

– ONE YEAR LATER –

"I'm starting to think this surprise of yours is *not* anal sex," Ian says as I pull him forward, his eyes closed and a wide smile on his face.

"It's not," I confirm. "And I told you that the minute you asked. Which was two seconds after I told you I had a surprise for you."

He firmly nods. "Yup. Don't need a summary. Need my surprise."

With a sigh, I look back and, satisfied, turn to Ian. "Okay. Open your eyes."

Slowly and dramatically, he does. First one, then the other. With a puzzled expression, he looks behind me, then to our left and right. "What . . . what am I missing?"

"Something huge," I say as I point my thumb behind me.

"The joke's almost too easy." He squares his shoulders, then his eyes squint. "Hmm. I . . . That's a ridiculous, ridiculous name."

Rubbing my forehead, I glance at the horse fountain behind Ian. Water is pouring down from the sculptures' mouths into a large pool underneath, and around it a slew of tourists are throwing coins in the water. Ian did it, too, of course. He said he wished for anal sex, which is indisputable proof that the fountain does not work.

"It's because, if you spell *desserts* backward . . ." I sigh loudly. "Never mind. Let's go in."

We open the door, which has the logo of a girl in a pink dress under the bakery's name, and, once inside, my trained eyes quickly spot the pastries behind the counter. The whole place is beautiful, with white counters and warm wooden floors. Plants hang overhead, and the back wall is a chocolate waterfall I'll definitely need to keep Ian away from.

"I love my surprise. Love it. I have no idea what it is, but boy, am I grateful." Ian's lips kiss the top of my ear. "Thank you, beautiful."

Rubbing his arm, I explain, "This is the place that made Barb's cake. The bakery you kept asking about?"

"Oh." His face crumples. "Well, I didn't really *eat* that cake. But I definitely saw it." He tilts his head. "Maybe. From afar. It was white."

"No, it was not." I tug his hand and pull him closer to the counter. "It's about time you try it. And I know you don't love cake, but you were also sure mushrooms were as disgusting as peas, and now you love them."

"I *do* love them," he considers. "I'm in. Let's get cake. We wouldn't be here if it wasn't for cake." Pointing at a slice of Black Forest, he hums. "That one looks good."

"I booked a nuptial cake tasting for us. Only lactose-free cakes."

Ian's confused eyes meet mine. "I'm pretty sure we're already married. You're not going to make me do it twice, are you?"

I chuckle, thinking of our wedding day. I still don't know how Ian managed not to frown *once*. Not at the speeches, which were awkward at best; not at the props for the wedding pictures; not at the monogrammed cookies or the first dance. He smiled and looked as happy as he could ever be and totally didn't let me throw the bouquet.

Which worked out just fine, because I handed it to Martha.

"No, no other wedding." I dreamily look into my husband's blue eyes. "We've had enough weddings for a lifetime."

"More than a lifetime." He leans closer, his nose grazing mine. "But I'd marry you every day, forever, if that's what you wanted."

I grin and close my eyes as his lips find mine. I love it when we smile mouth to mouth. His tongue gently grazes my own, his hand on my neck as his thumb brushes my cheek, and the fountain might actually be a wishing well, because I'd give him anything right now. Anything. Even anal.

"Errrr . . . *Hello?*"

I flinch away from Ian, then look down at the tiny human next to us. She has gorgeous dark hair and chocolate-brown eyes and is wearing a shirt with the bakery's logo. I look left and right for the owners—*parents.* The parents. I'm sure children aren't supposed to be alone when they are this small.

Ian crouches down, a big smile on his handsome face. "Well, finally, there you are. I was starting to think nobody worked in this place. We'd like one hundred slices of cake to go, please."

"One hundred?" she asks, a giggle sputtering out of her lips. Obviously, Ian is a kids' person. "That's too much cake!"

"Oh, *really*?" he says playfully. "Excuse me, but it looks to me like you could use a sales class or two. Rule number one: never tell your customers to buy less cake."

Throwing a curious look at me, she hooks her finger into her mouth. "I don't work here," she explains.

"You *don't*?" Ian's eyes widen.

"No. It's my dad's work."

"Ooooh." Ian nods. "What's your name?"

She hesitates, giving him a shy smile as she rocks from one foot to the other. "Nevaeh. Like Heaven but backward."

"Wow. My name, backward, is just Nai."

"That's silly."

"It really is." Ian stands, then turns to me and whispers, "What's with the backward-words thing?"

Just as I shrug, someone enters the bakery from the back. We both turn around and, holy fuck, that is one hell of a handsome man right there. Dark hair and dark eyes, just like his daughter. But he's also tall, wide-shouldered, and covered in flour. Which helps.

"Good afternoon." His eyes dart to Nevaeh. "What did Daddy say about greeting customers alone?" She smiles mischievously and runs to the back, and only then do the man's eyes meet mine. "Sorry for making you wait. It's flu season and I'm out of personnel."

I give him a quick shake of my head, but I'm still flabbergasted that a man this handsome exists. I mean, Ian's just as gorgeous, but I've had time to get used to his beauty. This is hitting me all at once.

"You, sir, are one very handsome man," Ian says. "Are you seeing that?" he adds as he turns to me with a surprised look.

Oh, Ian.

"Excuse my *husband*," I say when the man's eyes narrow into a dangerous glare. "He's . . . he has no filter. Just says anything that enters his brain."

After a quick glance at me, the man focuses on Ian again.

"He—" I cup the back of Ian's head. "There's just a big, happy daisy field in here."

The man smiles at me, and releasing a deep breath, I relax a little. I'm ready to bet he isn't the one who usually handles clients, or this place wouldn't be as famous as it is. "What can I help you with?"

Ian points to the board. "My wife booked a nuptial cake tasting."

"Congratulations," the man mumbles. "Wait—your wife? Are you getting married again?"

"No, we—it's . . ." I shake my head. "I doubt you'll remember, but you made a nuptial cake for my friend about two years ago. Barbara Wilkow."

"Of course." The man's smile is genuine now. "Strawberry shortcake and white chocolate ganache with pink sugar paste." When my brows raise, he shrugs. "I have a great memory." His eyes dart from Ian to me, and he nods. "Well, sit down wherever. I'll check your order and bring over the first samples." Turning around, he approaches the coffee machine. "Can I offer you something to drink in the meantime?"

The door opens, the bell overhead ringing as a woman comes in like fury. *"Sorry-sorry-sorry-sorry.* I know, I'm sorry." She approaches the man and kisses him on the lips. "Please don't go all Mr. Asshole on me: Marina needed—"

"Marina knows how to handle herself far too well, and you've been overworking yourself." He leans closer and returns the kiss. It's not the passing kiss of a couple who've been together for years and are just saying hello. No, sir. It's a full, loving kiss that almost makes me uncomfortable but stops just before it does. It's full of love, full of—

I turn to Ian, and he's wide-eyed, staring at me. These two are that couple! The couple at the Quinns' wedding! The way they look at each other is just the same as how Ian stares at me. And I'm sure it's how I stare at him.

Once the woman faces us, she smiles wide. "You must be Amelie and Ian. Wedding cake tasting, right? Can I get you anything to drink?"

"We're good, thank you," I say. We walk through the bakery,

and I see beyond a pair of glass doors a gorgeous courtyard garden with tall columns and vines wrapped around them all the way to the skylight on the roof.

Turning to Ian, I smile excitedly. "Want to sit outside?"

"Martha's planning a party for her anniversary," I tell Ian as he looks worriedly at a coffee cake slice. I'm almost done with my half, but I'm used to him taking some time to try new things when it comes to food.

"Oh. In Creswell?"

I nod, then take a sip of water. "Two weeks from now."

"Cool. We can also stop by and see your dad. It's been a while."

Since our wedding. We've kept in contact, mostly through texts, apart from his birthday and mine, when we spoke on the phone. Though I'd like to say things are all better, I'm not sure they'll ever be. Not completely. "We would pass through Mayfield too."

Ian's eyes narrow, and he sticks his fork into the cake and shoves it into his mouth without a second thought. *Interesting.* Bringing up unpleasant topics speeds up the cake-eating process.

"Hmm—nope." He spits it into a napkin, then dramatically sticks his tongue out. "I'm not having this at my wedding."

Fair enough. I was probably shooting a little too high with the hazelnuts and cinnamon. "More for me," I say, and pull the plate closer. Moving a slice of red velvet in front of him, I nod in encouragement. "You'll love this one."

"Hmm."

Okay, so I probably shouldn't have mentioned his father. It's a recipe for bad moods lately. The thing is, I see the way it affects him. I can pinpoint the exact moment William comes to his mind, because his eyes fill with grief and nostalgia. I hate to see him like that, and, just as importantly, I don't think his father will ever stop harassing me with his apology texts unless they have a conversation.

"You can take your time," I say softly as I set my fork down. "But at some point you'll have to talk to him, right? Forgive and forget?"

"Yes. And it's not like I don't miss him. But every time I think about talking to him, I remember what he did to you, and . . ."

I notice the way his Adam's apple bobs up and down, then the thick emotions in his eyes, and put my hand on his. "In his twisted way, he did it to protect you."

"I know he did, but . . ." He blinks faster, his jaw tensing. "I need more time."

"No Mayfield, then. Not until you're ready."

I set the empty plate aside, then dig into the red velvet cake. I'm glad I didn't have any lunch, because I won't be leaving this table until all eight slices of cake are gone. I might lick the plates too. This guy really knows his baking.

"So where's our honeymoon bringing us next?"

I smile, tilting my head as I think of potential stops between Roseberg and Creswell. "There's Willow Falls. I was just reading an article about this amusement park they opened nearby."

"Sold," he says immediately, his bad mood only a memory now. "We can leave tomorrow."

Just as he digs his fork into the red velvet cake, the door to the bakery opens, and Heaven, the baker's wife, comes out with a tray filled to the brim. She distributes the orders around the courtyard, which is nearly full of customers even though it's almost closing time, then comes over to our table. "How are you guys doing?"

I turn to Ian, who looks like he's about to spit out another piece of cake, and widen my eyes in warning until he swallows. "We're doing great. Your husband is a marvelous baker."

"It makes up for his grumpiness."

Using the occasion to excuse myself, I walk back into the bakery, where Shane, the baker, is serving a client. He turns to me. "Bathroom's the first door to the right."

"Oh, no. I don't need the bathroom. I actually wanted to . . ." His dark eyes pierce mine, and I lose track of my thoughts for a second. This guy can be intimidating. "I wanted to compliment you on your desserts. I worked as a chef for fifteen years and I don't think I've ever eaten better cakes than the ones you served us today."

He blushes slightly as he closes a paper box, hands it to the man waiting on the other side of the counter, and says, "Thank you." Then, turning, he gives me a warm smile and says, "And thank *you*."

"You're welcome."

I approach the counter, studying the pastries behind the plexiglass. There are rows of his famous homemade Oreos, and though I've never tried one, I've seen them on social media plenty. They went viral a while back, and they've been all over the web since.

"Where do you work?"

"Hmm?"

"You said you're a chef?" He cocks a brow. "Where?"

"Oh, not right now. Ian and I plan to open something together one day, but . . . we've been enjoying being married and free for a while. He's working as a consultant here and there, and I'm . . ."

I shrug, smiling dreamily. "I'm on a mission to have him try all vegetables at least once."

Shane settles both hands on the counter. "I take it he's not a chef."

"Definitely not." I look at the croissants. "European butter?"

"Of course. European dessert."

With a smile, I nod. I like Shane.

I walk back to the garden, where Heaven has taken my seat at the table, and it sounds like they're talking about movies. As soon as Ian sees me, his smile widens, and his eyes take on their usual glimmer once they settle on me. It's unmistakable. "Hey, wife. Is everything all right?"

"I just needed to compliment the chef, because these cakes are . . ." As Heaven stands, I gesture to her to sit down again. "Please, stay."

When Ian pulls me onto his lap, Heaven smiles. "Ian was telling me you're a chef."

"I am, yes."

"You know, Shane and I actually own this building, and there's this property that recently got vacated. A restaurant."

"Really?"

Heaven nods. "Right there." She looks to the left, and once I turn to the spot she's pointing to, my breath hitches and shivers run through my body. And Ian's reaction must be similar, because I feel his chest rise sharply against my back, then slowly fall.

The restaurant is empty, and the insignia on top is gone too; only the screws left. But on the large window facing the garden, there's the illustration of a big, beautiful, yellow . . . daisy.

I twist, my fingers tightening on the back of Ian's neck, and dragging my eyes away from destiny itself, I focus on him. There's a single tear rolling down his cheek, but as he blinks, another one falls.

I kiss his cheek, then his forehead, the tip of his nose, his eyes. Until he looks at me, and I need no words to know.

Turning to Heaven, I nod. "We'll take it."

THE EN—

New notification.

Daisy
@daisyofficial

Guess what? We've opened a restaurant!

04:34 PM · Aug 12 · Twitter for iPhone

245   156   874   1.2K

THE END

Acknowledgments

I never expected that I'd be writing this section a second time. I call this novel "the book that changed my life," and none of it would have been possible without every single person mentioned herein, and so many more whom I can't possibly fit in.

Writing this story has been the most beautiful and challenging experience of my life, and I'm so thankful so many of you loved it. I'm grateful you shouted about it from rooftops, promoted it, and helped me get it into the hands of such a wonderful agent, editor, and publishing house.

Thank you for giving *The Wedding Menu* new life.

Caitlin. Without you, I wouldn't be writing these words. Thank you for believing in me and my book and for knowing exactly whom to entrust it with. Thank you for being there through every doubt and question. I couldn't have wished for a better agent.

Carrie, my editor, and the whole team at Gallery Books and Simon & Schuster. Thank you for taking a chance on me and working so hard to get *The Wedding Menu* in front of new readers.

The heroes who tackled this book when it was unedited, unpolished, and, oh, so very different: my (first) beta readers,

Victoria J, Valerie A, and Catherine. Your help was incredibly precious and made this book what it is today.

For their super-exclusive, early ARC reading, which, really, was them spotting potential typos in English and French: Heather and Romane.

Britt, editor of the indie version of *The Wedding Menu*. Your work remains the foundation that made all of this possible, and I can't thank you enough.

I'd also like to acknowledge Meg Jones, who, with her *Dicktionary*, inspired me to add a "Whine List."

Oksana, Madison, Lucca, Amanda, and Liv, readers and friends, thank you for your continuous support and unwavering faith in me and my work.

An honorable mention to my friends Chiara, Stefania, and Mariangela, my soul sisters.

Carmen, for buying every book and reading them with the assistance of Google Translate. *Grazie*.

My brother and his beautiful family, Laura and Dami. Thank you for buying my books, for asking about my publishing journey, and for always sending congratulations at every new milestone. And thank you for giving me the most beautiful nephew.

My partner, Caroline, for letting me ramble about past and future timelines until I found a solution to my issue of the day, only to come back twenty minutes later and explain why it wouldn't work. *Jag älskar dig*.

My parents, for supporting me every way they can and for their know-how. Thank you for not even thinking twice before offering to drop everything and travel across the continent when you knew I was going through the motions.

And since it really does take a village, I'd like to thank mine. The group of authors who made me feel less alone in an industry that can be very isolating. The authors who've lent an ear, given me advice, listened to my rants, encouraged me, and checked in when I needed it the most. You're all, in some way or another, an integral part of my life and my publishing career. Thank you for making this process easier.

Katie Golightly, Elodie Colliard, Jillian Meadows, Meg Jones, Caroline Frank, Lindsey Lanza, Heather Garvin, Stephanie Alves, Elliot Fletcher, Rebecca Quinn, Peyton Corinne, WH Lockwood. And, of course, LH Blake, who's been my number one cheerleader, friend, and reader since the beginning.

I can't think of a kinder and more talented group of people. Thank you for being a part of my journey and allowing me to be a part of yours.

And, finally, to my readers.

Thank you for reading this book. I hope you found exactly what you needed in Amelie and Ian's story. I wouldn't be here without every single one of you, and I love you all.

About the Author

Letizia Lorini is an Italian rom-com author who's based in a quaint town with pretty canals in southern Sweden: Malmö. There, she lives in her lovely apartment with her partner and their fluffy Japanese Spitz.

Her books portray imperfect people falling in love as they navigate messy, entangled, and hilarious situations. She loves writing swoony, laugh-out-loud, emotional love stories that will keep you on the edge of your seat.

When she's not writing or reading romances, she's cooking up some new story, drawing, or watching '90s movies. She's also a criminologist, speaks three languages, and loves coffee far more than her doctor approves of.